APOCALYPSE REAVER

BOOK ONE

TOBASCOASAKO

Apocalypse Reaver
Book One
Copyright © 2025 TobascoAsako

ISBN: 979-8-88993-065-5

Written by TobascoAsako
Edited by Taylor Kilgour
Cover by Kartstudio
Illustrations by Aepuru Arts

Published 2025 by MoonQuill
Arlington, VA
www.moonquill.com

TABLE OF CONTENTS

Chapter 1

STRANDS OF FATE

The war started at the behest of the elves when they were still one people. The First Children spoke of the great devourer, the herald of the end that would consume all things and leave this world a shriveled husk of rock. They predicted that Mana, the god-gift that flowed through all things, the giver of life and hope of the future, would be ended by this grave new threat.

— On the Cataclysm by an unknown Quassian Scholar, circa 103 AC.

Between dreams and reality exists a place where the mind can wander freely, unencumbered by the constraints of this world. It is a place of imagination. There I had flown over vast plains of grass filled with exotic creatures, walled cities protected by stout, armored knights, and witnessed the majesty of desert-dwelling sandworms.

A cold breeze entered through the open window, bringing with it the sounds of an awakening city. Inside, the radio blared out the morning news, the announcer's sonorous voice filling the emptiness of my room to wake me.

Lately, the dreams had been growing more vivid, more real. I mused this as I forced myself to get out of bed, nearly tripping over a pile of books in my rush to the sink, flailing my hands to keep balance like some demented cartoon character. Staring into the mirror, my mind turned once more to the dreams. How stimulating would it be to live in a world like that?

After quickly brushing my teeth and dressing, I searched my mini fridge. The investigation revealed a half-eaten chocolate bar and a loaf with mold merrily growing on it. I scarfed the bar down while placing the moldy loaf in my bag alongside books I would need for the day.

Moving to the door, a new letter from the building's management caught my eye. I already knew it was going to ask me to pay this month's rent, which was two weeks late. My last job didn't pay as well as it had promised, so I would have to beg or borrow money from friends this month—or, heaven forbid, from my parents. How could they charge so much for such a terrible room? The roof leaked, and the place was damp all winter.

Making sure to lock the door, I decided to take the long way to school through the park. A jogger passed by, who, judging by the music blasting from her headphones, was determined to destroy her eardrums. For a moment I was sure I heard the sound of an army marching to the beat of war, until the harsh honk of a car replaced a warhorse's neigh as a stray cat crossed the road.

Snapping out of it, I crossed into the park and was greeted by familiar birdsong. People seldom used the park at this time in the morning, and for a few precious moments it felt like this section of the park was truly mine. Lately I had had the notion that my life was spiraling out of control, a feeling the birdsong eased.

My phone buzzed, breaking the peace of the morning. More spam. The display picture was the same, a picture of *her*. My recent breakup had done more damage to my confidence than I cared to admit, and it had started to affect my studies and job. I replayed in my mind the phone conversation with her again, my curt "Okay," before putting the phone down. Should I have begged instead? Bought a present with my nonexistent funds? Round and round the scenarios swirled.

Torturing myself with these thoughts, I continued walking through the park until I reached a small pond. Ducks drifted across the brown surface, quacking and occasionally diving down to feed, tufted bottoms in the air. A few silhouettes of fish lurked in the murky depths. Reaching into my bag for the moldy loaf, I began to feed the ducks and fish.

A frenzy of activity whirled wherever I threw the bread, and I smiled as two birds squabbled over a larger piece. I was just about to throw another piece when a large shadow appeared beneath the birds, a shape growing so suddenly in size that I was forced to step back in surprise. Something flew towards me, and I instinctively closed my eyes. I could have sworn that water grazed my cheek, but when I opened my eyes, there was nothing but the peaceful scene of ducks and fish. Shaken, I threw the rest of the loaf into the pond, then took off.

Feeling disoriented, I hurried to my lecture, making it with a little time to spare. I had few friends, and none of them had chosen this particular course, so I found my customary corner near the back and sat down to prepare. My mind began wandering again to the dreams and my encounter in the park. *Overactive imagination,* I thought. Too rich a diet of video games and fantasy books by far.

The history lecturer's loud voice, as it had done so many times in the past, brought me back to reality. I tried to focus on his words, but an errant thought drew me to picture fields of the most brilliant emerald grass, a viridian sea swaying in the wind.

Grass...? I could hear the susurration of each blade dancing to the cool spring breeze. The taste of the crisp, clean air pervaded my imagination, a striking contrast to the acrid aftertaste of the city. I saw a small hill with what looked like a large acacia tree overlooking it, a vision that would make for the most perfect of landscape pictures. I yearned to go there. I stepped, only to find myself back in the hall as the lecturer listed the reasons for the fall of an empire.

Occasionally casting a glance at a girl a few seats away on my right, I listened with half an ear to the professor. Hair like burnt gold cascaded around her shoulders and framed a heart-shaped face with eyes of cornflower blue. A cute button nose, a little upturned, was perfectly positioned above blossom-soft pink lips. I knew her name, as I had heard her friends greet her once, but I had never had the courage to introduce myself. Sighing, I entered an almost zen-like autopilot for the rest of the lecture as my subconscious took in all the relevant data.

After the lecture finished, I checked my timetable on my phone. The next class would be in the late afternoon, providing me time to carry out a few errands in town. Checking my calendar and smiling to myself, I was reminded that I had scheduled to play a game online with a friend later in the evening, but first I needed to go to the post office to pick up a package.

Whistling an off-key tune, I made my way to my next destination to find that a long lunchtime queue had already formed. Patiently, I waited in line, part of the tune on repeat in my mind until my turn came.

The cashier was a bespectacled, mousy woman of middle years, hair tied in a tight bun with small streaks of gray just beginning to appear. She pretended to carefully check over my details before handing me a small brown package and an invoice for import tax. I grudgingly counted out the necessary money. As an aside, I asked her the cost of sending a package back to its country of origin.

With an irritated sigh, she replied, "Well, you will have to choose between—"

"Choose!" a voice thundered somewhere behind me. Eyes wild, I searched for the source.

"—will be more expensive but faster..." I half heard the post clerk continue.

"Choose!" the voice thundered even louder, and this time there was a burning sensation in my heart and lungs. It felt as if chains were constricting them, squeezing ever tighter. I leaned against the counter for support as I fought for breath. *I did take my medicine this morning, didn't I?*

I panicked, before remembering my rush to leave early. Screaming a silent "No," my eyes glazed over, and I fell to my knees. Some people in the queue behind me rushed to help. The last thing I remember was the clerk's change of expression from annoyance, to worry, then to perturbing awe. As the pain intensified, I felt something important give way inside.

This is what death is, I thought, as I felt a sensation of falling. I was traveling through a place filled with a bright incandescence before I was wrenched into a new reality. Suddenly next to me was... the girl from the lecture hall? Cornflower eyes, once so warm and soft, now seemed cold, and the lines of her mouth and lips had hardened.

A wave of disorientation passed over me, and I could hear a ringing in my head before her features fully shifted. In front of me was the perfect ideal of classical female beauty, like the Ancient Greek statues of yore. It felt so strange, yet somehow absolutely right—as if this were fate, the final piece of a puzzle slotting into place.

A veiled face of perfect symmetry and form stood before me. Piercing cobalt eyes, familiar, yet utterly alien, were framed by delicate oval features. Her loose gown, similar to a Roman stola, billowed slightly, as if floating in the water around a more luscious figure. Beneath a lovely high nose, sensuous, crimson-stained lips hinted at the beginning of a playful smile. Panic rising, I began to question what this experience truly was. The encounter was so distant from anything I could have ever imagined in any vapid daydream.

"You have been chosen." Her voice held the lightness of an angel, yet carried an ominous echo of ages long past.

Through some intangible power, I sank to my knees, overwhelmed by reverence. I could not bring myself to raise my head. I was not a religious man, but a corner of my heart knew I was in the presence of absolute divinity.

"I am justice, and you shall be my herald," the goddess proclaimed, for there could be no doubt that she was a goddess. "All that you do will be in my name. You will be the avatar of my will."

My heart missed a beat with every declaration, and I could do nothing but yield under that divine gaze. Still, where bravery failed, panic and fear rallied.

"Why?" I croaked.

"You have been judged and have not been found wanting. A life lived without sin and in service to your fellow man. A soul that is compatible with our needs, forged anew to be a tool of the righteous. This will be our covenant."

A soft warmth spread throughout my body. It was purpose, and every word she had spoken struck my soul with a hammer's force. A sorrow-tinged smile grew across her face, and my soul rose with joy as tears tracked their way down my cheeks. I was not worthy of such regard.

She lifted my face. "Let it not be said there is no justice without mercy. Though it will cost me greatly, you will be given a day to face the trials to come. Prepare yourself, my Champion. I am Avaria."

The last utterance held such lament that I felt nothing but deep shame that I was unworthy of such benevolence. Slowly, the warmth faded from my soul as my dream began to dissipate. The peace was followed by the jarring sensation of falling.

Tendrils of shadow ripped through me, stabbing into my soul. I flailed my limbs in a desperate attempt to escape, but the tendrils only tightened their grip and pulled me ever closer to the source of their origin, a yawning abyssal void. I screamed and thrashed, my desperate cries echoing across the blackness.

Despite my panic, a glimmer of understanding flickered to life. Avaria had chosen me as her own. Surely she would not abandon me now, in my darkest hour. Renewed strength fueled my struggle against the tendrils. But it was all for naught. With a sudden force, I was pulled into the maw.

My being was stretched and compressed. The darkness was so absolute that it was more than just the absence of light. And there lurked a presence, breathing behind my neck, yet at the same time all around me. The embers of my recent divine revelation still burned low, allowing me to utter a word.

"Who...?"

A voice rumbled with laughter.

"Are you a god?" My words were a pathetic squeak.

Laughter sounded again. "I am no mere god," the voice intoned, followed by a long pause that could hold the time of the rise and fall of empires. "I am a higher Truth. The final Truth of all things." With these words, I felt my very sense of self shredded and rewritten.

"That Avaria is a mere mortal, and a flawed concept. She has chosen and claimed you for her own, but in her mercy broke the rules. She thought to bend the Concord. To gift you the time to ready yourself for the great trials. To give you an advantage. To give that world hope. What a foolish child, to think we would not notice. No respite can be given in the rules of the Great Game. I claim you now, child of Earth."

Sibilant whispers skittered across my mind, shaping it so I might better understand the being and prevent my mind from shattering against the cliffs of insanity I stood upon.

The whispers, echoes of the great being, spoke directly in my mind, their voices like sharpened glass. Every word was a lesson in pain.

"We will gift you nothing but our curse. We care nothing for your success or failure. We will simply try again, as this moment will fold into itself once more. Know utterly the futility of your existence. However, we will gift you a curse. I give you pain. Take this and know a fleeting joy, mortal. The pain I give to you, you will give to others, as is the nature of your being. The pain will guide your growth and understanding in your new world. As it once was, so shall it all be again."

Then agony filled me across a moment of eternity and flayed the fibers of my soul. All thoughts of the goddess burned away, and the moment stretched forever. All I could do was hear the hollow laughter of a thousand uncaring gods.

Chapter 2

A CHOICE

I sojourn now in the blessed lands of the Rawesan for a time, the birthplace of Her church. Many are the prophets who venture into the deep deserts in search of guidance, but few ever return with the divine scripture. Those who do are often blessed with the Gift-spark and write on parchment, paper, or vellum the instruction of the divine so that others may know greater communion with Her.

— The Fanciful Travels by Beron de Laney, 376 AC.

As suddenly as my soul torture had begun, it stopped. I sensed a shift, and I was no longer there, but elsewhere. Vertigo overtook me, and I fell face forwards into what felt like earth and grass. Curled in a fetal position, I whimpered as the aftershock of pain played across my mortal body.

Shadowy purple tendrils continued to whip across my consciousness, but fainter now, slowly replaced by a plethora of error messages. I kept on begging for the agony and torment to end, until exhaustion finally claimed me. I fell into a nightmare-fueled sleep filled with visions of the deaths of everyone I had ever loved or known.

* * *

I awoke naked and gibbering nonsense to an uncaring universe. Dull sunlight pounded my senses as I tried unsuccessfully to raise myself on fever-drunk feet. Failing pitifully, I instead retreated to curl on a soft bed of grass.

Rocking back and forth to a rhythm known only to the mad, I chanted, "Not real, not real," to myself. Over and over, a litany to a world that did not care.

Looking across the sea of green, I saw it was a gray and dark day with clouds, pregnant with rain, on the distant horizon. At the edges of my vision, the hint of shadowy things scuttled back into the recesses of my mind. Across from me in the near distance, I saw a picture from what felt like a lifetime long past: the imposing tree on the hill. I was vulnerable, naked, and alone in a place known only to my madness.

Memories from another place smashed into my consciousness as a high trill of sound flooded my senses. Willing the world to go away, I wrapped my head in my hands and closed my eyes.

Then, as inexorable as time itself, a message played across my inner eye in a bold script.

CHOOSE YOUR CALLING.

Flustered, I could not help but be drawn to the message. As my awareness brushed against understanding, new text was shown to me.

INITIATE, and below, another choice, **STUDENT**.

Just as I was musing on the incongruity of "Student," the text flashed static across my vision, and there was a ringing in my ears. The "Student" option had changed to display "Acolyte." Could I get any crazier? I felt in my bones that I had to choose quickly or there would be dire consequences.

I knew in my gut that the "Acolyte" must be some sort of hidden class. Those were usually harder to play but tended to have some real endgame advantages if you could master their skills. With nothing else to go on—no wikis, guides, or even friends to explain the choices in front of me—I selected Acolyte.

I heard a rumble from within as text blazed and imprinted across my mind. A rushing sense of power filled me, a feeling of completeness.

STATUS

    Calling: [Error] Lv. 1 Acolyte of [Error]

    Strength: 8

    Dexterity: 8

    Constitution: 8

    Intelligence: 8

    Wisdom: 8

    Charisma: 8

    Luck: 8

SKILLS AND PROFICIENCIES

    Pain Nullification Lv. 1

SPELLS AND MAGIC

    None

GIFTS

    None

Experience to Lv. 2: 0/100

It looked like the user interface, or UI, of one of the many games I would play. What was this? Pain nullification? Shock and indignation rose to the fore of my mind with this notification of a skill. Before I could fully comprehend it, new numerical markers blossomed in the lower-left corner of my vision.

Health: 5/6

Stamina: 16/16

Mana: 2/6

Feeling vulnerable with my nakedness, I pinched myself to make sure this was no dream, then pinched again harder to draw a little blood. *This must be a game. This cannot be real,* I thought.

My mind teetered once again on the brink of insanity, sibilant whispers reassuring me that it was real, which were followed by a far-off scream of a distant divinity. At the edges of my vision, I could sense the impression of dark, shadowy tendrils, ever moving and just out of sight.

The pain proved this was genuine, that I must be here. Was this really the place of my dreams? An escape from the doldrums of a pedestrian life? The idea both disturbed and thrilled me. Looking at my hand, I curled my fingers into a fist before straightening them again. What power awaited me in such a world? Love? Immortality?

As I contemplated the bewildering scale of my circumstance, the next message appeared.

New Quest: First Steps

I was once again struck by the importance of the message. With earnest effort, I rose to my feet and trudged towards the tree on the hill. Each step was heavy and painful as I made my way barefoot to the place where the revelation had occurred.

After what felt like an eternity, I finally arrived and took a deep breath, gazing upon the scene.

A majestic tree, looking like some sort of acacia but with bladed green leaves, stood tall, its branches rising from its great trunk like an accusation against the heavens. The air around it was saturated with a strong pine scent mixed with the sweet fragrance of lemon blossoms. Beneath its generous boughs, a crude stone altar stood. At its foot, fallen from its place, lay a stone carving of a female figure, a crude facsimile of the goddess.

"Avaria," I croaked, caught somewhere between desperation and joy.

There was no answer. Yet, I thought I heard again the screaming of a distant female voice. Shaking my head, I wondered what madness on top of madness was possessing me.

There, an echo. A tinkling echo of joyful laughter.

"Who are you?" I asked in a quiet, hopeful voice to no one.

"I am power strike."

Impressions of a female voice tickled my mind, a resonance close to my ear that left me shivering in excitement. Renderings of war and conflict, the press of the melee, an image of a peasant bringing down a cruel warlord, and an unsung hero alone atop the battlements unleashing savage blows against unspeakable horrors—all of this played across my inner vision.

A solemn note entered my mindscape. A soft choir of angels. A cry of anguish and salvation. The music built up to a crescendo until there was a new voice.

"I am Heal." The voice was gentle and authoritative, with all the kindness of a mother.

New images were brought to my mind: those of a man, bleeding by the road, only to be saved by a blue light; and a dying man, coughing blood, only to rise again. They were a wish to rectify a little of the pain and hurt of the world.

I felt the budding of real, earnest hope. Like a game, I was being given my initial class skills. With these powers I could grow to be a mighty paladin, slaying all who stood before me, advancing in Strength and making the world a better place.

Then something very wrong invaded the last remnants of tranquility. A sense of uncaring, of unbridled change and boundless hunger. Shadowy tendrils began to play against the edges of my mind once again, demanding attention.

"I am Rust..." a voice uttered in a sibilant, gravelly tone behind me.

I turned around and found nothing, met instead with dark, hollow laughter. Images assaulted my senses, violating my sense of self. They were of a forlorn sword, rusting as a grave marker to a forgotten soldier. Its serrated blade, marked with red rust the color of dried blood, was so corroded that it had failed to cut through the hide of a majestic beast.

Then a pause, pregnant with all the future of a dead promise.

Shaken but undaunted, I optimistically chose not to look past the gift. This was just another skill that had appeared before me, albeit a little darker and edgier. Applying my gamer logic, this was probably a debuff that reduced the damage of enemy weapons.

"But first... you must look... must look!" thundered the voice, now sounding a thousand strong. The shadowy tendrils forced my attention to the places at the edges of my vision.

Curse of [Error]: -20% to all starting attributes.

Gilt in black was an error message, the name of my curse.

"What is my name?" demanded the voices, insistent and wheedling.

I coughed blood as I was struck by a blow as sharp as any saber.

"What is my name?" the legion cried out again. They had grown increasingly unrelenting, infused with a wrath that spoke of the death throes of a supernova and echoed with the silence of the grave. Visions of decaying flesh and the slow decline of alien civilizations flooded my consciousness.

"I don't know!" I wailed, my voice harsh as I screamed with all my might.

"What is my name? What is my name? What is my name?" The question rang out again and again, and each utterance was a hammerblow to my psyche. New visions flooded my mind: of the cosmos, explosions of light, the scattering of stars, and the cruel end of all things. I even saw the heat death of the universe.

In the bottom left of my vision, I saw that my Health was plummeting. A flash of inspiration struck me then, fueled by utter desperation. *An endless spiral of lost energy to chaos...* read a fragment of a half-remembered communion with the ultimate end of all things.

"Entropy... you are Entropy!" I cried in a last-gasp bid to live.

Impressions appeared of a smile that was a tear in reality, a galaxy wide, as the true name of my curse was revealed.

Curse of Entropy: -20% to all starting attributes.

A myriad of new system messages then flashed across my vision with the cessation of the pain. Finally, I saw a simple line of text at the end that made me smile in satisfaction as darkness once again claimed one of its own.

Quest Complete: First Steps

Chapter 3

STRUGGLE

The diviners and the truth seers of the elves called for war against a small country far to the west, across the Untouched Seas, who were ruled by a mage-king they divined would bring about the end times. The High King of the Elves, acknowledging the words of the prophecy, sent his envoys to the realms of man and throughout the civilized lands.

— On the Cataclysm by an unknown Quassian Scholar, circa 103 AC.

I awoke naked, sodden, and shivering, my teeth rattling in my skull as I fought a futile battle against the cold. The joy I had felt upon being transported to a new world had evaporated like morning dew under the harsh sun, replaced by the bitter memories of the night before. Even my dreams had turned into a new form of subtle torture.

The dream of the old world, and the events that had led me to this cursed place, were an unwelcome reminder of all I had lost. For a moment I indulged in self-pity, lamenting how quickly I had come to call it the "old world." Thankfully, the last remnants of the dream were dissipating, driven away by a score of minor aches and discomforts that roused me to full wakefulness.

This world was full of pain and suffering greater than anything I had known before. My discomfort demanded that I look with my inner gaze at the notifications.

100 experience gained.
New Skill: Power Strike Lv. 1

New Spells: Heal Lv. 1, Rust Lv. 1
Lv. 2 attained - 3 unassigned attributes have been distributed automatically.

STATUS
    Calling: [Error] Lv. 2 Acolyte of Avaria
    Strength: 8
    Dexterity: 8
    Constitution: 9
    Intelligence: 8
    Wisdom: 8
    Charisma: 8
    Luck: 10
SKILLS AND PROFICIENCIES
    Pain Nullification Lv. 1
    Power Strike Lv. 1
SPELLS AND MAGIC
    Heal Lv. 1
    Rust Lv. 1
GIFTS
    Curse of Entropy: -20% to all starting attributes.
    Experience to Lv. 3: 100/220

I scrambled closer to the tree, sitting against its hard trunk. Gathering myself, I closed my eyes and tried to draw a deep, even breath. Gazing to the bottom-left corner of my vision, where my Health, Stamina, and Mana were represented, I scanned my new Status.

Health: 5/13
Stamina: 14/16
Mana: 4/6

My thoughts scattered as I realized my Health was just over a third of its maximum. This must be responsible for the stabbing pain that throbbed all over my body. It was incomparable, of course, to the banquet of agony I had previously gorged on.

I noticed the irony that two of my randomly assigned points were allocated to Luck. This was my new reality. I was stuck in a cursed game that felt like a thousand other games I had played throughout my life.

I could not stifle a manic laugh. Great shakes filled me with pain as the madness tore through my being, but my hysteria ceased when I realized my Health had dropped by one point. I had been ripped across time and space to die of exposure under a tree in this unknown and alien world; I needed to think rationally before insanity overtook me again.

I needed to regain my Health. My eyes darted around, panic scrambling my thoughts as I desperately sought something that could save me from this predicament.

"Heal!" I desperately shouted, willing for something—anything—to save me.

A pulling sensation shifted energy through my body, followed by a hint of soft warmth, then nothing. Echoes of absolute nothingness. Magic was tantalizingly out of reach; my spell had failed.

"What can I do?" I puzzled to myself as despair began to rise again.

As if in answer, lines of warped text flickered across my vision—binaric script from a corrupted machine that mirrored the broken nature of my reality. Slowly, the chaos settled, forming something I could recognize: a mathematical puzzle. Was this the game's way of telling me I needed to solve it to unlock the key to my magic?

The first puzzle was simple, a clear pattern begging to be recognized. But as I progressed, the puzzles grew harder, twisted into a kind of sinister mini game. I could feel something—or someone—testing me.

Unbidden memories of a long-forgotten mathematics lesson returned to me. My mind reviewed the calculations involved in factoring polynomials, and double-decked equations. Bitterly I smiled, surprised at how much I could comprehend in my new mental state.

And then, as I solved another puzzle, they ceased.

You have gained 1 Intelligence.

The message floated across my vision. Incredulously, I looked at my Status, noticing that my available Mana had increased to five. "What does this all mean?" I wondered as another wave of pain struck.

Shivering, I rose on shaky legs, leaning against the tree to survey my surroundings. Under the tree lay the familiar sight of the dilapidated altar with the fallen statue of the goddess. Yet, as he looked down at his feet, he noticed something unfamiliar: a bundle of roughly spun cloth.

The third person... I must be losing it.

I gathered the bundle and opened it. Inside was a coarse robe of similar fabric to the cloth bundle. Hastily, I scrambled to put the robes on my still-shivering body, ignoring the itchy sensation that reminded me of sackcloth. Tying the robe closed, I felt an immediate sense of security. A tear tracked down my face as the constant hum of vulnerability finally lessened.

Gritting my teeth, I forced myself to focus. The world I was in resembled a game. There were rules, and I needed to find and test out every aspect as soon as possible. I wanted to live, in defiance of all the suffering I had experienced.

Looking at my Status again, I confirmed I had five available Mana. Perhaps I had needed more Mana to cast the spell, and the earlier dull pain was the result of a miscast? Some games I knew had a chance of spell failure, especially for novice magic users. Was that it? No, it couldn't be. Last time I had definitely felt something when I tried to cast Heal, so I would not give up.

"Heal!" I shouted out to the world and willed myself to be made whole.

Once again, I felt a power shift and flow sluggishly through me. However, this time, an unpleasant ripping sensation coursed through my insides, followed by a healing warmth. My Mana had bottomed out to zero, but my Health had increased by two points, to nearly half.

Everything felt like such a burden, and my earlier enthusiasm was fleeing as a painful attack assaulted my mind. Stabbing needles beat against my brain as I wearily struggled back to the tree and sat. My breath began to slow. I fought against closing eyelids that weighed like a mountain, remembering a platitude from a previous life before they shut.

"The serenity to accept the things you cannot change," I whispered. "How apt…"

You have gained 1 Wisdom.

Chapter 4

GROWTH

When facing a manticore, it is prudent to note that the beast has few to no blind spots. The scaly hide is dense and thick and will repel most non-magical weapons, though across the belly one's weapon may find purchase.

One must also observe that, despite being a beast, it has some capability with the arcane, with an ability to cast elemental magics from the fire and ice domains. I would recommend a party of at least five highly skilled adventurers to best one of these fearsome creatures.

— Monsters of the Mortal Realms by K. D. Fidditch.

Groggily, I woke to the night. Stars shone in the sky like a beautiful sparkling tapestry adorned with shining pearls, and I saw a single oversized blue moon through the boughs of the tree. Squinting, I fancied I could perceive great craters on the moon's surface. Its light bathed the world with a soft, ethereal glow in shades of blue and silver, and the grass rustled in the chilly night breeze.

Pulling my thoughts away from the stunning beauty that surrounded me, I slowly hugged my knees to my chest, trying to draw some warmth from the bitter cold. Shivering, I forced myself to peruse my notifications, verifying the changes to my character. I noticed that despite the increase in Wisdom, my maximum Mana had not changed.

Nevertheless, I now stood at the full six points of Mana. Could it be that the Wisdom attribute affected Mana regeneration? More significantly,

I breathed a sigh of relief as I observed that my Health had climbed to eight after my rest and the agonizing healing spell. In my slumber, I had also attained a mysterious skill called "endure" at level one.

STATUS

    Calling: [Error] Lv. 2 Acolyte of Avaria

    Strength: 8

    Dexterity: 8

    Constitution: 9

    Intelligence: 9

    Wisdom: 9

    Charisma: 8

    Luck: 10

SKILLS AND PROFICIENCIES

    Pain Nullification Lv. 1

    Power Strike Lv. 1

    Endure Lv. 1

SPELLS AND MAGIC

    Heal Lv. 1

    Rust Lv. 1

GIFTS

    Curse of Entropy: -20% to all starting attributes.

Experience to Lv. 3: 100/220

Health: 8/13

Stamina: 14/16

Mana: 6/6

Feeling miserable, I hesitated to try to cast Heal again, as I had not enjoyed the unpleasant ripping sensation I had felt when I last cast the spell.

As I pondered my situation, I analyzed my absurd circumstances. In some games, the system penalized players if they reached zero in a statistic.

A lack of Stamina would hinder movement, depleted Mana would impede spellcasting, and zero Health would result in death.

My conclusion was that I did not want to perish, and therefore I had to endure the pain once more to restore more of my Health. I tried to convince myself that the discomfort was akin to receiving a painful injection. Hopefully, the pain from the previous spellcast was a result of depleting my Mana completely, but the only way to find out was to try again.

Wincing at the expected agony to come, I gingerly uttered, "Heal," and focused all my will on the spell. Once again, I felt a shift of some sort of energy, and an uncomfortable pulling sensation. Expecting daggers to assault my mind, I scrunched up my eyes and clenched my fists tightly.

A soothing warmth flooded my body, but there was blessedly no suffering. Glancing at my Status, I saw my Health had increased by a further two points, bringing it to a much safer ten. I breathed deeply as tension left my body. My Mana had dropped to one; I felt a little lightheaded, but there was no excruciating pain.

Fighting against a wave of mental fatigue, I tightened my robe and struggled to my feet. If this was indeed a game world, then this coarse robe was likely my pathetic starting gear. I also made a mental note to investigate the mystery skill, "endure," later. However, the growling in my stomach and the dryness in my throat reminded me of my immediate, more pressing needs.

Searching around the stone shrine, I was prompted with another quest.

New Quest: Restore the Shrine of Avaria? Yes/No

No, I thought, quickly dismissing the intrusive notification from my inner vision. I owed nothing to the supposed "goddess" who had callously plucked me from my comfortable life and thrust me into this harsh and unforgiving world.

My immediate needs took precedence; I had to find food, water, and some sort of protection. I shivered as I remembered my encounter with Avaria in another life. The cold realization that she had all but stripped me of my free will with feelings of forced adulation struck me to the core. That such a being had deigned to mold me into a mere instrument of their indomitable will was a terrifying thought.

With the moon high in the sky, there was plenty of light to see by. I searched around the altar and found a broken spear. It was split in two about halfway up the haft, and the spearhead seemed to be made of sharp stone, bound to the shaft by sinew.

I now had one of humanity's oldest and most trusted tools as a weapon. Two halves of one, anyway. Buoyed by my discovery, I searched more of the area, revealing a rolled-up piece of leather parchment, tied with what looked like rawhide string.

Untying the cord, I noticed there were further knots on the string at varying points down its length. Under the moonlit sky, I wondered if there was enough light to see by as I slowly unraveled the cloth. I was not to be disappointed.

Written across a thin piece of animal hide, esoteric symbols glowed a dull red. Fractals and other geometric shapes writhed and changed across the surface. I traced my fingers along the shapes, awed by what I saw, feeling an electric sensation playing across their tips. A smile rose to my face unbidden as a voice whispered and a new notification flashed across my inner vision.

Learn the spell Identify? Yes/No

"Yes!" I shouted, the inner child and gamer within me feeling a rush of accomplishment.

Another presence made itself felt with images of moldy tomes in a forgotten library, an explorer, holding a torch, searching the dark ruins of a long-lost civilization, and a wise sage poring over a veritable mountain of scrolls.

"I am 'Identify.' Call, and the mysteries of this world you will know," an echo of a scholarly voice whispered, the sound slowly dissipating in the recesses of my mind.

The esoteric symbols stopped moving, and their glow faded as the scroll began to crumble into dust.

You have learned Identify Lv. 1.

Finally, a success in this inscrutable new world. I dared not cast this new spell just yet, as memories of my previous experience still haunted me. To play it safe, I decided to wait until I had full Mana.

Giving myself a mental pat on the back, I began humming the victory tune from my favorite game. Still, my night was far from over, for I needed to explore my surroundings more.

Walking behind the altar, I saw a sight that brought relief to my weary soul. At the foot of the hill, a small pond glistened silver. *Water,* I thought as I licked my dry lips, until I noticed small shapes moving around the shore of the midnight pool.

I clutched both halves of the broken spear to my chest as I cautiously moved down the hill at a half-crouch. My heart was beating fast as I stopped perhaps forty paces before the pond. There, I saw dark, fish-like shapes about half a meter high and two meters long with high-crested dorsal fins.

On the far side, some were swimming lazily in the pond, while others basked in the moon's glow, making odd, yet undeniably musical, mating calls. The creatures reminded me of mudskippers I had once seen in a nature documentary.

So alien was the scene in front of me that I took pause. As quietly as I could, I lowered myself to the ground. Crawling along the soft, moist grass, I edged ever closer to the pond. Thirst drove my actions, a maddening thing that demanded haste, but I mastered it as I slowly made for the water's edge. I quested forwards on hands and knees, my fingers sampling earth and grass before they found fine-grained sand and finally water.

Resisting the all-conquering thirst for a moment more, I peered at my reflection in the water, hazy in the moonlight. Wild and frazzled short hair framed a gaunt, clean-shaven face. It was hard to see, yet everything felt even more real than my old world. It was as if everything were set to a higher resolution. Gingerly, I touched my face, and a small wave disturbed my crystalline reflection.

Snapping out of my reverie, I cupped my hands and drank from the silvery water. Slurping quickly, uncaring of the world, sweet, blessed relief entered me as I slaked my thirst. I continued to drink heavily as another ripple lapped against the shore of the pond, this time one not of my own making.

A few paces away from me, two googly eyes on thick stalks rose up from the water. Bubbles formed where its mouth lay just under the surface, then a ball of water shot with great speed towards me. I flinched and ducked down, making myself as small as possible as the solid ball of liquid passed over me. A moment later I heard its splash. Adrenaline flooded my system, and my fingers gripped my scavenged weapons.

This close to the creature, I felt an equal mixture of sudden surprise, wonder, and fear, which was soon overridden by another scalding-hot emotion. Perhaps it was the constant agony I had been suffering, or possibly my frustration against an uncaring universe, but at that moment I felt a rage I had never felt before. Hot anger boiled within me, screaming for an outlet as I scrambled to my feet and launched myself at the oversized fish.

My eyes rapidly scanned over the piscine form—the size of a large wolfdog—looking for places to attack. I loudly splashed into the waters, breaking the serene tranquility of the night as I struck, stabbing with the half-spear in my left and swinging the broken haft like a club with my right.

As I engaged the strange creature, I noticed new bubbles had formed again just below the surface.

A part of me registered the surprise drawn infinitesimally slowly on the fish's face as my twin blows hit it with a force filled with all my desperation. The fish creature made a gurgling scream as it reactively launched another ball at my midsection. At this range, the creature could not miss, and it felt like a cricket ball had impacted against my chest. The pain only spurred my frenzy to greater heights as I repeatedly stabbed and clobbered the creature with both halves of my scavenged spear. A dark purplish film stained the roiling waters, and I gave a last savage twist with the spearhead as the creature turned tail to flee.

Panting heavily, I noticed more of the foul creatures entering the pond and swimming towards me with considerable speed. Drawing rapid, panicked breaths, I ran, desperation giving speed to my flight from the water. My robe was a cold, sodden, heavy thing that impeded my escape.

I heard splashes on the ground to my right and left before one of the water balls clipped me on the left shoulder, almost making me drop the half-spear. Doubling my pace as I struggled up the hill, I spared a glance at my Status with my inner eye. My Stamina was around half, and my Health stood at just under two-thirds. It would have to be enough.

A frantic final dash led me to hide behind the tree. My heart was hammering in my chest as I peered down at the ugly fish creatures below.

The monsters moved slowly on land, and for that I gave a silent thanks. They seemed to have stopped near the bottom of the hill, a scant few meters from the shore. Panting, I continued to look at them, willing them to withdraw. After what seemed like an eternity—but what could have only been mere minutes—they turned back as one towards the pond and slipped into the silvery waters.

I cried, breathing a long sigh of relief before new notifications flashed in front of me, bringing a sly grimace to my lips.

You have slain [Unknown]. 10 experience gained.
You have gained 1 Dexterity.
You have gained 1 Strength.
You have learned Stealth Lv. 1.

It seemed like today, I did get the one that got away.

Chapter 5

TESTING THEORIES

Although humans were short-lived in comparison to the elder race, they were as numerous as the trees in the forest, and were almost as ferocious as the barbaric orcs of the Long Hills. The League and the Old Empire ceased their endemic wars, united with the promise of gifts of powerful elven artifacts and mithril bullion.

— *On the Cataclysm* by an unknown Quassian Scholar, circa 103 AC.

Looking at the night sky, I saw an ocean of shimmering stars accompanied by a large, solitary moon that served as a fine contrast to their brilliance. For all its beauty, however, something was wrong. Though no student of astronomy, I could not identify a single familiar constellation or guiding star. This unexpected feeling of displacement and isolation compounded my misery.

The plan was to stay awake for the rest of the night to keep watch on the pond below. However, this intent shattered when faced with the cruel reality of my tired body. Exhausted, my eyes felt like lead, as the exertions of the past hours had left me cold and shivering. Slowly and inexorably, like the turning of the seasons, I closed my eyes and faded off into a troubled sleep.

I gradually awoke as the morning sunlight filtered through the branches of the tree and danced across my eyes. Rushing to panicked wakefulness, I looked around with wild eyes, searching for threats. However, all that lay before me was a sea of grass stretching as far as the eye could see beneath a cloudless sky. Sometime in the night, my robe had dried out and I was, at least, no longer shivering. The warm sun shone down as I attempted to gather myself towards some semblance of calm.

This was no idyllic fantasy land where the hero would be guided by the hand to become strong enough to face his destiny. No, this was a brutal world that taught in pain and suffering. Those who could not pass muster would die.

Checking my notifications, it seemed that I had gained another point of Constitution in the night. I hypothesized I had gained this single point due to my current harsh conditions, and that this was the reason my maximum Health and Stamina had increased. From this, it would be logical to assume I could increase my Health by both increasing in basic level and improving my Constitution attribute.

Muttering to myself, I swore to increase my Constitution as often as I could. I simply did not want to feel the awful, numbing pain of being at low Health anymore. Upon checking the rest of my Status, I noticed that I had acquired a new skill, rest, which was at level one.

It seemed I could gain skills from even the most inconsequential things. I observed that my Health was only slightly below the maximum, and my Mana and Stamina were both at full. I craved more knowledge about the world I had found myself in. I needed more data. It was time to experiment.

STATUS

Calling: [Error] Lv. 2 Acolyte of Avaria

Strength: 9

Dexterity: 9

Constitution: 10

Intelligence: 9

Wisdom: 9

Charisma: 8

Luck: 10

SKILLS AND PROFICIENCIES

Pain Nullification Lv. 1

Power Strike Lv. 1

Endure Lv. 1

Stealth Lv. 1

Rest Lv. 1

SPELLS AND MAGIC

Heal Lv. 1

Rust Lv. 1

Identify Lv. 1

GIFTS

Curse of Entropy: -20% to all starting attributes.

Experience to Lv. 3: 110/220

Health: 13/14

Stamina: 19/19

Mana: 6/6

I analyzed my current Status. If this was a game, apart from the horrible start, I was in a satisfactory position. I had likely completed one of the early stages of a grueling "tutorial."

My cautious nature willed me to cast Heal to top off my Health, but the curious gamer inside of me wanted to experiment with Identify, my new spell.

With a slight spring to my step, I made my way around the tree to look down at where the mudskippers were. Finding a medium-sized specimen on the far side of the pond, I uttered, "Identify," and willed the monster's secrets to be known to me. I felt the now-familiar shifting and pulling sensation, and my Mana was channeled into the spell as it coursed through my body. But this time, instead of releasing within me, it was funneled towards my chosen creature.

Bibsis Lv. 1
Health: 8/8

"Bibsis," I muttered to myself, fighting the frustration of being unable to see all of its relevant stats, such as Strength, Dexterity, and Constitution. Drawing a deep breath, I tried to calm myself. It was probably physically weaker than I was, but I had no idea if it had spells or special abilities apart from the water balls. However, at least I now knew the name, Health, and relative level of the creatures I had faced, which further reinforced my hypothesis that this area was some sort of tutorial zone.

I decided to continue casting Identify for confirmation. However, with each use of the spell, my Mana decreased by one without revealing additional information. As I continued to cast the spell, I could feel a pressure mounting in my head.

On the fourth casting, I was overcome by a sense of dizziness similar to the time I had used Heal twice. Thankfully, there was no accompanying sharp, stabbing pain, or overwhelming exhaustion like when my Mana had dropped to zero.

Upon careful examination, I concluded that all the creatures I had targeted with Identify were only level one. I breathed a sigh of relief, realizing that if I had been in a high-level area, my prospects would have been exceedingly grim.

Taking a small break from my experiments, I left the weapons I had scavenged by the small shrine and made my way down the hill to relieve myself on the other side of the pond. When I returned to the tree and altar, I resolved to try out the "power strike" skill next.

I took a few deep breaths to prepare myself. I picked up the half-spear in a loose grip and practiced jabbing at the air in front of me. Then, with all the strength I could muster, I shouted, "Power strike!" while thrusting forwards. Nothing happened. Undeterred, I continued to attack the air while shouting the skill's name.

After several fruitless minutes of exertion, my Stamina had depleted to about half. I hurled the half-spear to the ground and threw a punch at the nearby tree, screaming "Power strike!" at the top of my lungs. My left fist shot out at an alarming speed, pulling my body along with it.

The impact caused chips of bark to scatter, and I felt something in my wrist snap. The excruciating pain was too much to bear as I crumpled into a fetal position on the ground, clutching my injured wrist to my chest with my good hand. Blood trickled down my knuckles, a stark contrast to the color of my skin. It was a vivid reminder that I could bleed in this world, just as I had in the other.

After what felt like an eternity, I summoned the strength to stand up and leaned against the tree for support. I drew shallow breaths through gritted teeth as I half-screamed in agony. Closing my eyes, I recited the births and deaths of long-dead leaders, battles that changed my homeland, and the rise and fall of ages, rebellions, and revolutions. It was a mnemonic tool to help me distract myself from the pain.

While the world I found myself in was game-like in nature, some things were unquestionably not. Unlike controlling a character with a mouse and keyboard, I was well and truly immersed in the "game," and felt pain with every foolish mistake. Despite this reality presenting itself like a game, the consequences of my actions were very real.

You have gained 1 Intelligence.

I let out a wry laugh between waves of pain. Closing my eyes and whimpering forlornly, I decided to rest and focus on restoring my Mana.

For the rest of the morning and a significant part of the afternoon, I cast Heal whenever possible, determined to bring myself back to full Health. I theorized that my maximum Mana had increased by one point, likely due to the recent boost in my Intelligence.

When my Health reached around eleven or twelve, my wrist snapped back into place with a painful crunch, which was then soothed by the remaining aura of my healing spell. Finally, sometime in the late afternoon, I was back to full Health.

An injury that would have taken at least a month and a half to heal in my previous life was fully rectified here in about half a day, thanks to my magical abilities. I found it preposterous, and yet some part of me could not deny the reality of my situation. The pain, if anything, reminded me that this was all-too-horribly real. Still, I could not help but marvel at the miracles I had performed. "Magic..." I whispered in a hushed, reverent tone.

In a previous life, I had read that "Any sufficiently advanced technology is indistinguishable from magic." Could nanobots or some other super technology be responsible for the "magic" and this game-like world? Were my struggles merely entertainment for some weird interstellar audience? But these questions only served to perturb me, so I brushed them from my mind. Survival was my imminent concern, and I refused to die.

The first pangs of hunger hit me as the sun dipped ever lower in the sky. I waited for my Mana to reach full again before picking up both halves of the broken primitive spear.

Absently, I considered casting Identify on my weapons, but thought better of it, as it was painfully obvious what I held in my hands. My ominous Rust spell was also perhaps worth experimenting with at a later time, for I could not see anything in my local environs that would precipitate its use.

I needed all my resources to do what I planned to do next. I needed to grow, and growing, in this world, meant killing.

Chapter 6

HUNT AND HARVEST

The berry of the galebush is sweet and nutritious, attracting fauna and adventurers alike. However, unless thoroughly cooked, the seed will spontaneously sprout within a few hours, causing an almost certain and gruesome death. This is likely a mechanism to provide the new seedling with fertilizer for the next part of its life cycle.

If the being somehow survives the "sprouting," they will slowly turn into a volatile and strange chimera of plant and animal. One such creature was the infamous sun bear of the Duskdown Forest, which terrorized the local territories for many years before a group of Knights Penitent brought it down.

— Monsters of the Mortal Realms by K. D. Fidditch.

My twin weapons in hand, I crept down the hill towards the pond with a furtiveness I never knew I possessed. Walking along the edges of my feet, heel to toe, I mused that my newly acquired stealth skill was already bearing fruit; I instinctively knew how to bend my knees just enough to absorb as much sound as possible.

I slunk along the shore of the pond on my belly. Taking cover behind some shallow rushes, I observed the scene before me.

Across the opposite shore, the amphibious bibsi basked under the late-afternoon sky, occasionally making musical gurgling noises. The school of monsters consisted of creatures the size of an enormous breed of dog, along with smaller juvenile specimens.

I forced each drawn breath to be slow and even while I formulated a plan. Some of the juveniles were playing in the shallows near the shore. I needed to surprise one of them, kill it, then retreat back to the relative safety of the shrine.

Waiting in position, I trusted my stealth skill to hide me from the monsters. After an indeterminable length of time, I grew impatient and picked up a scattering of fine sand, throwing it a short distance from my hiding place, towards the water's surface.

Two adult bibsi broke away from the main school, swimming lazily to investigate where I had thrown the sand. They gurgle-chirped to each other before diving below the surface, swimming to look for the source of the disturbance.

After a minute or two, one of the creatures swam back to the main school, babbling to the others. The remaining monster, about the size of a large hound, beached itself on the shore, rolling onto its side and closing its googly eyes in contented relaxation. *Perfect,* I thought. *Time to use one of my combat skills.*

I rushed out of my position to attack the monster. Instead of shouting out power strike, I invoked it using my mental voice, and targeted the lone, basking bibsis. With my left hand holding the half-spear, I thrust it through the creature's flapping gills.

There was a moment of resistance as my Stamina drained by ten points. Then a driving sensation, different from a spell reaction, traveled through my body and along my arm, guiding my weapon to its fated target.

The stone spearhead passed cleanly through the gills and into the bibsis's brain matter, bypassing the cartilage of its skull with a squelching noise. I followed up by striking the creature's stilling body along its length with the other half of the spear, using it like a wooden club. To my savage satisfaction, the forceful blows scattered muddy brown scales across the shore.

Quickly, I pulled the half-spear from the bibsis's cranium and scanned my surroundings for any oncoming monsters, but none approached. Taking a deep breath, I was gratified to receive a notification of the creature's death, which granted me another ten experience points. I assumed my initial attack had been a critical hit, given the powerful impact.

A dark liquid rapidly congealed on the shore underneath the fish monster's head, with blood, thick like tar, staining the sand. I tried to drag the creature away from the edge of the pond, but soon realized the impossibility of such a task, as the monster was too heavy to move.

Hunger was upon me, and I needed to eat as soon as possible. With the spear's edge serving as a makeshift butchery tool, I began cutting near the tail end of the fish. Piercing first and then sawing across, I deftly avoided bone and cartilage to carve out large chunks of meat from the corpse. With a chunk in each hand and the spear halves tucked under my armpits, I hastily made my way up the hill to the altar.

Upon arriving, I dropped my weapons, then tore into the chunks of flesh like a wild animal. At first I barely registered the taste, due to my intense hunger and the flesh's toughness, but as I ate a second piece, my stomach finally began to settle.

It was then that I noticed the slightly slimy texture, but the meat had a rich flavor. It reminded me of what it might be like to eat a raw frog, and the thought almost made me vomit in disgust. Nonetheless, I continued to devour the rest of my barbaric meal.

Finishing off the last piece, blood congealing down the front of my robe, I crept down again to the rest of the carcass with more practiced ease. I crouched over the remains of the creature and began to clumsily butcher a few more chunks, then ran back up the hill to place the fresh meat upon the altar. On my third run, I stopped to drink some of the cool water from the pond and washed as best as I could the slimy blood from my hands.

Hoping to farm experience and gain new skills, I repeatedly employed my ambush tactic throughout the night. I lost count of the times I had clumsily attracted too many of the creatures and was forced to rush back up to the altar, dodging and weaving in a crazy zigzag pattern. Despite my efforts, I was occasionally hit by an errant solid water ball, and I had to pause to heal myself to restore the damage of bruised flesh and broken bones.

Occasionally, after landing a solid hit, I would cast Identify to gauge the amount of damage I was dealing. It seemed my half-spear was doing between four and six damage, while my impromptu club was rather weak, dealing only one to two damage. Perhaps I was taking penalties for dual wielding, or for not being proficient with my equipped weapons?

Still pondering the mechanics of my new world, I climbed back up to the hill and succumbed to sleep just as the rosy-fingered dawn broke through the sky.

Upon waking up, I rubbed my weary eyes and hastily devoured a few bites of bibsis flesh. Cautiously, I made my way down to the pond to quench my thirst. After checking that my Health and Stamina were fully restored, I repeated the tactics of the previous day. All was fine until, in the warm early afternoon, I was hit by two water balls in quick succession.

Strangely, the first one didn't hurt at all, while the second one hit me with excruciating pain. A pattern began to emerge in my mind as I tried to decipher some of the game's rules. After resting and healing myself to full Health, I deliberately endured two more water ball attacks without trying to dodge. It would almost be my downfall.

The first shot hit me in the stomach, knocking out more than half my Health. Then the next struck, rattling my brain. Concussed and disoriented, I somehow made it back up to the altar, where I cast another Heal spell, hoping to clear my head and prevent a potential brain injury.

My dangerous experiment did, however, prove one thing: I would feel no pain with the first hit *if* I was at maximum Health. Finally, I had an explanation for my mysterious skill, "pain nullification." I had to remind myself this was not some form of invulnerability, as I could still take damage from attacks. Nonetheless, anything that reduced the pain from this horrible world was sorely welcome.

Leaning against the comforting security of the tree, I took stock of the situation and reviewed my current gains.

STATUS

Calling: [Error] Lv. 2 Acolyte of Avaria

Strength: 9

Dexterity: 10

Constitution: 12

Intelligence: 10

Wisdom: 9

Charisma: 8

Luck: 11

SKILLS AND PROFICIENCIES

Pain Nullification Lv. 1

Power Strike Lv. 1

Endure Lv. 1

Stealth Lv. 1

Rest Lv. 1

Backstab Lv. 1

Dodge Lv. 1

Polearms Lv. 1

SPELLS AND MAGIC

Heal Lv. 1

Rust Lv. 1

Identify Lv. 1

GIFTS

Curse of Entropy: -20% to all starting attributes.

Experience to Lv. 3: 170/220

Health: 16/16

Stamina: 21/21
Mana: 7/7

A day and a half of a consistent loop of receiving damage and healing myself had increased my Constitution by another two points, raising both my maximum Stamina and Health. I also discovered that my Dexterity had climbed to ten somewhere along the line. Additionally, I noticed that the average damage I inflicted with my half-spear had increased by one point after using Identify before a solid hit on one of the monsters. Unfortunately, I had not gained any Wisdom or Intelligence, likely due to my exclusive use of physical attacks.

Interestingly, I had also acquired three new skills. Two of the more enigmatic ones, "dodge" and "backstab," were at level one, similar to my beginner skills. I assumed that I had obtained the dodge skill by avoiding the countless water balls that had been spat at me. Backstab could have resulted from my success in launching surprise attacks against the bibsi. I speculated that this skill was responsible for the occasional spikes of one or two damage points I had inflicted on the oversized fish when I managed to catch them off guard. Finally, it was logical to assume that my third new skill, "polearms," was acquired from my extensive and exclusive use of the scavenged spear.

Thank goodness I had been an avid gamer in the old world. Without that skill set, I would have had little frame of reference for this bizarre experience. Shaking my head in disbelief, I noticed I had also inexplicably gained an extra point of Luck. I had only a vague idea of how that attribute would affect my current predicament.

Circumstances were certainly not perfect—far from it—but they were definitely improving. I felt a glimmer of consolation that I was beginning to understand the world I was in. It was satisfying to work out some of the rules I had to play by. There was no internet or wiki here with easy answers. Yet despite all of this, I was enthusiastic about the future.

Tomorrow was another day, and I had five more monsters to slay to level up.

Chapter 7

PROGRESS

The Under-Kingdoms were slower to answer the call, but dwarven greed eventually won over ancient enmity, and they flocked to the banner under elvenkind. The dragons of the mountains and the sky, understanding the threat the mage-king possessed, grudgingly promised aid, though in their pride they would suffer none to command them.
— *On the Cataclysm* by an unknown Quassian Scholar, circa 103 AC.

I awoke to the pleasant aroma of pine and lemon blossoms as I slowly opened my eyes, feeling both fearful and optimistic about what was in store for me. All around me were featureless flat plains of endless green that met the azure horizon somewhere in the far distance. This would become a problem when I eventually decided to leave my place of relative comfort. However, that was a concern for another day. For now, I had five fish to fry.

The bibsi were now one level lower than me, making them relatively easy prey. My strategy was a simple one: distract some of them, take down one, and retreat as quickly as possible back up the hill. It was a tactic I had used countless times in my gaming days to clear areas teeming with powerful enemies. The problem was that I had no baseline to work with to gauge my relative strength in this brave new world.

I needed to gain a better understanding of the rules governing this world. It was imperative to uncover how to improve my skills, as this directly impacted my survival in both the immediate and long term. Would focused practice and repetition enable me to advance them? The fact that the bibsi I had identified were all at level one indicated the possibility of more formidable monsters out there.

Like in fiction, I tried shouting "log out," and "disconnect," once even yelling, "Alexa, log me out," willing myself out of my newfound world with pure force of will. It quickly became clear, however, that this was not a virtual reality—or at least there was no way for me to confirm it.

With my experiments complete, I resolved to spend the rest of the day working on improving my skills and spells in any way possible.

As I walked over to the stone altar, I couldn't help but notice the chunks of meat had become putrid and malodorous. I hurled them as far as I could down the hill, away from the nearby pond. It seemed I would have to feed both my bodily hunger and my desire to increase in power with the lives of a few more of the fish creatures.

Creeping confidently along the edges of the pond with my newfound stealth, I channeled my built-up frustration against these low-level creatures that had dared to harm me. Like an animal that had been beaten too many times, rage filled me as I lured the creatures in small groups towards me. I ambushed the slow and the weak as they retreated back to their side of the water.

My spear felt steadier in my hand, my attacks more calculated and precise, as I struck at them from my hiding place among the rushes. I would violently thrust, pierce, slice, and bludgeon the unsuspecting bibsi until I received a notification of their demise. Butchering only what I needed for the day, I consumed my morning meal slimy and raw. Half-forcing each piece down my gullet as quickly as I could, I was ever watchful against attack.

On my third ambush, I failed spectacularly. Hit in the face by one of their water balls, I felt nothing before a second cannoned into me full on the chest, making me drop my half-spear in the shallow waters. I fumbled, searching for it in the cool waters, gasping all the while in agonized breaths.

Half-blind with pain, my questing hands found the familiar wooden haft, and I beat a hasty retreat.

As I fled, I received another ball of water to my back that took out another chunk of my Health and caused me to scream. Healing myself, and determined to reach level three, I ventured back again, albeit more cautiously.

After a few more hours filled with pain and death, I was granted the much-anticipated notification.

You have reached Lv. 3.
3 unassigned attribute points.
1 unassigned skill point.

In the bottom-right corner of my vision, the writhing, shadowy tendril returned, obscuring a few of the numbers before blossoming into a cascade of indecipherable digits. A short countdown appeared, and the numbers began dropping with each beat of my heart.

Nine... Eight... Seven...

Panicked, I willed all of my unassigned attribute points into Constitution.

Six... Five...

A surge of energy rose from my stomach to my extremities, leaving a feeling of exhilaration. My breath came a little easier, and the chill of the cold waters through my sodden robes seemed more distant.

Three... Two...

With scant seconds to think and choose, I quickly looked within myself, searching for the presence of Heal and focusing on it. The countdown ended, but in my haste, at the same time I had selected Constitution for improvement I had also foolishly cast Heal, despite already being at full Health. I did not know what would happen if I did not allocate my points before the countdown ended, but I felt the price for learning such knowledge would be too steep.

"A waste," I cursed quietly as I checked my Status, confirming the changes to my character.

STATUS

Calling: [Error] Lv. 3 Acolyte of Avaria

Strength: 9

Dexterity: 10

Constitution: 15

Intelligence: 10

Wisdom: 9

Charisma: 8

Luck: 11

SKILLS AND PROFICIENCIES

Pain Nullification Lv. 1

Power Strike Lv. 1

Endure Lv. 1

Stealth Lv. 1

Rest Lv. 1

Backstab Lv. 1

Dodge Lv. 1

Polearms Lv. 1

SPELLS AND MAGIC

Heal Lv. 2

Rust Lv. 1

Identify Lv. 1

GIFTS

Curse of Entropy: -20% to all starting attributes.
Experience to Lv. 4: 220/364
Health: 29/29
Stamina: 24/24
Mana: 5/7

My Health had risen to a staggering twenty-nine points and my Stamina to twenty-four. Also, I could now increase the power of my spells and abilities by leveling up. I whooped for joy, the sense of accomplishment banishing my recent brushes with death and unbridled, unceasing violence. I posited that I would gain Health for each level regardless of my Constitution, and I vowed to test this theory on my next level promotion.

Bolstered with renewed confidence and seeking more gains, I cast Identify on the large, flowering tree in front of me.

Aeyory Tree: [Unknown]

The result was less remarkable than I had expected. Apart from identifying the name of the tree, I realized that magic was no substitute for basic human observation. With four Mana points left, I decided to cast Identify on another object close to me, which ended up being the fallen statuette lying at the feet of the stone altar. The now familiar—yet still uncomfortable—sensation of Mana flowed around and then out of my body towards the object.

Statuette of Avaria: [Unknown]

Again, the spell gave me little that I could not have deduced on my own. Growling in frustration, I cast the spell again in my mind, focusing now on the blazing sun high in the sky. The name of a star roared across my vision like an exploding supernova.

Sahel (Star): [Error]

This was followed by an infinite stream of numbers and raw data that flooded the hollows of my mind, threatening to tear it asunder with its scope. Clutching my head in agony, I screamed once more to the heavens in a primal, bestial shout of the purest pain.

When it was finally over, I found myself on the ground, rocking back and forth while clutching my knees to my chest. Somewhere amidst the pain and shock, the thought, *Why didn't pain nullification work?* repeated itself in rhythm with my rocking. Despite the foolishness of it, I cast the spell once more, this time at the stone half-spear to my left. What did a little more pain matter anyway?

Broken Half of an Ancestor Spear
Durability: 27/53

I smiled a crazy grin of the mad and the broken as a notification flashed across my vision before the pain and exhaustion took me once again.

You have gained 1 Intelligence.
You have learned Identify Lv. 2.

I grinned at my bitter triumph. I had succeeded in increasing the level of not just one spell, but two.

Chapter 8

SURPRISE AND RESPITE

The fae of the deep woods and the places of the In-Between honored ancient pacts and promises, presenting their best warriors and life mages. They also gave unto the First Children great stores of witchwood lumber, grown from the giant, sentient trees that had roots in both worlds so that the elven craftsmen might make living ships to travel the deeps. The forces under the command of the Elven high king were named the Eastern Alliance as an entire continent prepared for war.

— *On the Cataclysm* by an unknown Quassian Scholar, circa 103 AC.

I awoke first to a kick in the stomach, to which I felt nothing except a mute impact. This was followed by another strike to the small of my back, and this time I very much felt it. I let out a howl of agony and struggled to open my eyes as my hand reached out for a weapon that was no longer there.

As my vision cleared, I saw that I was surrounded by four individuals dressed in heavy fur-trimmed leathers and chainmail. Shock filled me as I realized this was my first encounter with other people, and they did not appear to be at all friendly. Through the pain, I tried to explain that I meant no harm, that this must all be some sort of mistake. But all that escaped my lips were wheezing coughs.

One of the men, whom I presumed to be the leader, wore a plumed iron nasal helm. He spat out a mixture of invectives, curses, and orders in a guttural language filled with far too many consonants. As I glanced at the other men, my eyes were drawn to the cruel weapons hanging from their belts.

Their assortment of weapons, from cavalry sabers to crude-looking clubs, heightened their menacing presence. One of them held my broken half-spear reverently; I subconsciously reached for it, only to receive a stinging backhand to the face.

The men were laughing cruelly at me, no doubt viewing me as no threat. Grasping at straws, I mentally targeted the leader of the small group and cast Identify to try and regain some control of the situation.

Bogurchu Batbayar - Waverider (Human Lv. 12)
Health: 142/144
Stamina: 36/37
Mana: 8/8

The men continued to taunt me, their eyes filled with undisguised scorn. One of their brutish numbers straddled my back, pushing my face into the ground and muffling my cries of pain. I was overpowered like a child, and he grabbed my hair, forcing my head up and shouting at me in a rage-filled voice. Hot saliva droplets sprayed onto my face as he snarled at me in an unknown language. I imagined I could pick up one in three of his insults from his tone—something to do with my mother, animals, or perhaps slavery.

Another of the men, squat and heavily muscled but bow-legged in the manner of experienced horsemen, kneeled before my face. Looking closely at him, I saw cruel black Asiatic eyes and a jagged scar running across his nose on a face that was pockmarked with the ravages of acne. His hands were callused and rough from a hard life, but he ran them almost gently through my dirty hair, muttering soft tones of perverse appreciation.

Then, from behind, I felt hands slipping up the hem of my robe, and another pair grabbed my buttocks firmly. Panicked, I tried to twist away, futilely flailing and kicking with my limbs. The men jeered and laughed, trading whoops and hollers with one another.

With an angry grunt, Bogurchu pushed the man off my back. Enraged, the man issued a feral challenge to the leader, snarling with pent-up lust. Bogurchu, with a firm voice that brooked no rebellion, barked at the man until his eyes were downcast, and he grunted in frustration, stepping away from me.

They gagged me with a dirty cloth that tasted like ash and rot. The brutes then covered my head with a crude sackcloth before tightly tying my limbs with rough rope. As I struggled to breathe, a blow landed on the back of my head, causing me to lose a significant amount of Health. Finally, I succumbed to merciful unconsciousness.

* * *

Awakening to darkness, my first sensations were of the acrid stench of the sackcloth, like a mix of rotten vegetables and spoiled milk. I became aware of the rocking motion of what seemed to be some sort of vehicle or wagon. Pain radiated from the back of my head and a ringing sensation persisted in my brain, providing a mild distraction from my numb limbs and the blood trickling down my neck.

The hood was ripped from my head and a rough canteen was brought to my lips. I drank fervently, the stale water tasting of leather, before coughing a little to the men's crude jeers. Two pairs of hands from behind set me down upon the ground, and I could see that the animal in front of me was just a horse. It reminded me of the steppe ponies I had seen in cultural documentaries, but a few hands taller with stronger, more muscular flanks that promised great strength and endurance.

Tied behind the animal, I was forced into a shuffling, stumbling walk, half-dragging against the rope that bound me. Looking wearily in front of me, I saw the strangest of sights.

Before me was a sprawling city of tents surrounded by a high wooden palisade and a deep earthen ditch filled with sharpened stakes. Pairs of men armed with fine long lances patrolled the ramparts. There were four gates at what I presumed were the cardinal points of a compass. Gasping, I saw that in the center was what could only be described as a great ark of a ship, like some leviathan of the ocean that had been beached.

Its neighbor was a large golden-domed white structure, reminiscent of the grand mosques I had seen back on Earth. Around the Ark, four main streets of hard-packed earth, sporadically paved with bleach-white stone, flowed from the city's center. Scattered across the tents were a few rare stone and wooden buildings one and two stories tall.

Towards the east lay a primordial forest, golden and green in the late-afternoon light. The smoke of many charcoal-burners at the forest's edge rose lazily into the air. Near the forest I spied a quarry, or a mining pit, filled with workers toiling away at the alabaster rock.

Taken together, the nomadic tents, rough stone buildings, and presence of primitive industry defied direct categorization. But the academic in me placed the level of civilization at around the eleventh or twelfth century, and a rough guess would establish the population at perhaps twenty to thirty thousand.

Performing these rough calculations in my head, I was filled with a renewed sense of wonder, realizing that this single area was bigger in scale than the entirety of any of the adventure role-playing games I had played back on Earth.

As I stopped in my tracks, lost in wonder, someone kicked me from behind, forcing me to hurry and keep pace with the horse.

It was sundown when we finally approached the southern gate, weary and exhausted. Bogurchu exchanged words with the group of guards at the entrance before handing a length of knotted leather string and a single copper coin to a young boy, who scampered into the city.

The streets were hard-packed mud with occasional deep ruts. Shutters were closing as the city prepared for the night, and the sounds of city life filled the air. I could hear the sounds of when humanity is pressed together—the arguments, the minor violence, the crying of babies.

Close by, I saw a long line of miserable pale-skinned muscular men being led down a street in chains, their eyes devoid of hope. They passed us just as we walked by a large tent filled with music and merriment. It was their equivalent of a tavern, I presumed. Occasionally, a mounted patrol would pass us, and Bogurchu would salute them with a closed fist over his chest.

Finally, we arrived at our destination: a squat building of rough-cut stone, around two stories high. Every window of the building had wooden shutters and cast-iron bars. Two guards stood at the entrance, looking bored and tired in the way of men who had performed the same duty many times over. They saluted our leader before lazily making way for our party.

Inside, a stubby, bored-looking man was reading characters written on animal hide at a desk. He looked up and gave us a quick nod as we passed before I was roughly shoved into a stone cell. The hinges of the stout iron door squealed in protest as it closed with an ominous clang, signaling the finality of my imprisonment.

Through the bars of the cell, I saw the guards turn to leave, jauntily stepping away as if from a job well accomplished. Further down from my cell, the sound of playful laughter could be heard. Men were giving each other a ribbing, only to be tersely cut short by an authoritative voice.

My new environment consisted of a small cell with a pile of straw in one corner. In the other corner there were two buckets, one filled with water and the other empty. The walls were made from solid stone of uniform length and shape, the gaps filled with damp, rotting mortar. A small window, secured with iron bars just above my head, let a drizzle of twilight into my new, dank dwelling.

I moved to the straw in the corner and sat down, feeling almost catatonic. Glancing at my Health reminded me that I had suffered great damage from my beating earlier. Silently, I cast Heal, noticing that my spell was healing me for five points of Health, a vast improvement over the previous iteration. This helped alleviate some of the aches that were running through my body.

However, magic could do little for the bitter humiliation and the hope that had been cut savagely short. Huddled in the corner on the pile of straw, I hugged myself in the cold, damp cell. I longed to return to the comfort and security of my old life. Frustrated by the absolute powerlessness I had experienced, I wept myself to a troubled sleep, filled with grim dreams of cruel men.

Chapter 9

INTROSPECTION

Prophecy is a rare talent, granted only to a select few by the River God. The ability to glimpse the future, by classical definition, implies a linear and well-defined path. However, if one could truly know the future, even for a moment, it would mean that destiny is predetermined and immutable.

The truth, however, is far more complex. Time flows like a river, but it is not a straight and unalterable course. Instead, it is a meandering current that curves around islands of primordial Chaos and Entropy that taint the very fabric of our existence.

The gift of prophecy is unique in that those who possess it can see many, but not all, possible threads of the future. With their own will and agency, they can eliminate unwanted paths, thus serving the temple of the God of the Wend and Way. In this way, the oracular visionaries can guide the course of events towards a more favorable outcome.

— On the Prophecy of the Gods by Gideon de Salavia, 376 AC.

The next day, I was jolted awake by shouting. One of the guards slid a tray of food into my cell. My stomach rumbled as I picked up the meal.

The tray had a crudely carved wooden bowl filled with some sort of thick gruel. I hesitantly tasted the liquid, uneasy at the meaty chunks within. The flavor was bland with the texture of chewed, salty cardboard, but I still hungrily slurped down the rough repast. It was my first "civilized" meal in this new world.

The meal did wonders for my mental state. For better or worse, I had encountered civilization. According to my Identify spell, the inhabitants were human, and being fed meant they were not planning on killing me—at least not immediately.

Despite my recent "cultural exchange" with the locals, I was, for some bizarre reason, cautiously optimistic. I felt, or rather hoped, that there was at least a little room to maneuver and improve my fate. This was a very different situation from killing murderous amphibious fish. Yet, humans could be every bit as cruel as monsters. I remembered yesterday's savage beating and swore vengeance against the men who had found me.

I now had the chance to review my situation and take stock. The previous day was just an unskippable story event. After a good rest, my Health had been restored to just a little under my maximum, and my Mana and Stamina were both full. I noticed that, likely due to the beatings and forced march, I had gained a point of Constitution.

Almost automatically, I cast Heal, a habit ingrained from a lifetime of playing online role-playing games to maintain my Health. This time, the familiar sensation of magic enveloped me with a new twist. The movements and sensations were slower and stronger, like water building up pressure behind a dam. A warm pulse flowed through my core, unlike any previous casting, leaving me feeling a little tired when the spell finally ended.

You have learned Silent Casting Lv. 1.

So instinctive was my casting that I had forgotten to say "Heal," the verbal component of the spell. I had simply willed the spell to be. Wonder filled me as I considered the implications of this new ability, a potential ace in future encounters. They would be unaware of what spells, if any, I was going to unleash upon them. However, I did note that this method of casting took a little extra time, perhaps a few seconds—an eternity in combat.

"*Carpe Diem.*" One of my father's familiar quotes rose unbidden to my mind. It meant "Seize the day," and I intended to take full advantage of my situation, despite the dire straits I found myself in. Stealthily, I moved to the bars of my cell, checking that no guards were watching my next move.

I decided to train my body while waiting for my Mana to recover. I began a series of exercises: jumping jacks, push-ups, crunches, and even using the barred window frame for pull-ups. Every time I lifted myself up, chin above the shutter's bottom ledge, I caught a glimpse of the small square outside, now empty, and the main thoroughfare that ran alongside it.

I continued to push myself until my Stamina reached zero, arms screaming with effort. Still straining with all my will, I tasted blood at the back of my throat as I finished my last pull-up. Panting heavily, I realized I had pushed myself so hard that I had caused some damage to my Health, dropping it by a single point.

Resting and allowing my Stamina to recover, I seized the opportunity to sharpen my mind. I sat cross-legged atop the straw heap, closed my eyes, and delved into a reflective exercise, scrutinizing my actions in this world so far. What could I have done differently? What crucial lessons had I gleaned?

Taking a deep breath, I plunged deeper into my past, attempting to summon long-lost fragments of information from half-remembered lessons. I pondered a host of topics, ranging from mathematics and science to economics, history, astronomy, and religion.

I drew upon my mental faculties to focus on the realm of science, reexamining what I knew about atoms, particles, charge, and bonds. These were the very building blocks of the material world I once knew, and I worked diligently to reinforce my previous knowledge and understanding.

And for my tireless efforts, I was to be rewarded.

You have gained 1 Intelligence.

The notification flashed across my mind, and I laughed with pure joy. The local culture I had encountered was nowhere near as developed as my own world. As a student in the modern world, I stood upon thousands of years of accumulated knowledge and wisdom. What was taught so casually in a classroom would take me far beyond the scholars of this small settlement, perhaps even of this world. I realized that I might have finally found my edge to surviving in this cruel place.

Throughout the day, I continued in much the same way, training both my mind and body in the cell, thankful for the security of its walls. During my training, I gained a single point each in Constitution and Strength.

Every time a small voice urged me to lie down and take a rest, I thought of Bogurchu and the scarred man. Remembering the touch of his fingers across my face brought a shiver of revulsion, and I redoubled my efforts. My body was becoming stronger, my limbs felt more powerful, my movements more graceful, and my breathing a little steadier when I pushed myself to the fullest.

However, the most striking change of all was in my mental faculties. As my Intelligence attribute grew, I found that I could recollect things more clearly, and concepts I had been taught but did not fully understand came more easily to me. This allowed me to increase my Intelligence attribute further, which propelled even more clarity of thought.

Breathing deeply, I settled myself. If Intelligence was learning, knowledge, and retention, then Wisdom must surely be the correct application of that knowledge. With my newly sharpened intellect, I recalled the parables of Aesop and the dialogues of Plato, who urged the pursuit of virtue as an intrinsic good, and the probing inquiries of Socrates, who challenged citizens to examine the moral foundations of their beliefs. Yet I did not stop there; I considered Aristotle's notion of the "golden mean," where moral virtue lies between excess and deficiency. There, I was reminded of how the Stoics—Epictetus, Seneca, and Marcus Aurelius— advised the cultivation of inner fortitude and rational discernment in the face of life's hardships. I even reflected on Confucius's emphasis on proper conduct, an Asian line of philosophy that I usually had no truck with, and the noble aims of cultivating benevolence and righteousness. As I situated these arguments within the tapestry of my own new reality, I saw more clearly, if ever so slightly, man's place in the universe. And as the day turned to dusk, I was rewarded for my efforts with a notification that I had gained a point in Wisdom.

Opening my eyes, I noticed that at some point during my meditations, a new tray of food had been delivered. Checking the contents, I saw what looked like the sorry remains of a root vegetable placed in with my gruel. I had to take sustenance wherever I could find it, so I promptly devoured my meal, leaving the tray by the entrance to my cell. It would do me no favors to antagonize my jailers by making their job more difficult.

The idea of planning some sort of daring escape at this stage struck me as similarly foolhardy. My encounter with Bogurchu and his men had left an indelible mark of fear on me. I made excuses to myself, doubting I would last long on my own in this high-level zone, and decided to play it safe and wait for the next story event on this quest arc. For now, I needed to improve myself and get stronger.

With the pale moon of this world casting an Argentine blue light into my cell, I continued my mental training well into the night, when my thoughts started to drift towards my past. I remembered that it was likely my ex-girlfriend's birthday today, and I silently wished her the very best, wherever she may be. I wondered if time flowed differently in this world compared to my old one; for all I knew, the days were longer here, and it was becoming increasingly difficult to keep track of time. But I was wise enough now to know it was neither of our faults that things had ended the way they did.

After all, life and circumstances could turn anyone into a monster.

Chapter 10

CORRIDORS OF THE MIND

The language of the knots served as the Tide Children's solution to a life spent braving the cold gray seas. Parchment and paper were far too susceptible to rot in the salt-laden air. Instead, they wove intricate patterns into lengths of twine, silk, cordage, or any combination thereof, each knot communicating a surprising level of detail and meaning.

To my untrained eye, this method of recording information seemed slow and unwieldy, but I realized it was likely a mere reflection of my own shortcomings as one who was not born to a life upon the ever-shifting waves.

— *The Fanciful Travels* by Beron de Laney, 376 AC.

The following morning was spent a little differently from the last. I began with a basic breakfast, followed by vigorous physical training consisting mostly of calisthenics. As I completely drained my Stamina, I healed the damage to my Health with magic. At the end of this brutal session, I was awarded with an increase to my Constitution.

I then continued the mental training of my Intelligence and Wisdom, slipping back into the knowledge and lessons of my old world. I still had a few ideas on how to increase my Charisma and Luck, but my attempt to alter the former through interactions with my jailers failed when they pointedly chose to ignore me.

Late in the morning, the sounds of the bustling city filtered into my cell. I watched the busy scene of people going about their daily lives from my window, and, as I finished my set of pull-ups, a flash of inspiration came to me.

A little way outside my cell, in a small square, a market was forming. Sellers had set up many stalls with a wide variety of goods, ranging from the mundane to the exotic: pots and pans, arms and armor, tropical fruit, and even menacing, alien-looking creatures caged in bars of cold steel.

The merchants hawked their wares with guttural cries, no doubt espousing the quality of their goods and offering bargains. The smell of cooking meat wafted into my cell, and I felt a rumbling in my stomach, which I chose to ignore.

Regret filled me as I held myself up to the bars, my gateway to the outside world. I spotted a middle-aged turbaned man in furs arguing jovially with a woman clad in fancy colorful clothes of amber and gold. I steeled myself as I prepared to cast a spell. Focusing again on the man, I shifted my attention to the words he was speaking; I blocked everything else out of my mind and cast Identify.

A swath of information poured into my understanding for the brief few seconds I connected with him, the man's words translating into my native English. Practicing the new words with my tongue, I had difficulty mimicking the coarse, guttural tones and inflections. I was astonished to find that I could recall his words with almost crystal clarity, a feat I would have found impossible in my foreign-language classes back home.

I fired off Identify spells at random conversations, sating my curiosity and increasing my vocabulary, but also thankfully distracting me from thoughts of home. Driven by a need to understand the men I had sworn vengeance against, I vowed to learn all I could of their primitive language.

After a second round of mental training and rest, I once again pulled myself up to the bars, draining a little of my Stamina. The market was closing for the day, with people breaking down stalls and packing away their goods, but I was still able to catch some words.

As I continued to listen, I began to understand more of the language, this time without the aid of magic. Whether it was due to the lingering effect of repeated use of the spell or my growing intellect, I had begun to grasp the language's structure.

Each word was a key to a door that opened new meaning, and every assembled pattern of grammar a corridor that revealed higher concepts of the language. A notification confirmed my progress with another increase in my Intelligence, and I took a moment to congratulate myself for my creative use of magic to learn their language, armoring myself with a false sense of superiority as a thin defense against the powerlessness of my situation.

During a lull in prison life, I noticed that the local fauna had decided to pay a visit to my cell. Small, insect-like creatures scuttled into view, about the size of a large coin, featuring considerable mandibles, two-joint thoraxes, and two pairs of legs attached to an upcurved abdomen. Inquisitively, two or three of them would skitter about my cell when I was perfectly still.

I threw small, loose stones that had fallen off the wall at them, making a game of it. With a lucky strike, I was able to injure and slow one of them. I finished the injured creature with a quick stomp. Blue viscera stained the stone floor, but I was not rewarded with any experience points. The mini games of this world were a bit of a letdown.

I undertook another hard round of physical training, earning an increase of one point in both Dexterity and Strength.

Before resting for the night, I decided to look at my character sheet. I was pleased with the gains across my attributes; thanks to my herculean regimen, my Constitution sat at eighteen points. Also, I noticed that I had considerably boosted my Intelligence and gained a smaller bump in Wisdom, no doubt due to my meditations.

Casting magic and the active pursuit of understanding had also increased my maximum Mana. The hike in my physical attributes had bumped up my Health and Stamina, and I had gained a marginal increase of twenty points of experience for my efforts.

It appeared that in this world, there were three ways to gain experience: quests, practicing skills, and cold-blooded killing. The last reminded me of the party that had found me, and I vehemently swore to turn them into experience points.

With my efforts, I had more or less countered the effects of my initial curse. Nodding in satisfaction with the growth of my mental faculties, I curled up on my pile of straw and faded away to an exhausted, dreamless sleep.

STATUS

Calling: [Error] Lv. 3 Acolyte of Avaria

Strength: 11

Dexterity: 11

Constitution: 18

Intelligence: 15

Wisdom: 11

Charisma: 8

Luck: 11

SKILLS AND PROFICIENCIES

Pain Nullification Lv. 1

Power Strike Lv. 1

Endure Lv. 1

Stealth Lv. 1

Rest Lv. 1

Backstab Lv. 1

Dodge Lv. 1

Polearms Lv. 1

SPELLS AND MAGIC

Heal Lv. 2

Rust Lv. 1

Identify Lv. 2

Silent Casting Lv. 1

GIFTS

Curse of Entropy: -20% to all starting attributes.

Experience to Lv. 4: 240/364

Health: 29/33

Stamina: 2/28

Mana: 1/10

Chapter 11

ARBITRARY JUSTICE

After many years, the great horde started their journey across the vast Untouched Seas, unmolested by the scaled leviathans of the deep. The dragons had negotiated their safe passage, securing it in the ancient way of their kind. The serpents of the sky and sea were to be bound together once more.

— On the Cataclysm by an unknown Quassian Scholar, circa 103 AC.

I was not in any immediate danger, but the monotony of life stuck behind bars, unable to enjoy the wider world, was taking its toll. I wanted to be free, but for the time being, I had to content myself with a little experimentation and training. It seemed that magical healing, as tested with rigorous exercise, could relieve the body of muscle fatigue when cast. As long as I had the Stamina, Mana, and will, I could engage in a torturous loop of self-improvement. However, it seemed that fate had other plans in store for me.

On the third day of my incarceration, instead of one of the guards, a boy just on the cusp of adulthood appeared to deliver my first meal. Exhausted after a strenuous bout of exercise, I was sitting cross-legged in the corner of my cell when the sound of the meal tray disturbed me.

As I stirred from my meditations on the nature of the state's responsibility to the people, my eyes met his, and he backed away from the bars of my cell. He had short, cropped hair between a dark brown and true black, a button nose slightly set in a round face with a weak jaw, and panicked brown eyes that had opened in surprise like wide saucers. He wore a brown ill-fitting woolen tunic two sizes too big for him with large buttons made of horn, and coarse linen trousers. The overall impression was of a startled mouse surprised by a cat.

Feigning calm, I cast Identify on the boy.

Jongshoi Aigiam - Trainee Warrior (Human Lv. 6)
Health: 48/48
Stamina: 22/22
Mana: 6/6

My Identify spell failed to reveal his primary attributes. However, I could discern that he likely had little in the way of Constitution despite being at a higher level than me, due to his comparatively low Stamina. Perhaps he was a "glass cannon" with a ridiculous amount of Strength, but I doubted it. Furthermore, having such a low amount of Mana indicated that he was not the sharpest tool in the shed.

In an attempt to appear approachable, I smiled to greet him, my voice unsteady and hesitant.

"Jongshao," I called out in a halting voice, likely butchering the language.

His eyes only opened wider. He cried out words of alarm, scrabbling to get as far away from me as possible. Two of the guards promptly marched to my cell. Armored in a mixture of half-plate and sturdy leathers, with mean eyes and meaner weaponry, one of them rapped loudly on the bars with a dagger.

I glared at the guards as they turned their backs to leave, realizing why Jongshoi had panicked: never had I asked him for his name, and I cursed my mistake. I did not know how this culture viewed magic; perhaps he thought I was a witch who had cursed him. My cell was no longer a safe haven from the world. Suddenly, the idea of trying to make a daring escape had become more appealing than waiting passively for circumstances to change.

It seemed that my unlucky encounter with Jongshoi was an omen of further misfortune, as later, despite almost bursting a blood vessel with my efforts in training, I gained no bonuses to my attributes. Perhaps this was due to the game becoming exponentially more difficult as I progressed? I berated myself, realizing I could not think of this as a game. This was a world, filled with all-too-real pain and suffering.

Pulling myself up onto the barred window ledge, I resumed my quest to learn their alien language. By the end of my session, with the help of my magic and increased language ability, I could understand about seven out of ten words in spoken conversation. I was now able to demonstrate feats of learning that would have impressed even the most talented of linguists in my previous life.

The city's name was Ansan, a frontier mining town by the standards of my world, and it was famous for two things.

First, the mammoth ship located in the city center. Legend had it that the ship was placed there as the waters receded after a cataclysmic event known as the "Breaking" or "Scouring." However, it remained shrouded in mystery as to how or when this event had occurred. Nowadays, the ship served as the seat of local governance for the people known in their language as the "Children of the Tides." They were originally a maritime people before the Breaking.

The second point of notoriety for the city was its burgeoning slave trade. Ansan's flesh markets, slave pits, and fighting dens were infamous among the trade caravans that frequented the city. The Children of the Tides were a martial people whose economy revolved around a constant state of war and slavery.

Outside the city, near the forest, were mines rich with ore, worked on by slaves who were brought in by the Children's never-ending wars. Marketplace rumors hinted at recent movement in the Sainba, the primordial forest to the east of the city. Strange, chittering creatures had been sighted along its borders by charcoal-burners who made their living at its edges, disrupting the supply of precious fuel for the mines. This had resulted in a visible increase in military patrols in the area, and the air was tense, taut as a bowstring ready to be released. Straining my ears, I had also heard hushed and cryptic rumors that a local place of some religious significance had been desecrated, causing consternation among the warrior classes.

I found it odd that there was no mention of levels, attributes, experience, or magic. Were any of these subjects a local taboo?

A few hours later, I had another visitor. I heard the clank of armored feet and the scream of tortured hinges as my cell door opened. Without any ceremony, a new group entered my prison: a veritable hag of an old woman, flanked by two guards whom I did not recognize.

The crone was a small, hunched thing, clothed in robes the color of fresh-turned earth. She wore animal necklaces and fetishes made of the bones, teeth, and claws of unidentified beasts around her neck. In her left hand was a walking stick made of gnarled wood, with black feathers placed along its tip. Her hair was lank and light gray, and dribbled down across her face and shoulders. A hawk-like nose, thin, narrow lips, and black piercing eyes gave the overall impression of a shriveled, mystic raptor.

Her burly guards, clad in a mixture of unadorned plate, chainmail, and riding leathers, funneled past her. One of them carried a thick orange cloth rug of some sort, which he laid across the middle of my cell. She indicated for her guards to position themselves behind her, standing to her left and right.

The guard to her right, who had a porcine face with a large, bulbous nose, idly explored the depths of one of his nasal cavities through his open-faced helm. Finding no treasure, he wiped his hand on his leather tassets before fixing me with a menacing glare. As he shot daggers at me, the woman hitched up the hem of her robe and, with a small cough, sat cross-legged on the rug.

I started to offer a half-hearted greeting, but she cut me off with a raised hand and gestured for me to sit. Timidly, I sat down on the rug across from her. She smiled at me in the way a snake eyes up a rabbit. Looking me directly in the eyes, she tried to greet me in a language that resembled Latin but was heavily accented. Confusion must have shown on my face as she switched back to her native language.

"Outlander," accused the old crone in a lilting soprano voice that was surprisingly firm, belying her advanced age. She noticed the dawn of understanding written across my features. "Do you know why you are here?"

I began to mouth a reply, but she interrupted. "I am Navigator Olai of the Second Fleet. You have caused quite a stir and no end of trouble. Jongshoi accuses you of witchcraft, but from his tale, I deduced that you probably gleaned his name from his inane conversations with one of his father's friends here. They gossip like little unmarried girls! Did you know the foolish boy begged and skipped one of his duties to view the strange outlander? We must move up the schedule for his Blooding, put a little bit of spine into the lad."

As I was ruminating about my failure with Jongshoi, one of her scrawny arms shot out like a snake and grabbed my face just under my chin with surprising strength. The guards moved their hands to the weapons at their hips as she tilted my head at a slight angle, examining me with cool, calculating eyes.

"Too pale to be a Qisnian, and too short to be an Imperial," she said, now looking at my soft, uncalloused hands. "Perhaps a runaway house slave or some noble's get? What possessed you to desecrate the shrine, break the Spear of the First Ancestor, and burn the words of the Covenant? And, to make matters worse, why did you kill the sacred Rain-Bringers and partake of their flesh?" Her fingers tapped my chest with each accusation.

"I didn't—" I started, but the hag didn't let me finish.

"You would deny this? Each of these crimes alone warrants death." My face grew flushed, and one of her thin eyebrows arched as she continued. "You were the only intelligent being, and I use this term very loosely, in a day's ride of the shrine. The Sea Council has come to a conclusion, despite your mysterious origins, to dispose of you—"

"I didn't desecrate your shrine, and I didn't break the spear. They were like that when I found them. Please, you have to understand!" I begged as I reached out to her.

The guards began to draw their weapons, but she raised her hand, stopping them mid-motion. "Your pronunciation is lamentable. Like an Imperial dog farting out what it thinks is speech. And even if this were true," she said in a softer voice, "what of your other crimes?"

My mind scrambled to make a plausible excuse in those precious few moments and drew a solid blank at the trap she had laid with her framing.

"I would have had you killed mercifully, by sharp blade or poison. We are not savages, after all. But the Commodore and the Captains are loath to waste resources, and they wish to make an example of you." She sighed in tired resignation. "What is your name, young man, that we may announce during your sentence on the sands?"

I felt pins and needles in my brain in response to her innocent question. I wracked my mind, trying to remember my name, but no matter how hard I tried it eluded me, like trying to grasp motes of light. Panic was just beginning to set in before I remembered that this must be the part where my character got to choose their name. I quickly settled on one from my other world. His legend was that of the first hero, of which all others were but pale copies. His name would become legend in this world, too.

"Gilgamesh," I said with a confidence that I hoped hid the quiver in my voice.

Out of one of the folds of her clothes, she drew a many-knotted cord of crimson the color of freshly spilled blood on snow. Running her hand along its length, as if reading, a lump formed in my throat as she pronounced my sentence in a distant, authoritative voice.

"Gilgamesh. You have been judged of crimes against the people. Their eyes have turned from you. Still, you have been granted a chance to redeem yourself of these vile deeds. When Sahel is at her highest tomorrow, you will be brought to the sands of the Winnowing. Your death will blood our next generation of warriors. Should you find the favor of the gods, you will be allowed to live the life of a slave. May the divines watch over you."

Her words lingered in my mind as she rose abruptly on creaking joints, shooing away her guards' proffered aid. They departed as swiftly as they had arrived, abandoning the carpet on the ground. Though my ingrained sense of etiquette urged me to remind them of their forgetfulness, the bars of my cell closed with the finality of a judge's gavel.

Chapter 12

THE SWORD OF DAMOCLES

The queen's first egg was to be presented in ten turns of the seasons as a new bride. Such was the desperation of the Alliance with the fate of the world on their shoulders. The dragons, in their great pride, would never forget what the "lesser races" had forced upon them, and their resentment would only grow with the passage of time.

— On the Cataclysm by an unknown Quassian Scholar, circa 103 AC.

Calm. I sought calm amidst the battlefield of my thoughts. A thousand times I replayed my exchange with Jongshoi and Navigator Olai. Was there anything I could have done to steer the conversation in a different direction? To find a different path, a different strand of fate to cling to? I circled my cell, ruminating ceaselessly as the dawn's rosy glow kindled the horizon. Soon after, the hush of the night was replaced by the clamor of industry and commerce.

My breakfast was a death row inmate's last meal without the flavor. Despite all my efforts, my last training session only resulted in a single point increase in Strength. This led to a small boost in Health, and from that I deduced that Strength's threshold for increasing Health was every four points. Strength, Dexterity, and Constitution all played a role in determining my endurance and Stamina, though I had not yet calculated to what degree.

I smiled wryly, thinking that if I were back home, I would have sifted through the message boards, forums, and wikis to confirm my theory. Here,

I had only myself to rely on. I checked my character sheet as I prepared to face the rest of the day. It appeared I had also gained an additional ten experience points, and my character sheet had been updated with the name I had chosen. Once again, I marveled at the game-like nature of this world, far removed from my old one.

STATUS

Calling: Gilgamesh Lv. 3 Acolyte of Avaria

Strength: 12

Dexterity: 11

Constitution: 18

Intelligence: 15

Wisdom: 11

Charisma: 8

Luck: 11

SKILLS AND PROFICIENCIES

Pain Nullification Lv. 1

Power Strike Lv. 1

Endure Lv. 1

Stealth Lv. 1

Rest Lv. 1

Backstab Lv. 1

Dodge Lv. 1

Polearms Lv. 1

SPELLS AND MAGIC

Heal Lv. 2

Rust Lv. 1

Identify Lv. 2

Silent Casting Lv. 1

GIFTS

Curse of Entropy: -20% to all starting attributes.

Experience to Lv. 4: 250/364
Health: 36/36
Stamina: 29/29
Mana: 10/10

There would be no point in training now—I needed to face my trial with a fresh mind and body. I had little doubt I would be pushed to the limit with the odds stacked against me. As my time approached, however, I refused to give in to fear. I overruled the thoughts that hung over me like the Sword of Damocles.

I tried to formulate a strategy for my upcoming combat. Between my Mana and my level two Heal spell, I had forty-one points of effective Health, provided I wasn't instantly killed by a single attack. It was actually a respectable forty-six points if I was willing to brave the pain and disorientation of bottoming out my Mana, although I conceded that this might not be feasible in a combat situation. Perhaps I could use it with my pain nullification skill to some sort of advantage?

Power strike was a skill I could use three times before I started taking potentially serious damage to my Health, but I worried whether I would be strong enough to inflict significant harm against my enemies. How tough, exactly, was the average human in this world? Bogurchu seemed like the sort who was hard as nails, with his tremendous 144 points of Health. Dread filled me at the thought of having to face someone like that.

On the bright side, Navigator Olai mentioned that the "Winnowing" was some sort of test for their younger members, which could mean that my opponents would not be as tough as Bogurchu. For all I knew, I could be facing Jongshoi, or other boys like him. However, whoever I faced, they would almost certainly be a higher level than me. For all intents and purposes, I was like a newborn in this world.

Yet if I managed to survive, I would no doubt gain a significant amount of experience. My hands began to shake as I realized I might have to take another human life to stay alive. Was it in me? I resolved that if it came down to a choice between my life and someone else's, I would not play the role of a martyr.

After about an hour or so, two armored men entered my cell, wearing wolf-masked face helms and outfitted in overlapping plates that resembled beetle chitin. Each of them carried a long two-pronged device that exuded an aura of tightly coiled menace.

I weighed my options, considering that this might be the prime moment to make a break for freedom. However, indecision took over, and I missed my chance as one of them caught me by the neck and began dragging me out of the cell.

I raised my hands in the universal sign of surrender and exclaimed in their language that I would walk willingly. However, they just grunted in the way of busy men and tugged harder on my leash.

Once I was out of the cell, the other guard attached his man-catcher around my neck, and they began pushing me with the length of their polearms, directing me towards the outside street. When we reached the main entrance, the bright morning sun greeted me, causing me to squint and slow down a fraction against its light. Two guards standing post at the door stifled their chuckles as my bare feet touched the hard-packed earth of the street. My escort suddenly stopped behind me, pushing me slightly down and indicating a space on my left by my feet.

"Put them on," one of them growled in a surly voice as I noticed a pair of worn leather sandals lying by the entrance, perhaps a size too big for me.

I kneeled down and slowly put them on, my fingers unsure with the buckles and intricate straps. I was tempted to use Identify on my new footwear but thought better of it; I would need every scrap of Mana for my upcoming challenge.

After I finished putting them on, my escort shouted for me to keep walking. Their voices were clipped and harsh as they pushed me again with their long man-catchers. I could feel the hard stone floor through the thin soles of my sandals.

The market outside my prison cell was a cacophony of colors and sounds, a lively display of human commerce and interaction. Merchants of all kinds vied for attention, their voices rising in a chaotic symphony of salesmanship. Some spoke in hushed tones, conspiring with potential customers, while others bellowed out their wares with all the fervor of street preachers.

A magician caught my eye during this swirl of activity. He drew a silken blue cloth from the ear of a blushing young woman, eliciting gasps and applause from the crowd gathered around him. I watched with curious detachment, wondering if the magic was real or merely an illusion created by sleight of hand.

As I made my way through the throngs, moving beyond the market and onto the main street, a young girl caught sight of me. Her cherubic face turned towards her mother, and she pointed in my direction, her eyes wide with wonder. "Is that the outlander?" she asked, her voice ringing out above the din.

Her mother quickly hushed her, casting a furtive glance in my direction before hurrying away. But the girl lingered for a moment, pulling at her mother's hand and stealing one last look at me before disappearing into the crowd.

The people we passed who were milling about on the main thoroughfare paid us little heed, their gazes sliding off us like water off a smooth stone. It was clear that our presence here was nothing new to them—they had seen it all before.

A small brown mongrel dog caught our attention as it began to bark, its single white eyespot contrasting sharply against its matted fur. The dog's yapping drew a disheveled man out of a nearby tent, stumbling and lurching like a drunken sailor. He was followed by screams and hurled objects, much to the amusement of his neighbors.

Despite the strangeness of our situation, it was clear that humanity was still humanity in this new world. The petty squabbles and crude humor of these people were no different from those of the world I had left behind.

We strode past a multitude of round tents made from hides and oilcloth, their shapes reminiscent of the yurts of the Mongolian steppes. Some boasted intricate patterns, with threads of green and red intertwining like waves on the open sea. But for the most part, they were dull, squat things.

I would have liked to have had a better look at some of them, but my eyes were drawn instead to a building made of clean-cut white stone. A symbol of a crossed sword over a wooden torch hung above the iron-banded entrance, marking it as some kind of armory or weapons shop.

Just as we passed, the door burst open and a hulking giant of a man stumbled out, his massive form filling the doorway. A greatsword was strapped to his back, nearly as long as he was tall, and he drew it with a mocking roar of rage. His ham-sized hands gripped the leather-bound hilt under a cross guard just over the width of the blade, the weapon's shallow fuller running about three-quarters up its length. As he waved the sword back at the people inside the building, shouting unknown curses, I could not help but marvel at its craftsmanship. The double-edged blade gleamed in the sunlight, and I could sense the power and weight of the weapon, even from a distance.

Following the giant of a man was a thin figure draped in loose dark blue robes, with golden esoteric patterns sewn into the fabric around the sleeves and hem. He wore a wide-brimmed conical hat with the tip slightly folded, looking every bit like a wizard out of a role-playing fantasy game as he joined in his friend's laughter.

As they exited the building, a platinum-blonde woman stormed out behind them, shaking with fury and fists clenched at her sides. Clad from neck to toe in plate and mail armor, a white tabard with a golden chalice hung loosely over her armored chest. A flanged mace, with sharp spikes protruding from its head, was slung from a belt made of thick iron rings. She delivered a powerful punch to the bare shoulder of the barbarian man, but the force of her own blow unbalanced her, nearly causing her to stumble. The giant of a man only laughed harder at her momentary loss of composure.

A typical adventuring party, I thought, before my escort shouted at me to pick up the pace. For a long while, I could still hear the woman berating the man in what sounded like a form of Latin until we passed another market square and the sounds of their argument were drowned out by the hubbub of the city.

We took a left turn from the main avenue and continued through the labyrinth of tents. As we progressed, the object of our journey came into sharp focus: a colossal circular structure crafted entirely from massive wooden logs, fashioned in the style of a primitive Roman arena. A small market had formed around the periphery of the building, and the air was thick with a sense of festivity as the din of commerce grew louder with each step.

The throng of people surrounding us began to part as we made our way through a myriad of colorful stalls. In our wake, I could hear the murmurs and whispers of the populace as they debated my fate.

Finally, we arrived at the arena's entrance. Its colossal iron portcullis, resembling the jaws of some beast that had devoured a multitude of humans, loomed before us. guards draped themselves lazily around the entrance, leaning against great glaives of banded wood and bladed steel. As I stepped through the threshold, a chill crept into my bones, and I felt the gnawing sensation of dread in the pit of my stomach that I had been marked for sacrifice to this place.

I was shoved roughly into a wooden cell, and again I was left alone with my thoughts.

"Yet another cell," I grumbled. My eyes took a moment to adjust to the dimly lit room, and when they did, I realized I was very much in deep trouble. A small slat in the door allowed a sliver of sunlight to penetrate the gloom, illuminating the sandy floor of the cell. Above, a series of cables, winches, and pulleys were attached to the door, no doubt designed to lift it when it was my turn to fight.

I could hear the murmurs of a crowd through the opening and quickly made my way over to see what was causing the commotion. Looking through the open slat, I could see a roughly circular arena with a white sand floor. Above the sands rose a fenced wooden stand area made of rough-hewn logs. The audience was a mix of unarmed citizens and armored martial types, all shouting and cheering as an armored warrior entered with a swagger that exuded confidence and skill.

I was surprised by a sudden grinding noise as the wooden reinforced door to the cell on my right was raised. Quickly looking back through my window to the arena, I observed a ceremony official with a colorful plumed helmet and a bronze breastplate throwing a gray weapon into the arena's center. A scrawny figure, clad in rags, abruptly darted from the cell to the center of the sand, scooping up the weapon with thin, weak arms as if it were the most precious thing in the world before adopting his best fighting stance. The crowd roared their approval.

The shape on closer inspection was a pitifully poor specimen of a man. His beard and hair were a long and unkempt brown, and his eyes were wild with panic. He was holding a straight steel or iron short sword with both hands in front of him, arms locked and stiff.

Across from him, the armored warrior closed his helm and hefted a large shield in his left arm. Holding a curved backsword in his right hand, he executed a few simple flourishes before walking languidly up to his opponent. The crowd's cheers and jeers faded into a distant hum as the warrior closed in on his prey. For every step forwards he took, the wild man took a step back.

The armored warrior reached the center of the arena and gave a wild, ululating battle cry, which was met by a great roar from the crowd as he charged. The rag-clad man broke and panicked. He threw his sword down and tried to clamber up the stanchions. After his second failed attempt, he gave up and retrieved his short sword with shaking hands, his eyes now filled with the look of a cornered animal.

Clad in heavy armor, the warrior moved closer with fast but sure steps. Sprinting, he aimed a cool, methodical cut at the poor soul in rags, who threw up his sword to block the blow. His effort was in vain as the warrior's long curved blade cut a crescent through the air, leaving a red line across the man's chest.

Screaming in pain and shock, the thin man crumpled to his knees, lifeblood pouring through his hands. Like a gardener plucking weeds, the armored man put an end to his misery with a simple flick of the wrist, cutting across his throat to sever the thread of his life. Turning to the crowd, he raised one closed fist in salute, and an approving roar erupted. Another of the Children of the Tides had been blooded this day.

Despite the violently surreal scene playing out in front of me, I could not help but wonder how many experience points the victorious warrior had gained from killing his opponent. It was a callous thought, but one that revealed the brutal nature of this place.

As soon as the man fell to the ground, the victor picked up the defeated man's short sword in his other hand and turned back to his corner, walking through the gates at the far end to riotous applause. On the sands, a group of young boys between the ages of ten and fifteen hurriedly dragged the corpse away in preparation for the next bout.

This scene would repeat itself ten more times as the doors to my left and right were opened one by one. Blood was spilled on the sand, and a bitter harvest was reaped. Some prisoners surrendered without a struggle, huddling in their cells, and were butchered like livestock. Others fought with all their might and were cut down in a gruesome display of force.

One desperate soul even tried to outrun his fate, but the spectators' jeers were little comfort as he met his end like an animal. It was a stark reminder that in this world, as in any other, power was the only currency that truly mattered. The unfairness of it all made my blood boil.

As the door to my cell slowly rose with the grinding of gears, an official from above threw a weapon into the sands. It traced a graceful arc, glittering as it reached its zenith before falling to signal the start of the Blooding. It was a kill-or-be-killed scenario, and it seemed the universe agreed, as a new quest notification flashed across my inner vision.

New Quest: Kill Jongshoi and survive the Blooding

Chapter 13

A TEST OF IRON

*Our enemies are the whetstone upon which we hone our bodies and
minds. Ever striving to reach perfection, until all that is left is only that
which is required.*

— The Living Sword by Fen Vaigorus, circa 520 AC.

Repeating the mantra that this was just a game, I was able to suppress a
blossoming panic that had taken root in my mind. Unlike the previous
contestants, through some stroke of luck or the devil's meddling, I
knew who I was facing. And with my character sheet I was aware of my own
abilities—I wouldn't have to waste Mana on an initial Identify.

I sped towards the center of the arena, eager to obtain the instrument
of death that awaited me. With every step, my determination to complete
my quest grew stronger. As I rushed, I stumbled slightly before grabbing a
short infantry-stabbing spear. The polearm had a shaft length of just over a
meter, with a long and wide-bladed leaf-shaped metal spearhead. Whether
it was my expertise in polearms or simply the need to feel secure with a
weapon in hand, the spear was a reassuring and solid weight.

Jongshoi lacked the grace and calm confidence of the other warriors I
had witnessed bloodying themselves in the arena. He looked skittish, like an
animal about to bolt. He made his way to the center cautiously, where I
waited, now trying to exude an aura of calm, like a gazelle approaching a
watering hole for the first time. But he was no lion, no roaring warrior
thirsting to prove himself by wetting his blade in the blood of his victims.
The fear of violence could be seen in his eyes, and in another world I would

have held no ill will towards him. But I was here, and he was merely a steppingstone for me to reach greater heights of power and the freedom that brought.

The unblooded would-be warrior was garbed in armor of heavy scale and plate. His hauberk bore circular scales akin to those of a monstrous fish, buffed to a shine that mirrored the high afternoon sun. Interlocking plated steel pieces draped over his shoulders and arms, and metal gauntlets with round steel nubs encased his knuckles. Thick iron leggings and greaves covered his lower half, and an intimidating plumed open-faced helm that depicted a roaring lion completed his ensemble.

A spiked oval shield, reminiscent of the scutum, rested upon his left arm, while on his right he brandished a small straight-stabbing sword reminiscent of the Roman gladius.

But despite his formidable equipment, the young boy looked out of place, like a rabbit that had grown horns and fangs. For he looked untested in battle, and the weight of his armor and weaponry seemed to burden him more than lend him strength.

Jongshoi was already breathing heavily, each exhale a ragged spurt in the hot sun, no doubt in part because he was suffering from some equipment penalties due to wearing such heavy armor. I, on the other hand, was only equipped with my initial robes and could move much more freely. A glimmer of a battle plan began to form.

He came at me first with a tired, hesitant probing thrust that I was easily able to step away from. I returned with my own weak thrust to his center, aiming to preserve my Stamina. He blocked it easily with his shield, turning aside my blow, then returned with another thrust of his short sword that I was able to avoid with my greater reach. Since I was unarmored, I had to be careful, but he, on the other hand, looked like he could certainly take a hit or two.

Piercing the boy's defenses was proving almost impossible. However, he simply could not land a blow on me as I darted backwards after one of my own failed attacks. Then something changed. After deftly deflecting one of my rapid jabs, Jongshoi cried, "Shield Bash!" before lunging forwards with his shield, breaking through my feeble guard. The spike of the "scutum" tore a bloody gash across my left arm, and my Health dropped by five points. Worst of all, I was left feeling stunned and disoriented, my world spinning as I struggled to gather myself.

My enemy moved into his follow-up, a little awkwardly but deadly nonetheless. With a panicked fury, he struck at me, raising his sword arm, and screamed, "Power strike!" Barely able to shake off my fugue, I raised the haft of my spear just in time to meet his down-coming blade. Strong sharp steel met the wooden haft of my spear, causing a sharp crack and sending splinters flying from the point of impact as his attack savagely split my weapon. His skill-enhanced blow continued its deadly arc, tracing a red line across my chest. A sharp pain blossomed within me, and my Health dropped by another thirteen points as I stumbled backwards.

Jongshoi breathed heavily, barely able to stand on his feet and his sword arm faltering. Blood ran from his nose and mouth, as he had pushed his body well beyond its physical limits. I knew that feeling well. With the remains of my weapon in a death grip, I grinned savagely, knowing his desperate gambit had failed.

He had likely depleted his Stamina with his continuous use of skills, while I still had a healthy amount remaining. And I had magic. I needed to keep the pressure on. Through the red haze of pain, I continued to throw jabs and light slashes with my half-spear and broken spear haft. My adversary was barely able to defend himself. And to add to his troubles, his exhaustion was probably draining away his Health.

Using the Silent Casting, I cast the Heal spell and felt the energy spread through my body, like the warm touch of a lover. Surprisingly, my Health increased by seven points, and I absently concluded that my spell must heal a proportional amount of damage instead of a set amount.

My opponent's eyes widened in surprise as I stood a bit taller, the bleeding now stemmed by magic, my weapons sure in my hands. The crowd grew bestial and wild, shouting epithets at us. In my own desperate bid for survival, I charged him, as the crowd above gasped in surprise that I still yet lived.

Raising my broken spear haft like a club, I started raining blows on his shield. I threw a jab with my left weapon, which he met with a weak parry of his sword before I called forth the power strike skill, the energy of its release like an arrow from a war bow.

My blow skidded across his hauberk, ripping out a few scales, and went upwards to savagely cut his face. His youthful, innocent features were now made into a vision of horrible deformity. He screamed, crying out in utter animal pain as he dropped his sword and reached for his face.

My own breathing was starting to come heavy and ragged, and I knew I had to press my advantage and finish this quickly. Tossing aside the broken spear haft, I bull-rushed him clumsily to the ground. His face was a gory mess. He tried reaching for a sword that was no longer there before blindly swinging at me, punching at me with his plated gauntlets. His blows scarcely registered across my trunk as we were simply too close, and he was barely able to cause a single point of damage despite his superior Strength.

Nevertheless, his blows still caused me pain, which kept my blood hot and angry. Grappling him with my right, I raised my half-spear in my left like a knife over the remains of his face and used another power strike. The spearhead hammered down, punching through teeth and bone in an explosion of crimson.

Suddenly my opponent was still, his blood staining the pearl sands like vermilion ink on fresh snow. A great hush fell across the arena. I recovered my half-spear from Jongshoi's mangled face. It came out with a sickening sound, the spearhead covered in blood and pink viscera. Just as I did so, a long list of notifications flashed across my mind—my reward for committing murder.

You have slain Jongshoi Aigiam. 100 experience gained.
You have gained 1 Strength.
You have gained 1 Dexterity.
You have gained 1 Constitution.
You have gained 1 Wisdom.
You have gained 1 Intelligence.
You have gained 1 Luck.
You have learned Dual Wield Lv. 1.
You have learned Critical-Hit Mastery Lv. 1.
You have learned Power Strike Lv. 2.
You have learned Endure Lv. 2.
You have learned Dodge Lv. 2.
You have learned Polearms Lv. 2.

Quest Complete: Kill Jongshoi and survive the Blooding. 200 experience gained.
You have reached Lv. 5.
6 unassigned attribute points.
2 unassigned skill points.

As soon as the countdown began, I assigned all of my points into Constitution. Unarmored as I was, I needed to be able to take a hit, and an increased Constitution also granted me greater Stamina, which allowed me to train my other physical attributes. As for my skill points, I needed to focus on the spell that seemed to be my main advantage: Heal. Some people prefer to play their character as a jack-of-all-trades—and the temptation was certainly there—but with pain and potential death as my constant companions, my focus was on survival. I quickly checked the changes to my character sheet, confirming them with an exhausted nod.

STATUS

Calling: Gilgamesh Lv. 5 Acolyte of Avaria

Strength: 13

Dexterity: 12

Constitution: 25

Intelligence: 16

Wisdom: 12

Charisma: 8

Luck: 12

SKILLS AND PROFICIENCIES

Pain Nullification Lv. 1

Power Strike Lv. 2

Endure Lv. 2

Stealth Lv. 1

Rest Lv. 1

Backstab Lv. 1

Dodge Lv. 2

Polearms Lv. 2

Dual Wield Lv. 1

Critical-Hit Mastery Lv. 1

SPELLS AND MAGIC

Heal Lv. 4

Rust Lv. 1

Identify Lv. 2

Silent Casting Lv. 1

GIFTS

Curse of Entropy: -20% to all starting attributes.

Experience to Lv. 6: 550/743

Health: 24/78

Stamina: 6/37

Mana: 5/11

Through all of this an explosion of hushed silence filled the arena, as if a profane and blasphemous word had been uttered in a sacred temple. Then I heard the wailing of a woman somewhere up in the stands, her grief smashing the fragile silence with its anguish.

So piercing was her lament that my eyes were drawn to her, a slender form with gold circlets woven throughout her hair, a counterpoint to the strands' raven darkness. Even at this distance, I could tell her features were wracked with overwhelming sorrow.

The official who presided over the event was still, like a statue frozen in bronze, his face through his plumed open helm a picture of shock. I surveyed the crowd and found in my questing gaze a group of robed women rattling bone effigies about them like mantles. There amongst them stood Navigator Olai, who stared at me with her sharp gaze, a cold black ocean of daggers.

The men came for me then, sure in their stride, my fate now written in the characters that spelled slave. Bare muscular chests glistened bronze in the afternoon light as they held long man-catcher poles and cruel barbed nets. I offered no resistance, as I had already played my part. As it was in my old world, the powerless were, even in victory, never truly winners.

They led me away. But before I was swallowed up, I noticed that one of Bogurchu's men, the pockmarked man who had tried to lay hands on me, was staring at me with hate-filled eyes.

Chapter 14

THE CHARACTERS OF A SLAVE

They were met on the beaches by envoys of the unknown mage-king under the banner of peace. Their decapitated heads were sent back wrapped in spider silk and sweet-scented with aeyory blossoms, a traditional declaration of total war in the east.

— On the Cataclysm by an unknown Quassian Scholar, circa 103 AC.

The area stank with the general effluence of the city and the newly enslaved and packed humanity. It was grief in all its stages. Some were choleric with rage, defiance a bright torch in their hearts. Others were catatonic with shock or grief, some wailing and crying a river of tears. A rare few had accepted with serenity their new station in life.

Naked, we were prodded, pulled, and scrutinized by rough men and women with licentious hands. Our teeth were closely examined for decay, and our bodies for disease. Those of us still holding on to our previous lives were taught otherwise with the crack of a three-pronged leather whip.

All my life, slavery had been just an academic subject. Its most blatant manifestations were buried in the past, and though it persisted in some corners of the globe, slavery bore no relevance to my privileged existence in the West. Yet in this place, I was receiving an education of a different sort— one that left scars on my body and imprinted lessons that no mere history class or award-winning documentary could ever aspire to impart.

Two days had passed since I had been brought to this pit of human suffering. I had overheard some gossip about my fate as I was being led. Some of my captors had wagered that, against all tradition, I would be poisoned, or have a subtle knife plunged between my ribs. Others thought I was destined to be broken in the mines.

I was determined not to break. The fire of defiance smoldered like an ember within me, although it was almost extinguished when I heard another man's screams as orange metal met his pliant skin, melting a red-hot mark in the shape of a flowing wave. Nevertheless, I clung to a strange blend of rage and hope as I received a new mission. As I read the words, I felt like I was witnessing a divine revelation, and I knew the gods had not yet abandoned me.

New Quest: Escape from the slavery pits of Ansan

I would not be a slave to mere NPCs.

Narcissistic fantasies crossed my mind as to what I would do when I escaped and wreaked vengeance on these slavers, only for them to retreat, whimpering, to the back of my mind with each crack of the whip. Still, I managed to hold on to the notion. In the old world I was free, and I would be so again.

The comeliest of the men and women were lined up to the right, slave brands to be replaced with a tattooist's art. They were fated to be the concubines or playthings for these cruel people. Whether fire or ink, however, we were all still slaves.

I stared at the man who branded me without the defiance that would have invited a lashing, nor did I react to the searing touch of the hot metal that had reduced so many before me to sobbing wrecks. Instead I felt total apathy, as if this were just a routine procedure that was, at most, a mild annoyance. Pain nullification allowed me to experience this small mercy, and I had made sure to be at full Health before the branding took place, using precious Mana to do so.

They shouted at each other, trying to confirm whether someone in their mercy had administered drugs to numb my pain. I had shown no expression, which visibly unnerved them.

My brander yelled at me to keep moving. Another person applied a foul-smelling green paste to my newly opened wound, which felt as though I was being stung and salved at the same time. After that, we were ushered to another open-air enclosure by the cruel slavers' barking commands. There, we were made to strip and don new clothes consisting of simple, coarse linen tunics, baggy trousers, and leather sandals with hobnailed soles. The more violent and rebellious slaves were separated from us and grouped on the left.

The wooden-fenced pen was surrounded by dark-bearded guards who were silent, stern, and clad in dirty chainmail and leather armor. They carried a variety of blunt instruments, ranging from cudgels to wicked-looking maces and flails. One of the guards, a particularly brutish specimen, stood nearly two meters tall and wielded a giant pole flail studded with deadly iron. He occasionally made jokes with his peers about how long it would take to break the weaker-looking slaves or how he would enjoy shattering bones with his weapon, which he affectionately called "Wife-Beater."

After we were all herded into the pen, which had a hard-packed earth floor from the passage of hundreds of feet, we were forced to form lines and columns. Many of us held an arm to our fresh brand, whimpering in pain. Not all of us were fully compliant, and the guards gleefully beat the troublemakers into submission. Extra licks of the whip were thrown in for good measure, leaving a few new slaves bloodied and bruised.

Suddenly, the guards snapped to attention as a corpulent man entered the holding area. He wore a light red turban trimmed with fur, with a ruby at its center, and clothes cut from the finest silk. His round girth was emphasized by a sash of vermilion red that strained to contain his prodigious bulk. Two sparkling, jovial eyes were set in his face, orbs of icy blue against a backdrop of olive skin. His mouth lit up in a satisfied smile as he surveyed the slaves.

He spoke to us then in a voice filled with genuine joy, as if he had just enjoyed a particularly satisfying bowel movement, which was so incongruous to our suffering and pain.

"Greetings, friends, one and all. My name is Hassan. Welcome to the first days of joining the family of the Children. Life aboard will be harsh but fair. All must play their part on the great waves. By low or high tide, work and you will be fed. But understand that laziness will be met with the kiss of the whip. Know well, then, that either will give us great satisfaction!"

The fat man guffawed as his jeweled fingers sparkled and danced in time to the heavy heaves of his laughter. The guards dutifully laughed along with him, having played this part many times before.

Initially I was puzzled at their use of a mariner-like lexicon before remembering that their whole culture was based on seafaring people, now trapped inland by world-shattering events. I brushed aside these mistaken thoughts and focused on the portly, yet jovial man.

"Work well and live content," he ended, my attention having wandered for part of his speech.

After Hassan's introduction, we were manacled and chained together before being frog-marched out of the pen. Now that I had some time to gather my wits from the pain and mental exhaustion, I recognized where we were. Across from me, to what I presumed to be the east, a breathtaking vista of golds and reds painted a riot of color across gigantic trees. I stopped in my tracks to drink in some of the natural beauty, only to be pulled along once again by the cruel chains around my ankles that cut through my reprieve.

We began our descent down a wide dirt track that wound ever downwards, cutting through hard alabaster stone. Eventually we passed a checkpoint, where guards lounged about their posts only to be playfully shouted at and brought to attention by our escort.

As our large group of slaves made our way through, the sounds of metalworking and industry grew ever louder—the clang of hammers striking metal, the roar of coal-fired furnaces, interspersed with the occasional crack of the whip and a painful scream. The smell came next, an acrid scent that crept up on the nostrils before finally overwhelming them.

They led us to a pile of pickaxes, shovels, and other miscellaneous mining equipment. The guards then removed the manacles from our wrists before gesturing for us to quickly pick up a tool. As I bent to take up a crude mining pick, I heard a sudden war cry rise above the sounds of the mine.

A blond-bearded animal of a man, with hair grown long in wild dreadlocks, screamed in fury as he brandished a pickaxe, attempting to strike down the closest guard. He was hindered by chains still attached to the other slaves, dragging them along with him.

A guard nonchalantly—with ease born of many years of practice—clubbed him across the back of the head with a blackjack. He fell to the ground like a great sack of meat. The flames of rebellion were instantly smothered, casting a pall over the rest of the slaves, stifling any thoughts of further defiance. The blond man was unchained from his line and roughly carted off by the guards.

Our group was now thoroughly cowed, with some of us beaten and all of us still suffering from our recent branding. An individual approached us then, reed-thin and stooped like a wading bird. He lacked the musculature and solidity of his peers but exuded a strong bureaucratic aura.

Carrying a tablet and stylus, he directed our group with a pointed and oddly shrill voice, through his thin lips, to the mine shaft cut deep into the rock to our left. The noise from the industry around the mines was oppressively loud, so I could not hear his exact words, but our guards nodded to his authority. My Mana had since recovered from the Winnowing, and I decided to silently cast my Identify spell on him.

Degei Ganbataar - Slave Overseer (Human Lv. 8)

Health: 72/72
Stamina: 27/27
Mana: 12/12

Interesting, I thought. The overseer, despite being three levels higher than me, seemed to be weaker overall, except for a little bit more Mana. I deduced that he must be a wily individual to have risen to his current authority. I cursed inwardly for not taking the opportunity to Identify Hassan as well.

As we continued to pass by the overseer on our way to the open mine shaft, my column was forced to a halt as Degei raised an arm. The slave behind me was trembling, panicked vibrations traveling along the length of the chain that connected us like a cruel Morse code. The overseer moved closer to me, his black eyes cruel and inquisitive, before checking something on his tablet and making some notes.

"No trouble from you, slave. Work, and if the gods are kind, you may live to see the end of the year," he said, voice emotionless. He waved for the line to continue, and I was jostled forwards. A few of the slaves in front of me threw me wary glances before moving, pulled inexorably by the others in front.

Chapter 15

THE MASTER DWARF

Of all the other races, I find the dwarves closest to true men. Though slightly longer lived, they are not as eternal as the elves; yet for all of that, they have always seemed to be more solid, more grounded in the now. What truly brings us close is our love for the fruit of the deep ground, the sparkle of gems, and the lure of gold. It is through mutual greed that we find common parlance.

— Attributed to Duchess Jessalyn, the Unifier of the Lost Duchy, circa 240 AC.

I gripped my mining pick tightly in my hands, finding comfort in its solid weight. Attacking the guards at this moment would be foolish; I needed more information before making a move. With a firmer grip on the handle, I trudged forwards, vowing to someday be free.

As we descended further down the gaping maw of the mine shaft, the air grew cooler. Wooden support beams held up the shaft at ten-meter intervals, and the echoes of our footsteps and clanking chains reverberated down the passage. A dull blue light emitted from the ceiling of the shaft, a blue opal gem pulsing softly. My curiosity got the better of me, and I cast Identify on it.

Zajasite Lightstone
Durability: 187/240

Despite the drain on my Mana, I didn't feel as debilitated or sluggish as the last time I had pushed myself magically. With my curiosity momentarily sated, I observed that none of the other slaves even cast a glance at the gem as we passed.

After another ten minutes of descent, I could hear the sound of mining picks striking stone, mixed with voices exhorting slaves to give greater effort. We reached a fork in the mine system and the guards separated us again, my group funneling down the right-hand passage.

As we continued down the right fork, I could not help but feel a sense of dread. Suddenly, there was a small tremor, and fine rock dust fell from the ceiling. A light pattering of soft alabaster dusted the slaves in front of me as the whole line paused. After the tremors stopped, we continued further down, urged on by a cracking whip. I forced away my claustrophobia.

The clinking sounds grew louder as we passed mining slaves on either side of the shaft. They chipped away at the soft white rock under the watchful eye of another group of guards. Their mining tools rose and fell in a steady cadence. Some of the older slaves shoveled what looked like raw, rough metal ore into large wicker baskets. Once the baskets were full, they were hoisted onto the slaves' backs with straps around their shoulders, like primitive backpacks.

A man spoke to the slaves, calling an end to their shift. His features were difficult to discern in the pale blue light, but I recognized him as a preferred slave or foreman, unshackled except for an iron collar with gold trim around his neck. Three-quarters of the slaves grabbed the wicker baskets full of heavy ore and made their way back up the way we had come from. The man with the special iron collar barked out orders for the remaining workers to instruct us in our duties, then confirmed that they understood with a stern, questioning look. One of the slaves was a little slow in his reply. The whip cracked out close to him, more for intimidation than inflicting pain.

Those who remained came over to us then. One of them, a burly man who was shorter than me, demonstrated how to use a pick. He grabbed it with hands wide apart, rolled it across his shoulders, then brought his hands together as he struck the white rock. I watched closely as he worked, noticing he was wide but without an inch of fat on him. A long-braided beard of indeterminate color fell to near his waist, tied at the end with what looked like a small disc of metal that followed the movements of his body.

"Now do," my new mentor said slowly, as if instructing a child in the guttural language of the Children, gesturing for me to follow his actions.

I gripped my tool as he had and brought it down against the rock, cutting deep. The burly man grunted in confirmation, and we worked together, striking almost in rhythm with one another. As we toiled away, I felt my Stamina gradually depleting, but I wasn't sweating as much as I used to from similar exertions in my previous life.

After an hour or two, I lost track of time in the soft blue darkness of the mines until I saw a boy going down the line, passing a ladle of water for us to drink. Though the water was stale with a distinct coppery aftertaste, when it was finally my turn, I greedily slurped it up like it was sweet ambrosia. When I had finished, the boy whispered a surprising "Thank you" to me before hurrying down the line to give another worker his fill of the water.

In a surprisingly shrill voice, the foreman barked, "Break now! For only two turns of the glass!" before taking a swig from a small hip flask at his waist, drawing stares of envy from the other slaves.

I took this as an invitation to sit down on the cool rock floor, laying my tool by my side. My hands were chafing from the strenuous activity, but my Stamina had recovered a little. Looking at the dwarf, who had now worked a double shift, I decided to speak to him.

"Would you"—I drew another shallow breath—"mind telling me your name?"

"Manners be to introduce yourself before asking for someone's name," he replied brusquely, eyes pointedly avoiding me before he sighed through gritted teeth. "Though I reckon manners be different in the lands of men.

Name's Durhit Coal, of the Beacon Mountains. Your own?" He spoke the last with a raised inflection, still refusing to make eye contact.

The lands of men? I wondered what he meant by that. His comment caught me a little off guard before I forced myself to think about his question. My subconscious mind was almost able to grasp my old name but then hit a dead end when I focused on it. Grasping at straws, I remembered my moniker in this world.

"Gilgamesh of Uruk," I said haltingly, the unfamiliarity of my new name leaving a strange taste on my tongue.

"Never heard of an Uruk." He raised a bushy eyebrow. "Sounds too foreign for my liking. You're from far away from here, little manling? Across the seas, perhaps?"

"Further than you could ever imagine. Across a sea of stars," I replied, trying my best to sound mysterious and poetic. The dwarf's face contorted as he tried to make sense of my words, but we were interrupted.

"Back to work, dogs!" The words lacked anger, more said out of rote. They were lines repeated so many times they had lost most of their bite. However, the crack of the whip that soon followed had not.

We continued our work in silence. My Stamina dropped low, and my arms had begun to feel like lead weights when I received a notification.

You have learned Mining Lv. 1.
You have gained 1 Strength.

I was not too thrilled about gaining the mining skill, but an increase in Strength was always welcome.

The foreman called for the end of our shift in an almost high soprano, and our group began to gather the ore in wicker baskets before starting our march out of the mines. At the previous fork, we met the other group and formed a long line up the shaft, our footsteps echoing in the soft blue darkness.

We continued upwards and finally reached the entrance, the cool night air a balm for our exhaustion. The sound of the forges and smelters had grown somewhat dimmer than during the day but had not stilled completely. A slave stumbled at the entrance, exhaustion finally taking him, but he was helped along by his fellows. It was a show of blossoming camaraderie from the shared forced labor, and a fitting end to my first shift as a slave.

Chapter 16

NEW LODGINGS

The great Arks, living ships of near-indestructible magical witchwood, made excellent time across the water, their massive bulk now pushed and pulled by the gigantic leviathans that made the deep places of the sea their home. Great cheers were raised when the ships made landfall on the western continent.

— *On the Cataclysm* by an unknown Quassian Scholar, circa 103 AC.

Half a day of grueling labor had been an exhausting—yet strangely relaxing—experience. There, in the mine, it was just my pick and I waging a never-ending war against the rock. It reminded me of the time when I had washed dishes for a summer job. The dirty plates piled high with leftover delectables, more arriving throughout the night until close. Muscle memory would take over, and the mind was free to think of other things.

The pull of the chain from the line snapped me from my reverie, and my hobbled feet almost stumbled as we were led to our next destination. The heavy ore-filled wicker basket's straps cut painfully into my shoulders as we moved. Passing by a sorting area, we deposited the load as instructed before continuing our weary march.

We arrived at our final destination, a compound surrounded by tall walls of smoothly quarried stone. A single gate led into the place, and we were herded through like tired cattle after a long day of grazing. On our left, as we entered the walled slave pens, flowing water ran across a rough-cut line in the stone floor. It rushed fast, like a mountain stream, before disappearing into a large metal grate running into the ground.

As we passed by, elderly slaves of both sexes hunched over, washing clothes and other miscellaneous items, their eyes held low. We were corralled into another area, where we handed over our tools to some official-looking guards, who counted and recorded them on tablets. Another group of cruel-eyed guards took us to an area with slaves in various states of undress, washing in the cool open air with cupped hands along the stream.

"Wash here. Relieve yourself down by the grate," instructed a guard with a large pole flail, his voice bestial in its promise of danger. It appeared my captors had some idea of the importance of hygiene, if nothing else.

Even here, at the bottom rung of society, a pecking order was established. Those who were more belligerent or stronger took a place near the water's source, while others made do further downstream with the dirtier remnants. With my bladder painfully swollen, I made my way down to the grate to relieve myself.

After fulfilling my bodily needs, I moved back upstream to a place with cleaner water, but a huge block of a man shoved me back with a grunt. Tilting my neck upwards, I saw blond hair hanging in loose locks, dripping water. A chiseled jaw and aquiline nose were set in a face that looked carved from hard stone, and his cold, glacier-blue eyes dared me to try again.

"I am the first to wash," he drawled in a low voice, almost like a warning growl from a bear. He raised a fist at me before turning away and going down to the water to bathe, cocky, slow, and sure in his arrogant stride.

The sudden threat of violence caused a spike of adrenaline, and my face flushed with anger. I checked my Status, preparing to reply in turn with violence, when a familiar gravelly voice piped behind me, "Don't mind him, lad. Just wait your turn. We'll all get there eventually. The guards will beat you twice as hard if they see you fighting here."

Turning around, I recognized the wide frame of Durhit, his eyes dull with exhaustion. I was in no shape to enter combat anyway, and the threat of punishment kept me in check for all but a split second.

I was about to thank him for his sage advice, but something gnawed at me—a seed of violence that had been born in the arena. Having faced bullies before, I felt it necessary to show at least some form of resistance. It wasn't just about who got to clean themselves first anymore. If I accepted this treatment, I would be accepting it for the rest of my time here. I'd had enough of it in my old world.

Absently, I also noticed my recent gain in Strength had led to a slight increase in my Health and Stamina, and I had gained a modest amount of experience from toiling in the mines. Would it be enough for what I had in mind?

Health: 58/80

Stamina: 24/38

Mana: 1/11

I pushed past some of the waiting slaves and found my target washing himself. At first I only intended to prove that I was not easily cowed; however, his vulnerability as he lowered his face to the water inspired something darker. My sudden transportation, the constant smorgasbord of pain just to survive, the ever-present threat of death, and my recently awarded victory at the arena unlocked something I think all of us possess deep inside.

I threw a punch with all my weight as I splashed into the water, aiming for the space just above the nape of his neck. With a closed fist full of rage, I connected with a meaty wallop. By some stroke of luck, the titan of a man fell into the water, stunned. Falling on top of him, I grabbed his head and kept smashing it against the cold hard stone. The water began to turn crimson, and the slaves parted from me like Moses before the Red Sea, fear etched in their stupid bovine eyes. I got up quietly, walked a little further from the spreading crimson, then washed my face in cleaner water.

After splashing my face a few times, notifications flashed across my inner vision, and I could not help but laugh. It appeared my karate classes as a teenager had paid off, and a green belt equated to about skill level three.

You have slain a Human. 240 experience gained.
You have learned Backstab Lv. 2.
You have learned Unarmed Combat.
You have learned Unarmed Combat Lv. 2.
You have learned Unarmed Combat Lv. 3.
You have learned Critical-Hit Mastery Lv. 2.
You have gained 1 Strength.
You have gained 1 Dexterity.
You have gained 1 Luck.
You have reached Lv. 6.
3 unassigned attribute points.
1 unassigned skill point.

Something inside of me probably broke then as I kept laughing at the sheer absurdity of my new reality. This was a world that rewarded violence and death. If this wasn't a game, then what was it? The notifications confirmed it; I had killed a no-name human NPC and was rewarded for it.

The guards came for me then, a cautious respect in their eyes, wielding long-poled man-catchers and wicked whips. I was mentally exhausted, my pent-up anger and frustration fully spent in my cathartic explosion of violence. Raising my hands, I accepted my fate, hurriedly increasing my Strength and my Heal spell.

They beat me.

Like good workmen, they went about their task diligently, going over me with effortless rhythm. I was dragged to another cell, raised high up on chains attached to my manacled wrists. With my Health already quite low, I was forced to endure the lash. Many times I thought the pain was too great and I felt myself sinking into the blessed refuge of unconsciousness, but they were experts in their craft and would not allow me to fall into insensibility, splashing me with water or targeting a particularly sensitive nerve with their cruel irons until finally, after what seemed like an eternity of suffering, my throat hoarse from long-running screams, they left me to welter in the dark.

It was then I received a new notification. A poor consolation prize.

You have gained 1 Constitution.

Chapter 17

DISCIPLINE AND PUNISHMENT

When the ever-creeping ice drifts further south, the inhabitants of the North dread the arrival of what they call the "Time of Trials." It is a period marked by an unforgiving cold that drives the fearsome tribes to become more aggressive in their bid to keep their hold on power and resources.

The barbarians, with their unrelenting will and superior battle skills, embark on raids against neighboring tribes. When successful, they take their defeated enemies as slaves and sell them into bondage. But when defeat befalls them, they resort to a brutal custom: they sell their own excess children into slavery to make up for their losses.

This is a time of hardship and struggle for these people, as they are forced to adapt to the harsh conditions of their environment and the ruthless demands of their own society. But amidst the chaos and violence, there is also a fierce spirit of resilience and determination that has kept them alive for generations.

— The Fanciful Travels by Beron de Laney, 376 AC.

A shockingly cold splash hit my bruised and battered body, jolting me from my exhausted slumber. My eyes were heavy, and they refused to open until a sharp slap stung my left cheek. I saw that a large iron collar had been fitted around my neck, and through my partially open eyes I noticed Degei, the overseer, looking down his nose at me with disdain. Two tall guards carrying cudgels flanked him, adding to his air of authority. With a sigh, the weedy man began to explain my new situation.

"You are the most troublesome bilge rat of an outlander. That Nord you killed was a good worker, and it will reflect poorly on our quotas. Good slaves are hard to replace!" Degei exclaimed, punctuating his statement by lightly slapping me, as if disciplining a dog. "Though he was a bit of a troublemaker himself... but I digress. As a survivor of the Winnowing, I knew you would give me a net full of troubles, but right on your first day?"

The slave overseer took my silence as acknowledgment and continued in his educated voice, "This is a witchbound slave collar. If you cause trouble, you will feel pain. If you become lazy, you will feel greater pain. If you try to escape, you will feel agony until our waveriders collect you. If you cause violence to a free man, you will die."

With this, he tilted my head back and forced a red liquid down my throat from a thin glass vial. The taste was somewhere between old socks and rotten cheese, with a surprisingly sweet undertone of cherry. I half-gagged down the foul concoction. My Health, which had been hovering around fourteen, rose by twenty points as I felt a different, yet somehow familiar, warmth diffuse through my body, and I realized I was being force-fed a healing potion. If this world was a game, it really was the work of a sick creator.

Degei raised the rest of the vial to my lips, but I moved away from it.

He slapped me again before explaining, slowly and in a voice as cold and uncaring as a winter day, "These potions are valuable. Spill a single drop, and I will have you beaten within an inch of your life." He pronounced each syllable with the finality of a prophet's last words. My eyes grew wide, and I forced myself to nod in understanding.

The taste was, of course, horrible, and I almost coughed and gagged. However, this time I welcomed the warmth that straightened my limbs and healed my broken muscles and bones. But it did nothing for my splintered soul.

"Good little bilge rat," he remarked, patting me across the cheek in some form of twisted affection.

A smile almost unconsciously formed across my face, such was my reaction to any show of positive emotion in this new world, however distorted. Something was definitely wrong with me. I fought down the burgeoning feeling of gratitude. The rebellious part of myself, the part that had always hated the skewed system, refused to give in to the seeds of a pernicious, newly forming Stockholm syndrome.

While looking down to avoid meeting his eyes, wishing to hide the glimmer of rebellion they held, I looked over my Status and character sheet.

STATUS

    Calling: Gilgamesh Lv. 6 Acolyte of Avaria

    Strength: 18

    Dexterity: 13

    Constitution: 26

    Intelligence: 16

    Wisdom: 12

    Charisma: 8

    Luck: 13

SKILLS AND PROFICIENCIES

    Pain Nullification Lv. 1

    Power Strike Lv. 2

    Endure Lv. 2

    Stealth Lv. 1

    Rest Lv. 1

    Backstab Lv. 2

    Dodge Lv. 2

    Polearms Lv. 2

    Dual Wield Lv. 1

    Critical-Hit Mastery Lv. 2

Mining Lv. 1

Unarmed Combat Lv. 3

SPELLS AND MAGIC

Heal Lv. 5

Rust Lv. 1

Identify Lv. 2

Silent Casting Lv. 1

GIFTS

Curse of Entropy: -20% to all starting attributes.

Experience to Lv. 7: 810/991

Health: 54/105

Stamina: 12/41

Mana: 6/11

The healing potions had raised my Health to just over half, though my Stamina was still perilously low, and I could feel tiredness weighing down my limbs. I had the Mana for a healing spell, but something in my gut told me it would not be wise to cast a healing spell in front of Degei, Silent Casting skill or not. The overseer checked over my naked form, nodding at the requisite level of violence my torturers had used. His guards flanked him, solid and silent, like two stone sentinels.

Patting my head like a good broken dog, he turned around and indicated for me to follow as his guards left the cell, both of them giving me looks that promised violence on a whim.

I lifted a manacled hand to shield myself from the light of two almost smokeless torches. Degei gave me a satisfied smile, like an owner who had trained a pet to do a new trick, and he pointed off down the way to a group of slaves huddled on the packed earth eating their evening repast.

"Go, outlander. Eat your meal. Tomorrow you will be working a double shift—no, triple shift!" His eyes lit up with glee. "Enjoy your new home, and be a good boy."

Still shackled at the hands and hobbling, I slowly made my way to the group of slaves huddled on the packed earth eating their evening meal, my escort following me halfway. With my eyes downcast, the slaves would occasionally steal hesitant glances in my direction before continuing with their meals. However, a small youth held my gaze for longer than the others, his features conflicted with warring emotions before snorting and returning to his meal.

Approaching a small trestle table stacked half-full of crude, chipped earthenware bowls and rough wooden spoons, I saw a cauldron filled with a thick, gruel-like paste being overseen by a world-weary old crone of a woman. The scene before me gave the impression of a witch boiling up a new concoction, but my stomach rumbled, and I found the smell of cooking food inviting. I shuffled forwards, grabbed a bowl and spoon, and greeted the old woman.

"Good day to you, madam," I said in a polite, neutral voice. However, I was met with a cackle that only solidified my original impression of her.

"Not a madam, just little old Adita," she managed to utter between cackles. "You're the lad they speak of who survived the Winnowing and did that giant Harun in for looking at you funny, they say. Here, give me your bowl if you want some food. Give you a little extra too, for cutting the thread of one of the little masters."

I handed her my bowl, a little hesitant. "Why am I even still alive?"

She grunted. "They can't kill you, boy. Least, not directly anyway, by their own hands. You sure ain't made any friends though—that young pup was probably someone's get. Still, you survived the trial on the sands. In their reckoning, you are now a blooded warrior and member of their tribe." She cackled before continuing, "A lifetime in the mine will break you. Seen it too many times before. The masters be a practical lot, so you'll be paying the blood price one way or another." She punctuated her explanation by dolloping two ladles of slop into my bowl before spitting a huge wad of phlegm into the fire.

"Thank you for the food," I humbly replied, the words sticking a little in my throat at the simple display of common human kindness.

I went to sit alone in a quiet corner, where I made sure to eat slowly. I had already experienced extreme hunger once before, so I knew the importance of allowing my digestion to adjust to the new food. My mind wandered as I ate, considering the potential bacteria and other biological dangers that just existing in this new world posed, but between my magic, the recent potion, and my relatively high Constitution, I had yet to feel any of the ill effects from this world's smaller denizens.

Before I knew it, and despite trying to eat slowly, I had finished my crude, yet filling meal. About a dozen meters away, a thin streamlet flowed across a crack in the rock before running down into a grate, similar to what I had seen when I entered the compound. I bent down to wash my earthenware bowl and wooden spoon before noticing a slightly familiar face, dark eyes looking intently at me.

"Did you really kill Harun?" the young boy asked with quiet determination.

Blinking a few times at the sudden question, I looked up at him quizzically.

"Harun the Iron? They say you killed him because you're a murderer. They put the slave mark on you for killing one of your own, a kinslayer. They say you killed him because you think that even here in the pens, you're still a master," the boy continued, speaking like a judge reading out a sentence and already convinced of his own justice.

So surprised was I by how irresponsibly rumors had twisted the truth that I could offer no solid defense to his accusations. The boy noticed the dawning understanding in my eye and mistook it for acceptance of his words, causing his chin to quiver with repressed emotion. "My name is Gunne, son of Gudlaug, and I will have my vengeance," he said, looking me in the eyes with his fists clenched.

An apology that was rising as an automatic reflex reaction was suddenly stymied by his pronouncement of revenge. This whole world had offered enough suffering and pain for three lifetimes, and the only kindness I had received so far was from some sort of cooking witch who hated our masters more than she hated me. What should have been guilt was replaced by anger and scorn.

"He died like a sow in heat being plowed by a horse," I spat out, making sure to thread disdain through my words. Although somewhat random, the collection of insults felt fitting and inventive in this context. "I am Gilgamesh, and you'll die as he did, sniveling and crying for the comfort of your mother. You are nothing but an N-P-C."

I emphasized each syllable of the last word deliberately and slowly, laced with whatever icy threat I could muster, though I doubted he understood the meaning.

I was glad to notice his eyes had widened. Standing, I looked at him, seeing now nothing but a scared boy who had dared to challenge a killer. He almost fell back then as he turned to run, and some of the other slaves whispered among themselves. A seed of darkness had been planted within me then, and it felt satisfying to have sown fear rather than to have been subjected to it. It was empowering, even to hold sway over someone weaker than myself. For a moment, it had washed away the memories of the torment I had suffered.

Looking around at the other slaves, I made sure to hold their eyes just long enough to show strength, but not long enough to provoke a challenge. I returned to finish my chore. Once done, I moved slowly back towards Adita and handed her my now clean utensils, to which she gave me a short nod of appreciation.

The others, sensing there would be no similar entertainment this night, followed suit before drifting off towards a simple flat-roofed building. It resembled a sort of stable for housing a large number of animals. A single wooden entrance and wooden shutters were the only decorations on its front facade.

Following a herd instinct, I made my way to the tail end of the group and accompanied them inside. It was dark inside with the lack of lighting, but I could still make out crude wooden pallets at certain intervals on a hard-packed earthen floor. Some of the slaves had already claimed their spots, but I hazarded a rough guess that there was at least one free space today.

I settled down on a simple pallet a little way from the corner. Remembering that I had enough Mana for healing, I took the time to cast Heal silently amid the flatulence, snores, and myriad noises that humans make in a packed space near one another. Grinning to myself, I noticed that the strength of my spell had increased significantly and was now healing me for just over a third of my total Health.

Health: 90/105

Stamina: 22/41

Mana: 1/11

This reaffirmed my decision to focus my points instead of trying to be a jack-of-all-trades, which filled me with a hint of peace—a small thread of order in the midst of chaos. I had finally found enough serenity to face another tomorrow.

Chapter 18

THE GRIND

Spies from the Alliance and divine scrying showed that the mage-king was actually no king at all. In fact, he was seen to be more of a steward and servant of the people, and was chosen by the majority of them, which was a concept that was alien and foreign to the members of the Alliance. The system of government was seen as preposterous—for who in their right mind would allow the common man to dictate the rules of power above their station?

— On the Cataclysm by an unknown Quassian Scholar, circa 103 AC.

Dark things plagued me in my dreams and stalked me through my own imagination. Sharp things that pierced, stabbed, or bludgeoned me while their cruel laughter echoed in my mind. Oily tentacles whispered raspy, sweet promises as they caressed my cheek, only to wrap around my neck and suffocate me as they plunged down my throat.

I awoke during the night several times, flailing my limbs against invisible assailants before I finally slipped into a deeper slumber.

A worker inadvertently banged against my wooden pallet, rousing me from the last vestiges of my unsettled sleep. The slaves moved in silence, akin to well-trained soldiers about to embark on a dawn raid. Glancing out at the open wooden entrance, still dark before the first light of sunrise, I saw them arrange themselves into passably neat columns and rows, watched by our overseers.

I quickly followed suit, not wanting to draw the ire of our masters or the promised pain of my new collar. As I rose, I noticed a few insect-like creatures with double thoraxes and large mandibles scuttling into safety from the stampede of humanity and disappearing into various holes and corners. They seemed vaguely familiar.

Making my way outside, I noticed there was at least one positive: despite my disturbed sleep, I had fully regenerated all of my Status points.

Health: 105/105

Stamina: 41/41

Mana: 11/11

Falling into line, our slave drivers exhorted the benefits of hard work and the promise of pain to the lazy among us. However, they lacked the oratory skills and finesse of Hassan, the corpulent man who possessed a charismatic voice. Although we had been—quite literally—part of his captive audience, my attention was drawn to him whenever he spoke. Listening to our slave drivers with only half an ear, I cast Identify on my new collar.

Iron Slave Collar of Obedience

Durability: 400/400

Something about the name of my slave collar niggled at my subconscious as we descended into the mine shafts to repeat the drudgery.

During the day, while others along my line were rotated out and allowed a reprieve, I was compelled to continue working. I encountered Durhit again during my last shift, but I was so exhausted that I could barely manage a simple grunt in greeting.

So determined was I to avoid the collar's promise that I practically assaulted the white rock. Throughout the day, I carved great chunks from it with my growing Strength. I had made progress, gaining a single point in both Constitution and Strength. Fear had driven me so hard—and so good was my conditioning—that I had lost a few points of Health, as I had pushed my Stamina to the limit. Although I did not make any gains in mining, which I did not care much for anyway, I still earned a nominal amount of experience for my level.

Taking my evening meal, Adita made sure to stack my bowl full. I sat quietly in a secluded corner. No one looked at me, and I took the time to review my character sheet.

STATUS

    Calling: Gilgamesh Lv. 6 Acolyte of Avaria

    Strength: 19

    Dexterity: 13

    Constitution: 27

    Intelligence: 16

    Wisdom: 12

    Charisma: 8

    Luck: 13

SKILLS AND PROFICIENCIES

    Pain Nullification Lv. 1

    Power Strike Lv. 2

    Endure Lv. 2

    Stealth Lv. 1

    Rest Lv. 1

    Backstab Lv. 2

    Dodge Lv. 2

    Polearms Lv. 2

    Dual Wield Lv. 1

    Critical-Hit Mastery Lv. 2

    Mining Lv. 1

    Unarmed Combat Lv. 3

SPELLS AND MAGIC

Heal Lv. 5

Rust Lv. 1

Identify Lv. 2

Silent Casting Lv. 1

GIFTS

Curse of Entropy: -20% to all starting attributes.

Experience to Lv. 7: 830/991

Health: 87/109

Stamina: 7/43

Mana: 10/11

Good, I thought. The increases in Health and Stamina were always welcome.

Now that I was finally allowed a moment's respite, my limbs felt like they were made of solid lead. As I watched the slaves go about their evening meal and chat among themselves, I heard a language that sounded similar to the one Navigator Olai had first used when she was interviewing me.

It was much more musical and lilting, like a singsong version of a Latin language. I sat back and cast a few Identify spells at the words, increasing my knowledge with every cast. I stopped after the ninth spell, unwilling to push myself to undergo what I had begun to term as "Mana sickness." Through my spells, I gained a very crude understanding of the language and attained some basic knowledge of its grammatical structure.

Distracted, I touched my Iron Slave Collar of Obedience with a wandering finger and was met with a sharp stab of pain that ran along my spine and through my limbs like wild, unbridled lightning. I almost wretched up my evening meal, but my instinct to survive forced me to keep it down, despite my eyes filling with tears. My Health had fallen by two points, which felt completely disproportionate to the agony I had been inflicted with. The message was clear; I was not to touch the collar. The name of the heavy yoke around my neck, "Iron Slave Collar," stirred something in the depths of my mind. However, like a falling leaf that escapes your grasp the harder you try to catch it, the connection eluded me.

Shaking my head in resignation, I washed my bowl and spoon in the running water. As I took a drink, I spied a familiar sight. A fierce, wild man with a collar like my own, looking like some sort of half-tamed animal, was sitting away from me. He was the man from our slave indoctrination, the one who had dared to resist.

Blond dreadlocks hung across his neck like a lion's mane. His eyes were like smoldering blue coals filled with icy fire. They locked with mine for a moment before he pointed at the heavy iron collar around his neck. I moved over to him, feeling somehow that we were kindred spirits.

The wildman rose and slapped me on the back as I came closer, a mischievous smile on his face. He guffawed as he greeted me. "You are a troublemaker! The yoke does not sit so lightly about your neck, no? I am Kidu, raider of the Three Bears Clan." He pointed to his left breast and declared in a loud voice, "Like you, I am not a slave," almost as a challenge to the other gathered slaves.

"You have a slave brand just like the rest of us, *Your Highness*, just with a bit of extra-heavy jewelry!" someone in the back jeered.

Kidu scoffed. "Come, let us ignore these sheep. Let us talk like men. How did you come to be in this thrice-cursed hell hole?"

I told him about my encounters with the dark entities of the void and my meeting with Avaria. The overwhelming need to spill the emotions that had bottled up inside me caused me to disregard any inhibitions I may have had. Although I knew on some logical level that it was the wrong choice, logic is merely a servant of emotion. But for some reason, I chose not to disclose that I was from another world, instead stating that I had completely lost my memories before arriving at the shrine. Kidu listened attentively, nodding as if he had expected something like this.

"You are one of the God-touched. Some in my tribe go into the madness of revelation. Limbs shake, and they drool like mad dogs, though different to the Berserk. They are honored among our people. Your gift must have been too great, so your tribe offered you to Vari, Chooser of the Slain, in some form of appeasement." He spoke these words in a thoughtful seriousness that was incongruous with his wild appearance.

He must have mistaken the look of confusion that crossed my face as sadness, for he tried to brighten my mood.

"You missed your chance to fight the endless battle in the heavens, my friend! But I am fortunate to make your acquaintance, Gilgamesh of Uruk. Perhaps with a little divine guidance, we may yet make our way out of our troubles, yes?" he said, more as a statement than a question as he slapped me on the back in encouragement.

"Yes, let's get out of this thrice-cursed hell hole. One way or another," I replied, nodding. A few slaves nearby shook their heads. No doubt we were not the first to make such a vow.

"Do you know anything about levels?" I asked him as nonchalantly as possible.

"Levels?" His eyebrows furrowed. "Like how high something is?"

"No, no, to determine one's Strength. Experience points and such? How do you get more skillful or stronger?"

"Friend, truly you must be God-touched. I know no such thing of levels, but there are ranks in the armies of men. Points of experience? I guess as one practices at some things, one will get better at it," he replied earnestly, not truly understanding the line of my questioning.

I continued to question him about his past during the brief moments before we were ushered off to sleep. The locals did not understand the "system" responsible for my growth, but I did manage to gather that they were possibly affected by it. Kidu mentioned that some warriors of his clan seemed to become physically stronger as they proved themselves in battles or successful hunts.

He also spoke of older beasts and creatures that grew stronger over time. He told me about monstrous ice drakes in the frozen north that became more vicious and malevolent with each passing year, preying on the herds of the tribes until a group of determined hunters or adventurers could take them down.

I took note that perhaps the NPCs of this world had more organic growth in their strength and development, since our conversation highlighted that they had no knowledge of this game world's "system." I, on the other hand, could guide my own progress to a certain extent as I leveled up. This would give me a great advantage as I hopefully continued to grow in power.

Going through the doors to the slave stables, we chose pallets next to each other for some form of security against the true slaves. Exhausted, I fell asleep.

I awoke sometime in the night, plagued once again by dreams of dark, stalking things. Thinking of Kidu and his fantastical homeland in the frozen north, I was half-tempted to see if he was also awake, but I was interrupted by the sound of two creatures seeking solace in the night. Finally, their rut finished, and I was once again lulled into the land of dark dreams.

The next day was very much like the previous one. The wildman and I, who were obvious troublemakers, were separated into different teams. After the rest, I had regained all my Status points and received a new notification informing me that my concentrated efforts to sleep had increased my rest level to two.

I fell into line and toiled in the light blue gloom of the mines. During my second shift, Durhit worked next to me. As I hacked away at the white stone with my crude pickaxe, focused on my work, Durhit paused for a moment and spoke to me quietly while our whip-carrying minders looked the other way.

"I've never seen a fellow dwarf… let alone a human like you… hack away at the stone like that. Have you made an enemy of the Earth Mother?"

Durhit said from behind his bushy beard, his barrel chest straining with each breath.

Intrigued by his use of the word "dwarf" and with plenty of Mana to spare, I decided to cast my Identify spell on him.

Durhit Coal - Sapper (Dwarf Lv. 14)
Health: 273/280
Stamina: 42/50
Mana: 11/11

I could see that Durhit had a prodigious amount of Health—truly formidable—probably due to his dwarven Constitution. Dwarves were always famously hardy in modern fantasy depictions, so it was little surprise to me that this paradigm applied to this world too. Also, the dwarf still had most of his Stamina and had dug out more rock than me. In comparison, I had already burned through more than half of my own Stamina as I pounded furiously at the stone. I half-heartedly concluded that his sapper class explained his more economical mining.

Striking the alabaster rock, I grunted before answering Durhit. "This is 'grinding,' sir dwarf. I need to build up my Strength if I am ever to escape."

Durhit pretended to understand my response, no doubt thinking I was perhaps a little touched in the head. Come to think of it, an infection caused by the myriad wounds I had suffered, and my questionable diet may well have caused a riot within my body and addled my mind. I mentally shrugged to myself as I rolled my shoulders. Perhaps this was all just a fever dream?

This line of thinking would produce no real answers, so I focused back on my work, striking out against my enemy, the alabaster stone. Mimicking the dwarf, I raised my pickaxe slower and used more of the tool's weight than my own muscle when striking the rock. Subconsciously, an unspoken bond was formed between us as we toiled under a blue glow, and just as Durhit was relieved of his shift, I was rewarded with a notification.

You have learned Hammers Lv. 1.
You have learned Mining Lv. 2.
You have gained 1 Strength.

Humming a catchy tune from my own world between strokes to break up the monotony, I continued my assault on the rock. Some of the slaves around me took up the tune before we were silenced by the crack of whips on pliant flesh.

The dwarf noticed my smile, however, and just shook his head at my antics as he slung his pickaxe over his shoulder and left. I continued to hum the tune, albeit under my breath, in discreet defiance. Like Kidu, I was not a slave in my heart.

Chapter 19

TALK OF THE PAST

Deep within the primal forests, dragonroot, also known as the widow's mercy, is harvested under the watchful eye of the giant jaderock bees. These monstrously large bees, according to the observations of the researchers of Quas, require the poison produced by the flowers to crown a new queen among their number. Such is the importance of dragonroot that alchemists from far and wide seek it out for use in their elixirs and concoctions. Legends even tell of the dragon slayers of old who coated their weapons with a deadly paste made from the root, granting them the power to vanquish their scaly foes.

— The Fanciful Travels by Beron de Laney, 376 AC.

When my shifts were finally over, the exhaustion I felt could still not quite dampen my good spirits. I made sure to hide my smile from the guards, who looked at me as if I were deranged, and I made sure to smile too at each slave who met my eyes. Some of the poor slaves even hesitantly smiled back.

"You look to be in good spirits, boy. Did something good happen in those godforsaken mines? Maybe you poked about in a different shaft!" Adita jibed jovially, laughing at her own crude joke.

"No, no, Madam Adita. Nothing of that nature, but I see that this evening's meal looks as delicious as ever," I replied adroitly, my good spirits lighting my eyes.

"Told you I'm not a madam, not one of those high-nobility types, and flattery will get you nowhere!" She cackled as she dolloped an extra portion into my bowl. "Old Monta caught himself a little delicious rockcrab by the latifundium, threw that in today."

You have gained 1 Charisma.

I smiled knowingly, taking my bowl filled to the brim with the questionable stew. The gain in Charisma was extraneous to my current dire circumstances. My mind was more focused on the fact that the game's internal logic had translated Adita's words into the Ancient Roman word for slave quarters, an oddity that puzzled me as I began eating my evening meal.

Soon, a familiar hulking manacled shape hobbled over. I rose and clasped his arm at the elbow, which he returned in greeting. "Welcome, Kidu the Raider." I grinned at him, my neck having to tilt upwards to meet his cold blue eyes.

"And you, Gilgamesh of Uruk," he chortled, settling his bulk down cross-legged on the hard-packed earth.

"I have questions..." I began hesitantly.

"Of course, you do, God-touched. As long as we do not debate Quassian philosophy, I welcome them. Perhaps through answering them, you will gain some insight into your past," he said sympathetically, his voice colored with compassion as I joined him on the ground.

We talked for a while. Kidu confirmed that he had no knowledge of the strange mental script, which I had dubbed the "UI" or "User Interface," a script that apparently only I could see. He viewed my interpretation of the UI's messages as some form of communication from the divine.

I also learned from Kidu that the language of the Children of the Tides was simply called "Trade", and that the guttural language was almost the *lingua franca* for this region. He considered my pronunciation of Trade to be above average, indicating that my grasp of the spoken language had improved by leaps and bounds. The singsong language that I had some experience with was called "High Quassian," and was also spoken by the desert people of the South.

In time, the large man shared his tale with me. I found out that Kidu was from the far frozen North. His tribe was a nomadic people who hunted massive creatures called the cronir. The cronir traveled across the tundra in vast herds, like caribou, and were sometimes preyed upon by vicious ice drakes. His tribe had lost several skirmishes, and the allocation of hunting rights to rival tribes had further weakened them. The windspeakers of his tribe, a group of elderly and wise individuals who kept the oral traditions of the Three Bears, advised the chief to send a raiding party to the South.

The chief had sent Kidu, who even then had a reputation for being a belligerent troublemaker, along with a few other fractious youths to form a party and travel south as raiders. The leader had planned for them to bring exotic riches from the warm, verdant lands back home so they could trade for favors and hunting rights from the other tribes.

However, in a frontier town near the frozen wastes, they had been duped by shady characters in the local drinking den promising them the location of a rich caravan that was scheduled to pass through. Instead of a profitable raid, they were assaulted in the night while in their drunken stupor, stripped of their weapons, and sold into slavery to the said caravan.

Due to his fractious and violent nature, Kidu had been sold and traded from master to master many times. Eventually, he had changed hands so many times that he had finally made it to Ansan, the jewel of the grass sea of the Grieving Lands and a gateway to the Wilds.

Spying Durhit with a group of tired-looking men, I called him over. At a distance, his face looked like he had just swallowed a sour plum as he made his way to us. Suspicion warred with a need to make a connection across his bearded face. In the end, despite initial reluctance, the need to find some form of solace won.

"Be a little quieter, manling. The guards here are sensitive to those with loud tongues," grumbled the dwarf.

I held my hands up in mock acquiescence, still grinning.

"I've never seen a human—plenty of dwarves, but never a human—so happy pounding away at rock. I swear he is a little queer in the head," he grumbled again.

"Then you have probably never heard of the gold rush," I replied. The dwarf's eyes widened almost comically at my mention of gold. "Men would cross oceans, plains, and deserts in their search for gold," I tried to intone as wisely as possible.

"Aye, that is well known, that man's greed for gold can rival even a dwarven Deeptaker's." Durhit nodded sagely into his bowl, his long beard almost brushing into the stew.

"I know you are God-touched, but at times you sound like my tribe's windspeakers, Gilgamesh of Uruk. Are you a scholar?" interjected the wildman, his voice surprisingly serious in its earnestness.

A bittersweet smile formed on my face. I shook my head as the lie found its way to my lips. "No, Kidu of the Three Bears, though I have heard a few things here and there." Already treading on dangerous ground with my mention of the California gold rush, I grew wary that continuing this line of conversation would lead me to share more about my origins.

"Your tribe will enjoy many good years with their offering to give not only a God-touched but also a man wiser than his years to the Chooser of the Slain," Kidu said with a nod, accepting my lie completely.

"How about you, mysterious manling? What brought you here to the great Ansan?" the dwarf inquired, bushy eyebrows raising a fraction.

Thankfully, Kidu interjected, eager to tell my story to the dwarf, with just a little bit of joy in the telling. He embellished little, except for my fight in the arena. According to the savage-looking man, instead of killing a green and untested youth, I had slain a scarred, seasoned warrior, his blade pitted with the clash of many battles.

"And what brings a stone-eater so far from your mountain halls?" the wildman finished.

The dwarf's face scrunched in irritation before looking down, troubled, as if trying to retrieve the memory from the ground itself. In time, he told his tale. "A bunch of lads and I signed as mercenaries for Lord Hayles, the manling, against one of his neighbors, Lord Farilse. Something about an exorbitant port tax that one of Hayles's ships refused to pay for. This led to City Lord Farilse seizing his vessel, the *Pride of Iron*, that was berthed in his port."

Something ticked at the back of my mind with the ship's name, but I quickly turned my attention back to the dwarf's tale.

"The port of Seaguard had strong, high walls and even stronger coastal defenses, and little Lord Hayles decided he needed a bit of dwarven ingenuity to do something about the defenses. A messy affair if there ever was one…" He spat on the ground before continuing. "Good rights to pillage and steady coin are a siren song to any dwarf worth his ore, so we marched under Hayle's banner with the baggage train. But Farilse was a cunning one, and he hired mercenaries of his own. Hateful pointy-eared scum, dark elves, quiet like shadows, fell upon the baggage train nearby, gutting the sentries and picket lines with not so much as a sound.

"My own mate, Kabruk, was taken down right before my eyes, one of their cursed black blades across his throat as he tried to raise the alarm. I gave as good a reckoning as any of the stoneborn, and I perhaps got a few of them with my trusty hammer. Like hitting leaves and twigs, those dark elves are. They faded away like morning mist just as the first light hit, and the damage they had done was great. They had hit our baggage train and killed our girabis, poor blundering beasts, and just like that, our whole venture was hamstrung. A curse of ash and ruin on the sharp ears!

"The blackguard Farilse never faced us in open battle after that. He hit us again and again and finally forced Hayles's surrender." The dwarf paused for a moment, as if the memory caused him bittersweet pain.

"My sister Evenes could only afford the ransom for her man, Nolat. I don't blame her in truth, as it was more my idea to go about on that slag heap of an adventure. She promised that once she and Nolat started work on the new claim they had, they'd find a way to pay my bond price. But with no way to pay my immediate ransom, Farilse soon sold us to a passing slaver caravan. Those vultures are always about the edges of war, like flies to a fresh corpse. Now, here I am in Ansan, mining iron ore for manlings to make weapons to wage war upon one another."

Something must have struck a chord with the wildman, as he silently patted the dwarf on the shoulder, only to be brushed off brusquely. I, too, fell silent, though for another reason. Something the dwarf had said had set off something in my mind, like suddenly remembering an important memory.

Then I found it—Rust, the spell. Like a slippery eel, it had always wriggled its way from my attention. Circumstances had meant I never had any leeway to experiment with its use. Determined now, I called out to it and was met by resistance.

Black slithering things crossed the edges of my vision and cold sibilant whispers caressed my ears, making me shiver as electricity traveled down the nape of my neck. A sense of wrongness so profound and utterly inimical to all things filled me.

Wanting to release this dark energy as soon as possible, I eyed a random slave engaged in evening conversation. Focusing on my target, I surreptitiously cast the spell at his manacled feet.

Black lines of power left me then, seemingly invisible to everyone else, wrapping around the chains like velvet lightning as he continued talking. The whispers slowly left me, the feeling of wrongness lessening, but I could still see the dark lightning working its way around my target's iron chains. Gradually now, the lightning danced around the metal slowly and steadily, like a funeral procession.

Where it touched, a few dots of orange and red could be seen, as the metal was oxidized at an accelerated rate. The spell had only cost me a single point of Mana.

I had found the key to my chains.

I made every effort to hide the grin on my face as I looked back at my companions, who wore questioning looks as I suddenly rose to my feet. Explaining to them that I thought I had seen the ghost of a familiar face, they nodded sympathetically at my false hope, and Durhit shared that he had often done a similar thing when new dwarves were welcomed to the mines.

We talked about small things of little importance, and I learned more of the common knowledge of this world. The name of the world I found myself in was called many things by its innumerable people, but here in this area, known colloquially as the "Grieving Lands" due to the sudden tumultuous storms that were endemic to the region in the later months of the year, the locals called the world "Gesthe." This meant "Garden" in the language of the First People, as the elves liked to call themselves. The Grieving Lands were but a small part of an enormous world that was broken up into massive continents, which according to Durhit were the bones of land dragons.

We talked also of strange and fanciful places. Durhit spoke of his home, the Beacon Mountains, an active volcanic range. The fiery chasms would frequently erupt with flame and ash. I couldn't help but ponder what kind of people would willingly inhabit such a perilous environment.

Somewhere in the conversation, there was talk of a place to the far west called the "Glass Fire Sea." Sailors feared navigating its treacherous waters as great crystalline glass formations floated on its surface, burning any ship that got too close to a blackened husk.

Despite the danger, some savvy—or desperate—captains were willing to take the risk, venturing forth under the cloak of moonless nights to collect precious fragments of the glass. Such treasures were highly sought after by the great universities of Quas, willing to pay a high price for the rare and valuable material.

The flames of adventure were lit once more in my heart, and I could feel a desperate need to be free taking deeper root there. However, before too long, we were herded back into the slave stables. Before going to sleep, I sat up and cast Rust silently, picturing iron manacles, and released the energy in random directions in the room. The black lightning from my spell was invisible even to me in the darkness. I knew the spell was being cast as I could see my Mana drop in steady increments, and on the ninth cast, I was rewarded with a notification.

You have gained 1 Intelligence.

Lying back down on my cot, I perused my character Status. Like the other day, I had gained some nominal experience from mining. But more importantly, I now had the tools to make a bid for freedom. I needed the patience to see my growing plans through, and it felt like my chains chafed more than usual now that a path to liberty could be seen. I yearned to feel and experience the best this fantasy world had to offer, and not just be a slave to destiny.

STATUS

    Calling: Gilgamesh Lv. 6 Acolyte of Avaria

    Strength: 20

    Dexterity: 13

    Constitution: 27

    Intelligence: 17

    Wisdom: 12

    Charisma: 9

    Luck: 13

SKILLS AND PROFICIENCIES

Pain Nullification Lv. 1

Power Strike Lv. 2

Endure Lv. 2

Stealth Lv. 1

Rest Lv. 2

Backstab Lv. 2

Dodge Lv. 2

Polearms Lv. 2

Dual Wield Lv. 1

Critical-Hit Mastery Lv. 2

Mining Lv. 2

Unarmed Combat Lv. 3

Hammers Lv. 1

SPELLS AND MAGIC

Heal Lv. 5

Rust Lv. 1

Identify Lv. 2

Silent Casting Lv. 1

GIFTS

Curse of Entropy: -20% to all starting attributes.

Experience to Lv. 7: 850/991

Health: 92/111

Stamina: 13/43

Mana: 1/11

Chapter 20

A TIME TO HEAL

But the spies and scouts of the unknown kingdom had not been idle, and they discovered horrifying facts that only hardened the resolve of the people to resist. Many of those who were brought across the ocean were in fact slaves.

Men and women who had pulled at the great oars, who had cleaned and scrubbed the decks, tended the fires, cooked the meals that fed the armies, and a thousand more labors, were chattel with the hateful mark of slavery inscribed upon their bodies.

— On the Cataclysm by an unknown Quassian Scholar, circa 103 AC.

I found myself being awoken the next morning by Durhit, concern etched across his features as he shook me roughly. I cleared the sleepy cobwebs from my mind as I rose to my daily grind. All of my Status points had regenerated, as expected. Looking around, I was pleased to note that the manacles on some of the slaves were covered in rust spots. *Slow and steady wins the race,* I thought.

Once I had gathered myself, I fell into line and received the daily speech from the overseer before we filed out to the mines. However, I was suddenly accosted by Degei, and our whole line was forced to stop because of me.

"How can you be in such good spirits this morning, you bilge rat? Triple shifts over a few days would test even a stunty stone-eater dwarf! Yet, I have talked to your watchers, and they say you work like a demon-possessed. There is something about you that I don't like. Know that I am watching you… and lower your eyes, slave!" He shouted the last words as he backhanded me across the face with a wooden cudgel, drawing blood.

I was taken more by surprise than actual pain. Since I was at full Health, I felt nothing due to my pain nullification skill. The strike had reduced my Health by only eight points, but I lowered my eyes anyway to avoid further antagonizing the cruel man. I remembered to grit my teeth in feigned pain.

The overseer, satisfied now that I looked the part of a thoroughly cowed slave, shrilled with smug superiority, "At least we will get some good labor out of you. Do work your little heart out, bilge rat."

He motioned for the line to move off, and we continued back to our daily grind. The guards were now keenly watching me, their hands gripping their weapons just a little tighter as we passed by them on our way to the mines. Half in defiance and half out of pure curiosity, I pictured one of the guards, now out of my direct line of sight.

I cast Rust at him, remembering his pockmarked face and lazy left eye. I felt the buildup of dark energy growing steadily more painful as dark things writhed at the periphery of my vision. But unfortunately, the spell failed. Panicked, I mentally targeted his metal breastplate. My heart was beating in my chest as the familiar sense of wrongness left me upon finishing the cast. Black lightning erupted from my hands, lashing towards the guard behind me, and my Mana was depleted by a single point.

Pausing in relief, I almost tripped over my own sandaled feet as I was suddenly pulled forwards by the worker in front of me. I realized that no one could see the visual effects of my Rust spell. Also, it looked to have no effect when cast directly against living creatures as opposed to objects that contained or were made from iron.

In a strange logical way, I supposed it made sense. Mentally girding my loins, I decided to spend the day as I had the others by working on my Strength and grinding up some experience.

My first shift passed without incident. As the workers along my line made their way out of the mine, I made sure to cast Rust a further four times, delaying each cast to measure the maximum distance of the spell. For the fourth cast, as I targeted a slave with a game leg about sixty meters away, I was struck by a familiar painful buildup: the spell had failed to take hold.

I quickly released the pent-up magic into the leg manacles of a miner closer to me, who was two places down the line from those who had replaced the first shift. I concluded that the spell—at level one, at least—possessed a range between forty and fifty meters at a very rough guess. I kept five points in reserve to cast Heal in case I suffered any "accidents" while working, with one point as a buffer against Mana sickness.

The day ended with my usual exhaustion, and my Health was in the low seventies. I had pushed my body to the extreme, even using power strike once against the rock when our minders were not looking. Much to my delight, the wicked blow had carved a great gouge through the rock. Though it had burned through my precious Stamina, I did not regret the action, as it allowed me to vent a little of my frustrations by imagining smashing the pickaxe against Degei's smug face.

At the evening meal, the other slaves still looked at me with fear in their eyes. No doubt the tales of my encounter with the Nord man-mountain Harun the Iron and my successful showing at the Winnowing had grown. Still, I was never the most popular person in a group in my old life, so it did not bother me too much. *Better to be feared than to live in fear,* I considered to myself, a rather Machiavellian line of thinking.

Despite all of this, I did have some companions, if not friends: the dwarf and the wildman. In the manner of those at the bottom rung of a society's ladder, we had bonded, perhaps subconsciously clinging to a false sense of superiority. The wildman with his unbroken spirit, the dwarf with his diligent pride, and as for me, I knew that I had come from a more civilized world. A certain glumness came over me then, as I had made no gains in Strength from my time in the mines, though I had still gained a small amount of experience.

Kidu and Durhit were not talkative that evening. I ascribed their reticence to the general rigor of a slave's life. After the evening meal, and just before it was time for sleep, I washed off the dirt and grime from a day's arduous work as best I could.

Before sleeping, I cast Heal on myself, and my knotted muscles relaxed. Small wounds that I had never noticed before healed across my body. A tiny stony fragment, perhaps from my overenthusiastic strikes against the rock, clattered to the earthen ground, pushed out by regenerating flesh. A warm balm washed over me, more soothing than any song, and took away the aches and pains of the day.

But it could not take away a feeling of bitterness that welled up inside at the thought of more backbreaking work.

Chapter 21

A CHANGE OF CIRCUMSTANCE

The Eastern Alliance vastly underestimated the depths to which a free people would resist an oppressor, and troops of the kingdom now known to be called the Republic of Arastia fought with great zeal and fervor. They knew what fate awaited every single man, woman, and child should they become a conquered people.

— *On the Cataclysm* by an unknown Quassian Scholar, circa 103 AC.

My magic healed my body, but in my vanity, I noticed it did nothing for the accumulating marks and scars. The days followed one another in a slow, steady rhythm, with little change for the next three. Work, eat, work, heal, and sleep were the parts of my monotonous routine.

However, on the fourth day, I took my morning toilet a little earlier than usual due to waking from a nightmare of being pursued by sharp-bladed dark things. I could just make out a woman of middling years, with a face set with hard lines of grief, making her way to Degei before his regular motivational morning speech.

Gold circles were threaded throughout her raven-black hair and tinkled as she walked. I could not help but feel that her features were familiar, but in my morning state, my mind failed to make a connection. A small leather purse was exchanged, and Degei nodded solemnly to the woman, raising the purse a little higher with both hands before stuffing it into the loose folds of his clothes.

Subsequently, I was made to work even harder in the mines that day. I now labored four shifts, with only a few hours of rest after my evening meal before I joined another slave gang to toil away in the dark blue depths. I was being worked to death. My mind, in its own twisted humor, joked that my new schedule gave me little time to have words and socialize with my newfound companions. But despite my circumstances working against me, we were able to exchange occasional snippets at brief intervals in the day.

I made sure to pace myself, but this new grueling menu of work meant that I had to dedicate five points of Mana every day just to keep my body in working condition. However, thanks to this new forced work plan, I had started to gain rapidly in attribute points and skills. I had gained two points of Strength and another skill point in hammers.

My near-sleepless nights earned me another point in Constitution and raised both my endure and rest skills. I had earnestly tried to raise my Rust spell and was rewarded with an increase in Intelligence and Wisdom, as well as finally raising the spell to level two. More importantly, thanks to my labors, I was gaining a modicum of experience. Putting aside my nightmarish conditions, the avid gamer inside of me actually looked forward to the next day and the opportunity to earn even more experience.

One small moment of levity that lightened my spirits for a day was a guard being berated by Degei for the state of his equipment. Unbeknownst to him, I had been casting Rust on his gear. He looked genuinely shocked at the state of his armor and weapons as the overseer gave him a dressing down.

I had also secretly cast Rust on Kidu's collar with some trepidation one evening before my spell had leveled up and gained in power. He showed no ill effect as he lay in his deep slumber, snoring wildly like a bear. I was satisfied to observe that there were a few splotches of rust about the edges of his collar the next day.

From these observations, I concluded that it would be safe to cast Rust on my own collar. Through gritted teeth, I cast it that same evening to no ill effects, save for the usual feeling of wrongness and a very slight warm feeling around my neck where the metal contacted my skin. I had learned to effectively block out the sibilant whispers that seemed to come from just behind me when I cast Rust.

This experience, in my mind at least, proved how adaptable humans were. We have the ability to compartmentalize even the most peculiar things. It made me wonder if those who participated in the brutal slave trade business were able to go home at the end of the day with a smile on their face and love in their eyes. Did the same hand that wielded the whip also caress the head of an innocent child?

Though mentally exhausted, I was indeed growing stronger. What didn't kill me could only make me stronger, I would mutter to myself, remembering the famous quote from Nietzsche. I needed to make my way out of here and escape. I was reasonably certain that Degei was already trying to kill me indirectly, and at this rate, who knew how much longer I would last? It was only my magic, my prodigious Constitution, and Adita's sympathy that had allowed me to survive so far under my conditions.

I knew that Constitution influenced Health and overall resilience, but could that extend to resistance against disease? To resistance to the general frailties of the human condition? I was still young, of course, but I wondered—could near immortality be possible for me if I pushed the attribute to its extreme? It was certainly a tantalizing line of thinking.

However, this was, of course, all predicated on this world being real...

Just as I was mulling these thoughts over, there was a rumble that quaked through the ground. The sounds of clanging industry stopped as the reverberations shook the encampment, and a sense of panic infected the air. The earthquake—for it could be nothing else—rattled the building around me as a stampede of slaves made for the single entrance. Rising quickly on unsteady feet, I hurried to join them in exiting the stables.

Before long, guards woken from their sleep stormed into the pens, with a tired-looking Degei in tow. The guards violently ordered us to form orderly lines, the licks from a club or whip more threatening than the shaking of the earth as we waited for the rumblings to subside. I could hear the ignorant slaves whisper to each other something about land dragons stirring, the Earth Mother being angry, and other such superstitious nonsense.

The locals probably had no idea about the mechanics of tectonic activities and continental drift. However, a small part of me did wonder if perhaps maybe, just maybe, it could be the work of actual land dragons.

"Get back to sleep, the lot of you! Work tomorrow! Back! Back I say, dogs!" Degei ordered, half-shouting, his words enforced with the stinging crack of studded leather.

I made my way back inside along with the other slaves, our common fear of Degei overriding our dread of the angry earth. That's how well some of us had been broken by fear of the whip.

Lying on my pallet, I tried to whisper to Kidu, but the snoring noises from his direction confirmed he was already asleep; it would be churlish of me to steal him from it. Turning to my right, I whispered to Durhit. I could barely make out his craggy face in the gloom, and he responded with an annoyed grunt.

"Best be going to sleep, manling. Tomorrow will be the hardest, darkest day yet, mark my words," he said in an attempt at a quiet voice before turning on his side and facing away from me, closing off all further avenues of inquiry.

Apprehensive and annoyed, I cast Rust impulsively at my collar. I felt the familiar uncomfortable and inimical sensation flow throughout my body before I released it into the slave collar on my neck. The whispers had become stronger, and the crackle of the black lightning's pulses felt increasingly like the heartbeat of a living creature now that the spell had increased in level.

The collar on my neck grew unbearably hot, sizzling my skin and filling the air with a sickeningly appetizing smell. It skirted the borders of agony, taking a chunk off my Health before it subsided to just merely painfully hot.

I gritted my teeth at the unexpected sensation, the strength of the reaction taking me completely by surprise. But there, alone in the darkness, I was unwilling to let out a sound and draw attention to myself. I hugged myself pathetically against the pain.

And then I thought I heard something crack or give way in the collar, like the sound of an errant foot slowly stepping on an expensive and fragile toy. I could feel a coarse, sandy sensation where the metal met my neck. Tentative fingers shook as they reached to confirm the state of my collar, but I stopped them just before they brushed against the slowly cooling surface, remembering the pain from when I had touched it before. My mind scrambled for a solution to my predicament before I remembered an old staple of mine—Identify. Perhaps in this way, I could at least check the durability of the collar. Guiding my magic to the collar, I made a welcome discovery.

Iron Slave Collar
Durability: 294/400

My hands were shaking, hesitant and unsure, as if unwilling to test the truth of a mirage in a desert, but I touched the collar anyway. Nothing happened. Sweet, blessed relief, nothing happened, no pain, no lightning shock. Touching the collar again several times to affirm my discovery, I began to cry silent tears of joy.

Even in my heightened emotional state, my mind sought to explain what had happened. The "Iron Slave Collar of Obedience" had lost its suffix and was now just a simple "Iron Slave Collar." Though I was never particularly gifted in science, my improved Intelligence had helped me attain this sudden realization.

The rapid oxidation of my iron collar caused by my improved Rust spell had released a great deal of heat in an exothermic reaction, which had inflicted me with first- or second-degree burns. This could be a boon, in that the effects of the level two spell were more rapid and significant.

On the other hand, this also meant that it would now be difficult for me to apply the spell against enemies without their knowledge. I hoped that the dark energies released when I cast the spell remained invisible, and with some chagrin, I noticed that the spell had cost an additional point of Mana.

The coarse, sandy feeling around the area below my neck was probably oxide or rust that had shaken loose. I hypothesized that the degradation of the collar likely interfered with its delicate mechanics or magical circuitry, or whatever crazy system they used to keep a person in a state of slavery in this magical world.

Fearing a potential tetanus infection despite my relatively high Constitution, I quickly cast Heal on myself. I checked the status of my character to distract myself, as the feeling of my skin knitting over was most uncomfortable; however, the soothing balm soon spread throughout my body and assuaged my concerns. With only four points of Mana remaining, and an unknown amount of time before I would probably be called to an even more grueling day, I decided to rest.

Though my talks with Durhit and Kidu had stoked the desire for adventure, my own actions this evening had lit a burning need within that was growing into a blaze—the need to be free. I found it laughably ironic that the thing I had so casually taken for granted in my old world was the thing I craved the most here.

The universe appeared to have agreed with my actions.

You have gained 1 Wisdom.

Chapter 22

DANGEROUS CONDITIONS

The people of the New Empire say that the best slaves are those who are born into slavery, as they have known nothing else besides the discipline of the whip and the benevolence of a master. These chattels will often work much harder, and are one of the pillars of a well-run house. For surely iron and steel may rust, but the threat of punishment, once learned, is until death.

— *The Fanciful Travels* by Beron de Laney, 376 AC.

It seemed like I had just closed my eyes when a cruel steel-capped boot kicked me in the stomach, dealing about six points of damage. One of my minders, a narrow-eyed and spiteful-looking man dressed in a motley collection of rust-speckled chains and leather, had attempted to wake me before, and this was his second kick. Perhaps there was a disadvantage to the pain nullification skill after all.

To avoid any further harassment, I got to my feet as quickly as my sleep-starved body allowed me. Like a child used to being caned, I followed the group as they made their way out of the building as fast as possible. The distant sound of industry that had pervaded the area around the mines had significantly quietened after the first quake. The disappearance of the sound of clanging metal and belching bellows lent a certain solemn atmosphere to our morning gathering. As our minders grouped us into passable rows, another small rumble of the earth threatened to shatter the serenity of the morning. A scared slave screamed in a pitch higher than usual.

After a crack of the whip had reduced the vocal slave to a curled, gibbering wreck on the floor, a group of rough-looking individuals of various races and skin colors, perhaps a dozen strong, entered the assembly grounds. Some were tall and muscular, like meaty slabs that had discovered the fine art of walking on two legs. Others were whipcord thin, lean, and quick of movement. A few dwarves were scattered about their number, dour and stout, with bushy eyebrows and long beards of assorted colors.

Most interesting of all was what I recognized as an orc, who hulked over the rest of the group. He was an olive-green bestial being of layered muscles and had sharp, jutting tusks that rose from an extended underbite. On his sloped, scarred head, a single topknot of purple hair completed the fierce appearance, and his fists, the size of small boulders, clenched and relaxed repeatedly at his side—a sign of barely restrained animalistic fury.

The majority had bodies scarred with the loving kiss of the whip and eyes hard and unforgiving as cruel winter. Some had the demeanor of those who had been victims of great cruelty, and in suffering those cruelties wanted to pass them on tenfold to the weaker and more vulnerable. And all bore a thick iron slave collar almost identical to my own.

Kidu and I were herded off to join this new group, long sticks from our watchers guiding our way with a few savage flicks, which led Kidu to snarl at them. This in turn caused the wildman to utter a sharp, high-pitched yelp as the magic of his collar, neutralizing a perceived threat to its masters, worked to send great waves of lightning agony to its host.

Miraculously, I was able to support the massive man—who was still spasming with pain—and we both somehow made it over to the new group. Upon joining them, we were met with calculating stares that seemed to be judging if we were to be part of their pack or simply new prey.

Surprisingly, an uncollared Durhit also joined our party. Dwarven expertise with stone was a valuable commodity in our next venture, I figured.

Now separated from the main group of slaves, Overseer Degei addressed our wolf pack of troublemakers himself, flanked by his usual burly guards. Unlike the earlier occasion, the guards seemed tense, scanning our motley crew of individuals with practiced gazes, searching for any threats against their master. I lowered my eyes to avoid drawing attention, which evoked a few snickers from the hardened crowd around me.

"The recent shakings of the earth have caused a collapse in one of the portside shafts near a particularly valuable vein of ore," Overseer Degei began in a voice that contradicted his small size. "Under the guidance of this dwarf"—he nodded in Durhit's direction before continuing—"you will work to clear the shaft of fallen debris and open the way for industry once more. In good time, all of you will be allowed a turn with a female from our breeding stock of your choice, and two days of rest. However, should we fall behind, you will be left to the kind ministrations of our most experienced flesh sculptors with no food for a week." He finished the last sentence with an aplomb only those granted the mantle of authority for many years could marshal.

It was the carrot-and-stick approach, then. My new group began to make their way to the mines, some with avid lust on their features. The orc was most horrifying of all, looking like a wild beast in heat as he greedily picked up a mining pick and shovel in each of his giant hands. As I made a move to grab a familiar pickaxe, Durhit placed a gentle hand on my shoulder and shook his head. He handed me a shovel and a large, sturdy-looking wicker basket to place around my shoulders.

"Dangerous work, this. You'll be wanting to stay back as far as possible. Might not be improving your chances by much, but they will be improved nonetheless," he said in his sage, gravelly voice.

Grudgingly, I took his advice and placed the basket about my shoulders, giving my thanks before catching up with the rest of the group, which consisted of four mean-looking guards who carried an assortment of intimidating blunt and bladed weapons. These men were to be our escort.

As we approached the dark, dank passage, Durhit made his way to the front of the group. Our escorts stationed themselves at the entrance, exchanging worried glances with each other as they counted our numbers on an abacus before we stepped foot into the mine's gaping maw. Near the entrance, we could see scattered tools and other debris left behind by the slaves and their overseers who had abandoned their posts when the earthquake struck.

As we ventured deeper into the mines, we took the furthest left tunnel but soon realized that some of the wooden beams supporting the ceiling were askew and broken in places, with large slabs of rock and earthen debris half-blocking our path. This sight cast a worrying pall over the group; no one wanted to be trapped under hundreds of tons of earth and rock.

To address this concern, Durhit quickly ordered supports to be laid at various locations. With his and the other dwarves' guidance, our team efficiently placed lumber to buttress the ceiling and help prevent a potential cave-in. However, as we worked, another small tremor shook the mines, causing a light dusting of rock powder to fall from the ceiling and heightening everyone's apprehension. Even the orc paused and sniffed the air as fear and lust warred across his porcine features.

"Just a little shake, nothing to worry about. The faster we get this done, the faster we can get out of this cursed hole," one of the dwarves said.

However, his attempt at reassurance was met with a sharp retort from one of the gigantic human meat slabs. "That's what your sire said to your dam, you stunty bastard!"

The other dwarves gave the human a hard look, clearly sensitive about their height. Despite this, the rest of us laughed at the jibe, breaking the sudden tension in the air as we returned to our work.

I tried to push out of my mind the fact that several metric tons of earth and rock were hanging above our heads. I had never been particularly comfortable in confined spaces, and the recent quake had tested my nerves.

A part of me felt close to breaking, knowing that nothing in my skill set or arsenal of spells could aid us in the sudden and random event of a cave-in.

Chapter 23

LUCKY STRIKE

From the land of towering steel spires and venomous mists shall it emerge, its hunger insatiable, never quenched by the bountiful harvest of the shifting sands. Nay, it shall make its way to the sea that is but a memory, trapped and entombed in halls of white as pure as milk.

A grave, long forgotten and left to the ages, shall stir once more, its power unleashed to claim the final reckoning. A scion of the ravenous people, born to bring destruction and ruin to all that stands before it. False justice and chaos its only companions, heralding the coming of the apocalypse.

The harbinger of the ultimate cataclysm, it shall not rest until all that was once known is consumed by its wrath. None shall escape the doom that it brings, for its power is absolute and its hunger unending. The end is nigh, and no man, woman, or child shall be spared its merciless fury.

— Attributed to the Wrack Witch before her execution, circa 245 AC.

Our group eventually reached a part of the shaft where a large amount of stone had fallen from the ceiling, obstructing further passage to the deeper parts of the mine. Some of the other dwarves suggested digging around the shaft to create a small connecting tunnel, but Durhit decided we should place additional beams to support the roof while we break up the larger pieces of stone and clear the way.

The work was strenuous, but our group worked quickly under the skilled guidance of the dwarves, without the need for the extra motivation of a whip. I was shoveling gravel and loose debris into my wicker basket when a man of average height approached me. He had a lean and feral appearance, with scars running down his limbs. A receding hairline, thinning hair, and bald spot on the top of his head gave him the look of a tonsured monk. He greeted me with a rakish smile and began to talk.

"Haven't seen your type before around here. Name's Elwin, Elwin Tucker," he said with a cheerful tone that seemed out of place in the setting. He then placed his shovel in his left hand and reached out to shake my hand with his callused grip.

I returned the shake with moderate enthusiasm and replied, "I've never been to these parts before, but I think the hospitality and accommodations could use some improvement. I would very much like to end my journey in these lands." A small smile began to form at the corner of my mouth, and I found his friendly attitude infectious. "My name is Gilgamesh. Gilgamesh of Uruk."

"Hah! I'll drink to that, Gil, if only there was anything to drink. You don't mind if I call you Gil, do you? There's no escaping now that they've got you." He pointed to his heavy iron collar. "You could put one of these things on a giant, and it wouldn't be going anywhere fast!"

"I wouldn't know about that." My tongue loosened under his charisma, and I had to make an effort to stop myself from continuing foolishly. "I mean, I've never had one of these lovely pieces of jewelry on me before," I finished a little lamely.

The man looked at me quizzically before returning to his work. "Not for lack of trying on my part," he said, gesturing to his collar. "I've tried many things with this. I've hit it with something, tried getting my mates to hit it with something, and that took some doing. I've even tried grinding it against some hard rock, and let me tell you, that is not an easy task. It felt like I was sawing away at my own neck! But everything ended in pain." He shoveled another load of dirt and gravel. "Once, I was even able to get a good distance away from this lovely holiday spot. But I was caught by those cursed Tides, writhing on the ground in pain so great that I'm sure my bastard children's children will feel it. They had a good laugh at that."

The temptation to reveal to him that there might be a way out of our situation grew stronger, but I knew I had to keep that particular card close to my chest. I had only just met him, and I began to wonder if this was some sort of test. I had absolutely no reason to trust this man despite his friendly demeanor.

Venturing to change the topic, I gave him a brief summary of my origins, leaving out the detail about coming from Earth. Unlike Kidu and Durhit, he appeared a bit skeptical about my story but was nonetheless understanding of my fabricated memory loss. At some point during the conversation, Kidu, who was busy breaking up rocks nearby, began to interject, correcting some of the details to fit his own version of events.

The brutish orc was carving up the stones in front of him, a pickaxe in each hand, and gouged through the stone with consummate ease and fury. Kidu responded in turn, blond dreadlocks swinging with each mighty flourish of his mining tool, and a sort of rivalry grew between the two. Elwin and I hurried to keep gathering the smaller stones and detritus out of the way.

During a small lull in the work, even the formidable Kidu had to begrudgingly concede victory to the orc. Impressed by Kidu's performance, I decided to discreetly cast my Identify spell on him as he breathed in and out like the bellows of a forge. I was a bit surprised that I had not thought to do so earlier.

Kidu Kreshin - Hunter (Human Lv. 11)
Health: 211/214
Stamina: 2/47
Mana: 5/5

Kidu's statistics were impressive, and it was no wonder how he was able to keep up with the orc for as long as he had. His class designation of hunter made sense from his tales of his home, his skills no doubt honed by dealing with the great beasts that lived there.

We asked Elwin about his own origins. The temptation to cast the spell on him as he began his little tale was strong, but I decided to refrain until we were at a safer locale.

"My tale is a simple one. I was a forester for a lord. My whole family had been foresters since way back in the March Reaches of Aranthia," he began in his naturally friendly tone. "Our lot in life was to protect the lord's game from the hungry types and the occasional Goblin. One year, after perhaps the bitterest winter and poorest harvest of the ages, I found out that one of my neighbor's sons had been putting a little extra in his game bag. Wilf, Silf, I can't even remember his name now... It seems like another lifetime. But I do remember that it was hard to enforce Reach justice, which called for death for the crime of poaching. All of this was for a lord whom I had only met once, to punish a man who had a starving family and a wailing bairn. I let it go, and perhaps even snuck him a bit of coin every now and then." He paused for a moment, as if gathering himself.

"It began with poaching, and it seemed that poaching was a steppingstone to banditry for young Wilf. Needless to say, someone who was deep in their cups told someone else, and then a different someone pointed a finger at me. The Arbitrator said I was responsible for the crimes of the man whom I had willingly turned a blind eye to, that I was some sort of corrupt civil servant. I was sold off to pay for someone else's crime and as a demonstration of the lord's authority. And here I am, toiling under the earth, when I should be under the boughs of the trees, breathing in the clean forest air." Elwin tried to finish in resignation, but he couldn't quite help adding, "Which sure beats the stench of you lads. The bunch of you could kill a full-grown buck just standing downwind. I'd probably be dead already if my nose wasn't!"

We replied with a weak laugh as a dour, gray-bearded dwarf gestured for us to get back to work with a scowl and a wave of a shovel that scraped the ceiling, coating his beard with fine white rock dust that looked like blue snow in the gloom.

"On my honor, I wish for nothing more than to be free and wreak vengeance on the Children!" Kidu declared in his simplistic way, his voice filled with strong determination as he resumed carving up the rock, no doubt imagining he was caving in the faces of the Children of the Tides.

A few hours later, we had finally cleared enough of the shaft's obstructions for two abreast to walk through. Under the blue glow of the zajasite lightstones, we allowed ourselves a small break to rest our tired and sore muscles. Durhit sent Elwin back up to the surface to call for much-needed supplies.

A group of younger slaves, led by Elwin, returned to us later. Water bearers brought with them baskets of bread, which we scarfed down almost as quickly as they handed them out. A familiar face passed, his eyes hot with rage but downturned in fear.

"Gunne," I said, recognizing him. The boy flinched, surprised I had remembered his name. "Son of Gundlaug. Will you have your revenge this day?" I continued slowly, my tone filled with petty spite.

To his credit, he didn't rise to the provocation, silently handing out my portion of bread just as Durhit arrived to check up on us.

"Don't be terrorizing the lad too much. We are..." he began, but was cut off as the earth suddenly rumbled and the walls shook as if receiving blows from mighty fists.

Losing my balance, I was tossed against the wall, accidentally striking a slave with my shovel and sending him to the ground. Powerful vibrations shook the mines, causing our hastily made supports to quiver against the seismic forces and stone dust to fall from the ceiling. Somewhere in the chaos, I could hear wailing and panicked screaming as the earth continued to convulse like an angry and uncaring god.

Suddenly, one of the supports exploded under the strain like a tree in the coldest winter, making a sound like a gunshot and adding to the cacophony of chaos. This triggered a chain reaction as rocks began to fall from the ceiling. First, small loose stones and gravel hit with a rattling sound, followed by hulking, jagged boulders that added to the disorder and caused injuries in the blue-stained pandemonium. As I looked down, I was met with horror as the slave I had accidentally struck was smashed by a large rock, utterly squashed under its great weight.

You have slain a Human. 95 experience gained.
You have gained 1 Luck.
You have gained 1 Dexterity.
You have reached Lv. 7.
3 unassigned attribute points.
1 unassigned skill point.

Even as the earth rumbled in its rage, rocks falling everywhere, I frantically navigated through the interface to assign my skills. In a split-second decision, I added a skill point to dodge and, as was my custom, allocated all of my attribute points to Constitution. Being a fraction more agile, I was able to avoid another falling rock, and even pushed Kidu out of the way of a large plummeting white stone.

Then the world went black, and I knew no more.

Chapter 24

SMALL MERCIES

With the cost in blood ever rising as the war raged on, the leader of the Alliance, the elven high king, even offered amnesty to the Republic on the condition that they surrender their leader in chains. This was met with derision by the senate, and their envoy was sent back with a message that there would be no surrender to the savage barbarians from across the seas.

— On the Cataclysm by an unknown Quassian Scholar, circa 103 AC.

Black things that stabbed while whispering sweet promises of release plagued me as I woke up with a feral scream. Disorientation filled me as I looked around the blue gloom. The insides of my skull felt like mashed jelly as I tried to take stock of my situation. Gingerly, I touched the back of my head to find it crusted with dried blood.

I winced inwardly as I checked my Status and character, noticing I had sustained considerable damage in the last quake. Chuckling to myself, I remembered that I had gained a level and a few attribute points when I had inadvertently killed a fellow slave. Looking over the rest of my character sheet, I confirmed my gains.

STATUS
    Calling: Gilgamesh Lv. 7 Acolyte of Avaria
    Strength: 22
    Dexterity: 14

    Constitution: 31

    Intelligence: 18

    Wisdom: 14

    Charisma: 9

    Luck: 14

SKILLS AND PROFICIENCIES

    Pain Nullification Lv. 1

    Power Strike Lv. 2

    Endure Lv. 3

    Stealth Lv. 1

    Rest Lv. 3

    Backstab Lv. 2

    Dodge Lv. 3

    Polearms Lv. 2

    Dual Wield Lv. 1

    Critical-Hit Mastery Lv. 2

    Mining Lv. 2

    Unarmed Combat Lv. 3

    Hammers Lv. 2

SPELLS AND MAGIC

    Heal Lv. 5

    Rust Lv. 2

    Identify Lv. 2

    Silent Casting Lv. 1

GIFTS

    Curse of Entropy: -20% to all starting attributes.

Experience to Lv. 8: 1065/1289

Health: 93/147

Stamina: 45/49

Mana: 12/12

It appeared that my short sojourn into unconsciousness had counted as a rest. This had thankfully regenerated most of my Stamina, Mana, and even some of my Health. Even in my weakened state, I would be more than a match for a few bibsi.

Groggily, I tried to rise, only to be stopped when I realized my right leg was trapped. A slab of white stone had fallen across it, stained blue in the zajasite glow. I tried to push off the rock and was met with a sharp pain that competed with my other agonies. Straining ever harder against the cold stone slab, I finally managed to move it off, which was accompanied by a grinding noise that I hoped was not the sound of breaking bone.

Whimpering a little, I tried to gather myself, finding it difficult to cast Heal through the pain. Finally, after a few long, agonizing seconds, I was able to complete the spell with a short mental shout as it filled me with familiar warmth. My leg wondrously healed before me, bringing me almost to full Health. I felt a wave of relief at putting nearly all my level-up skill points into the Heal spell.

Taking a moment to collect my wits after that arduous experience, I looked around at what was left of the tunnel. Great slabs of stone had fallen randomly and crushed and killed most of the slaves. The path to the surface was completely blocked; there would be no rescue from that direction. My eyes cast through the dark, searching for familiar shapes and faces before alighting on the great bulk that could only have been Kidu.

Scrambling to his side, I could see that he was covered in gashes and cuts across his massive limbs and trunk, his linen tunic bloodstained in many places. By the grace of the gods, Kidu was still breathing, his massive chest rising and falling, albeit erratically. His breath was raspy and strained.

Focusing my power, I cast Heal. Now, instead of pulling the power inwards, I pushed it outside of myself and through my hands into the giant's body. I watched the healing power flow through Kidu's body, closing several of his wounds, and let out a relieved sigh. As he began to breathe easier, I sat down cross-legged beside the large man, mentally exhausted.

A sound halfway between a whimper and a wail distracted me from my reverie, and I turned in its direction. Leaving Kidu's side, I made my way to the pitiful sound. In the gloom, I spied Durhit's short, solid shape hunched over a small form. As I came closer, I saw that the small shape was in fact a person. It was none other than Gunne, son of Gudlaug, the boy barely into his teens who had sworn vengeance against me for killing Harun.

Looking back at my actions, I was somewhat perturbed by what I had done to the man Gunne had idolized. Did the crime of cutting in line merit such a violent reaction? Had this world already changed me to such a frightening degree? Still, the experience from his death probably had been instrumental in helping me survive this far. This world rewarded killers, after all.

Gunne was whimpering weakly, his lithe, youthful body half-crushed by rocks, a puddle of red forming around him. Durhit was holding his hand gently, offering soft, meaningless words of comfort to him in his final moments. Durhit then looked up at me, and I imagined his eyes were a little shiny with the start of tears.

"The boy is in great pain. I have seen this before... in the field." He paused for a moment. "I can't do it again. And you are... well, you know..."

I raised a single eyebrow, which he may not have noticed.

"Take away his suffering. He might be a long time dying otherwise." Cowardice and weakness were threaded into his plea.

I looked down at the boy and his mangled body, and—perhaps a little too eagerly—I picked up a mining pick from a pile of loose rubble. Its point glinted wickedly in the gloom. I wanted this pathetic NPC to suffer for a long time, to feel even a fraction of the pain and humiliation he had inflicted on me when he dared to threaten me. However, I mentally shrugged my shoulders. It was free experience, after all, and Durhit was practically begging me to do it.

Without further ceremony, I met Gunne's widening eyes with a cold gaze as I slowly raised the pickaxe. His hands clenched, and his mewling grew more desperate. Durhit began saying something like, "It's going to be all right," or some other pointless tripe as I brought the pickaxe down into Gunne's skull in cathartic anger, smashing what remained of his youthful features.

You have slain Gunne. 70 experience gained.

Chapter 25

GIVE AND TAKE

The Great Below, the Everdark, and the Realm of Shadowed Rock are just a few names given to the great expanse that lies beneath the surface. The dwarven miners of old were said to have first made entry there even before the Cataclysm. Great artifacts from bygone ages are said to lie there, guarded by monsters and natives who have only known the embrace of the night. Adventurers from the guild have been sent on countless expeditions to map out its depths, searching for a fabled treasure trove said to lie in a place called the "Inverse Mountain."

— *The Fanciful Travels* by Beron de Laney, 376 AC.

Something broke in Durhit then, as he began to cry silent tears. I was simply disappointed that Gunne's death was only worth seventy experience points and did not bring about any improvements to my attributes or skills. Gunne, almost useless to the end. For a fleeting second, I also wondered how much experience I could get if I were to finish off Kidu in his weakened state...

"Pull yourself together, Durhit," I said as I pretended to console him, placing my hand on his shoulder. "We need to get out of here before the tunnel collapses completely."

"Gunne was a good boy," he said, rubbing his eyes. "He always showed up on time, always had a smile on his face. You know he had a beautiful singing voice? That's why that bastard Harun took him under his wing. He was a good lad who didn't deserve to die like this."

"Are you okay… I mean, all right, Durhit?" He had looked at me quizzically as I subconsciously used the unfamiliar English word. "Kidu is in a bad way, and we need to move him. I can't heave his great bulk alone," I said, pointing to the wildman's prone form.

Something in my words spoke to his sense of responsibility as a leader, and he rose up on his two short legs. He gave a final mournful look at Gunne's remains, filled with sadness, before slapping himself on the face with both palms.

"You speak the truth, Gilgamesh. Let us get Kidu to a place of safety and search for other survivors. In the undermines, a quake like this is usually followed by others, often more deadly than the first," he said in his rough voice, setting his shoulders and walking purposefully towards Kidu's location.

Together, we managed to move Kidu as far as we could down the tunnels before having to stop and rest. We quickly turned back to search for any other survivors. I began to shout, but Durhit immediately stopped me, clasping his rough hand firmly over my mouth.

"You don't want to be shouting after a cave-in. Quakes are bad enough, could bring down the whole thing on us!" he warned sternly, looking at me intensely.

I nodded my understanding, and we continued our search for survivors in low voices, listening carefully for any signs. Durhit picked up a fallen zajasite stone, casting its light around the area. The blue glow of the stone threw up strange shadows in the darkness.

As the dwarf searched, I decided to do something to improve my situation. Not wanting to hurt myself, I focused on a single link of the manacles around my legs and slowly released the Rust spell, barely registering the scratchy alien whispers and the radiated heat. Black lightning flowed down into the metal, corroding and eating away at it. After some time, the energy subsided to a light thrumming, and I called out to Durhit softly, making my way towards his moving light.

Tripping on something, a hand suddenly gripped my ankle. I let out a shrieked yelp that drew the dwarf's attention. Looking down in surprise, I could just about discern Elwin's features, covered as he was in rock dust and dirt. The man looked like some sort of Mud or Earth Elemental.

"Could you check where you're stepping?" Elwin said with a grimace before coughing. "Also, a little help, if you would be so kind?"

Durhit quickly made his way over, helping me raise Elwin up as we supported him on both sides. His arms draped loosely around our shoulders as we moved him further down the tunnel.

"Wait here and keep an eye on these two. I'll go back and look for anything useful to keep us alive in this mess," the dwarf said in a commanding voice, and I nodded in agreement.

"Well, thanks a lot back there. Now, instead of dying quickly, I get to die slow. Not like we can go anywhere too far with these," Elwin said, darkly pointing at his collar. "And not like our glorious masters will be sending a rescue party down a dangerous mine to get some trouble slaves! Glad the big man made it through. At least we'll all be eating well before we die of thirst," he finished with a dispirited sigh that echoed in the gloom.

The situation was dire; the threat of being buried alive was very real, and I needed all the help I could get. The time for keeping things close to my chest was over—I needed to roll the dice.

"There might be a way to neutralize these collars," I said, slowly and hesitantly. Unease crept over me with my sudden confession.

"I told you before, lad, I've tried just about everything except for magic..." He paused, understanding dawning in his eyes. "The big man said something about you being God-touched," he uttered solemnly.

"There is, however, a problem. It might be a little painful, and I need to rest before I make the attempt."

"Ha! I knew it all along. I knew you were hiding something big. A lad like you could have never taken out a Nord like Harun if you didn't have something special in you," he said, his voice animated with childish excitement.

"But first I'll need something from you."

I raised a hand, and he stopped yammering almost instantly. Give and take, the simple language of transactions, was what a man like Elwin understood. "Tell me what you know about magic," I breathed, trying to contain my eagerness for this esoteric knowledge.

"Can't say I know much myself," he began, before noticing my expression. "And I don't know anything more than what is commonly known. Also, I don't think this is the best time to be wagging tongues. But that bit of magic you used just there, I've never heard of its like before, and I don't really see how it's going to help us get out of this little predicament. That is, unless you've got a few other different tricks in the bag?" An edge of desperation had replaced his usual good humor.

He was right. Now, perhaps, was not the best time to be having this conversation. But I thirsted for any scrap of information. Was the man holding out and hiding something from me?

I looked him in the eye, now not quite trusting the man. After casting Identify on him, my suspicions were confirmed.

Elwin Tucker - Rogue (Human Lv. 12)
Health: 74/132
Stamina: 27/38
Mana: 10/10

Most certainly not a forester, then, which meant I probably couldn't trust his spiel about his tragic past. For all I knew, he could have been the poacher turned bandit in his little story. But challenging him on this would be of little advantage to me at this moment, and I would have to reveal another of my abilities if I did so.

The man had basically told me nothing. Something in my gut told me not to trust the charismatic rogue fully just yet. I was able to take some assurance that, from seeing his attributes, I was probably a little stronger than him physically. A good thing to keep in mind if it came to blows.

"Thank you," I replied weakly. "I need rest to gather my strength. Can you and Durhit watch over me and Kidu?" I leaned against the rock for support.

"You do whatever you need to. Now that I know you can help me get away from this cursed hole, I'll be guarding you with my life, even if the Dark Lady pays a visit!" Elwin thumped his chest with a fist.

The reference to the Dark Lady did not ring a bell for me, but I figured it must be some grim entity held in terror in this world. Speaking to him had opened up more questions than answers, but at least I could be sure of his motives. Our only hope was to work through this together, or we would all die here, underground.

A few beats of my heart later, I heard movement. It was Durhit with the zajasite crystal, its dull blue glow illuminating the walls slightly. He declared this length of the tunnel structurally sound. Deciding to roll fate's die, I finally relaxed my shoulders and tried to rest. Soon enough, I would fall into the clutches of a nightmare of drowning under a blanket of dark, choking earth.

Chapter 26

THE DARKEST HOURS

The subterranean depths are not to be trifled with, for they are home to a multitude of creatures that would make even the bravest of men tremble. The darkness down there is eternal, and those that dwell within it have evolved to navigate it with senses beyond our understanding. Some are pallid and sightless, while others possess an array of heightened senses that make them deadly predators.

There are whispers of a creature that surpasses all others in its power and ferocity: the great crawler. Though its existence is little more than rumor, its supposed presence has been felt through the quakes it causes as it tunnels through the rock and earth. It is said that the monster is the stuff of nightmares, a beast so terrifying that even the hardiest of adventurers dare not venture into its domain.

Many believe that the tales of earth dragons are nothing more than the ramblings of ignorant peasants, but perhaps there is some truth to their words. For who can say what beasts lie in the depths of the earth, waiting to unleash their fury upon the surface world?

— Monsters of the Mortal Realms by K. D. Fidditch.

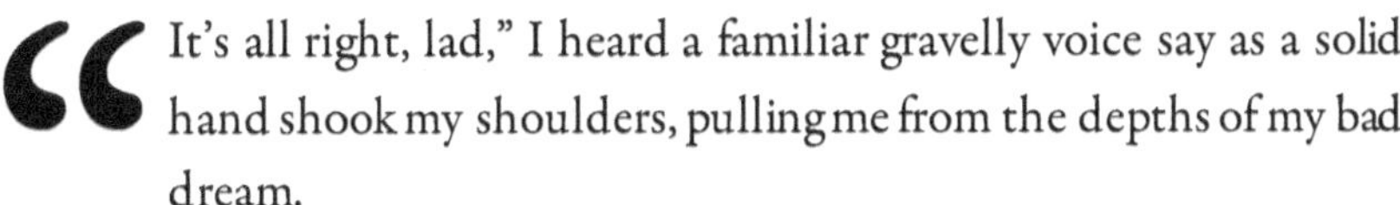

"It's all right, lad," I heard a familiar gravelly voice say as a solid hand shook my shoulders, pulling me from the depths of my bad dream.

Groggily, I rubbed my face awake and saw Durhit's ash-gray eyes looking intently at me, cold in the zajasite's blue light. Turning to my left and right, I could see Kidu standing with his arms crossed, hulking and taciturn in the gloom. Elwin Tucker, the rogue, practically jumped up when he saw that I was awake.

"Can you do it?" he asked almost childishly, his desire glowing in his eyes and written in the dark lines of his face.

I checked the bottom left of my vision, confirming that my Mana had risen, but not to full.

Health: 147/147
Stamina: 49/49
Mana: 9/12

Answering Elwin's question with one of my own, I croaked, my voice dry, "How long did I rest for?"

"About an hour, I would say," Durhit answered. "Even for us, it's hard to keep track of time when you're in the earth's embrace."

"Hmm... Nothing related, but I always wondered, why do they call you little dwarves stone-eaters?" Elwin asked offhandedly.

Even in the gloom, Durhit's scowl could be clearly seen. "Because you manlings believe that such is a dwarf's greed that he would rather eat stone than pay for food!"

"Your collar. I can... I can... do something to it. Break its mechanisms, I think," I all but blurted to change the subject, unwilling to let the situation escalate.

All attention suddenly turned to me, and I felt the full onslaught of their gazes. Kidu uncrossed his arms and tried to give his best impression of a whisper, but his voice ended up booming and echoing in the darkness. "You have a way? This is the truth of it?"

I nodded. "Try touching your collar; please trust me. Not you, Elwin!" I quickly snapped as Elwin made to touch his collar, stopping just before making contact.

Gingerly, Kidu touched his own collar. I knew for a fact that I had cast Rust on his collar once before, albeit at level one. Hiding my panic as best I could, I realized that I should have cast Identify on his collar before urging him to touch it. I breathed a mental sigh of relief when he suffered no ill effects.

"Now many of the Tides will die thanks to you, Gilgamesh the God-touched. I swear it to be so. For this gift of freedom, I do also swear from this day forth we are brothers. My spear and bow will be yours, always," he vowed solemnly, looking me steadily in the eyes.

"All right, now how about me?" Elwin chimed in, raw eagerness lacing his voice.

"This might hurt a little... Well, actually, to be honest with you, this may hurt a lot. You will want to be seated for this," I cautioned.

Elwin acknowledged my instructions and sat down on the rocky floor. Anticipating the potential pain, he ripped some fabric from the short sleeve of his tunic, rolled it up, and bit on it before nodding to me. I motioned for Kidu to restrain Elwin before looking at the rogue once more in the eyes.

"You sure of this?" I asked, knowing his answer before I had even finished. He nodded emphatically, his eyes steady with resolve.

Casting my magic, I heard the familiar dark whispers as an oily feeling of wrongness pervaded my body. The energy felt almost gleeful now, as if wishing to be released. Holding my dominant hand forwards, I unleashed the pent-up energy into Elwin's slave collar.

Black energy, visible only to me, danced across the metal and swirled ever faster in a crescendo of movement. At first, Elwin looked as if nothing were wrong, until his eyes opened in what must have been great pain. A muffled scream reached his lips as he bit down. He closed his mouth tight against the rising heat of the collar.

A slight tinge of ozone laced the air as esoteric energies devoured the metal, releasing stored energies within. This continued for long moments. The energy released from weeks of oxidation, compressed into such a short time frame, was hurting Elwin.

Eventually, the roiling energies subsided to a soft thrumming, and the rogue's head lolled, his mental and physical endurance at its limits. The smell of lightly charred flesh filled the small space. Durhit, in his wisdom, splashed some precious water from a scavenged canteen where metal met the skin of the man. It hissed as it hit the hot, now inert metal, and caused Elwin to wake up with a resounding scream that could be heard even through his gag.

I moved quickly to his side, placing both hands around his neck to cast Heal. At first it seemed reluctant to follow my will. Nonetheless, after a tense few moments, I was ultimately able to channel the positive energies into the struggling man. The warm power ameliorated his pain and suffering, and the cuts and bruises along his face healed before our very eyes, visible even in the dark gloom.

Finally, as the spell ended, he spat out the wad of cloth and took deep breaths, like a man who had come too close to dying on a distant shore.

The hulking Kidu looked at me and nodded, affirming his own wisdom. "By the ancestor spirits, you truly are God-touched. Now I know that I was right to join my spear to yours," the proud wildman proclaimed.

Durhit looked confused, conflicting emotions warring across his features before he spoke a single word with the impact of a gunshot.

"Gunne," he whispered.

"Gunne, son of Gudlaug, swore a blood feud against my spear brother. Under what obligation was he to help that brat? Better to die free than to die as a slave," snarled Kidu, fierce in his protectiveness, like a mother bear.

"He was just a child who had fallen in with a..." Durhit stammered, surprised at Kidu's sudden unequivocal defense.

"Healing... like this... is expensive," wheezed Elwin, slowly recovering from my ministrations. He touched his collar for confirmation and breathed a sigh of relief when no lightning pain paralyzed him. "Gil here was under no responsibility to help the boy. You know that the good brothers at the temples charge a fortune for his kind of healing!"

"Just... we could have saved him," the dwarf said somberly, his shoulders sagging in surrender.

Seeking to clear up the situation, I decided to speak up and say my piece.

"Durhit, I truly believed the boy was beyond saving. The healing you think could have saved him, I simply could not do," I said, looking to Elwin for support. "I could not have done it with the energies I had at the time," I added, lying with ease.

"I have known many liars, and I would stake my life and immortal soul on it that Gil here speaks the truth," Elwin said before taking a breath, which seemed to come a little easier now. "As Kidu says, it's better he died quick and clean than the slow, tortured life of a slave. Besides, what else was he to do?"

I looked at Durhit, challenging him to disagree, but he said nothing. It must have been some sort of test because I received a notification that I had gained another point in Charisma.

You have gained 1 Charisma.

The old dwarf took a sip of water from a canteen before passing it around to the rest of us. We each drank greedily in turn, the stale water having a slightly leathery taste as it cleared our palates.

The dwarf reached into a wicker basket and produced a single loaf of bread, which he divided into four equal pieces, then handed out a chunk to each of us. We ate this humble meal in silence, the recent events on our minds.

"Well, what do we do now?" Elwin asked tentatively, looking to Durhit for direction.

With no answer forthcoming, I took the lead and made a suggestion. "First, we need to break these chains," I said, holding up my manacled hands and pointing to the chains at my feet.

Even Durhit perked up at my proposal, which had given us all a clear purpose.

Placing my hands on a sharp boulder, I turned to Kidu and asked, "Would you do me the honor of breaking my bondage?"

Grinning with almost childish glee, Kidu picked up a heavy pickaxe. Lifting it overhead, he brought it down in a massive swing that crushed through the iron links. His strike caused a mighty clank to echo down the shaft, and his pickaxe gouged a further few inches into the hard rock.

The others stared in wonder at his prodigious strength. Smiling down at me, Kidu gestured for me to place the chains of my legs on the rock, and he struck down again with all of his great strength. The chains had been weakened by my Rust spell, and they split apart like ripe fruit, freeing me. At long last, freedom.

Even in the blue gloom, I could have sworn that the eyes of the others brightened a little.

Next, Kidu solemnly placed his own chains on the rock, almost reverently gesturing for me to break his chains. I picked up another scavenged pickaxe and, unsure if my unaided Strength would be enough, raised the mining tool above my head and silently released a power strike.

The results were suitably impressive. I utterly obliterated the chains and shattered the rock beneath them, almost splitting the small boulder in two with a single blow. Wiping my brow and feigning greater fatigue than I truly felt, I smiled at my companions with bravado.

Kidu thanked me with all the air of a priest at communion. Knuckles facing outwards, he touched the place between his eyes with an open hand, which I gathered to mean a sign of respect and gratitude.

"Now, let's see if we can find a way out of here," I said, looking around at the dank, narrow tunnel walls. All I wanted to do was get as far away from there as possible.

Elwin and Durhit, however, were more focused on the business of smashing their own chains. Kidu and Elwin searched to help Durhit find another suitable piece of rock.

* * *

After what seemed like an eternity, but was probably less than half an hour, we were all able to break our chains. Elwin's bonds had proven to be particularly resistant, and the dwarf and the wildman had to take turns smashing at the stubborn links. Finally, we were all free. Although the remains of our manacles still encircled our wrists and ankles, our spirits were much lifted.

As we rested in the blue gloom, Durhit made sure to gather some fallen zajasite stones. He asked Kidu to carefully smash one from the ceiling and handed each of us a glowing blue stone, giving us a source of light.

"I hate to sound annoying, but what do we do now?" Elwin asked the group, although he looked mostly in my direction.

"We need to find water," the dwarf suggested. The area around here be known for its underground streams and rivers. If we can find one deeper down, we may be able to find a way out of here, but..."

"There is always a 'but,' though, isn't there?" said the rogue saucily. "By all means, speak on, sir dwarf. I am just delighting in my newfound liberty for a moment."

"In the deep places, a few workers were said to have gone missing. Strange tunnels were formed that no overseer was responsible for digging," the dwarf explained. "I believe the deep places are dangerous, so we should proceed with caution. But it could be our only way out. Going back the way we came would take almost a lifetime of digging through that mountain of rubble."

"I'd rather try for it than standing around here waiting to die of starvation. I say that we go for it!" chirped Elwin, while Kidu simply grunted.

I nodded to the dwarf, giving him leadership of the group. "Lead on. I bow to your expertise and wisdom. I have no understanding of these deep places as your people do."

"Thank you all. Given this old dwarf a little bit of hope back, you have," Durhit replied, some of his earlier confidence returning to his voice.

Although I was low on Mana, I thought about asking the group for another rest, but their eagerness to leave was infectious. With that, we gathered up what equipment and scant supplies of water and food we had and ventured deeper into the earth.

Chapter 27

A BID FOR TRUE FREEDOM

Incensed by the refusal of what he thought was a reasonable offer of amnesty, the High King of the Elves begged once more with the dragon queen for aid, offering a dragon egg's weight in precious silvery mithril. Greed sinking its claws into her reptilian heart, she commanded that flights of dragons launch into the sky and rain death and destruction on the Republic.

— On the Cataclysm by an unknown Quassian Scholar, circa 103 AC.

We trudged silently down the long tunnels for perhaps an hour or two, the small zajasite stones in our hands casting strange blue shadows in the gloom. As I looked to the bottom left of my vision, I noticed that my Mana had mysteriously risen to three points and I had also received a new notification.

You have learned Mana Regeneration Lv. 1.

I was grateful for the new skill, and its effects were pretty self-explanatory. The mystery to me, however, was how it had been triggered. Was it due to my constant draining of Mana and then resting? Did it stack with my rest skill? I pondered these questions fruitlessly until I almost bumped into Durhit, who had raised a hand, signaling a stop.

Up ahead, in the semidarkness, there was an offshoot tunnel. It was almost perfectly circular and smaller in diameter than the tunnel we were currently in. The dwarf raised a finger to his mouth, gesturing for silence as he looked down into the gloom. Slowly, we understood the need for caution as we strained our ears, catching the impression of an insectile clicking noise. As stealthily as possible, I ventured to the lip of the new tunnel and gazed down, holding my piece of glowing zajasite like an icon of faith close to my chest.

What I saw could only be described as *other*. A pair of dark four-armed creatures, just over a meter high, stood on two reverse-jointed legs. Their feet had sharp-looking claws, and a bony cranium sat on a squat, almost nonexistent neck. Large hairy antennae protruded from their craniums where eyes would normally be, which twitched as if tasting the air. Instead of a mouth, four deadly mandibles formed a cross shape, clicking together as they communicated with one another.

Two long double-jointed arms extended from their shoulders, which ended in sharp-looking bone spurs that resembled scythe blades. From their chests, smaller, yet more dexterous arms ended with three clawed fingers and an opposable digit for possible manipulation. The creatures' bodies were armored with pale ridged, chitinous scales, thicker along their backs and trunks and finer along their joints.

The creatures chittered to each other in their unknowable language, their moth-like heads and antennae moving around as if searching. I noticed a bead of sweat forming on Durhit's brow as he moved closer, his body tense, like a drawn bow. Everyone gripped their worn mining tools, ready for a potential fight. My heart was beating like a war drum. An unknown part of me almost welcomed this potentially cathartic conflict, an alien counterpoint to the fear I felt in equal measure in that cold darkness.

"Echo-Stalkers," the dwarf muttered under his breath, causing Elwin to flinch and take a step back, inadvertently kicking a small pebble. Almost instantly, the pair of insectile creatures turned in our direction, their antennae swishing almost spasmodically. Their chittering grew in volume, loud in the silence of the tunnel as they stalked closer towards us, their scythe-blade arms menacing the air.

Adrenaline began pumping through my system as I cast Identify at the rightmost echo-stalker to try and gauge the scope of the oncoming threat.

Echo-Stalker - Drone Lv. 6
Health: 45/45
Stamina: 23/24
Mana: 4/4

Without warning, their antennae stiffened, and the chittering stopped as they charged towards us, their leaping gait bounding across the distance. Mesmerized by their sudden burst of speed, I saw the right echo-stalker run across the wall of the tunnel as it sprang straight at me, dual scythe blades raised to stab through my chest. It was met suddenly by a rock thrown with lightning speed by our rogue, landing smack into the center of its mandibles, half-stunning it as it missed its fatal strike.

Snapping out of my fugue, I raised my own weapon to smash down in a deadly arc with the strength of a power strike behind it. The force of the blow was so powerful that the chains at my wrists hit the creature before rebounding and striking me lightly across my own forearms. As it tried to rise on unsteady limbs, I ended its suffering with a blow to its mangled head, killing it.

You have slain an Echo-Stalker. 30 experience gained.

The notification of its death brought a rush of elation through my veins, fierce and unrelenting.

Looking around for any remaining threats, I saw that Kidu and Durhit had surrounded the remaining drone. Its own speed and eagerness to reach us had been its downfall. Kidu had been able to flank the monster, striking at it as it leaped. The force of his blow shattered one of its scythe-like arms, leaving it dangling uselessly at its side. The hunter and the sapper worked in silent tandem, each delivering their own precise, probing strikes with the utmost caution.

Elwin held another stone in his hand, testing its weight while he waited for an opening. Sensing my approach, the drone chittered wildly, mandibles clacking as it raised its head in threat. That was all the opening Elwin needed. He promptly threw his projectile, hitting an antenna square on, causing it to nearly snap off.

We all charged the drone then, even Elwin, who picked up a shovel to join the fray. Our group struck it with everything we had, making it crash to the ground in a bundle of mangled, flailing limbs. We did not stop hitting it until it finally stilled, and I received another death notification.

You have slain an Echo-Stalker. 15 experience gained.
You have gained 1 Dexterity.

The fight could not have lasted for more than a minute, but the surge of adrenaline and the aftermath of spent combat fervor had left my hands trembling. We stood there, our chests heaving as we sought to catch our breaths, hands resting on our knees in an effort to recover.

"Well, that was certainly something," the rogue quipped, trying to mask his earlier fear.

But the bearded dwarf's expression was grim and dour as he said, "Those two were just a scout pair. There will be more of them ahead... a lot more."

The wildman, unfazed by the danger ahead, simply shrugged and said matter-of-factly, "They'll make for fine trophies."

He proceeded to tear off the scythe blades from the drone's lifeless body with ease before carefully placing them in his wicker basket. However, when he made a move to remove the insect heads, he quickly changed his mind, shaking his head.

Peering into the gloom, now that the immediate threat had been neutralized, we saw that the tunnel connected to a circular room, large and wide. Within it was a vast concave floor resembling a pit that dipped shallowly towards its center. Without so much as a whisper, we cautiously entered the space, our senses alert for any sign of peril lurking within.

Casting our weak blue lights at the edges, we walked along the circumference, only to find the room filled with old bones, loose rocks, and a miscellany of detritus. The whole area must have been a great garbage pit for the underground monsters.

Seeing that no further tunnels branched from the room, the dwarf decided to explore further. Skidding down, followed by loose pebbles, Durhit made his way to the center of the room. As we followed in his wake, the crunch of animal bones beneath our feet sent shivers down our spines. Large and small, the bones were of species unknown to us, intermingled with the occasional cracked human skull, a grim reminder of the fate that may yet soon befall us.

"So, this is where the lost miners ended up," Durhit mused, his attention diverted as he lifted a humanoid skull for closer inspection. "Some of us even thought they had found a way out. No matter, let us search and see if we can find anything useful."

We swiftly followed his lead, scouring the trash heap for any useful items. What surprised us were the occasional remnants of once-colorful garments that were strewn among the bones, a stark contrast to our own drab slave linens.

As I examined a particularly large femur, my attention was drawn to the remains of a crude doll lying nearby. The toy had small horn buttons for its mouth and eyes and was no doubt once a beloved possession of some innocent child.

Elwin sifted through the refuse and uncovered a plain, rusty iron dagger, which he quickly concealed up his sleeve. Kidu, meanwhile, discovered a rotten bow that nearly crumbled to dust in his grip.

After searching for a while longer, Durhit found something and tossed it my way, exclaiming, "Should be about your size, manling!"

Caught off guard, I fumbled with the object, my hands clumsily passing it back and forth in a rather comical fashion. Eventually, I regained my composure and examined what he had given me. It was a conical open-faced bronze helmet, tarnished and dull. The piece of armor seemed nothing more than an old, albeit serviceable helm. Durhit gestured for me to try it on, and I obliged him.

Undoubtedly, I must have looked a little foolish, clad in nothing but slave linens and a simple bronze helmet, but my limited knowledge of warfare had taught me that protecting the head was of the utmost importance. To my recollection, the helmet was the first piece of armor that any soldier worth their salt would invest in. The leather straps had long since rotted away, making the helm feel loose on my head, but it was certainly better than nothing.

Continuing our search through the rubble, I stumbled upon an iron spear lying next to an almost fully intact skeleton. The spear had seen better days, its diamond-shaped spearhead pitted with rust and corrosion. Kidu cast envious glances at the weapon, clearly longing to wield it.

I had hoped for a more formidable weapon than my reliable pickaxe, which—despite its power—was difficult to handle in combat. Nevertheless, I yielded to Kidu's evident fascination with the spear and handed it to him. After all, he probably had more expertise in wielding it than I did, and with his massive frame, his reach would be lethal.

In a gesture of appreciation, Kidu handed me a pair of surprisingly well-preserved leather gloves. I donned them, feeling a slight loss of Dexterity but knowing it would have little impact on my combat style. After all, the pickaxe was not the most subtle of weapons.

The rogue had discovered a pouch filled with small copper coins. Despite the fact that there was nowhere to spend the money, we agreed to split it among ourselves. Much to Elwin's chagrin, we each ended up with ten copper pieces. Durhit skillfully fashioned basic money bags out of scraps of torn, formerly colorful fabric that lay strewn about. Over Elwin's weakening protestations, the dwarf handed a pouch filled with the coins to each of us.

Realizing that any further time spent searching through the rubbish den would be a waste, we clambered out and cautiously made our way back to the main shaft. We continued down the tunnel as stealthily as possible. Holding his new iron spear with both hands as a precaution against potential dangers, Kidu placed himself at our van.

Slipping further down into the tunnels, we stumbled upon the broken bodies of drones. Among the corpses, we noticed a larger, more menacing version of the echo-stalkers. These mutilated bodies had thicker, more heavily armored chitin carapaces with larger, extra-vicious scythe blades for their weapon arms. Some of the corpses were almost torn in two, while others had their skulls completely crushed by what must have been extreme blunt force trauma.

In the gloom, Elwin uttered, "What sort of creature could have done this?"

Chapter 28

LOSS

"There is always sun above the darkest of storm clouds."
— A saying from the Avian Guard.

"Only one thing could be responsible for this whirlwind of destruction: an orc in heat… gone berserk," the dwarf answered.

"Combine that with the pain from the collar, and you have a recipe for a natural disaster."

Remembering the orc's hulking physique and brutish appearance, it came as no surprise that he could wreak such destruction. I did not know which I feared most—coming into contact with more echo-stalkers or reuniting with our fearsome former team member.

Still, we were fortunate the berserker had cleared the way for us. We walked down the path until Durhit raised a hand to signal us to stop as we reached the entrance of another perfectly round tunnel. He sniffed the air and pressed his ear to the wall.

"Running water, and close," he said matter-of-factly, gesturing towards the new path. "Move quietly. Perhaps we can sneak by while the hive is distracted."

Similar to the main shaft, broken bodies of echo-stalkers lined this new path at almost uniform intervals. We passed by the shattered shaft and the head of a pickaxe, both halves of the tool buried in separate bodies that still oozed fresh ichor. The trail of destruction left behind by the maddened orc was impressive.

Following the breadcrumb trail of death and Durhit's unerring sense of direction, we navigated through the network of tunnels as quickly and quietly as possible in the gloom. Sometimes the dwarf led us downwards, but more often now he guided us in a slight ascent through abundant twists and turns.

We continued without incident until we finally heard the sound of free-flowing water, confirming the dwarf's prediction. Excitement coursed through us; we picked up our pace, abandoning the last vestiges of stealth as we powered down the tunnel.

Just as we turned the corner of the tunnel, we ran into two more drones and a new larger, more heavily armored and dangerous type of foe. I quickly dubbed this new enemy the "soldier" variant, which bristled with a cold threat as it gazed at us with its unfeeling arachnid eyes. They raised their deadly weapon arms and threatened us with death with their rapidly clicking mandibles.

The man-mountain Kidu needed no prompting and rushed our new enemies. He thrust his iron spear into the larger soldier echo-stalker before it could even mount a defense, stabbing it deeply. Momentarily distracted by Kidu's martial prowess, I almost allowed one of the drones to stab me in the chest. Luckily, I was able to dodge at the last moment. The chains at my wrists and ankles jangled as I turned a potentially lethal strike into just a glancing one. Still, my Health was reduced by a full twenty-three points.

Capitalizing on the glancing strike that left it now open, Durhit smashed it with his mining tool and gouged a great wound down its trunk with a mighty blow. Recovering from my shock, I swung my own pickaxe in a rough upwards strike that brained the insect, the point of my tool firmly lodging in its cranium.

You have slain an Echo-Stalker. 30 experience gained.

Mentally brushing aside the notification, I saw that Durhit had moved to help Kidu. The hunter was still dueling with the weakened but extremely dangerous soldier, his spear striking out like a darting snake while Durhit added a few attacks of his own to give him some openings.

I turned to see if Elwin needed any help, but he already had the situation well in hand. His opponent was bleeding from a multitude of wounds across its limbs, with one weapon arm drooping weakly as Elwin danced around it. The drone's antennae seemed to be following the rogue's knife as he passed it from hand to hand. Seeing it distracted—and wanting a slice of the experience—I raised my pickaxe. I smashed into it from behind with all my might with a power strike, which ended its life instantly, and another notification crossed my vision.

You have slain an Echo-Stalker. 30 experience gained.
You have gained 1 Dexterity.

Taking a quick breath, I turned to see what had become of Kidu and Durhit's fight, but was disappointed to see that they had already put down the savage beast. Feeling a little frustrated, I absently kicked a loose stone on the floor. I was just a few points away from my next level. Kidu bent down to rip out the beast's impressive scythe arms as another battle trophy, only to stop when the sound of further fighting drifted from down the path: a bestial roar of fury and frustrated rage.

"Don't you be telling me now that this is our next destination?" Elwin began weakly, looking a little paler even in the gloom.

"The sound of running water is coming down from there, so that is where we must be going, manling. Let's just pray to the Earth Mother and all the gods of the hearth that the orc can distract them for a little while longer," the dwarf replied grimly.

Faster we journeyed down our path until we could clearly hear the swift-flowing water and the sound of battle that was joining it. We continued past a corner to see that we had come to a cliff path, and a small dark river was running swiftly below us in a vast cavern that reached to an unending darkness. To our left, I could feel a weak breeze and taste the fresh air. But higher up along the path to our right lay a most impressive sight.

The lone orc juggernaut was frothing at the mouth as he battled an entire hive of echo-stalkers on the ledge, his great bestial war cries drowning out the sound of the rushing river. He held a pickaxe in his right hand that cut through rigid chitinous armor as if it were paper. In his left hand, he clasped a ripped-off scythe arm from a soldier, which he used to stab with lightning quickness at the never-ending horde of insectile monsters. He relentlessly smashed them left and right, causing many of them to plunge to their deaths in the swift current below.

"That way!" hissed Durhit, pointing emphatically to our left. "Go! Go!"

Just as we passed Durhit, a dark shape dropped from the ceiling, its chameleonic skin making it almost invisible in the gloom. It planted two sharpened scythe blades through Durhit's chest that burst out the other side. His eyes widened in shock and pain as he started coughing up blood.

With a great snarl, Kidu thrust his spear with both hands at the new monster, striking it squarely where its neck should be and twisting savagely as dark viscera exploded from its new wound. But despite its injury, the monster was still standing and fending off the rest of the hunter's strikes.

"No! No! No! No!" I screamed in rage and loss.

Durhit was one of my first friends and companions in this cruel, barbaric world. Memories of our shared comradeship flashed across my mind as I raised my hand to strike out at the monster. I swung a wild horizontal attack that connected solidly with its thorax, the chains at my wrists hitting it a moment later. The blow was so powerful that it smashed the creature aside as Durhit toppled to the ground.

You have slain an Echo-Stalker. 30 experience gained.
You have learned Flails Lv. 1.

I barely registered the death notification as I rushed to hold Durhit in my arms, all thoughts of the battle lost with my friend dying. I tried to summon a Heal spell, but with my Mana being so perilously low, it would not heed my call.

Hollowly, I read the notifications, looking for a way to save the dwarf. I found nothing, except for the fact that this game had counted the chains of my slavery as flails.

"My sister... Evenes... Bronzegate Hold... tell her..." the dwarf gasped his last through bloodstained lips.

Someone began shouting in my ear. I almost ignored it, but the voice was persistent.

"We've got to go, now!" Elwin yelled, attempting to drag me up, while Kidu stood guard over Durhit's corpse.

Stumbling to my feet, I gently released Durhit, noticing that the echo-stalkers had redoubled their assault. Some of them had climbed up the walls past the orc only to be met in turn by Kidu's swift spear, which skewered them against the cavern rock. Slowly, we began our fighting retreat, with the wildman taking up the rear guard.

In a fit of rage and frustration, I cast Rust on the orc's collar as a parting gift to let the last few moments of its life be that of a free creature. Luckily, I was in range, dark whispers barely audible to me as the magic took hold. I could barely feel the unwholesome energies as I released the spell's black lightning into the orc's slave collar.

This only incensed the creature to further heights of rage, its bestial roars echoing throughout the cavern, stunning the echo-stalkers in front of it with their intensity. Whether it was the adrenaline, my high Constitution, my new skill—Mana Regeneration—or simply my inability at that moment to feel, I did not notice the usual wave of fatigue that came with reaching zero Mana.

All thoughts of fighting left us then. Clutching our weapons tightly, we beat a hasty retreat. I held my helmet to my head and my pickaxe in my other hand as we sprinted through the cavern, following the ledge and the course of the river below.

The darkness of the cavern began to lighten, and we eventually burst out into glorious sunlight, which almost blinded us after what had felt like an eternity of darkness and blue gloom. The river fell from the cliff in a cascading waterfall that fed into a large lake. We all skidded to a stop to avoid falling off before we noticed an animal trail that cut down across the cliffs and into the woods. A notification appeared that brought hot tears of joy and grief to my eyes.

Quest Complete: Escape from the slavery pits of Ansan

Chapter 29

DIVINE GRACE

Though a small nation, it was a country of free thinkers. A nation where great strides had been made in the fields of magic. Even so, their mages, who were growing fewer in number, could not protect them from the constant barrage from the skies. Desperate, the Republic sanctioned the use of a newly researched form of magic that combined dark and life energies in an aberration of the natural order.

Necromancy, the art of raising the dead and bringing them back in some corrupted form of unlife.

— *On the Cataclysm* by an unknown Quassian Scholar, circa 103 AC.

400 experience gained.
You have gained 1 Luck.
You have reached Lv. 9.
6 unassigned attribute points.
2 unassigned skill points.

As we ran down the animal trail, I quickly put all my unassigned attribute points into Constitution, which raised my maximum Health to a lofty 216 points. My two unassigned skill points would prove to be a trickier proposition. I tried to allocate both points to Heal but was met instead with three choices from the UI.

Purify
Holy Aura

Greater Heal

I had no idea what Holy Aura would do, so with the timer ticking down, I made a snap decision and chose to put a single point in both Purify and Greater Heal. As soon as I made my choice, time seemed to stop, flowing at almost a hundredth of normal speed to my perception. Voices of angels rose, singing righteous hymns of blessing and redemption in perfect harmony and counterpoint to one another. My mind was filled with visions of winged beings guiding those at death's door back to the world of the living.

Next, I was to be blessed with a new vision of a man in long white flowing robes trimmed with gold. He was crowned with what looked like a bishop's miter and was giving a benediction to the sick, soft golden light weaving among their number and cleansing them of their ailments. The same man again, this time clad head to foot in heavy armor, with a large mace in one hand and a white heater shield in another, was wading through a sea of undead. The same golden light that cleansed the sick now unraveled the necromantic energies that bound them to this world.

As time finally started to flow back to the real, I understood in my gut the purpose of these visions. It was this world's way of explaining the use of the spells I was gaining. Finally, I was beginning to make some sense of the esoteric nature of this world.

Lost in my thoughts, I barely noticed when Kidu touched my shoulder, urging me forwards along the trail. I looked into his eyes and nodded, having now fully returned to the present.

"Come on, ladies! Let's get out of here!" shouted Elwin, a note of panic in his voice.

We ran as fast as we could going down the narrow trail, almost killing ourselves in our haste. Finally, we made it down to the lake into which the underground river was flowing. We took some time to regain our breath and drank deeply of the ice-cold waters. I then received a notice that both elated me and filled me with dread.

You have slain an Orc. 437 experience gained.

"Gather yourselves, we need to go soon. The orc is dead," I said with as much seriousness as I could. Almost gulping at my slip, I noticed the eyes of my companions looking at me questioningly. Luckily, I was saved from further inquiry as they just shrugged, probably thinking I had simply misspoken, as more pressing concerns weighed upon them.

You have reached Lv. 10.
3 unassigned attribute points.
1 unassigned skill point.

Even as I was telling them of the death of the orc, I was already assigning the points. Rust had all but saved my life in the slave pits, but I decided not to spend the skill point on it. My newly acquired spells were all still level one and *should* be easy to raise to at least level two through practice. Durhit's death had taught me a valuable, yet painful lesson in resource management, so I allocated the bonus point to Mana Regeneration in the hopes that it would also allow me to cast more spells outside of resting. To add a little more punch to my "build," I placed my attribute points into Strength.

Snapping back my attention to my companions, I noticed that, to their credit, they had not panicked. With almost military efficiency, Kidu quickly filled up our canteens with water, while Elwin stopped to drink directly from the river. Soon enough, we started running once more through the woods, parallel to the course of the flowing water. As we ran along the banks, we saw large, silvery willows growing along the banks, swaying softly at the water's edge.

Our passing disturbed the wildlife, causing brightly colored waterbirds to burst from the rushes. Further along, we came across a family of otter-like creatures. The animals were perhaps half a meter in length, each with six legs, basking in the afternoon sun along the warm banks of the river. They slipped into the running water as we passed, chittering at us in annoyance.

We kept running until a tributary joined the river we were following. Kidu advised that we should cross in an effort to shake off further pursuit. With no reason to question his advice, we forded at a shallow area, all of us floundering against the swift current. Exhausted, we finally waded over to the opposite bank.

In the distance, we could see thin columns of rising smoke. With no better options, we decided among ourselves that it would be as good a direction as any. Slowly, as we penetrated deeper into the woods, the deciduous earth-like trees gave way to veritable giants—huge sequoia-like trees that rose like towers questing towards the sky, dwarfing their smaller cousins. Their branches created such a thick canopy that they darkened everything beneath, casting a cool pall on the forest floor.

The underbrush was thinner here, allowing us to make greater speed. Up above us, birds fluttered among the great boughs in a riot of color, their musical songs competing with one another in a symphony of nature. Looking up from beneath the branches, I saw creatures running across the massive limbs of the trees and lithely jumping from branch to branch, some even sporting three sets of limbs. There seemed to be a whole world filled with life above us.

Slowing to a fast jog and noticing my look of wonderment, Elwin asked me, in more of a statement than a question, "First time seeing the Sainba?" He drew a deep breath before continuing. "I was lost for words too when I came down here once with a caravan in my youth. Don't have trees like that back home, do you?"

"No, we don't," I answered lamely, still gawking at the forest vista. "I mean... I don't remember."

Kidu signaled to stop. We were standing just before a strange-looking green growth that covered a thick root of one of the giant trees. Wide-bladed leaves in differing shades of green spread out from the base of the plant. The most impressive feature, however, was its great spiky open flowers. Like giant maws colored in a delicate pink, they rested on thin stalks of viridian, resembling an enormous venus flytrap.

Cutting himself slightly with the blade of his spear, Kidu smeared a few drops of blood onto a twig that he had picked from the forest floor. He then threw the bloodied twig casually at one of the open traps. The rapacious maw launched itself energetically, snapping shut with great force and swallowing the twig. He repeated this until all the vicious traps were closed, after which he walked up to the plant and cut the flowers from the stalk.

Picking up one of them, he opened it up before us, ripping it in two halves and removing the stuck twig. He offered Elwin and me one of the halves each.

"Sweet and good eating on these. Snap-honey," he said simply, gesturing for us to take a bite before turning back to gather the rest of the heads.

With some trepidation, I took a bite, my hunger winning over hesitation. An explosion of sweetness filled my mouth, and greedily I took another taste. The flavor was somewhere between wild honey and watermelon, and I ate it all with gusto, leaving only the inedible spikes. This was the first delicious food I had eaten since coming into this world, and it was my first meal since I had won my freedom. It appeared that Elwin shared my enthusiasm, as he had thoroughly ravaged his portion and was making his way to help Kidu collect the other heads. Oddly, when I had finished eating and made to join them, I noticed my Health had increased by a few points.

"I think it best that we make camp for the night," the hunter said as he scanned the forest with his icy blue eyes. "If they come this far, best we are rested. I'll take the first watch so you can both regain your wind." He sat against one of the great roots, his spear resting across his knees. The feral man looked positively in his element.

"Much appreciated, Kidu," I said, giving a nod in thanks that was mimicked by Elwin as we settled down into the softness of the moss-covered forest floor.

Finding a comfortable position, I removed my bronze helm from my head and placed it on the ground next to me. I closed my eyes for but a moment before falling into a deep sleep. From the darkness of my subconscious, I saw my fallen dwarven friend glowering at me with eyes filled with anger. The stout dwarf seemed to be screaming accusations at me, his mouth moving in a storm of silence. Suddenly, he was consumed by a seething mass of tentacled shadows. Just before he was completely devoured, his face broke free from the living darkness, and I could hear only two words.

"Bronzegate... Evenes."

Chapter 30

THE POWER TO CHOOSE

A lucky ballista bolt, shot from atop one of the border forts, was able to fell one of the lesser dragons from the sky, having pierced through its heart. Forged with all of Arastia's arcane might, the bespelled adamantine tip was able to punch through inches of rock-hard scale and thick muscle. The mages of the Republic, ecstatic at having acquired a vessel of indomitable power, poured all of their magical might into the dragon's now still corpse.

— On the Cataclysm by an unknown Quassian Scholar, circa 103 AC.

It began with the usual dark dreams, but soon I felt a shift in my dreamscape. The scenes of violence and promised pain changed with a jarring sensation. There was now a dusty attic or storage room strewn with a variety of objects and artifacts. They ranged from the unremarkable, like a baker's pin or a sewing kit, to exotic-looking lamps and fabulous weapons.

I knew then that this was not part of a dream, but some sort of vision sent by this world. Cobwebs clung to each side of the room, and a thin layer of gossamer gray dust coated everything. The dusty walls seemed to be made from an off-white wattle and daub, with wooden supports running through them. Mold and mildew were present in the corners.

The room seemed a little drained of color, as if it had been bleached out. Yet the items strewn about drew the eye in disconcerting ways. Somehow I knew the objects in this room were of great significance.

My hand was drawn to an iron dagger with short, upturned quillons, rusted and pitted with grime. I kneeled before it, seeking to understand the question it posed, then saw a message.

Assassin.

No, this was not for me. Though the thought of becoming a shadowy individual flitting across the rooftops and silently eliminating his target did hold a certain adolescent appeal, it was not the choice I would make. An assassin was a mere tool, a blade directed by another's hand.

My thoughts roamed, for no discernible reason, to my last faithful dog, Shadow, who had passed away the year before last. My pet had been a wonderful companion who somehow always knew how to lift my spirits. My focus was shifted by the dream, and I saw then, in the corner of my eye, a large worn leather collar studded with iron spikes. I went to see what choice this item would offer. Moving to grasp it, I stopped my hand just above it as a new message came to me in the same manner as the dagger.

Beast Tamer.

Interesting, I thought. The idea of taming great beasts seemed a tantalizing one. But with no idea how to go about doing so—or the dangers involved with the profession—I decided to reject the offer. Taming a wild creature was only half the battle. After all, there was the care and upkeep, which was a lifetime commitment. I simply did not have it in me to make the emotional investment, nor could I see how this choice would help me in my current circumstances. Though, idly, I did ponder whether it was possible to tame an echo-stalker...

I needed something more practical, with a bit more punch. As these very thoughts came to my mind, I found myself treading across cobwebs and dust in the dream. My attention was drawn to a pair of leather fighting gloves, stained and cracked with age, with vicious hobbed metal plates at the knuckles. I moved my hand cautiously towards them to see what choice the item represented.

Pugilist.

In many games the pugilist or monk classes were popular and valid choices, but why on earth would anyone actually choose to fight monsters and other evil creatures with just their fists? Surely, any weapon would be better than almost nothing at all? Supposedly they could improve their bodies to reach near superhuman heights, but I simply could not risk it. Yes, if this was all just a game I would be tempted, but this was not the time for idle experimentation.

I wandered across the room, my hands questing here and there, and I almost grasped the scabbard of what looked like a longsword. The scabbard had intricate floral patterns of spiked vines and alien flowers running along its length, faded and dull from the passage of time.

Warrior.

Far too pedestrian. I could admire the romance of following the path of the sword; however, in a world of swords and sorcery, choosing just to wave about a metal stick, no matter how skillfully, seemed rather banal. It was like choosing to eat at a familiar fast-food chain after flying to a faraway and exotic location. Why just use a long sharp stick when, in this world, magic seemed to be the equivalent of having a gun? Besides, I needed something that could leverage my magical abilities.

Gun...

Something about that word sparked something in my mind before swiftly fading into the haze of the dream.

As my feet took me to my next destination in the room, I wondered just how many choices were here before me. Was I allowed to return to a previous choice? These thoughts floated around my mind as I scanned the room, which I still couldn't quite place the size of. Small, yet large. Glancing down, I saw a long wooden rod before me, tipped with a cracked and broken amber gem. Its luster was dull and muted. Around the tip and just below the gem, bronze copper rings wound themselves loosely around the haft. *What is this?* I wondered as I kneeled in the dust to get closer to the item.

Mage.

This was more like it. Being a specialized magic user certainly held great appeal. It would significantly boost my prowess, allowing me to deal damage through esoteric means. But my stats, as I remembered them, were geared more towards that of a "tank" or "warrior" build, with most of my focus on Constitution and Strength.

Also, the survivability of the mage class was a consideration I had to contend with. In this savage and brutal world, I needed to be able to protect myself as much as possible. Was it Elwin who had once remarked that mages could be killed with simple arrows if they were not careful? Or was that a memory from a previous life? Regretfully, I had to reject this choice, as I needed a lot more durability and a boost to my healing spells if possible.

Something began to pull at me, almost incessant in its force, persuading me to rise once more. Slowly, as if the flow of time itself had grown sluggish, I began to walk mechanically to my next goal. A lone chair sat in a forgotten corner of the strange room with a drab, gray dustcover draped across its back. As I moved closer, I could see on the seat of the chair a tarnished silver medallion with delicate links for a chain. Small gems framed the noble profile of a veiled woman etched at the center of its surface. Like the coins of this world, the face was looking to the left.

Even before the message played across my thoughts, I had already begun to place the medallion around my neck.

Paladin.

Laughing, I couldn't help but realize that somehow this room was reacting to my thoughts. *Perfect for me,* I concluded to myself as the dull metal settled around me. Its luster started to return as it became warm to the touch. A paladin, a knightly champion and protector of the weak. In modern gaming representation, the paladin was depicted as a warrior in heavy armor who was both capable in the press of the melee while having the capacity to cast healing spells and blessings. This was exactly what I needed.

The room's grip on me began to fade, my environment becoming increasingly blurry as the last whispers of the dream started to slip away.

Just as I thought I would begin my journey back to wakefulness, my left hand reached out to a black, oily puddle, moving like a marionette against my will. A thin layer of gray dust coated the puddle's dark surface, and its forced invitation was the empty void. As my hand drew closer to the liquid night, a new message filled me with horror and existential dread.

Reaver.

Sharp tentacles flew from the puddle, growing in length and piercing my hand with a cold fire that burned through me and eviscerated all resistance. I could see black tendrils of darkness wriggle their way just under my skin, working a path of agony up through my arm and to the rest of my body.

At last, one of the questing tendrils of solid shadow found my heart. I felt a great lurch, as if falling from a great height, as the oily dark continued to ravage my very being. I screamed, still trapped in the haze of the dream.

Chapter 31

BLESSINGS AND CURSES

Slowly, like a grave flower blossoming, the dark energies flowed into the great lizard's cadaver, sloughing rotting flesh from thick and pristine white dragon bone. A new nightmare was born, arising with it the stench of a freshly turned grave and all the majesty of the winged tyrants of the sky. The first bone-dragon, Vizzeks, came into existence with a roar and the howl of a thousand lost, tortured souls.

— On the Cataclysm by an unknown Quassian Scholar, circa 103 AC.

Kidu was shaking me, worry and concern etched into his features, as Elwin hovered overhead. I was greeted by a plethora of messages and notifications that followed me from my dream. Somehow, I knew this was a crucial moment for me. The dream had been the stage for my first class change in this game.

You have selected Paladin as your Calling.
You have learned Purify Lv. 2.
You have learned Holy Aura Lv. 1.
You have learned Maces Lv. 1.
You have learned Shields Lv. 1.
You have learned Medium Armor Lv. 1.
You have learned Heavy Armor Lv. 1.
You have gained Gift - Mark of the Paladin.
You have gained 2 Wisdom.
You have selected Reaver as your Calling.

You have learned Rust Lv. 3.
You have learned Decay Lv. 1.
You have learned Drain Lv. 1.
You have learned Entropic Aura Lv. 1.
You have learned Axes Lv. 1.
You have learned Pain Nullification Lv. 2.
You have gained Gift - Touch of the Void.
You have lost 3 Strength.
You have lost 3 Constitution.

The flood of messages threatened to overwhelm my short-term memory. My thoughts were distracted by the sounds of the forest: unknown animals calling out to each other, hunting each other, mating with each other. With a hoarse voice, I responded to the awakening. "Give me a moment. I need to gather myself."

I sat up and took a few seconds to sort through my thoughts and take in the notifications. Night had fallen, and Kidu, by some miracle or dint of his wilderness survival skills, had started a fire from the fallen branches that carpeted the forest floor. Elwin was scanning the forest, wary that my screams may have brought something down to our camp.

Kidu, satisfied that I was all right, went back to tending the fire while munching on another of the carnivorous snap-honey heads. Taking a deep breath, I decided to review my situation. The first thing I noticed was, mercifully, that I was at full Health, Stamina, and Mana after my rest—fresh and ready to tackle the threats this cruel world would undoubtedly throw at me.

STATUS

    Calling: Gilgamesh Lv. 10 Paladin of Avaria / Reaver
    Strength: 22
    Dexterity: 16

Constitution: 34

Intelligence: 18

Wisdom: 16

Charisma: 10

Luck: 15

SKILLS AND PROFICIENCIES

Pain Nullification Lv. 2

Power Strike Lv. 2: 10

Endure Lv. 3

Stealth Lv. 1

Rest Lv. 3

Backstab Lv. 2

Dodge Lv. 3

Polearms Lv. 2

Dual Wield Lv. 1

Critical-Hit Mastery Lv. 2

Mining Lv. 2

Unarmed Combat Lv. 3

Hammers Lv. 2

Flails Lv. 1

Maces Lv. 1

Shields Lv. 1

Medium Armor Lv. 1

Heavy Armor Lv. 1

Axes Lv. 1

SPELLS AND MAGIC

Heal Lv. 5: 5

Rust Lv. 3: 2

Identify Lv. 2: 1

Silent Casting Lv. 1

Mana Regeneration Lv. 2

Purify Lv. 2: 3
Greater Heal Lv. 1
Holy Aura Lv. 1: 2
Decay Lv. 1
Drain Lv. 1
Entropic Aura Lv. 1

GIFTS

Curse of Entropy: -20% to all starting attributes.

Mark of the Paladin: 10% resistance to Dark/Holy magic. 5% resistance to Physical.

Touch of the Void: 10% reduced resistance to Holy/Fire magic, 20% resistance to Mental Effects, 15% immunity to Mental Effects.

Experience to Lv. 11: 2107/2583
Health: 225/225
Stamina: 53/53
Mana: 13/13

With the addition of my new skills and proficiencies, my character sheet had started to become cluttered. Also, in a strange, yet wholly welcome change, spells and abilities I had cast or used before now displayed their Mana or Stamina points cost on my character sheet.

I noticed too that my Gifts had an explanation detailing their effects. I was puzzled as to why now, of all times, my UI had changed. Also, I questioned why I had not received any visions to give some explanation for my new spells' functions. Perhaps it was because they were part of my Calling, or class choice, already? *Very unhelpful,* I mentally complained.

However, most disturbing of all was the fact I had lost the equivalent of two levels' worth of attribute points in Strength and Constitution. At a loss, I looked once more at my character sheet and saw that the reaver class had been forced upon me. This was, if the pain I had suffered in the dream was any clue, the reason for the reduction in my attribute points. This had the unfortunate effect of lowering my overall Health and Stamina.

The silver lining was the two new points of Wisdom from my paladin class, which provided an extra point in Mana. I would also have to pay more attention to the gains in my "secondary" attributes, such as Charisma and Luck. Somewhere along the way, I had stopped my mental tally of them. I had no way to measure their effect on my "character," and I had only so many mental resources to spare on worrying about less important attributes. And how did Luck even work? Would the universe bend itself slightly to suit my needs at high levels? Or did it just do something boring, like only work on critical hits?

The new skills and magic spells were welcome, but I could not deny that I felt a certain trepidation at the thought of trying them. The mentally unsettling effects of executing the Rust spell were still at the forefront of my mind.

Too many thoughts and questions spun around in me. Faced with yet more conundrums, my mind began to wander down the rutted path of an unrelated tangent. Taking a deep breath, I forced myself to focus.

Staring out into the distance, I ruminated on ways to test my new magic. I decided it would be wisest to first inform my companions about the latest developments.

"The gods have gifted me with new powers," I said suddenly, without preamble.

Kidu gave me a knowing nod and smile before intoning solemnly, "The gods often grant their favor after overcoming great trials. I, too, have felt their touch after our escape."

Elwin, on the other hand, simply raised an eyebrow, no doubt intrigued but willing to hold off his questions until later.

Truthfully, I had no idea what Kidu was talking about. Perhaps this was the hunter's way of interpreting a level-up and increase in power; he had, after all, cut a bloody swath during our escape.

"I would like to test out one of the spells. I don't think it's an offensive spell, but I don't exactly know what it does..." I said in a tone that inspired little confidence in my companions.

"Do what you must. We will help you observe," Kidu replied in his gruff voice.

"I think I am going to move a bit further back," Elwin said as he inched away from the crackling fire.

However, waving my hand in a set of arcane motions, I had already begun casting Holy Aura before Elwin could finish his retreat. I had decided against using the Silent Cast in conjunction with the spell to establish a baseline for the "normal" way of casting the magic. My fingers traced strange patterns in the air, and my voice started to chant a language I had never heard before. As I incanted the words, I noticed there was a slight echo, as if another being were chanting alongside me.

As my chant reached a crescendo, I uttered, "Holy Aura," and a single pulse of golden light expanded away from me, its epicenter. The immediate area around us was bathed in its light. Then the light finally settled around us, as if it were warding us against the darkness.

Kidu and Elwin held up their hands to inspect the golden light that had surrounded then wrapped itself around them. They looked incredulously as it played in intricate arcane patterns all about us. Then a small shock hit me as I looked closely at my Status bars; the spell had used two Mana, and my maximum Mana had also dropped by two. Quickly, I stopped the aura spell, and the golden glow softly disappeared.

My companions spun around, as if trying to determine to where the golden light was retreating. With a sigh of relief, I saw that my maximum Mana had risen again to thirteen, but my current Mana remained at eleven. *Intriguing,* I thought. What would happen if I tried to cast the spell again?

Kidu and Elwin looked distracted by the disappearance of the miraculous light. Seeing this and deciding it was better to beg for forgiveness rather than to seek approval, I cast the aura spell once again.

This time I invoked the spell while using my Silent Cast skill. I could feel a sense of resistance now, similar to a recalcitrant child going against their parents' wishes. It took a long while, perhaps six to eight seconds, before I could complete the spell, then a golden ambience bathed us once more. It certainly took a lot longer to cast without the somatic component of the spell, and, mentally, it was a lot more draining.

Looking at my Status, I could see now that my current Mana had dropped a further two points to nine, and my maximum Mana had again dropped back down to eleven. I gave a silent prayer of thanks that I had not damaged my Mana reserves permanently.

"Do you feel any different? Anything at all?" I asked my companions hesitantly.

"Apart from the pretty lights, nothing. Pretty impressive, though. Probably could make a few copper pieces at the next mummer's fair," piped Elwin, a little sarcastically.

"As the small one said. I am thinking that answers never come easy in the understanding of the ways of the gods," replied Kidu. "Perhaps this magic is a ward against evil and misfortune?"

Realizing his words contained surprising insight, I nodded to him in acknowledgment. "We also need to do something about these," I added, holding up the remains of my chains on both wrists. Casting Rust on metal that was in contact with my skin was a painful operation that I honestly did not want to repeat anytime soon.

Just as I was beginning to think about how to get out of this predicament, I noticed something about Elwin and Kidu. They were now free of the manacles that had bound their wrists and ankles!

"Yes, about that," Elwin began with a smug smile on his face. "We didn't want to disturb you while you were having your beauty sleep." He produced a thin sliver of metal from out of nowhere as he walked over to me.

Kneeling before me, he began working on my bindings, popping them loose from my ankles with dexterous ease.

"Strange skills for a forester," I said, looking him firmly in the eye.

"Let's just say I had a troubled youth," he replied in an even tone, dodging the subject as deftly as he had unlocked what remained of my bindings. "Now for your wrists."

I held out my wrists, and with an artisan's grace, he jigged and manipulated his crude sliver of metal into the sockets of the manacles. He released me from the iron in a matter of seconds, tutting as he worked.

Touching my liberated wrists, I reveled in the feeling of greater freedom now that the metal hindrances were finally gone.

"Thank you, Elwin, much appreciated. You are certainly a good man to know to get out of a bind," I said gratefully, testing my range of motion now that the chains and manacles were no longer there. "Now if only we could do something about these collars," I continued, smiling wryly as I pointed to the metal at my neck.

Kidu began to raise a pickaxe in his hand, his answer to my question clear, which drew a worried glance from our rogue. Almost jumping in surprise, I waved a hand to stop him from his obvious plan of action. Comically, this caused my loose helm to begin to slip, and I had to hold on to it to stop it from falling off.

"I don't think we need to resort to that just yet. I think my magic could weaken it a little more first," I almost shouted. It would also be a chance to test, albeit potentially painfully, the level of control I had with my spell.

"Your choice." He shrugged as he lay down to sleep on the green moss of the forest floor, throwing another loose branch into the crackling fire before closing his eyes.

Elwin threw me a worried glance. "You're not thinking of starting off with me, are you?"

"No, Elwin. Have no fear, at least for the moment. At the very worst, the spell will simply turn your collar into hot slag. I am fairly confident I can heal you through that," I said, sneaking him a mischievous grin. "Please keep an eye out in case anything goes wrong. Maybe keep some water close, eh?"

Even with a cloud of doubt staining my thoughts, I concentrated as best as I could and brought the magic to my center. I focused on tamping down the dark energies, trying to resist unleashing its full power. My tongue spoke eldritch words of dark things in a language not meant for mortal tongues, and Elwin looked visibly perturbed—with my mind fully engaged in staving off the stronger aspects of the spell, I had lacked the focus to use my Silent Casting skill.

My fingers, stilted in their movement, drew esoteric symbols in the air that left traces of ozone and oily dread blackness. Even as I went through the motions of casting the spell, a small part of my mind registered that Kidu had begun snoring already, the sounds of which would rival any great beast in a rut.

Just as the spell was about to reach a crescendo, the arcane power began to subside. Sensing the time was right, I released the black lightning into my collar, causing it to heat up, but not painfully so. I surmised that I had succeeded in my experiment of taming the dark, alien energies, as I had only lost a single point of Mana in casting the spell.

Smiling a cracked grin at the rogue, I said, "Well, it seems that wasn't too bad. I appear to have learned how to control myself a little." Elwin simply looked back quizzically at me.

Straining—and failing—to look down at the collar around my neck, I waited for the roiling energies to dissipate before casting Identify on the collar to see how much damage I had inflicted on its durability.

Iron Slave Collar
Durability: 258/400

Thirty-six points of durability damage. *Not bad,* I thought. Although the level two spell did more damage, it was extremely painful and required me to spend additional Mana on healing. This was the most efficient and safest way to go.

I gave Elwin a thumbs-up and smiled from ear to ear. Elwin looked like he had just sucked a sour plum before saying, "After all this, you want me to bugger myself? Can't say I can find the humor in it. There are places to go for that sort of thing."

"No, that's not what I meant at all! Where I come from, this is a sign of good luck... an indication of approval. You see, right now, I am rather pleased with myself," I said, holding up both thumbs with a smile.

"Thought you had no memories," the thief said in a slow, calculating voice before grumbling once again. "Bah, for that you'll be taking the next watch. Guess I'll have to be keeping another one of my eyes on you," he finished, continuing to gripe as he made a bed for himself from the leaves and moss on the cold forest floor. With an annoyed huff, he lay down.

"Of course..." I began, before noticing he had already turned away.

A few minutes later, he was already fast asleep, his breathing shallow and even.

Adjusting the loose helmet on my head, I stared up at the dark canopy, observing only one or two twinkling lights through the thick boughs. All around me I could hear the sounds of the forest as its denizens continued their nocturnal activities. The air was fresh and invigorating, full of the green smells of a vibrant forest, free from the stifling pollutants of my old world.

Alone with my thoughts, I began to reflect on my journey so far. Thinking back to my struggles with the amphibious bibsi, I realized just how much I had grown in power since coming to this strange new world. My time as a slave had forged my body and soul, and I was a vastly different man from when I had first arrived.

I realized the innocence I had once possessed was forever lost. I had killed, and more than once at that. This was a world that demanded it, even rewarded it. I knew in my heart this was no simple parody of a game: the scents, the sounds, the suffering… it was all too real. Yet despite all this, it was still a world that was beautifully virgin and full of wonder.

I thought, too, of Earth, and of the mediocre, yet somewhat tolerable life I had lived. Every day had been a struggle, but of a different sort. There I had to worry if I would be able to pay the bills on time; here I had to worry if I had enough Health, Stamina, and Mana to survive the next encounter with a monstrous creature. I chuckled to myself inwardly, thinking of the situations I had once considered stressful. Here I had grown tough, but I knew I had to grow even tougher still. With these thoughts, a few hours were lost.

I touched my collar, a reminder of the sights I had witnessed and the trials I had suffered. My first gift for slaying another sentient human being. This stubborn collar was just another hurdle I had to overcome. Focusing on Identify, I cast the spell on my collar once more, needing to confirm my progress from before.

Iron Slave Collar
Durability: 254/400

Intriguingly, the durability had dropped another four points. Was this from general wear and tear, or was it the lingering effects of the spell? "Curse" spells in games usually took a long time to fully take effect…

I had a feeling that it would do me no favors to wait, so with six points of Mana remaining, I continued to emit the weaker version of Rust onto my collar, ignoring the oily dark energies and weak whispers that followed each cast.

After the fifth use of the spell, wishing to avoid reaching zero Mana, I tried to snap the tortured metal with my bare hands, grunting loudly from the effort. A familiar hand the size of ham grasped my shoulder, and I turned to look at Kidu. His face was hard and unfamiliar in the dark flames, casting him as a monster, his blond dreadlocks like a wild medusan growth.

"A fine sentry you will make." He laughed in a not-too-unfriendly manner. "Please, let me..." His large hands reached for my neck.

For a split second, I feared that he wished to end my life, and my body involuntarily stiffened. Gently, he placed his giant hands on the collar around my neck before, with a great twist, he snapped the weakened, heavily corroded metal. It fell broken to the forest floor.

"Thank you, Kidu." Awe and appreciation echoed equally in my voice at his impressive strength.

"Freedom is more than payment enough," he said, even and stern before laughing and slapping me on the back. "But I would like to stay free for a little bit longer, so I will take the next watch!"

With the large man gesturing for me to sleep, I removed my helm and gloves, laying them down next to me before curling up into a ball. I touched where the metal had once met my neck, then looked at my wrists, now free of chains. Soon enough, sleep claimed me once again as the dark whispers followed me into her realm.

Chapter 32

PRIORITIES

With the birth of the bone-dragon, the winged dragons were horrified and unwilling to play any further part in the campaign. With the loss of one of their number, they felt the first pangs of fear from newfound mortality. The dragons left the mortal, short-lived races to their fate and flew back across the ocean to their high mountain homes. With their departure, the war began to grow into a grinding stalemate.
— *On the Cataclysm* by an unknown Quassian Scholar, circa 103 AC.

The sharp call of a morning bird rang through the forest, loud and shrill, piercing the veil of dreams and waking me from my slumber. Groggily, I shook myself awake, brushing aside the cobwebs in my mind. Aside from the forest noises, the first thing I noticed upon waking was the delicious smell of something roasting on the fire. Getting to my feet, I then sat down beside my companions, who were cooking a meal that looked suspiciously like gigantic insects on thin sticks. Sadly, I noticed that the pair had eaten all of the remaining sweet snap-honey heads.

"Good morning to you," Elwin said cheerfully.

I took one of the insect-sticks he offered me. Not wishing to be rude, I nodded in feigned gratitude. "Much obliged," I remarked, waiting for the rogue to eat a piece of his.

Elwin and Kidu both began to dig in as if it were the most normal thing in the world.

Closing my eyes firmly, I hesitantly took a bite. If I could eat freshly killed amphibious fish, the bibsi, then this should be easy.

The shell was crispy, and the white flesh was soft and tender. The taste was similar to that of freshwater shellfish. *Not bad,* I thought, *but it could do with a little seasoning.* Seeing my companions eat all the insect things, I decided to follow suit, pretending I was simply eating soft-shell crab as I crunched into the head of the oversized bug on a stick. Calories were calories.

"Do you like them?" Kidu inquired in a voice that couldn't help but rumble.

"Could do with a little more punch. Perhaps a little salt?" I said with a ghost of a smile. "But this is the first breakfast I have had as a free man, and it tastes better than any meal at a king's banquet!"

"I'll drink to that," added Elwin, lifting an imaginary cup in the air.

"Here, here!" I played along. "What was that I just ate?"

"A rockcrab. A bit different from the ones in the North. North rockcrab is better eating," Kidu informed me in a matter-of-fact tone. "These still not bad. Eating this reminds me of hunting with my clan."

"The same ones that came with you from the North?" I said carefully, afraid that this might be a sore spot for him.

Kidu grew taciturn and withdrawn before he answered. "Yes, those same people who came with me, not long ago. If I can, I wish to find them and release them from their bondage. Work and pay their brand price if necessary. Or have their masters pay the blood price, if I cannot. Their families deserve to be told of their fates. But most all, my soul seeks vengeance!" He almost growled the last words.

New Quest: Discover the fate of Kidu's companions? Yes/No

Both Elwin and I raised imaginary cups again as if to toast his last vow, but I had no true intention of helping an NPC in a quest that could potentially take years. How could I help others when I was struggling just to stay afloat? I had to be in a position to help myself first. Then there was the matter of who—or what—was giving out these "quests." Was it the fickle gods of this world? I had a feeling this "quest system" was a way for the divine forces of this world to control my actions.

Also, without knowing the parameters for the quest, dismissing it was the only choice. It sounded complicated; a mission of this nature was too much of a commitment. This was simply the stark reality of my situation.

I swore to myself I would only accept quests that were in line with my own goals. I would not be led around by the nose. This was my game, and I would play as I liked.

"Oh, Gil, since we are on the topic of freeing friends and so forth, what are you going to do about these?" Elwin said, pointing to his collar, bringing me back to the present. He had tried to say it as casually as possible, but he couldn't quite hide the eagerness in his voice.

"Right... I'll get right on it," I answered, giving the rogue a mocking salute and raising a hand as if to cast a spell in his direction.

Casting Rust had become a lot easier, though I still had to consciously rein in its power. I began to go through the motions of casting the spell, my tongue now more practiced in saying the eldritch words, and my gestures were more precise and fluid. I noticed, to my amusement, that Elwin still flinched at each utterance I made. Black lightning flowed from my hands to his collar. The whispers, these uninvited companions, echoed in my mind as they always did while the magic surged. The energies visibly ate into the metal, corroding it wherever the lightning touched. He squeezed his eyes shut, fearing the searing heat he thought was to come. Yet, unbeknownst to him, I had only cast the level one version of the spell.

Looking closely at Elwin's collar, I was left pleased with my handiwork. I did not need to use Identify to check the durability. I could see that the orange and red splotches, indicative of oxidization, had grown considerably and were their own testament to the effect of the spell. I turned to Kidu now and nodded at him, a gesture he returned. He accepted the spell much more stoically than Elwin, his trust in me absolute.

"How many times do you have to do that?" Elwin inquired.

"Honestly, I do not know. Casting this spell without causing harm to you is not easy. I do know that this spell significantly weakens the durability of the collar. I will continue to cast it as often as I can, whenever I can, until all of us are truly free." The apathy in my tone was reminiscent to that of my father.

The rogue shrugged before adding with a smile, "Can you do it again, then?"

* * *

In the end, I cast the weaker version of Rust two more times on both of them before we broke camp. I decided to keep more than half, the lion's share, of my Mana for emergencies. I hoped my Mana Regeneration skill would allow me to cast Rust a few more times as we moved.

As we made ready to break camp, Kidu and Elwin left their chains behind. Kidu, with a mighty roar, threw the remains of his former bindings into the bushes, while Elwin just let them lie next to the roots of a tree. I, on the other hand, decided to take a length with me as a reminder of the cruel and callous nature of this world.

We proceeded carefully through the forest in the direction of the distant smoke. Our eyes were constantly scanning the forest and searching for new threats. An hour or two passed by uneventfully before the world sought to test us again.

I was talking with Elwin, fishing for more information about this world when, without warning, something hard and moving fast impacted against his head. It knocked him down, almost comically, to the forest floor. In those fractious few seconds, all I could think about was that the object looked like a giant wooden seed.

More thuds echoed around us, and the wooden seed things continued to drop down as the branches swayed above us. Here and there, the heavy wooden balls fell from the canopy in staccato waves as a wind wove its way through the high branches, each one a missile of death and injury.

Instinctually, I thought first to run for my own safety, but clarity intervened. I could not survive the ordeals ahead alone, and so far Elwin had been a useful ally. With this as a priority, I quickly kneeled down next to him. The rogue lay supine on the ground, his chest still. I thought, almost instinctively, to perform first aid before I remembered we were in Gesthe, a land of magic.

I began to invoke the magic of the Heal spell and stole a look at his bloody head. As I did so, something told me that a simple Heal spell would not be enough. A different spell gently whispered to me, causing threads of a new idea to lace together to form a new tapestry. A vision of an angel saving someone from death's door came to the fore of my sight with crystal clarity.

Knowing what I had to do, I began to instead cast Greater Heal, until a giant seed struck my bronze helm. Shaking my head, I saw that the concussive force had caused almost twenty points of damage and probably would have completely interrupted my cast were it not for my pain nullification skill. Thankfully, I managed to maintain control over the divine energies and complete the spell. Today, at least, I was determined to not give the Reaper his due.

My voice rose in a steady cadence, sounding more like a hymn than a spell. I held my hands over Elwin's form and poured golden energies into the man. An echo accompanied my chanting, filling my soul with solemnity, and each syllable gave thanks to an unknown divine power.

Slowly—oh so slowly—the golden light began to mend his bloody head wound. I witnessed the magic as it closed the wound, drawing back the clotting blood and bone fragments and knitting skin together as his skull was restored to its original form. At last the spell ended and Elwin started to breathe evenly, clearly alive but still unconscious.

The wind had stopped as suddenly as it had started. No more of the heavy seeds fell to the forest floor, but a pervading sense of danger remained. We had to get out of there, and fast.

"Kidu, we need to find somewhere safe!" I shouted to the Northern hunter.

He gawked at me for a few moments before bursting into a blaze of action, running to search for sanctuary. With Kidu gone, I was alone with Elwin and constantly looking upwards, praying that the wind would not return. Luckily, Kidu came back a minute later, and between us, we dragged the unconscious rogue to a glade.

Sunlight bathed the moss-covered forest floor where one of the mighty trees had fallen. The light was a welcome rarity in the otherwise dark forest. Bushes and plants grew in a ring around the fallen titan, all reaching up in a race towards the sun. We went into the hollow of the gigantic tree, searching its cavernous interior first for threats. Next, we placed Elwin down, disturbing some creatures that chittered as they ran away from us.

The three of us rested then in our safe space, which smelled of earth and the slow rot of wood. Kidu looked over our new accommodations critically as he searched for hidden danger. The hollow must have passed some unspoken test, as the hunter grunted in satisfaction; however, all I saw was just another dank hole in a giant tree.

The adrenaline rush now slowly fading, I plopped myself down next to Elwin's comatose form. In the heat of the moment, I had saved the rogue because, overall, he added to my chances of survival. He was handy with a blade—and heavens, his class might be useful later on—but risking myself to save his life was decidedly alien to my nature. No, a hero did not just save people because they were "useful!" It would lessen me to think of people by just their utility. After all, Elwin was more than just an ally: he was a friend.

After a while, Elwin began to stir. I wondered what sort of effect his brain being smashed in would have on his personality. Possibly an improvement, I considered in dark jest. Just like the visions, it seemed that the Greater Heal spell really could save a person on Death's door.

Worryingly, Kidu began to shake the convalescing rogue. I knew from some half-remembered first aid course that his actions were not the most appropriate thing to do at this critical moment, but I didn't quite have the mental energy to stop him.

"What...?" Elwin mumbled with a slurred voice and unfocused eyes. He searched around for something—or someone—familiar.

"Be at ease, little man. You are safe here for the moment," Kidu said brusquely, if not unkindly.

"The Shallow River... I heard her bells... they were all calling for me," the rogue continued.

"Even the damn nuts in this forest are dangerous. You were hit by... a seed... or a bloody nut! What were those things?" I had tried to speak in a serious tone, but a ghost of a hysterical giggle entered my voice from the thought of the absurdity of the situation. Luckily, neither Kidu nor Elwin noticed my *faux pas*.

In the old world, I had heard of large, spiked fruit called durian killing a few people every year. I had read online that, statistically, they were more dangerous than sharks. *Ah, the Internet,* I thought. *What I would give to have access to that wealth of knowledge.*

Out of the corner of my eye, I looked down at Elwin. He had torn the sleeve from his linen tunic, exposing his arm and revealing that his slave brand had disappeared. Looking closer, I saw nothing but healthy, unscarred skin in the place of the brand.

"Kidu," I hissed loudly. "His arm... look!"

"By the ancestor spirits, the slave brand is gone!" Kidu exclaimed, his voice going up almost an octave in pure surprise.

Could it be that the Greater Heal spell had effects other than miraculous regeneration and healing? Was Elwin's hair a little thicker, the crow's feet around his eyes a little less pronounced? I brushed these thoughts aside as I realized I had a way to remove all the marks of our slavery.

Removing our slave brands through magical means would take up a lot of Mana. However, if I exploited my rest skill to squeeze out as much Mana as possible in the shortest amount of time, the process could be significantly sped up.

"Kidu, I will need to rest to regain my Mana," I began, a plan of action already forming in my mind. "If you can watch over us and find us something to eat, perhaps start a fire, it would be most appreciated. What was it that downed Elwin, anyway?" I added.

"That is hard task. Safeness or forage, that is a decision for you to make. As for the little man's attacker, I know not. At least with no trees above us, we should be away from those warm land nuts." He then looked at me, waiting for my order.

"Scout out the area near us and come back when you can. I am afraid to say I know nothing of making a fire, so be quick." I would have to trust that I could sleep lightly, or that Elwin would be able to come to his senses. With Elwin out of action and Kidu soon to be out scouting, I needed Mana more than anything. It was a risk, but with Kidu securing the area nearby, it was a risk I was willing to take. And as a bonus, it might help me with power leveling my Greater Heal spell.

Kidu took a quick drink from a canteen at his hip before rising to make his way out. Before he left the hollow, he nodded in my direction and said, "Be safe, and may the ancestors watch over you." With that, he leaped out into the forest, his spear leading the way.

I positioned myself just outside the entrance to the hollow of the tree, sitting cross-legged and willing myself into a half-doze as I attempted to clear my mind. With the sounds of the forest and worry plaguing me, sleep did not come easily.

Chapter 33

INTERRUPTION

The gods of this world are flawed, jealous, pitiful mewling creatures not worthy of our regard, let alone our worship. They toy with mortal dreams and desires to suit their whims and machinations.

The divines rage and war against each other in the "Great Game," with us mortals as nothing more than their pieces, their pawns, to be moved about the board. The strongest among their servants they imbue with a portion of their divine power and enslave them to their "holy" cause.

They call such blessed beings their "Champions." How do I know of this? The answer is simple: I am one such Champion, and I will break their game.

— A Record of Ash AND Ruin by Gilgamesh of Uruk.

Something was applying a sharp pressure to my arm, moving it left and right, up and down, in forceful motions. I opened my eyes quickly, thinking it was Kidu trying to wake me, only to find that a beast was savaging my arm. Screaming in shock rather than in pain, I saw that it resembled a six-legged furred creature that looked like a cross between an angry wolverine and a warthog.

Two forwards-facing tusks continued to stab at my arm and sharp canines worried at my skin as my Health steadily dropped. I punched the creature savagely between the eyes, striking reflexively with all my might. This just caused the beast to bite down harder, so I quickly drew upon a power strike, increasing the force behind my blow. It was a clean hit, forcing the creature to let go of my arm. It backed it off a few meters, its beady eyes still hungrily watching me.

My Health had dropped below eighty percent, and I was bleeding profusely. A world of agony filled my arm. Screaming again, I closed my eyes in pain, holding my bleeding arm with my other hand. It was all the opening the creature needed. It charged me again, like an enraged bull that saw the matador's cloak, almost leaping through the air with its animal speed. It slammed into me, reducing my Health even further. But its mouth, filled with jagged canines, was no longer seeking to bite me. It was then that I noticed a knife had sprouted from its neck, causing blood to start pooling around the wound.

Turning around to confirm who had thrown the blade, I saw Elwin give a faint, incorrigible smile from deeper within the hollow. Weakly, he raised his hand in a thumbs-up before blowing a raspberry in my direction. A notice filled my vision as the creature finally died.

You have slain [Unknown]. 35 experience gained.
You have gained 1 Strength.
You have gained 1 Dexterity.

"Another bloody... What was that thing? And thank you," I said in equal parts incredulity and appreciation.

Still flush with the shock of the encounter, the needs of the present forced me to quickly shove the unneeded emotion to the back of my mind. This encounter with a new monster was just another horror on a steadily growing list.

To dull the pain, I decided to cast Heal. Greater Heal was also an option, but a paranoid part of me insisted on saving my Mana. It was that same instinct all gamers share, the one that hoards resources for those inevitable "what-if" moments. Ruefully, I realized that if I kept this up, I would reach the final challenge of this world, lugging a warehouse of potions, an armory of weapons, and all sorts of odds and ends—just in case.

As I cast the spell on myself, I checked over my Status and was pleased to see that the gains to my attributes had gone a little way to mitigating my recent losses from the reaver class. Silently, the golden energies slowly filled my arm. Pain became a distant thing as the magic soothed it away like a warm balm that banished the sharp sting and caused torn muscles, ligaments, and tendons to knit themselves back together. I marveled at the wonder playing out before me, healing on a level far beyond anything in my own world.

"That thing will probably make good eating," the rogue said, intruding upon my thoughts. "But could you possibly be a good fellow and get me my knife back? I feel a little naked without it."

Hands still shaky, I gave a mocking salute and went to retrieve the weapon that had just saved my life.

Ripping the dagger out of the creature's neck, I took a moment to study the body. Beady eyes, now glazed in death, were set in a long and bestial porcine face. But unlike a hog, it had small black whiskers, and its ears were short and triangular. Two pairs of yellowed ivory tusks protruded from its feral mouth. Its hide was a thick, mottled brown, with bristly fur that was growing cooler to the touch. Three pairs of small—yet muscular—legs were tipped with claws that looked useful for both tearing at flesh and climbing trees. From its nose to its short, stumpy tail, it was roughly the size of a large alligator. I doubt I could have fended off such a beast in my old world.

Just as I had finished my observations, I asked Elwin, "What is this creature? This is the first time I've seen anything like it."

"That's a tree-laur, a juvenile male by the looks of it. Probably just left its nest a few months back. I best be about dressing the kill. Did you know that you scream like a girl?" Elwin jibed with a sigh.

I fought back a sliver of annoyance, smiling weakly in return and giving a perfunctory chuckle before growing serious. "Elwin! Thank heaven you are alive! Should you be up and about? What's my name? What's your name? How many fingers am I holding up?"

"I can remember my own name, remember your name too. The taste of my first hunt. Even my first lay with the village trollop! Bah, she was a fine one. Safe to say, I'm further in your debt after getting brained by a caru nut. Forgot they grew around these parts. 'When the wind blows, look up,' as the saying goes. Pah, my luck's turned since I met you!" He laughed. His mirth was infectious, and I joined him in it.

Just as we started to catch our breath, our recent trial by nature bonding us in deeper camaraderie, Kidu burst into the glade, bestial and wild. He locked eyes with me, paused for a moment, and, noticing the corpse with a casual glance, walked up to us.

"You are well I see, Elwin, Gilgamesh," he said, nodding to us both, kicking the corpse of the tree-laur absentmindedly. "It seems that things have been exciting since I was away, and you saved me the trouble of hunting something down." Kneeling beside the corpse, he gestured for me to hand over the knife, which just drew a shrug from Elwin, who was probably glad to be free of an arduous chore.

He dressed our kill cleanly and efficiently, like an experienced hand who had done the same job countless times before. He separated the cuts of meat, offal, and bone onto large, freshly cut green leaves. I left him to his industry as I felt a call of nature take me and excused myself from my companions.

After I returned from the bush, wishing for nothing more than the luxury of toilet paper, I saw that Kidu and Elwin had created a construct of wood and sticks to dry and smoke the meat over a crackling fire. How they started the fire was a mystery to me; I was, after all, a man of modern times, and thus had never undertaken such tasks in my life.

Kidu was busy scraping the fat from the tree-laur's pelt over a broad tree root with his spearhead, while Elwin was trying to hone the edge of his knife on a stone. If we were not all escaping from a system of slavery and blind, bladed, insect-like monsters, it would have been the picture of a typical campfire scene from a cheap fantasy novel.

"Hey, big man! You took a long time in the bushes. Was about to go track you, make sure the beasts from around these parts didn't get to you," chirped Elwin, looking up from his ministrations.

"It's important that we keep this fire going at all times, lest wild beasts come to investigate the scent of blood. Man has taught the wild to fear fire," Kidu uttered in a low, worried tone. "Though I fear the smoke may draw attention of a different kind."

I settled next to the crackling fire, too tired to notice the delicious smells of cooking meat but feeling safe in the pair's companionship. Smiling wryly at them, I added, "Let me do what I can for you both. I was never one to see a job only half-done."

And with that I began to cast Rust again, drawing worried looks from Elwin as he closed his eyes in a Pavlovian response to the dark words and mystical hand gestures that tickled at the limits of mortal comprehension. Kidu, on the other hand, continued with his work without a care, stretching out the pelt.

The dark and alien energies filled me, and I resisted the urge to unleash the full power of the spell on my companions, allowing only a trickle when it demanded a flood. I could see that the roiling black lightning had eaten into their collars, no doubt weakening them, and I began to feel the effects of Mana sickness as I bottomed out my reserves. This time, the effects were not nearly as debilitating as they were on the first try; they were now more a feeling of drowsiness with a need to rest.

As my head began to fall, I murmured, "I think I need to rest once more to gather my energies... So sleepy."

My companions simply nodded. The rush of adrenaline from defending myself had long left my system, and now Mana sickness flooded into its place. I didn't even take the time to remove my helm or gloves before I faded off to sleep.

My blessedly dreamless sleep was disturbed by a distant beast's call. Almost instinctively, I checked my Status, feeling a little alarmed at how easily I had accepted the realities of this world. My situation was totally absurd, my physical condition having been reduced to measurable numbers.

My physical and magical resources had both fully replenished. Yet despite this, I couldn't help but wonder if there was more to life than this near-constant struggle.

Looking around, I saw that Kidu was on watch, facing outwards from the fire, looking and listening for threats. Elwin was tucked up in a ball, sleeping quietly nearby. The big man noticed me and greeted me with a silent nod before asking, "Are you rested and well?"

"Yes, Kidu of the Three Bears. Thank you for taking this watch," I said in almost mock formality.

He didn't seem to notice, or simply chose to ignore my tone. "Elwin and I will take the watch tonight. This will allow you to focus your energies on restoring us." He pointed at his neck and slave brand. "We should not let the spear plow the field. But first, you must be hungry," he finished, offering me a portion of meat wrapped in a large leaf.

My stomach rumbled, which drew a small laugh from the massive man.

Though cold now, the meat from the tree-laur was delicious, if a little tough and stringy. Several times I had to spit out small chunks of indigestible gristle. After finishing my piece, I wiped my oily hands, slick with fat and grease, on my dirty tunic before focusing on my task. With half a mind bent on procrastination, I looked around the camp to notice that Kidu had strategically placed our zajasite stones to help dismiss some of the deeper shadows. Yet despite these precautions, I couldn't help but feel like something sinister was watching us.

I could see the wisdom behind Kidu's words. You needed to use the right person for the right job, and I had to do what only I could for our little team. Drawing upon my reserves, I cast Rust in succession on the pair, waiting for the turbulent energies to subside before repeating the spell.

Eventually, Kidu, sensing that his collar had weakened enough, tested his strength against the corroded metal.

The collar made a great snapping sound as he twisted it off his neck, resulting in small fragments of iron flying into the night. Waking Elwin to start his shift, Kidu unceremoniously snapped off his collar, too, much to the rogue's surprise and appreciation.

What surprised me was that now, even on zero Mana, I felt little of the effects of my earlier Mana sickness. My efforts at meditation just led me to fall asleep in a seated position. The task of clearing my mind of all thoughts proved too arduous in these troubled times.

Elwin woke me a few hours later when the fire had grown low, and the forest was a deeper dark. We added more fuel to the fire before he whispered in a low voice to ask me if I could repeat my magic on Kidu, freeing him from the mark of his hated bond. The man didn't need to ask twice; I was more than willing to erase all marks of our bondage.

Rolling up my frayed sleeves, I decided to experiment on my other, more robust companion. Holding my hands over a loudly snoring Kidu, I began to cast the Greater Heal spell, but this time without the singing and chanting. The magic resisted me greatly, and I had to create a mental image or construct of myself casting the spell before I could force the divine energies to come forth. The magic was slow and lethargic in emerging to do my bidding, but I was determined not to be denied and my will was iron.

The golden energy flowed into the massive man, running across and all over him. I could see small scars across his face and arms fade as the slave brand on his arm began to heal. The mark, once an angry red, grew to a healthy pink before completely vanishing into his natural skin color.

The spell had taken a long time to complete—far more lengthy than if I had cast it conventionally—but I still was able to finish it. At a rough guess, the whole process had taken a minute or two. Would raising my Silent Casting improve the spell's speed when cast in this way? Despite having to add another question to my growing list, I thought that all in all, my recent experiment was a success. In the glowing firelight, I swore I could see the hint of a bearded smile on Kidu's face as he slept.

Wanting to regenerate my Mana before dawn broke, I asked Elwin to continue his watch, explaining that I would need to gather myself if I was to be of more use in the morning. The rogue nodded to me, although his attention was focused completely on sharpening the knife he had acquired from the tunnels, treating it like a prized heirloom.

Adding another piece of wood to the small fire, I took a moment for myself, searching for answers in the dancing flames as I procrastinated. Part of me dreaded rest and sleep, even though I knew it was necessary to restore my resources and that tomorrow would come regardless.

Chapter 34

BLIND FAITH

The guild in the frontier regions is nothing more than a collection of opportunistic bandits, thieves, and failed mercenaries. They deem themselves monster hunters, heroes all, and the shield of the common peasantry. But tell me this: What hero is he who would not render assistance unless compensated in coin?

— The Fanciful Travels by Beron de Laney, 376 AC.

Here, unlike the deep dark of the forest, the sun was able to filter down through the branches of the lesser trees of the glade. The call of songbirds and the annoying chirping of insects filled the morning air as the creatures of the night made good their rest. Off towards what I presumed was the west, a plume of smoke rose just above the canopy of the trees.

The rogue and the hunter were having a meal of tree-laur haunch and discussing what to do next. Their discussion, more of a debate, was animated, with even the usually even-tempered Kidu showing a little anger.

"Morning, sleepyhead," said Elwin. "This great big lug thinks we should spend the rest of our lives out here in the wilderness, living off the land. I, for one, have had enough of the great outdoors. I want to actually enjoy my freedom. With your magic, we are no longer slaves! We should at least go and see whatever is causing that smoke. I'll go by myself if I have to!" the rogue finished emphatically.

"Elwin Tucker gives a plan with great risks. We are safe here, relatively so. There is sustenance in the forest if you are strong. Just a few days ago we were slaves in this land. I would not have it be so again," replied the wildman, clearly looking to me for direction.

I thought for a moment on both of their arguments before adding my own opinion. "Both of you make good points, though I, for one, find myself wary of further contact with the people of these lands. Still, one cannot live in the wilderness forever. We simply lack the tools and equipment to survive a winter here." I paused for a moment, digesting my companions' suggestions. "I say that we take the middle course and at least investigate what that smoke is together. This forest is too dangerous to traverse alone. Perhaps there will be people nearby. Perhaps they can help us. Perhaps they cannot. If there are people there then it might be possible to trade for something, or if not... we can take what we need," I added, looking them each in the eye.

They nodded in acquiescence before beginning to clear up the camp. The pair stamped out the fire, collected the glowing zajasite stones, and packed the recently smoked meat into our wicker baskets with an economy of movement that would have been impossible for me. Gripping our weapons in hand—Elwin with his knife, Kidu his spear, and I with my trusty pickaxe—we made our way through the forest towards the smoke.

We left the relative safety of the glade and moved deeper into the forest. Our surroundings became steadily darker as we pushed on. The sense of things leaping overhead and looking down at us never left my consciousness. We advanced quickly, though carefully, through the massive trees and slight undergrowth of the forest, making sure to scan for any threats from above or below.

At some point in our little expedition, Kidu held up a hand and called for us to stop. We had to wait for a herd of massive deer-like creatures, perhaps twenty or so strong, to finish crossing our path. They wended their way through a trail between the giant trees like lords and ladies of the forest.

They were majestic animals, almost three meters to the shoulder, heavily muscled, and their bodies were covered with chocolate-brown fur. Atop their long, graceful necks were large heads, from which four spiked horns grew. Their eyes were large, gentle, and brown. One of the animals stopped to look in our direction before moving off with the herd when the gigantic leader called out with an ululating cry.

Pausing in wonder at what I had just witnessed, I turned to the hunter and asked, "What were those things?"

"Southern cronir... smaller than the ones up north, with an extra pair of horns. Cronir make for good eating," he replied in a deep, hushed voice.

"To you, friend, everything makes good eating, and I would not want to tussle with the big one unless I had to... or was deep in the cups!" quipped the rogue jovially. This little exchange, it seemed, was as clear a signal as any for us to continue our march through the forest.

Finally, after what seemed like an excessively long time, we could start to hear the voices of real, actual people. We swiftly crouched down as we moved closer to the source of the smoke and sound of industry. Finding some cover, we peered through the bushes of the undergrowth and saw a small group of people undertaking myriad jobs in a large clearing. My eye was immediately drawn to some small mounds that had bluish smoke billowing from them. If my memories were anything to go by, the mounds could only be charcoal piles.

An old memory told me this was a sign that the wood inside was undergoing the change into charcoal. On a tangent, I remembered a lecture from a world away and softly mouthed, "*Köhlerglaube*," the word for blind faith in German, which had originated from the charcoal-burner profession.

In the old times, the ignorant peasants would blindly believe whatever the local priests dictated to them, as they had to spend the greater part of their attention on overseeing their piles. However, unlike the medieval peasants, I had little faith in the gods, let alone their priests.

I also remembered, from a distant lecture or seminar about medieval societies, that charcoal burning was seen as a lonely profession. The creation of charcoal was dirty work that needed constant supervision to ensure the wood burned at the correct temperature. Also, they needed to make the charcoal as close as possible to where they felled the trees, which meant that the charcoal-burners often lived far from the local centers of civilization.

Behind the piles stood several single-story log cabins. Around the smoking mounds, men were busy adding wood to make more charcoal.

A few of the men carried axes and heavy staves. They used these to chop up branches from the large fallen trees at the edge of the clearing or to poke holes into the charcoal piles to regulate the heat. It was a relief to note that only a few of their number carried sidearms, such as short swords or long fighting daggers.

The men were clothed in brown, gray, or black long-sleeved robes that were tied at the waist with wide, colorful sashes. A figure, clothed in blue in stark contrast to the other workers, barked orders at them before joining in the work. They all had the epicanthic folds of an Asiatic people, and the whole ensemble made me think of the old Mongolians of Earth.

Focusing on one of the nearest workers, I silently cast Identify on him.

Arban Bayarsaikhan - Charcoal Burner (Human Lv. 7)
Health: 75/77
Stamina: 18/28
Mana: 10/10

I did this again five more times, making sure to include the leader in blue. These were all the men who were in plain sight. I drew a breath of relief as I confirmed that they were all relatively low level, with the highest among them being only level eight and the lowest being level six. A ghost of a plan was beginning to form in my mind. Half wishing to confirm the strength of my companions against the workers and half simply for practice, I cast Identify on Kidu and Elwin.

Kidu Kreshin - Hunter (Human Lv. 12)
Health: 252/252
Stamina: 43/49
Mana: 5/5

Elwin Tucker - Rogue (Human Lv. 13)
Health: 152/152
Stamina: 27/40
Mana: 10/10

I had known it! The spell confirmed one of my sneaking suspicions that NPCs could also gain experience and level up. Kidu and Elwin had both gone up a level, and their basic parameters had improved significantly.

Furthermore, it confirmed to me why some of my previous kills had given me varying amounts of experience: it had been divided up among those who had credit for the kill. I also reckoned that my group, although smaller in number, had been significantly stronger in terms of raw attributes and levels than our vanquished enemies.

It was also pleasing to note that my investments in Constitution and Strength had meant I was getting closer to Kidu in terms of raw Health and Stamina. Yet despite this, I noted that I had seen little change to my actual physique, which I found most strange. Nor did it seem like there were any other visible changes, like a growth of a beard or hair length. Shrugging these thoughts aside as extraneous, I simply attributed these quirks to part of the rules for me in this strange game-like world.

I hissed to my companions, gesturing for a retreat. We moved out of sight and well out of earshot of the camp.

Once we were at a safe distance, I began to tell them my plan. "We observe them for the rest of the day just to make sure there are no surprises. Once we're sure of their numbers, we hit them at night, killing every single one of them."

"Not even going to talk to them? Just like that, kill a group of men minding their own business?" the rogue asked, surprisingly shocked.

I hadn't expected this level of empathy from him, an NPC.

"Where are we, Elwin? Think! We are on the run, wearing slave garments in a land whose culture is propped up by slavery. What do you honestly think would happen if we opened a line of dialogue with these savages? That they would welcome us with open arms and send us off on our way? Besides, we would lose the element of surprise," I replied vehemently. "Are you stupid? These are the people who enslaved me, enslaved you. Enslaved us. They don't see us as people. Are you so eager to face the kiss of the whip again? And you, Kidu. I thought the Three Bears to be an honorable clan. Did you not promise vengeance on *all* of the Tides?" I finished, my voice rising towards the end as I looked squarely at the wildman.

Elwin held up two hands placatingly as Kidu rose to my provocation and added, almost too eagerly, "I promised vengeance on the honor of my ancestors and my friends, and it is vengeance I will have. I will never again feel the crack of the slavers' whips against my back, nor the iron collar about my throat. If you wish to stand in the way of that..." The massive wildman growled at Elwin.

"But they outnumber us! And those weapons are real sharp-looking," murmured the rogue, uncertainty in his eyes.

"We have magic, and we are all proven fighters, much stronger than these scum," I responded confidently.

"How do you know?" he hissed.

I looked him carefully in the eye. "I know. Trust me, I just know. The gods have told me thus."

Kidu seemed to accept the explanation, but I could see concern still etched in the rogue's features.

"We're about to kill all these people... for what?" sputtered Elwin.

"Because we have to! Because I say so! I will kill these savages, and many more, if that is what it takes to stay free. Again, Elwin, these are the people who enslaved us!" I repeated, which drew a rumble of approval from the hunter. "As I said, we have little choice in the matter if we want to return to civilization. It's either this small crime of survival now, or a life forever on the run! Or, worse yet, to be a meal for some monstrous creature in these godforsaken lands. Better to be a bandit, thief, and criminal than a slave! Rest assured, Elwin, we will do this with or without you..."

Something in my last words must have struck deep within Elwin, for he was silent then. It was a stab at his past, and all the crueler for it. As I continued explaining the finer points of the plan, there were no further arguments from the rogue.

I sent Elwin to scout out the rest of the encampment, and during that time, after a light snack with Kidu of stringy, dry meat, I rested to regain my Mana.

Kidu had made a pair of crude weapons from the scythe-blade arms that he had ripped from the soldier echo-stalker in the tunnels. The handles were made of laur bone, and attached to it was strong sinew to keep the ever so slightly curved blade in place. A link from one of the chains formed a simple guard just above the hilt on both daggers to stop the hand from slipping when thrusting with the weapons. They were vicious and crude-looking tools of violence, measuring about forty or fifty centimeters from their handles to deadly tips.

Kidu had also fashioned a simple hide sheath for each of them. I tested the edge of the natural blade with a finger, drawing blood and causing a single point of damage to my Health. Overall, it was impressive craftsmanship for how quickly he had made it, and I wondered how this world would categorize these paired weapons in terms of skill proficiency.

Just as I had finished examining my newly made weapons and replacing my trusty pickaxe, I felt a tap on my left shoulder. Knowing this to be some sort of trick, I turned to my right, and there was Elwin, freshly returned from his reconnoitering just as the sun was beginning to set.

He gave us an unhappy grimace before delivering his report. "Eight men in total, I think, split between a day shift and a night shift. These are all free men. No slave brands from what I saw. Though, come to think of it, it would be difficult to train slaves for this kind of finicky work…" The rogue began to meander before we both looked at him. "Overall, though, they all seem to be lightly armed—axes, daggers, and short sword notwithstanding."

Settling in behind the cover of some thick bushes a good distance from the clearing, we waited for the night's darkness to deepen. Each of us tried to ease a measure of calm into nerves fraught with tension. I gripped my twin weapons tightly in my hands as my mind struggled with all sorts of variables and potential scenarios.

This was to be different from all my fights thus far, in which I had simply reacted according to circumstance. Up until now, it had always been fate that had forced my hand. This time, it would be premeditated and cold, a sensation I found both sickening and strangely thrilling.

Chapter 35

ALL THE BASES

"The gods give no gifts without exacting a toll." The ancient maxim rings true today, even in this forsaken age. And for the practitioners of magic, the price demanded by the divines for the loan of their power is steep indeed. As a mage's control over the arcane arts grows, so too does the Call—that insidious, seductive whisper that beckons them to become one with the very element they seek to master. Some would answer that Call with a pilgrimage to the water's depths, drowning in the embrace of the element they cherished above all others. Consumed by their very passion, some would seek the ultimate heat of the flame, offering themselves up to be consumed in a fiery dance of transcendence. Still others would entomb themselves alive in the very earth they commanded, seeking to become one with its secrets.

However, it is the anemancers, the Laughing Mad, who truly dare to walk the razor's edge of magic. They leap from great heights, bodies hurtling through the air, finally unable to resist the siren song of the wind. Madness, some call it. But to those who understand the true nature of magic, it is a sacrifice made in pursuit of the ultimate power, for not all who make the leap of faith meet their untimely end.

Yet even those with the strongest wills cannot hope to escape the demands of the cosmos forever. For the path of magic is a treacherous and thorny one, and only the most resolute can hope to walk it to its conclusion.

— Master Bertrand of the University of Quas.

Unluckily for us, the moon was high and bright among the veil of stars, casting a silvery light. The charcoal piles continued to emit their smoke, ghostly now under the moon's pale ambience and the sleepy watch of their minders. Our group moved from the tree cover of the woods towards the edge of the clearing and noticed that a solitary man had come towards us. I stiffened, standing completely still before checking on the position of my companions, only to see that Elwin had somehow slipped off.

Perhaps the rogue had suddenly caught a case of cold feet? The charcoal-burner kept moving towards us, oblivious to our presence. As he came closer, something dark—a ghost of a shadow—fell from the trees onto him without a sound. A glint of metal flashed in the moonlight. With Kidu, I rushed as quickly as possible the few yards towards the man to find Elwin standing over him. Blood emanated from a stab wound from the soon-to-be corpse's neck. Hoping I was not too late, I also stabbed the fallen man with my makeshift weapons to ensure his demise.

You have slain a Human. 25 experience gained.

Thankfully, I was able to get a hit in while his heart had still been pumping blood. I smirked in the darkness, realizing that this man had been worth even less experience than Gunne.

Just as I was about to discuss our next steps with our group, there was an explosion of activity from the opposite tree line, as if the man's death were some sort of trigger.

Familiar silhouettes bounded across from the giant trees in great leaping strides, calling to one another in their unnatural clicking language, weapon arms raised in deadly threat.

A man shouted a warning to his peers, and the other men grouped up hurriedly. The sounds of alarm were repeated across the camp as the rest of the men burst from the cabins, carrying a variety of arms and lethal implements.

A wave of chittering echo-stalkers descended upon them from the trees. Soon enough, there was a melee of steel against razor-sharp claws and piercing mandibles. The sound of battle and violence filled the previously tranquil night. Slowly, the sounds turned to shouts, then to screams of panic as the humans fought against their deadly foes.

I looked at the faces of my companions, their worried expressions clear in the moon's subtle light. The initial plan had gone completely to tatters, fate's arrow once again striking against us.

The echo-stalkers were the main threat. Humans, on the other hand, could be reasoned with. Then there was the matter of Durhit. In a split second, a decision was made. It was amazing what humans did when faced with a common enemy...

"We strike from behind and kill these echo-stalkers," I ordered. "Wait until they have all been drawn out and are fully engaged, then we hit them. Remember, these men... these things... were responsible for Durhit. No mercy! Be ready to follow my lead!"

I rushed towards the fight with a lack of hesitation that would have surprised my past self. The air was cool and refreshing as it brushed against my face, and in that moment of frozen time everything seemed so clear, as if my ears could distill every individual sound that cried out into the night.

The insect-like echo-stalkers had the numbers and savage ferocity, but the charcoal-burners had a surprising amount of discipline and skill as they fought back against them. Against this onslaught, the charcoal-burners started to regroup after their initial shock, and they rallied around their leaders.

The humans, even with their newfound discipline, were getting pushed back as the melee continued. Here, a claw would slash against exposed skin. There, a hand holding an axe or impromptu weapon would be punctured by sharp mandibles.

Still, the humans were able to inflict casualties against their multi-limbed foes. For every step taken in retreat, their weapons took a terrible toll on their enemies. Judging that the charcoal-burners' line had been weakened enough, I ordered my small group to charge.

Our group crashed into the rear of the echo-stalkers, entering the chaotic melee with silent violence that belied our rage. Stabbing with both of my weapons into the hard, chitinous back of one of the foul creatures, I found little resistance. A death notification of the creature floated across my vision. I dismissed it, as my full attention was required for the remaining monsters.

Since antiquity, humans had used nature's own tools against her, and I found immense joy in piercing the echo-stalkers' natural armor with their own weapons. Snarling like a feral creature, I dodged a barely visible slash meant for my arm. The move was more of an instinctive motion than a conscious decision.

Preparing to mete out some more punishment, I studied one of the creatures darting this way and that. Its erratic motions were difficult enough to follow, let alone line up an attack against. Noticing the antennae on its head were constantly pointed at me, I knew I was the sole focus of its attention. Keeping myself out of the measure of its slashing talons, I waited for an opening. I would not have to wait long, as the insect monster hunched low before launching itself to strike, the natural blades on its arms blue in the soft moonlight.

I lunged into the arc of its blow, coming beneath the creature and stabbing it with my dual blades through its chest with a power strike before slicing horizontally with both daggers—the blades still embedded in my opponent's flesh—in opposite directions. Such was the force of the finishing blow that I almost bisected the creature.

Somewhere in the grand melee, I could hear the charcoal-burners shout out the various names of their weapon skills, unleashing their techniques against the midnight horde. Double Strike, Rolling Chop, and a few others were among the skills that were screamed out desperately against the monsters.

I felt a clang against my helm, almost knocking it off my head before something sharp scraped across my shoulder blades and drew blood. Turning around with one blade outstretched to guard and the other held close, ready to stab, I saw a blurry outline that seemed to meld with the night. From its alien chittering, I deduced it to be one of the chameleonic strains of the creatures.

I fell back into a desperate strategy: a whirlwind of blows to overwhelm the monster. Still new to this world, my skill would be no match against such a lithe and lightning-fast creature. Where skill failed, raw savagery would have to prevail. I could barely see its outline, and each of my strikes felt like a literal stab in the dark.

Swinging with wild abandon, I continually missed the creature as it dodged and weaved like mist in the night. Just as I was gearing up to strike out at the creature again, I was saved from the results of my reckless strategy by Elwin, who appeared behind the creature as if by magic, stabbing it with a precise blow to the base of its neck.

Knowing better than to pause in combat, I swiftly turned on the balls of my feet, engaging a regular drone with my twin weapons against its natural armaments. I was faster, tougher, and stronger than the drone. I roared as I charged, my higher Dexterity allowing me to parry both of its falling arm blades with my daggers.

However, as I ducked under its vicious mandibles, I was met by its other pair of clawed arms. These tore through cloth and left bloody lines across my chest, causing me to lose a chunk of my Health. At the back of my mind, even in the heat of battle, I realized that I was not feeling any pain from the blows I had received. *It must be because my Health is still over eighty percent,* I thought, remembering the tree-laur and the exact threshold when the bleeding damage had begun to cause me great pain.

I did not have to wait long for my theory to be proven correct, because a sharp pain burst from my left leg as another echo-stalker struck from my blind spot. This forced me to keep my left weapon in a hastily made guard position to help fend off further attacks from this new threat.

However, I was still within my initial target's guard, so I used a power strike to try and skewer the monster with my right blade. My dagger hit true, and the crudely made metal pierced through its armored chest, with part of my fist burying itself in its body.

I booted it off with a savage kick, not caring to make sure it was dead, and turned to face my new opponent: the beast that had stabbed my leg. My Health points were falling precipitously due to bleed damage from the number of wounds I had received. I needed something to distract my enemies to let me disengage and heal myself.

Not seeing where Elwin had disappeared to, I shouted, "Kidu! To me!"

Kidu swiftly disengaged from his opponent by rapidly spinning his spear. The viper-swift blade formed a temporary circle of safety that swept away his opponents, and he found his way to my side. The hunter covered me with his bulk, keeping our enemies at bay.

I took this moment of respite to gather my magical energies and cast Heal vocally, prioritizing speed over anything else. The magic of the spell quickly filled my body with familiar, soothing energies and raised my Health to nearly full. I studied Kidu for a moment and saw that he was not in any need of healing, having only suffered minor cuts along his arms and legs.

Fully invigorated, Kidu and I rejoined the fray. Kidu's spear was like lightning, thrusts mixed in with wide circular motions that kept multiple opponents away and relieved a lot of the pressure from the charcoal-burners. Regarding the massive hunter as the principal threat, most of the echo-stalkers focused their attacks on him.

I took the opportunity to savage their now exposed flanks, slicing and stabbing here and there while they were busy attacking him. Kidu was a storm of violence as he went from sweeping cuts to savage jabs, smoothly mixing offense and defense with his weapon forms.

I glimpsed Elwin at the edges of the chaos, dancing among the melee between the charcoal-burners and the echo-stalkers. There he was, stabbing at the joints of an echo-stalker's natural armor at the moments when they were busy fighting a charcoal-burner. There he was again, plunging a blade into one of the insect-monster's eyes before fading back into the night in an impressive display of shadowy stealth and martial skill.

Alongside the surviving charcoal-burners, we began whittling away at the monsters' numbers. We gradually crushed them with our combined might, our enemies reduced to so many still-twitching corpses and, as such, they were converted into power-giving experience.

My Stamina was just under half when we finished stabbing the last of the echo-stalkers, and I was a little displeased that I had not leveled up after the encounter. Over half of the charcoal-burners had perished in the fight, and the remaining few looked tired but grateful to our party. The leader, who was clad in bloody blue robes, came up to me, offering his hand in gratitude.

With no belt or scabbard on which to hang my blade, I handed one of them to Elwin, who tested its balance as I walked up to meet the man.

Smiling oily, the leader spoke to us in a voice that was obsequious, yet condescending. "Thank you, travelers. Without your timely help this night, I am sure that perhaps we would have all perished. We owe you our lives, and you have rekindled my faith that all men are brothers against the dark things. May I offer you the humble hospitality of our camp?"

Even as he was speaking, a whisper in my subconscious suggested to me that he only wished me to let my guard down before trapping me once again into slavery. A twisted, logical part of my mind understood this to be the only possible way he could recover from the losses of this night.

So I stabbed him mercilessly in the neck.

You have slain Chagatai Nyamdor. 85 experience gained.

"You are no brother of mine," I spat vehemently at his corpse.

We had, after all, planned on killing them anyway. I didn't have the energy to answer a slew of questions; I was tired enough as it was. The wildman, on my signal, fell on the exhausted Children of the Tides with relish, releasing a battle cry that seemed to stun them. Elwin followed him two heartbeats later with his small, flashing blade that stabbed and stabbed into yielding flesh. With utter shock still on their faces, and with them offering little resistance, we slaughtered them to the man. I welcomed the experience as the last one fell.

Still shaking from the thrill and shock of battle, I realized I had been ignoring my notifications. Eager to check on my character's progress, I summoned my Status and scanned for any important changes I might have missed.

STATUS

> **Calling:** Gilgamesh Lv. 10 Paladin of Avaria / Reaver
> **Strength:** 24
> **Dexterity:** 18
> **Constitution:** 34
> **Intelligence:** 18
> **Wisdom:** 16
> **Charisma:** 10
> **Luck:** 15

SKILLS AND PROFICIENCIES

> Pain Nullification Lv. 2
> Power Strike Lv. 2: 10
> Endure Lv. 3
> Stealth Lv. 1
> Rest Lv. 3

Backstab Lv. 2

Dodge Lv. 3

Polearms Lv. 2

Dual Wield Lv. 2

Critical-Hit Mastery Lv. 2

Mining Lv. 2

Unarmed Combat Lv. 3

Hammers Lv. 2

Flails Lv. 1

Maces Lv. 1

Shields Lv. 1

Medium Armor Lv. 1

Heavy Armor Lv. 1

Axes Lv. 1

Daggers Lv. 1

SPELLS AND MAGIC

Heal Lv. 5: 5

Rust Lv. 3: 1–2

Identify Lv. 2: 1

Silent Casting Lv. 1

Mana Regeneration Lv. 2

Purify Lv. 2: 3 Visible

Greater Heal Lv. 1: 10

Holy Aura Lv. 1: 2

Decay Lv. 1

Drain Lv. 1

Entropic Aura Lv. 1

GIFTS

Curse of Entropy: -20% to all starting attributes.

Mark of the Paladin: 10% resistance to Dark/Holy magic. 5% resistance to Physical.

Touch of the Void: 10% reduced resistance to Holy/Fire magic, 20% resistance to Mental Effects, 15% immunity to Mental Effects.

Experience to Lv. 11: 2417/2583

Health: 196/230

Stamina: 15/55

Mana: 8/13

"Progress of my character?" What a strange turn of thought. This was *my* progress, and this was in no way a game. I focused more seriously now on my current situation.

A single point to Dexterity and Strength was both welcome and, at the same time, a little disappointing, since the growth rate of my attributes was slowing down, despite the ever more frenetic battles I had been fighting. And even after suffering a multitude of wounds in the heat of combat, my Constitution refused to budge.

Going over my skills, I noticed that my dual wield proficiency had increased by a level, thanks to my wild swings with the new weapons. These weapons must have been categorized as daggers by whatever system ruled this world. I knew this to be a fact as I had gained a new skill, "daggers," through their use. This skill, like all my other newly acquired skills from this world, was at level one.

I still had some spells that required testing, which I would leave until we had reached a safe place. My new gifts from my class choices would also need to be examined some other time, as I had more pressing needs.

"Leave the corpses where they are. Take no trophies, but loot the men. Leave the weapons on them for now. If they have coin, take some of it, but not all," I said, looking hard at our rogue, who looked like he was about to protest. "Please trust me... there is a method to my madness," I assured him between labored breaths.

Elwin shrugged his shoulders before he began rifling through the bodies. A few moments later, he was joined by Kidu, who spat on one of the corpses before going about the grisly task.

During the latter part of the fight, several times my notifications displayed the names of the men I had killed instead of the usual question marks. I wondered if they had any scripted family or friends to mourn them before swiftly brushing the thought aside.

I felt the smallest pinprick of guilt before I rationalized that their deaths, if they were truly alive in the first place, had been nothing more than a necessity for the survival of our group. It was a clichéd conviction, but we had simply done what we had to do. I did not have the time or emotional energy to cry over every defeated foe.

"Okay... I mean, all right," I said, looking at the corpses that had been killed by spear and knife. "Let's try and set the scene."

Moving to the corpses, I started the gruesome task of slashing or stabbing at the wounds that Kidu and Elwin had inflicted, attempting to make them look like they were simply the victims of the echo-stalkers. Understanding my intent, Elwin moved to join me, and we quickly finished our macabre work.

I nodded my permission to Elwin, who proceeded to pocket a fine steel dagger. The weapon was crafted beautifully, its blade a damask pattern that drew the eye with wavy lines etched into the smoked steel. I hoped it was of a common enough design in these parts to avoid drawing attention. Seeing that I could do with a better weapon, he removed the leader's short sword from his belt and passed it to me for my perusal. Rooting around the corpses, he soon found a long dagger to replace it with.

Drawing it from its unpatterned leather sheath, I examined the short sword under the large moon's silvery light. The lightly fullered blade was a little longer than my crude scythe dagger, around forty-five centimeters in length and ending in a triangular tip. A plain bronze cruciform guard protected the hands, and the handle of the weapon was made of dark-stained wood with a heavy iron or lead pommel. Testing its balance, I concluded that it would make a simple weapon, if not aesthetically pleasing.

Pleased with how it felt, I slid the blade back into its scabbard. When I struggled to fasten the cloth sword belt—those intricate knots were completely unfamiliar—Elwin stepped in to help, flashing a wry grin.

"Right bunch of trouble, you are! Feel like a mother helping out with her child's first mass murder," he said jokingly, though his eyes spoke a different story.

Kidu merely snorted at the attempted joke before saying, "Gil is no child, Elwin. He is wise enough to know that a wolf does not mourn a death of the herd, only of the pack. Besides, we had saved their lives from the monsters. They belonged to us to spend as we pleased," he said simply, a satisfied sparkle in his eyes. I couldn't help but note that the calculus of the North was a cold one indeed.

"Search the cabins for valuables and supplies. Try not to disturb the place too much and remember to leave a few things. I want this to look like nothing more than just a monster attack," I instructed the pair, looking at them each in turn.

After seeing them nod their understanding, I led them into the cabins. We were greeted by the sight of a few overturned chairs near tables with half-eaten food—the signs of hastily made exits. The insides of the dwellings were all sparsely furnished, with utilitarian furniture of wood or iron. The walls were uniformly unadorned, and a small fire burned merrily in each of the cabins in simple stone hearths. We eagerly searched the dressers and tables, going through the knickknacks and small things of the previous occupants. The rogue, by dint of his larcenous skills or instincts, uncovered a coin purse hidden under a loose floorboard. In this manner, we passed through each of the buildings, eagerly searching for items useful to us.

During this time, I was greeted by yet another mysterious notification.

New Quest: Do you wish to claim Nyamdor's Hold? Yes/No

I paused as I rifled through a dead man's nightstand, looking for hidden valuables, surprised once more by how gamified this world was. This small part of the forest must have been the property of the man in blue garments, Chagatai Nyamdor. Scoffing at the notification, I of course chose "No," and the message disappeared. The last thing I needed was something linking us to the massacre we had perpetrated.

I remembered the games I had played in my past in which you had to build up your settlement, pandering to an endless list of needs from helpless NPCs and micromanaging their pathetic daily lives for minor, pointless rewards. *No thank you,* I thought with finality as I continued my pillaging. Responsibility for a place that would tie me down was most certainly not my cup of tea.

The work was tedious but worthwhile. Our haul consisted of several bags, filled mostly with copper and bronze coins, and a purse filled with several silver pieces and four gold coins that Elwin had found under the loose floorboard. The rogue had replaced his iron dagger with another simple steel dagger of slightly higher quality, which he had discovered in one of the cupboards.

We also attained a good supply of food and general resources, taking what we could easily carry in large leather bags we had also pillaged. Most importantly, we were able to find new clothes—even for Kidu's massive bulk—all cut in the local fashion with wide silken sashes. We were even lucky enough to find some leather boots that were roughly our size, a huge upgrade over our simple sandals.

After changing, we burned our slave linens in the fire of one of the hearths. The whole process was solemn, like a funeral, or a pagan rite of passage. We had come so far, and we were now closer than ever to achieving true freedom as we watched our old garments being consumed by the hungry flames. My modern sensibilities now thoroughly put aside, I knew then that I would fight with everything I had to survive in this cruel and callous world.

Chapter 36

THE BENEFITS OF DAIRY

With casualties mounting on both sides, the Republic began to lose its appetite for war. Even with necromancy filling the holes of the army ranks, the constant attrition was beginning to wear away at the will of the people, with some even demanding they at least consider the elves' earlier offers of amnesty.

The steward of the Republic, hearing the people's cries and feeling the heavy weight of their expectations, searched for a solution that would expel the invaders from their land and bring an end to the war.

— On the Cataclysm by an unknown Quassian Scholar, circa 103 AC.

We rested in one of the cabins, eating and recovering a little of our Stamina, but we were not quite able to sleep. Before long, and taking measures to conceal any sign of our presence, we resumed our journey. We spotted a trail leading towards the west, which we followed for several hours. As we progressed, the colossal trees of Sainba gradually gave way to smaller deciduous trees, adorned with a rich blend of deep green and golden hues.

As the sun began to sink and twilight fell across the forest, the daytime calls of the birds were replaced by the howls of prowling night creatures. Kidu advised that we push on through the dark to place as much distance between ourselves and any potential pursuers, but one look at Elwin's haggard face put an end to that notion. Much to the rogue's relief, we moved off the trail to shelter under the trees and made camp for the night. We would have to hope that our blue-glowing zajasite chunks would provide a large enough deterrent against attack from the local fauna.

We ate a humble repast of trail bread and jerky, now lightly salted thanks to our pillage of the charcoal-burners' stores. Conversation was scant, if not absent altogether. The physical and emotional strain of taking human lives had taken its toll on our spirits, leaving us without the inclination for idle chatter. I volunteered to take the most unwanted duty, the middle watch. Normally, I would have been against this, but I viewed it now as the opportunity to practice casting my spells.

Before making camp for the night, and with some Mana to spare, I silently cast Heal on Kidu. I felt the warm energies leave my body as the divine magic healed him of the many small wounds he had acquired in the last engagement.

Feeling content and pleased with myself, I went just outside of the camp's zajasite glow to continue exploring my powers. I needed to learn quickly, as there was no way of knowing when the game would be throwing its next difficulty spike in my direction. To that end, I brought with me several pieces of loose metal—the few remains from our manacles, which I had kept for my next experiment.

Throwing a small chunk of metal to the ground, I began to channel the full raging force of the Rust spell. Even using the Silent Casting skill, the spell still came to me easily, if a little delayed. The alien whispers, once so unfamiliar to me, now tantalized me, their hidden meaning just out of reach. The dark power, previously so inimical, began to feel warm and welcome as it coursed through my body. Like a river just before bursting its banks, the spell reached a crescendo.

It was an almost manic completion.

I released the energies, and a stream of black lightning blasted into the piece of metal, which sizzled and heated in response.

Humming a soft tune, I patiently bided my time, allowing the Rust spell to dissipate and the metal to cool. I brought it closer to the faint blue light and examined the metal closely, discovering that it had become heavily corroded and remarkably brittle to the touch, the surface now riddled with rust the color of desiccated blood. Despite waiting several minutes for the heat to subside, I still discerned a lingering warmth through the old leather of my gloves.

To test the effective distance of the spell, I threw another small chunk of metal on the ground and walked further away from it, counting the steps in my mind. At seventy paces, I tried casting the spell, but the magic failed to latch on to the metal. I took another step towards the iron chunk, but still the magic failed to catch. I took another step, then another, until at perhaps fifty or so paces, a torrent of energy flew from my hand into the metal. This piece of iron, just like the last, hissed as the power of the spell ate into it. Even at this range the magic had lost none of its potency.

I knew now, for certain, the range of my Rust spell, and that increases in the spell level worked only for its strength. I repeated this experiment three more times, eager to level up the spell and boost either my Intelligence or Wisdom attributes, but luck was not on my side that evening.

With disappointment curdling in my stomach and Mana sickness adding to my tiredness, I returned to camp to get what rest I could. This drew neither a word nor a simple grunt of acknowledgment from Kidu, who was already awake to take the last watch. I spread out a looted bedroll and slipped into a blessedly dreamless and exhausted sleep.

* * *

The next morning, after a simple breakfast, we continued on the wooded trail with, again, only a few words shared between us. I surmised that Kidu and Elwin were likely thinking about our return to civilization. My thoughts, on the other hand, danced between how to test my new spells safely and the violent actions of the night before last.

With no sign of pursuit, we stopped for our midday meal. Our lunch consisted of hard cheese and even harder tack rations, which were mercifully softened and washed down with stale-tasting water. Despite traveling for most of the morning, I felt much better than when I had traversed through the woods in my simple leather sandals. The difference that good footwear could have on one's outlook on life was startling.

When our meal was finished, I turned to my companions and said, "I need your help once again with some new spells."

"How is this even possible?" Elwin exclaimed. "Did you discover a spell after the battle? Have the powers that be granted you new magic already? It is said that it takes a mage years of learning and dedicated effort, or a pious Cleric many seasons of devotion and prayer, to gain new spells! And you say that you have acquired more already?"

"He is God-touched," the hunter interjected, as if this were all the explanation necessary. "We will assist in whatever way we can..."

Elwin almost interrupted, but a single glance from the hunter silenced the rogue. "We owe you, after all, a great debt that can never be repaid," Kidu declared.

"Thank you, thank you both," I replied, my voice slightly thick with repressed emotion. "I will require you both to remain at a safe distance, but close enough to observe."

They nodded, Elwin a little more hesitantly than Kidu, before following me a little way from our place of rest. The sun shone bright and high, and not a cloud marred the sky. We walked to a small field of grass filled with white flowers poking up from between the blades. Checking that my companions were at a safe but observable distance, I began to cast one of my new spells.

A darkness and a fierce joy surged deep within me, coalescing into a force that demanded release. With a shudder, I gave in, letting the power course through my body and erupt. The void between heartbeats and atoms was filled with a frigid emptiness, and my being radiated with a dark and terrible energy. Like ripples on a stagnant pool, the gray pulses of power expanded outwards from me, spreading wider and wider in a circle before abruptly ceasing its expansion at a distance of around fifteen meters.

As I took in the reactions of my companions, it became clear that the effect had gone unnoticed by them. The energy, it seemed, was invisible to all but myself.

This was my Entropic Aura spell, and despite the impressive visual effects, I felt no difference. Like Holy Aura, this spell consumed two Mana to cast and decreased my maximum Mana by two points while channeling. After summoning my comrades, I verified that they had neither felt nor witnessed any alterations.

Elwin looked at me with a quizzical expression as I took out a piece of cheese to observe the possible effects of my aura spell upon it. After a minute or two, he said, "Are you all right, Gil? Thinking about getting into the dairy business by any chance?"

Kidu shot a sharp glance in Elwin's direction. "Hold your tongue, little man. Gilgamesh is in the midst of some great magic."

"Fear not," I replied, my attention fixed on the scene unfolding before me. "I am merely confirming something..."

Having expected to see some sort of entropic effect on the cheese, I was disappointed to note that there was no change to its visible condition. Just as I was plucking up the courage to give the cheese a taste test, I caught sight of the grass around my feet. Here, I noticed that some of the leaves had begun to wilt, their once lustrous greens now dull and faded, browning at the edges.

Wishing to test further the conditions of the spell, I tore a small piece of cheese off. In my mind, I voiced that I wished to throw it away and that it was no longer my property. Perhaps the magic only affected things that were not mine? After all, if I was dealing with the entropic forces of the universe, it would hardly do if my own weapons and equipment suffered.

I dropped the morsel at my feet. As I watched, it slowly began to decay, discoloring and breaking up into smaller and smaller pieces as what I assumed to be mold and bacteria assaulted it. It looked like the effects of time were being accelerated, like a time-lapse video, with what should have been days' worth of rot hastening over the course of just a few minutes. The piece of cheese still in my hand was showing no change, so I bit down on it to make sure it was still edible.

The cheese was, as I remembered, similar in flavor to a low-quality cheddar. Nothing special and no change. I quickly took a swig from my water flask to clean out the taste.

As I pondered over the curious results, inspiration struck me, and I decided to test another one of my newly acquired spells: Decay. As I cast the spell, a surge of oily darkness flowed through me, pulsating with a frenzied madness that almost made me recoil. I grappled with the dark energy, and with a swift gesture, I released it onto the piece of cheese in my hand.

To my amazement, black liquid tentacles that absorbed light erupted from my hand and ensnared the small piece of food. The tentacles writhed and pulsed in tune with the waves from my Entropic Aura, causing the chunk to decompose rapidly and release the smell of ammonia. Soon it was reduced to no more than crumbling dust, which an errant breeze blew away. It seemed that unless they were actively targeted, my spells would not adversely affect me or my possessions.

The spell had only cost me one point of Mana, but I was yet unsure about its place in my arsenal. Both of the spells seemed to be "smart," and did not negatively affect me. But would the same blanket rule apply to my companions? I needed to find out.

I shouted out to them, telling them that it was probably safe. Kidu came first, with Elwin trailing a few meters behind. Almost instinctively, Kidu stopped just before the rolling waves of Entropy, like an animal that had sniffed danger in the wind.

I beckoned him to come closer, and he did so, a fraction of hesitation in his stride. He was followed shortly by Elwin, who seemed totally oblivious to the aura. The pulses of Entropy broke against them like gentle waves on the shore and caused no harm.

"Something tells me of an emptiness here," the big man said with an air of mysticism as he looked around.

The statement worried me. Did NPCs have a way to detect magic? Was it some skill linked to Kidu's class? Or was it simply the wildman's animalistic instincts?

"Don't feel anything different. I was supposed to feel something, right?" chortled the rogue, playing with the handle of his dagger.

I invited them to sit next to me, and we spent perhaps twenty minutes under the sun in companionable silence before I cast Decay silently on Kidu. However, the spell seemed to resist entering the large man, almost as if it was beyond its scope. Luckily for me, Kidu seemed to be none the wiser.

The spell still needed a release, so I threw the rest of my cheese onto the ground. Willing the spell into that instead, the magic soon broke it down into a rotting mess, causing my companions to leap up in worry as the smell assaulted their senses. Thankfully, I was able to assure them that all was well by telling them that I was just testing out the same spell. They both looked at me, a little miffed that I had not given them any forewarning.

The grass closest to me was quite wilted now, and Kidu gazed at the vegetation before looking me in the eye. "Do you know what it is that you do?" he asked, genuine concern edging his voice.

"In truth, Kidu, this is why I requested your help. I am sure this is a spell that will help weaken my enemies," I said as I tore up some browning grass and showed it to him, hopefully dodging the question. "But I needed to know if it would affect my allies. Forgive me my small deception."

Elwin, visibly shaken, hurriedly got up and started to step away from me before Kidu stopped him, grasping him firmly by the arm.

"If we were being harmed, I would know it," explained Kidu. "And I have felt no ill effects from Gilgamesh's spell. Have you, Elwin of Tucker? Remember, we are here to help him understand his magic. Our debt is huge; we must give what small assistance we can. Many times now, thanks to his magic, have you not been saved?"

With a shrug, the rogue sat down. "Well, if you put it that way. But all this magic is making me nervous. Can't see it, after all. This esoteric arcane nonsense gives me a little of the shakes. How about it? Are we finished now, Gil?" the wiry man asked nervously.

I nodded at Elwin. "Yes, we are. I think this curse, or spell, or whatever it is, does not affect my allies. Only my enemies." I gave them another look over to make sure they had not suffered from the spell.

Not wishing to push my companions' largesse by insisting on more tests, I suggested we resume our travels. We continued our journey through the rest of the day, the trail gradually widening before we reached a simple earthen road that cut through the woods. Eventually, the trees of the forest gave way to endless grassland, stained golden and red in the dying light.

A flicker of movement caught my eye in the middle distance, but as quickly as it had appeared, it vanished without a trace. Kidu stopped in his tracks, his muscles tense, and he glanced for a moment, as if assessing the situation. Far away we could see the sprawling city of Ansan, our destination, just as the sun dipped beneath the horizon and twilight claimed the land.

I felt on my cheek the smallest impression of displaced air. Then a small group emerged as if from a thick mist, like phantoms, their presence jarring but barely registering in my mind. Something about them made me want to avert my gaze, to ignore their existence, but I fought against the compulsion and focused on their appearance.

They were a party of seven, cloaked and mysterious, and the bulge of hidden weapons about their lithe forms served as an unspoken threat. Was it my imagination, or did I catch a glimpse of pointed ears poking out from beneath one of their hoods? I shook my head out of a fugue and made sure to avoid eye contact or pay them further attention as we gave them a wide berth.

They passed us, and for a few moments, I could hear them cursing at each other in an unknown musical tongue. Were they hunting for us? Paranoia began to nibble away at me, and faraway-sounding whispers encouraged me to turn around and make an end of that group. *That would be foolish,* I thought to myself as I shook my head and waved aside the temptation. *Perhaps another time.*

Looking at my Status, I noticed that my maximum Mana was still at eleven... which meant I was still subconsciously channeling my Entropic Aura! The magic had a mind of its own, not wishing to recede from whence it had come. The slow dark waves were still there, pulsing, and almost invisible, even to me in the twilight. Fighting the temptation to turn around and horrified at my lack of control, I focused on trying to rein in both my panic and the entropic magic. Bringing the dark force to heel felt like trying to grasp at a slippery eel; the rogue magic wanted to stay on this plane of existence.

Closing my eyes for a moment, I began to bind it inexorably to my will, and was finally able to stop the spell. I was not the same man who had entered this world. My will and determination had grown with me. Sighing deeply in relief, I began to walk, before I felt a sharp pricking pressure at my throat—the pressure of a needle-pointed blade—and a soft feminine whisper in my ear.

"What are you, little day-spawn?"

Chapter 37

THE RULES OF THE ROAD

Ansan, known as the jewel of the Grieving Lands, is the seat of power of the Children of the Tides. The city has an insatiable hunger for slaves, which are its very lifeblood, acquired through both trade and their mercenary campaigns, where payment is more often demanded in flesh than in gold.

The city's greatest exports are the result of suffering and bloodshed. The high-quality iron from its mines and fine lumber harvested from the nearby Sainba Forest are its greatest assets and are famous throughout the known world. Lying along the Dust merchant route, the city is a veritable hub of trade. It is said that anything can be purchased in Ansan for the right price.

Beyond the Sainba lies the untamed frontier of the Wildlands, the hunting grounds of the Adventurers' Guild. It is a place of great danger, where only the bravest or the foolhardiest venture to collect rare and valuable materials.

— The Fanciful Travels by Beron de Laney, 376 AC.

I held my tongue. Out of the corners of my eyes, I could see that my companions had been similarly accosted by the hooded group. Slowly, we all raised our hands in surrender, completely powerless before them.

Two of their number came to face us, both lithe and predatory in their movements, talking to each other in a strange language. Their words were soft and lilting, and it was difficult to recognize if they were singing or speaking to one another. Needing to know what they were saying, I went through the mental gymnastics required to cast Identify silently on their words.

"One of the Tides's Honored Ones," said the one to the left, who was considerably shorter than the others. The figure turned in my direction. "A middlingly gifted one at that. We should just leave them here, and quickly. We need no more complications. Also, the death of an Honored One will…"

The words turned back into incomprehensible, yet pleasantly lilting singsong as my spell faded.

I noticed, even in my rising panic, that the smaller one in front of me was probably female. She had said something about me being gifted. I tried to parse its meaning, but the slight curves of her feminine form drew my eye, and I cursed inwardly at the momentary distraction. Curled blonde ringlets fell around eyes that held all the deadly playfulness of a cat toying with a doomed mouse.

The knife pressed a little harder against my throat, almost drawing blood, and drew me back to the desperation of my current predicament. "Gifted" must mean magic user, I concluded.

There seemed to be some disagreement about our fate between the two leaders. I had to know more about who had waylaid us, so I stole another glance at the small blonde one who had recognized me as a magic user. Desperately clutching at straws, I cast an Identify in her direction. The spell appeared to be resisted to some degree, taking far too long before providing some clarity.

Arimea Lostariot - Spellsinger (Wood Elf Lv. 19)
Health: 176/180
Stamina: 31/32
Mana: 13/17

I kept my expression neutral as I went over the information. At the same time, my eyes scanned left and right, in search of an opening. These were elves, but I had little idea how I could use that to my advantage to wriggle us out of this situation. My mind raced through every myth, legend, and modern portrayal of elves, but none offered any insight into how I might escape this situation. The only potential advantage I could recall was that elves were often physically weaker than humans, but that seemed of little use in our current predicament. Also, almost all my second-hand knowledge agreed that elves were as deadly as they were mysterious.

If the elf I had identified earlier was any indication, this group was not to be trifled with. Their strength was clear. But I had to keep searching for a way out, a glimmer of hope that might yet save us. I needed more information, so I cast Identify silently on their conversation again.

"Bah, the day-spawns' Honored Ones kill each other all the time in their futile power struggles. Make it look like another of their mindless killings," one of the elves, indistinguishable from the others, added to the conversation.

"We must keep up our efforts to find the Daughter of Chaos. She is close... Our informants at the guild... And this will be a poor salve for your revenge. Remember our mandate," said the one on the right in a clipped male voice, like a teacher reminding a child of a forgotten fact.

I was taken aback by the masculinity of his voice, for his face was more beautiful than it was handsome. Even in the poor light, a jagged scar that was intertwined with creases of concern did little to detract from that beauty. Though I could not fully understand him, I judged by his manner and tone that he was suppressing a deeply buried exasperation. Similar to his comrades, he possessed a lean and svelte frame, but was slightly broader at the shoulders than they were.

I burned through another point of Mana on deciphering their words as adrenaline surged through my veins, and beads of sweat formed on my brow in my struggle to focus on their conversation.

"They have seen our faces," Arimea said. "If we are to deal with them, be quick about it. We must hurry on. Time is of the essence, and seconds count. We must make it within the city boundary soon, for I cannot keep this veil up forever." I could hear a budding frustration in her musical voice.

"How did they even pierce your veil, Lady Lostariot? Such magics should be beyond the day-spawn," another of her attendants ventured.

You have gained 1 Wisdom.

Panic was beginning to seize me even as the notification flashed across my mind's view, and my bladder grew heavy in fear. Before I could cast another spell, the pair seemed to have reached a decision, made clear by the one on the right nodding to the elf behind me.

A knife cut a shallow slash across my throat, and I could feel a numbing sensation followed by my limbs locking up, paralyzed. I crumbled to the ground. Out of the corner of my eye, I saw my companions struck down in a similar fashion, falling to the elves' blades. The hooded terrors faded into the twilight gray, leaving us for dead.

Somewhere inside of me, a primal instinct—the simple desire to live at all costs—commanded me to take action. Yet, like a mouse who had escaped the claws and teeth of a predator, fear still ruled my heart and threatened to reduce me to a gibbering mess.

With a great effort of will, I stamped down on this mind-killing fear. Desperately, I searched my mind for a way to save my companions and myself. Surely this was not where my journey would end? My Health was rapidly dropping, and I felt a constriction about my heart. Was it possible their blades were poisoned?

The thought lingered, even as my lifeblood continued to pour out from my throat with every weakening pulse. Certainly, with my current Mana, I could cast Heal and save myself, but I would not have enough energy to save Kidu and Elwin. It would be a repeat of Durhit all over again. Without a word, I took a chance and cast one of my new spells, hoping my choice was correct.

Golden energies ever so slowly began to pulse from me, an echo of an angel's song ringing softly in my ear like a celestial lullaby. The glow spread over me, slowly closing the wound at my throat and repairing the damage done by the vile substances that had ravaged my body. The poisons remained within me, but their vicious bile had been blunted. My Health fluctuated in small ticks as the damage they were doing was mitigated by the slow healing.

The aura spell's energy left me feeling both warm and chilled in equal measure before it flowed over to my companions, soothing them as well. I could only pray that it would be enough. A notification appeared, telling me I had gained a point in Luck, but I dismissed it.

Staying on the ground in fear of the group's return, I waited for my shaking limbs to still themselves, hoping that the elves would not notice the glow and return to finish us off. I forced myself into a state of calm to check my Status. The attempt on my life had reduced my Health to around half, and my back-to-back uses of magic had put my Mana down to six points.

Like a newborn foal, I slowly got up and hobbled over to check on my companions. Kidu stirred his enormous bulk, and I felt great relief that my magic had worked in saving his life. Elwin looked to be in worse shape, his breathing shallow and his face pale. Using most of my remaining Mana, I cast Heal on him, which slowly brought the color back to his face.

Realizing that we had made it past the worst, I stopped channeling my aura spell and said, "Kidu, we must move. Those elves may return, and they have the advantage over us."

Within me, adrenaline was fighting a losing war with exhaustion. Kidu took several deep breaths, like a bull preparing to charge, before he moved with great effort to help me with Elwin, who had just begun to stir.

A mixture of disbelief, gratefulness, and awe dogged my companions' steps as we half ran, half shuffled towards a dip in the grassland where we could lie low and hope it was enough cover from prying eyes or ears. Every now and then, Elwin would look at his hands and whisper thanks and a prayer to some sort of "Dark Lady." Kidu would mutter to tell him to stay quiet while also secretly shooting me a look filled with wonder.

We settled down on the soft grass. I felt haggard and demoralized from the clear difference in the strength we had witnessed from the elves. We were like children before them.

Now in a relative place of safety, Kidu volunteered to take watch over Elwin to give him time to recover from his brush with death. I hunkered down next to them, shivering—more from fear than the cooling twilight air.

Hours passed, and I heard the hoot of a night owl somewhere in the distance. The peak of danger had now hopefully passed, and my thoughts turned to survival. If we were going to get through this, we needed the supplies in our bags. They represented all our worldly wealth, the wealth we would need to travel to more gentle climes, but the brush with death had unmanned me.

Kidu was keeping watch, but even in the dying light, I could tell he had lost some of his usual confidence and energy from the slump of his shoulders and the cast of his eyes. After putting him through so much, I almost felt guilty to be asking more of him.

"Kidu," I whispered, "we need to see if they have left anything behind. We need those things."

The hunter followed my eyes to the bags.

"Perhaps enough time has passed, and you are by far a better—"

"Yes, I see. I will go to see if those old ones have left and recover our things. You must stay with Elwin of Tucker. He may be needing further healing. Also, you make more noise than a rutting boar when you move, ha!" he added, some of his usual verve and confidence returning as he stood to his full impressive height.

Glad that I was able to save face, I nodded to him in thanks. In my current state, I could barely keep myself together, let alone venture out in the growing dark on a mission.

"Be safe, Kidu," I begged of him as he left.

"Fear not! They will not find me such easy prey this time!" he growled, then left me alone with Elwin.

My mind was filled with narcissistic fantasies of vengeance against the elves as I sat down on the dry grass next to the comatose rogue. Every minute alone left me feeling weak and vulnerable. I touched my neck, and recoiled at the memory of the blade slashing my throat. The remembrance put paid to my remaining thoughts of vengeance.

I did not know how much time had passed when suddenly there was a hand on my shoulder, which made me almost jump out of my skin.

"Be well, Gilgamesh!" a familiar voice said from behind me.

"Kidu! Thank heavens you have returned," I said, turning around.

Weighed down by our bags on his massive frame, it was clear the hunter had managed to return with our belongings. His appearance brought a glimmer of joy to my countenance, and I exhaled all my tension in sweet release.

"Yes, the old ones did not touch a thing. They are not worthy of respect, those who kill only for sport," he hissed angrily, dropping our bags down by his feet.

I helped in unrolling the stolen bedrolls. Between us, we maneuvered the unconscious form of Elwin into his bedding. He mumbled something about dice in his sleep, which gave me some measure of reassurance. If he could still talk, then there was hope that no enduring harm had been inflicted upon him.

Sick and tired of this stupid world, I curled up into a ball for the night. It took a long time for the dreams to find me.

Chapter 38

RETURN TO ANSAN

A man is judged by the quality of the weapon on his hip.
— *The Fanciful Travels* by Beron de Laney, 376 AC.

My dreams were of a different flavor this time. The tentacled creatures of the void did not disturb me, nor did the susurrations of the cruel whispers that promised an eternity of suffering. Instead, I endured a frustrating dream of battling hooded elves that moved like bottled lightning.

I tried attacking them with my short sword, but my limbs felt like they were moving through thick molasses. Again and again, the wicked creatures would harry me, stabbing and slashing with their evil, shining blades. My frustration was building up to a berserker rage until Kidu shook me awake, freeing me from my nightmare.

Groggily, I took over the watch, looking over at Elwin's sleeping form. I was physically refreshed but mentally exhausted. Anger, more than fear, was my primary emotion, and a small part of me hoped to encounter those elves again, to rend yielding flesh from their delicate bones.

However, in the deeper parts of my soul, I knew this was just an idle fantasy. If we met them again in our current state we would not be nearly as lucky. It was a humbling and abject lesson in the difference of power.

Staring out across the sea of grass, I whispered to myself, "One day," then began my watch. A cool night breeze made the shimmering blades sway softly in agreement with my vow.

* * *

During the long hours of watch, I busied myself by cycling Entropic Aura on and off to prove that I, and not it, was truly in control. So engrossed was I with my magic that I chose not to wake Elwin for his watch, which left me a little more tired than usual. However, as a result of my focused esoteric practice, I had increased the level of my Entropic Aura and, more importantly, was now better able to command its rebellious energies.

The next morning found our party in low spirits. Fear stalked at the back of my mind, and I nervously looked over my shoulder for any signs of pursuit. The previous night's encounter brought to the fore a feeling of impotence, akin to that felt when the collars were around our necks. The sun shone, and the birds sang their sweet melodies in the crisp morning air, but none of this could lift the pall of our close brush with the end.

After we had a simple breakfast of lightly salted traveler's bread—with not even a single word of thanks from Elwin—I decided to broach the topic of our next move. "Gentlemen, I believe it is time for us to discuss what to do next."

"Well, we certainly need to get out of this forsaken wilderness. Simple travelers aren't nearly as friendly as they used to be," replied Elwin sarcastically, hiding the worry in his voice.

"Just a few more enemies for the tribe," rumbled the big hunter threateningly before taking a swig of water from a canteen.

"I say we stick with our own kind—better the devil you know," Elwin suggested. "Best we make our way into the city and join up with a caravan, or get some supplies and gear and find a group traveling someplace else, once we get the lay of the land. Don't know about you lads, but I could do with a roof over my head for a little bit. A quick drink would not go amiss either."

"Better to be free in the forest than in chains in the city..." grumbled the big man.

"Very well, you both make good points," I said. "However, if we are to go with Elwin's plan, how are we to make good our entry into the city of Ansan? Our wealth is not without limits, and as Elwin wisely pointed out, it would be best for us to find friendlier climes as soon as—"

"Leave that to me," Elwin said. "City guards are always known for their grift, and we have a little coinage, more than enough to secure entry for three foreigners. Besides, people from all over come to Ansan, the jewel of the Grass Sea and gate to the Wilds of the Grieving Lands. What I would do for a real bed!"

I made a point of pretending to truly consider this before finally siding with the rogue. I would have to pray that my face would just be one among many. My notoriety from the arena was surely faded now from word of my supposed "death" in the mines. Still, I felt a little apprehensive to be going back to the city that had enslaved me. The irony was not lost on me that it was safer to be in the city in which I had been subjugated, rather than in the wilderness, where I could fall prey to dark beasts and proficient, chilling enemies. At least I would be among my own species.

"We enter Ansan and find a place to stay. Sell what we can for coin, then find transport out." I spoke this slowly in the best authoritative voice I could muster.

"All well and good, talking about getting in the city," Elwin said. "That's the easy part. But I would like to take a moment to discuss what in the blue hell happened yesterday? For a moment I was in the Shallow River, about to cross to the other side. Don't know about the big man here, but I was knee-deep in its dark water. What, or who, were those people or things last night? And what did you do to us that could pull us from the grasp of the Dark Lady? By the gods, we almost died! What exactly are you, and what are those powers that let you do this?" Elwin stared pointedly at me as he took a deep breath. "Let's start with something simple first. Gil here seems to have understood a little of what they were saying. Saw it, I did. Why did they attack us?"

Debating on telling them the whole truth, I carefully began to answer his line of inquiry. "They were elves—wood elves, to be precise—and they—"

Again, I was interrupted by Elwin. "Legendary, even among their own sort, the royal line of the First People of the Forest? The Warders of the Woods? They walk the lands of men again? Ha, you would make a fine bard for the royal court if you could get me to believe that," added the rogue in a sharp tone, which drew a snarl from the hunter.

"Enough, little man. Gilgamesh of the Uruks speaks the truth. Who else could have moved as they did? I am perhaps one of the greatest hunters of the Three Bears that has ever lived to walk on the ice, yet even I didn't sense a whisper before they were upon us. The old stories tell of sharp-eared people, great even among their own kind, that can walk as they do. If Gilgamesh says they are of the First People, then that makes for a good enough explanation for me."

"But why did—"

"Because they could," I said tersely, cutting Elwin off. "Because they're not human, their goals are alien and unknowable. But ultimately, I believe it was because they had the power to do so. Let's be grateful that they were in a hurry and didn't finish the job." I looked them both in the eye. "It is best that we focus on our current predicament. The whys and wherefores matter not in our quest for a bed for the night and a roof over our heads."

I said the last to humor Elwin, glad that I had diverted the topic from my own magic. I could almost feel invisible dice rolling to see if I had passed a check of some sort.

The pair nodded, with Elwin slightly narrowing his eyes, before they started to gather our things. While they were busy, I took a moment to confirm that it was only us in the immediate vicinity, as the light of the spell was somewhat of a spectacle that could draw unwanted attention. Seeing that the coast was clear, I silently cast Greater Heal on myself, eager to rid myself of the slave marks on my arm.

The divine energies wound about my form and erased the mark of my hated brand. The remaining light played about my companions, drawing a few gasps of surprise before softly disappearing.

When the pair finished with our preparations, we headed in the direction of the city with renewed vigor in our stride, the vestiges of my released magic making me light on my feet. Necessity had forced our hand, but I would make the most of the hand I was dealt.

About an hour away from the gates of the city, a heavily armed mounted patrol of Children passed our group. Their backs were straight as they clasped menacing-looking lances, their dark eyes looking to the horizon as if searching for something. We kept our eyes low. Even Kidu knew better than to cause trouble. Mercifully, they left us alone. My group must have looked like just a small band of innocent travelers, or perhaps farmers, looking for a better life in the city. The hawks were searching for other prey.

We joined a lengthy line of farmers, merchants, and general travelers all waiting to enter Ansan, the jewel of the Grass Sea. The line moved with a plodding slowness that ate up the minutes and hours, a testament to the efficiency of those manning the gates.

A small black-haired girl, in the awkward stage between girl and woman, was carried, like an imperial icon, on a palanquin by slaves from inside the city to the gate. She began to speak to the guards in an imperious tone in the local language of the Tides.

I could not hear the conversation directly, but I saw her doll-like features crease in annoyance as one of the guards at the gate kneeled before her palanquin and presented her with an intricately knotted silk string. Fuming in anger, she ordered her slaves to carry her quickly back into the city.

Unable to stem my curiosity—and ignoring Elwin's warning glare—I asked an old farmer wearing a wide-brimmed straw hat to explain what had just unfolded. The old man turned to give me a look over, no doubt questioning the discrepancy between my local clothes and my quite obvious ethnicity. One glance at Kidu, however, made him gulp in fear and answer my question.

"That be an Honored One, young man, those of the city who are strong in the Gift." He removed the straw hat from his head and clasped it to his chest. "Best not to draw the attention of the high folk. Only trouble for those of our station," he continued, eyes downcast.

I wanted to ask more, but Elwin was shaking his head, so I stilled my questioning tongue. The old man turned, now ignoring us.

"You don't want to be asking too many questions, not looking like that. In fact, it's best you don't ask any questions at all. Don't want to draw any more attention to us," the rogue said quietly, pointing to my clothes and the dull stains around my neck. "If you got any questions, let's ask them once we're safely inside."

Taking his advice, I kept quiet until our turn arrived. As I prepared to enter the city in which the yoke of slavery had been forced upon me, my thoughts became filled with trepidation. Would anyone recognize me? Or was I already considered dead, yet another victim of the system that fueled this city's wealth?

Suddenly, Elwin walked with a confident swagger to one of the bored-looking guards at the gate. His target was clad in an ill-fitting suit of piecemeal armor and armed with a crudely fashioned mace that showed signs of neglect. A terse exchange ensued between the two men, causing the guard's features to come alive with a spark of interest. Then, with a knowing glance in our direction, the rogue surreptitiously passed a few coins into the guardsman's open palm.

Moving towards the gate, for a moment I thought our plan had failed, or that Elwin had sold us out and we would have to fight our way free. I was soon disproved of this notion when the bored-looking guard offered, "You lot stink too much of the road. My cousin Taper runs an inn with a good bathhouse, just down this way, the Twisted Boar. Tell him Dagesh sent you." He winked, obviously pleased by his take this afternoon.

We passed the gates of the solid wood palisade, and I had to fight a sense of foreboding as my eyes caught the sight of the monolithic Ark at the center of the city in the distance, the seat of power and governance of the Children of the Tides. My nerves played merry hell with my heart, and I was worried I would be recognized by one of my former enslavers.

The stench of pressed humanity hit me, and my eyes furtively scanned everywhere, searching with dread for any familiar faces. To me, the local people all seemed to resemble my initial captors near the shrine of Avaria with their shifty, slanted Asian eyes that promised deceit or violence. Still, luck—or divine providence—was on our side, and our party drew no real notice.

Picking up our pace, we walked along the hard, earthen packed street. It was the main eastern thoroughfare of Ansan, and it felt odd walking here for the first time as a free man. I rationalized my good fortune with the fact that, in this barbaric and backwards society, being a slave had made me all but invisible. To them, I must have been just one face among thousands, quickly forgotten. I had weighed the risks of returning to the city against the life of a brigand in the Wilds. I convinced myself that this choice, though undoubtedly risky, allowed for potentially greater gain. Also, the lure of civilization was too great to ignore.

The mistake I had made was that of a modern civilized man. I had thought, in my error, that I was the center of the world and that its events and people revolved around me, the protagonist. However, nothing could be further from the truth. Even in this brand-new world, I existed in a place of astonishing indifference to almost everything I was. Everything I thought. Everything I did.

Unbeknownst to me, a more sinister impulse had guided me back to the city. One aspect of my decision was the recklessness born of youth—a rebellious spark that eagerly courted danger. Yet the other was far more ominous: a pledge of vengeance made what felt like ages ago, now grown cold and festering in the depths of my mind. It was a means to carve my existence into a cruel and callous world.

Chapter 39

THE TWISTED BOAR

In ages long forgotten, the Children of the Tides were the daring adventurers of the ancient oceans. They voyaged across the world, engaging in trade and pillaging along the coastlines of the many lands. But those days have passed, and their once mighty fleets and ships now exist only in memory. Instead, they have become semi-nomadic, with few permanent settlements, relying on their fast mounts and skill at arms for their military might. Having taken a life before their fourteenth year, every one of their waveriders is a blooded warrior.

In this modern era the Children of the Tides have reinvented themselves as mercenaries, offering their services to the highest bidder. To this day, they can field a substantial number of water mages, as their people still share a bond with the ocean. Their magisters, once skilled in the art of controlling the power of the depths, now employ their talents to aid their kin in their logistics. They supply the precious resource of potable water for their long and arduous campaigns.

— The Fanciful Travels by Beron de Laney, 376 AC.

Worry gnawed at me as we made our progress through the streets. I had to constantly remind myself that a smart criminal walks and does not run. This conflicted with another truth I had learned through modern media: the culprit almost always returns to the scene of the crime.

The foot traffic was heavy as we walked past the numerous tents and yurts lining the main boulevard, and a fine layer of dust coated almost everything. The smell of the city almost overwhelmed our noses, which were, by now, too accustomed to clean country air. Every now and then we would pass a stone or wooden building, but for the most part, they were relatively rare.

After making our way through the sweaty press of traffic, hands always on our valuables, we saw the sign of the Twisted Boar—a painted picture of a green boar being twisted in the hands of a leering giant on a wooden board. A strange sign for a strangely named inn.

The whole building looked relatively new, without the presence or signs of age of a structure that has long stood the test of the years. To the right of the building was a small one-story construction made of the local white stone, with a flat roof. Its chimney billowed out a small column of gray smoke—the baths of the establishment, no doubt. On the left of the building was an empty stable that had seen better days.

We entered the main establishment through a sturdy door, well-worn with use, to be greeted by the sight of a thin man behind a wooden counter polishing a horn stein. The ceiling was low, and the smell of spilled ale and recently cleaned vomit hung stale in the air. In the corner, two bearded, turbaned men sat around a glass pipe, taking turns sharing puffs of bluish smoke that twirled towards the ceiling.

At a small wooden table, a group of shifty-looking rat-eyed men sat, playing what looked like this world's version of cards. Dog-eared cards featuring unknown gods, monsters, and symbols were exchanged, placed, then exchanged again. Depending on their fortunes, the players' expressions changed from controlled neutrality to drunken consternation.

The willowy male behind the bar looked at us with eyes the color of chocolate. He was somewhere in his middle years, his once black hair now grown lank and thin. Narrow lips under a wide nose pursed as he nodded to us in the universal manner of all bartenders, somewhere between deference and amicability, before asking, "What can I get you folks?"

In a certain light, you could say he had a vague resemblance to the guard at the gate, but the association was tenuous at best. I was just about to speak, but Elwin beat me to it. "Innkeep, we are looking for a room—a private room, if you please—for the three of us."

"That'll be twenty bronze pieces a night for the lot of you, twenty-three if folk be needing to use the baths, which I highly suggest you do. You have the look of the road long traveled about you. Oh, and another bronze if you lot be needing your clothes to be laundered. Leave 'em with the boy, good lad he is. Three coppers for a meal when we're serving. Also, the name's Taper Athinad, at your service," he said perfunctorily.

As he detailed the prices, my brain performed some rough calculations. My time in the local jail, eavesdropping on the conversations of the market, had given me a rough idea of the value of the coins. As I spun the numbers in my mind, I made sure to study the innkeeper, searching his face for the signs of treachery, but finding none.

Luckily, this world's currency followed a simple decimal system. Having observed a woman buying two apples for a copper at the marketplace, in terms of buying power, I estimated that a single copper coin was worth approximately one pound. Ten coppers were then worth a bronze piece, and ten bronze coins were, in turn, worth a single silver piece, with ten silver pieces having the value of a rare gold coin.

I ran a finger over one of the silver coins as I was making my decision. On one side was the stylized version of a flowing wave, and on the other was a bust profile of an ancient woman terrifyingly similar to the goddess Avaria.

Like all of the coins, the edges of this one were smooth and uniform. Next to it was a similar-sized silver coin with a hole punched through its center. This was a "half-silver" piece. Like the silver coins, there were other denominations with a hole punched through their centers in both copper and bronze, though I had yet to encounter a half-gold piece.

Unlike the bronze and copper pieces, along the rim of both silver pieces was some script I could not yet decipher, written in a language I had not yet learned.

As my mind played about with the numbers, so too did it play around with the idea of casting a spell of Identification on the unknown script. However, idle curiosity was not a good enough cause to spend precious Mana.

Forcing myself to relax a little, I concluded that, overall, the inn's prices were reasonable. It was not worth looking for other accommodations. This place would serve our needs fine. The innkeeper was probably not out to get us, as we had never met before. These thoughts warred with my paranoia until I was finally able to get myself under control. What would be, would be, a mantra against the building pressure in my head. It was time to take a chance; the dice demanded to be rolled.

With my decision made, I nodded to Elwin, who then counted out a week's worth of lodging for us and put a little extra onto the counter. Just as the rogue finished, he asked Athinad in a quiet voice, "Bit far from home, Athinad? That's a southern name by the sound of it…"

He was met with a grunt by the innkeeper. "Travel bug took me, and my feet found themselves here. Nothing really about it. Now, what can I be getting you lads?"

"Just saying. Now, what we could do with is a little information. Perhaps to the tune of the comings and goings in the city? Perhaps a place where some strapping young men can earn a bit of coin? Maybe even a place to wind down… if you get my drift?" Elwin gave Athinad a knowing wink.

I couldn't help but think that this was rich talk coming from a man who had recently been enslaved, but then I realized it was part of his act, giving the impression of normality.

The innkeeper's brow furrowed, as if in concentration, before he deigned to answer the rogue. "Been a bunch of thieves operating around these parts recently, so keep a hand on your purses, I say. Small reward, too, from us local businesses if you're able to catch 'em. And there's always work down by the caravanserai—they're always looking for strong backs." He paused for a moment, looking us over. "Of course, those of... a more combative nature may find the odd job or two at the Adventurers' Guild."

With such a delivery, I almost expected an intrusive quest prompt, but none were forthcoming.

"And entertainment?" burst the rogue, the hunger for the diversions of the night clear in his eyes.

Coughing slightly, the innkeeper replied, "Well, there's usually a few games of chance and skill going round here, and there's a gambling house run by old Roi up by the Ark. But if you're into more bloodthirsty entertainment, there's the arena with its daily games."

Elwin looked at him, willing him to continue.

"Or... in the North Quarter is the pleasure district. Haven't had much in the way of time to actually get around to sampling its selections, business being business and all, so can't tell you much," he added as he cleaned a nonexistent stain from the counter.

Hurry up and get us our room already, I thought. The voices within painted a picture of me smashing Athinad's face in with a mining pick and taking in some delicious experience. Then I could loot his corpse for keys to the room, and there could also be money and treasure behind the bar...

"Your friend there, is he all right?" Taper asked Elwin in a low voice.

"We will take our rooms and a bath and, if possible, our clothes to be laundered," I interjected before Elwin could respond, pulling myself from murderous thoughts that were probably not my own. I sighed, glad that our plan was working.

The innkeeper gave me a relieved look, his shoulders visibly relaxing before handing me a set of copper keys. "Up the stairs, second door on the left."

I nodded, and our party made our way up wood stairs that creaked ominously under our weight. At the top of the stairway landing was a narrow corridor with doors on either side. We entered a surprisingly clean room. I was expecting three separate beds but was surprised to see instead a large single bed in the corner.

Simple wooden shutters, secured by a wooden bar, could be opened to let the light or fresh air in. A single chair, a side table by the bed, and three chamber pots in the opposite corner were the only other pieces of furniture in the room. A part of me had expected the locals to sleep like barbarians on the floor, so I was glad to have a proper, if shared, bed and a solid roof over my head that wasn't just a layer of rock and earth.

The tension that had been keeping me taut as a bowstring and on my feet threatened to leave as I thought of all the risks we had taken to reach this moment. However, rather than feeling truly safe, I simply felt an easing of the present danger.

We decided to take inventory. Our current scavenged and looted belongings included a few mining tools, our old weapons, a few assorted valuable objects and miscellany from the cabins, basic camping supplies, and, of course, the length of chain I had decided to keep. Four gold coins and thirteen silver pieces, with the rest of the coins in bronze and copper, were the sum of our current wealth.

The silver and gold we divvied up between us, Elwin looking unhappy at getting some of his share in bronze and copper. The group agreed that we should keep the rest of the copper and bronze for general expenses. At a rough calculation, I estimated their value to be at around five or six thousand pounds. The money in front of me, coupled with something that the innkeeper had said about gambling, sparked the beginning of an idea in my mind. I certainly didn't have enough funds to start a trade or business, but for the moment I had enough to survive for some time and find my feet in this world.

The group unanimously reaffirmed that we would treat our stay in Ansan as if we were in enemy territory. We would tread carefully with all our dealings here and try to keep a low profile, forgoing strong drink and other vices that could betray us. In that vein of thought, we decided it best that we go to the baths in pairs, with one of us staying in the room to watch over our gear.

I would be naked and vulnerable, but my modern sensibilities demanded at least some level of hygiene, as we assuredly stank of the road and the Wilds. Our marks of bondage were no more, leaving us as free men. Fretting incessantly would only lead me down a dark path of suspicion and delusion.

Elwin volunteered to try to find a fence to purchase our looted valuables later, once we had made ourselves more presentable. He also promised to trade for some new clothes; having some spares would always be welcome.

I first went to the baths with Elwin, entrusting Kidu to watch over our scavenged loot. A boy stood at a small counter near the baths—an eager, dark-haired, scrawny thing. We passed him the requisite coin to see to our clothes once we had placed them in the baskets. Bowing once, he hung some dull gray robes on two wooden pegs for us and left with our dirty garments.

We entered the baths proper through sliding doors. An old man, remarkably muscled, with jagged scars from past battles running across his body, rinsed himself before entering one of three large pools. Copying the man's example, we cleaned ourselves as best we could with cheap, coarse soap. As we scrubbed and scrubbed, the grime from our long travels slowly sloughed off us and, once we felt suitably clean, we entered one of the tepid pools. The feeling of embarrassment from my nakedness had long been scoured from me, but a sense of vulnerability remained, so Elwin and I would have to make quick our little bathing session.

For a moment I remembered Harun, comparing him to the old man. They were of a similar build, but would he pose a similar challenge? I played out the murderous scenario in my mind, and was even tempted to use an Identify spell on him, but finally decided against it. I needed to leave here and return to the relative safety of the room without incident.

Although a hurried one, the bath was doing wonders for my morale, and Elwin looked supremely happy to be clean again. Scratching behind his back, he turned and said cheerfully, "I always do enjoy my weekly bath."

I did my best to hide my grimace. Hygiene standards in this world were obviously not comparable to my own. Sighing, I simply smiled back at the rogue before slipping deeper into the warm water. Slowly, ever so slowly, the warm water began to soothe the myriad aches and pains of my recent travails in a way that magic simply could not replicate. Looking at my body, I noticed that despite receiving a number of wounds, I did not have a single scar on me. I touched the place where my slave brand should have been, only to find smooth skin.

Also, despite being at more than twice the Strength I was initially, there were still no significant changes to my physique. I had the same very average-looking body that I always had. A quick gander at Elwin's body showed a surprising lack of scars for a man of his trade, but an intricate tattoo of an unknown design ran from the nape of his neck along the line of his back. A few moments later, I realized my magic had probably gotten rid of his scars along with the slave brand.

Conforming with local customs and seduced by the relaxing pace, we moved into a hot drying room adjacent to the baths and sat on wooden benches. I didn't try to engage Elwin in any conversation, and simply replied to his attempts with noncommittal grunts and half-thought-out replies.

Once dry, we donned our loaned robes and went back to our room, where we relieved Kidu of his watch. Elwin, volunteering to take up the arduous duty of having another bath, quickly poured himself a glass of water from a pitcher by the bed before returning to bathe with the wildman.

Sitting on the bed, I finally had a little time to get my ducks in a row. I had traveled so far, only to return to the place of my imprisonment, albeit as a free man. I needed to get out of this city, sooner rather than later, once we had acquired sufficient resources. There still remained a chance, no matter how slim, that someone might recognize me. Perhaps that would never come to pass; after all, I was probably presumed dead after the cave-in. Still, I wanted to leave this barbaric city and go somewhere relatively more civilized. But to do that, I needed more cold, hard cash.

My short-term goals clear to me now, I spent an indeterminable amount of time running over a few things I had learned: the names of the creatures I had encountered, the people I had met, my brush with death... until my thoughts were interrupted by a knock on the door.

"Sir, your laundry is done," piped a squeaky voice that had shifted from a lower octave in the manner of adolescents just into their change.

That was pretty fast service, suspiciously so, I thought as I got to my feet.

Opening the door, I stiffened at the sight in front of me. The owner of the voice was the boy from before, but for a moment I saw Jongshoi's face superimposed over his features. Reflexively, I began to reach for a weapon that was not there, before catching myself, and instead reached for the purse at my waist. Passing him a bronze coin, I collected our clean laundry. He accepted the money gratefully and took Kidu's dirty garments, which the hunter had left outside the door. The boy was constantly bowing through all of this until, annoyed, I finally closed the door in his face.

Just as I was about to return alone to my thoughts, I was again interrupted, this time by my pair of companions bursting into the room. It seemed that I had forgotten to lock the door.

"I see all our belongings are still here. Congratulations on being able to stay awake!" joked Elwin as he plopped down next to me on the large bed.

Kidu seemed a little more relaxed than usual, the bath having miraculously healed some of the shadows behind his eyes, a feat that even my divine magic could not accomplish. More significantly, he had hacked off his beard, and the difference was rather astonishing. His features remained untamed and rugged, but he looked less like a primal thing and more like a civilized man.

"Why did you decide to do away with your beard, Kidu?" I asked on a whim, hoping I had not committed a social *faux pas*.

"A man grown in the North cuts his beard after a time of great shame or loss. This is how it has always been. It was I who led the raiding party south, and so the fault is with me. This is a small thing to remind myself that I am an unbearded youth," replied Kidu, his voice unnaturally quiet. "But I feel a little better now after that cleansing. We, too, have hot springs in the North, where the tribe will gather in the coldest of winters. This was most welcome." He lay down and, within moments, began to snore.

I touched my own face in sympathetic reaction, noting that despite the amount of time I had spent in this world, there was no evidence of even a hint of stubble.

"The inn's serving in an hour. Wake us up a little before then," requested Elwin, yawning almost exaggeratedly and cutting off any further conversation. "So sleepy..."

It seemed I was to take this watch, so I began to devise plans for future experimentation. I still needed to try out a spell or two in controlled conditions, and for that, I would need test subjects. Dark whispers intruded upon my ruminations and a jarring irrational thought played across my mind: Was the boy from the bath spying on our group? I played with an equally irrational idea of experimenting on the boy, but thought better of using somebody too close to my place of lodging. Thankfully, I was in a city full of strangers I cared little for.

Chapter 40

PRACTICE MAKES PERFECT

Research into the necromantic arts, sped up by the twins called Need and Necessity, had opened dark channels into another plane of existence. Here, the sibilant denizens of the void promised a quick end to the war with something that was translated by the magical researchers as the "Seed of Oblivion." Grasping at a chance of total victory, the leader of the Republic accepted the dark bargain and brought the Seed fully into the world.

— On the Cataclysm by an unknown Quassian Scholar, circa 103 AC.

I opened the shutters, drinking in the sights of the city before me. A steady flow of people traveled along the streets—a mix of travelers, merchants, and the occasional military patrol. These patrols were heavily armored and mounted on half-barded and intimidating horses. I gritted my teeth as I saw a chained line of miserable-looking slaves, their eyes hollow and their postures stooped in suffering. I was glad that Kidu was asleep, as I was unsure of how he would react upon seeing such a sight. I would need to have words with the large man to prevent him from potentially causing a scene in the future.

I watched the people of the city go by as my mind went back to the old world. Years of constant study into the depths of the night had made caffeinated drinks my constant companions. I realized that I could kill for a simple cup of caramel soy latte, both figuratively and literally.

After judging that about an hour had passed, more by instinct than calculation, I shook my companions awake. We changed back into our clothes, leaving the borrowed robes outside the room door. Kidu and I collected our meals on a tray from the innkeeper, paying him the required coins, which he took brusquely.

The inn's repast was a red stew, which had a rich, inviting smell, served in a simple earthenware bowl. Globs of unknown meat and the occasional shape of what must have been some sort of vegetable were in it. On the left of the bowl was a simple side of what looked to be a brown rye bread. The stew had a tangy taste, sharp and piquant, with an edge of hot spice. This was, without doubt, one of the better meals I had sampled in this world.

The meal was filling, and my companions and I ate it with such great gusto that we almost had to stop ourselves from licking the bowls clean. Politeness was so ingrained into my very being that I offered to return the trays. Descending the stairs, I went to the counter, where Athinad was still busy cleaning some mugs, and left the empty trays there. He gave me a small nod. Turning back to return to my room, I noticed that the denizens of the inn were all very deep in their cups.

A flashing glint of steel caught my eye as it flew like an arrow before embedding itself in a target on the far wall. The blade quivered from the force of the throw, causing a few whoops of joy and cries of disappointment from a small crowd. It seemed that the locals were engaged in a knife-throwing competition. My curiosity was piqued, and my earlier promise to treat this town as enemy territory was quickly forgotten as I made my way towards the crowd applauding the throw.

"Hey, hold up there, mate," slurred a rat-faced man, blocking my path. "Can't you see this is our little corner of the Boar?"

"No problems, Devon," Athinad called out from the bar at the other end of the room.

"Jus' being welcoming, Atty boy," Devon shot back, annoyance lacing his words like an irritated fishwife before he glanced nervously at the shortsword at my hip.

"Not looking for trouble, Master Devon," I said with feigned nonchalance. "Just interested in the game that you're playing. Looks rather fun. Perhaps I could have a try."

The man I was addressing, Devon, had a mop of unkempt dull brown hair framing a face that perhaps only a mother could love. Narrow slanted eyes and pronounced front teeth added to his impression of an avaricious rodent.

"Fun, eh? You hear that, boys? Looks fun it is. And a 'Master Devon' to boot! This lad's got a good eye for persons of quality, he does! Feels like I'm at court! So, you fancy trying your hand against the best in Ansan, eh? Hope you got the coin and stones to back that up!"

"Well, I never said anything of the sort." I chuckled and held my hands up in agreement. "Also, that would be difficult, as I have never thrown a blade before. You could at least make it a fair game if you taught me the rules and the basics of how to throw one."

Seeing the potentially easy target, the men lurking behind Devon grinned like sharks before a feast of chum and laughed along with me.

Devon rubbed his chin as he looked me over. "Well, that won't do at all, will it, lads? Can't be letting it get said that Devon the Dirk is a dishonorable sort to be taking coins from unwitting lads like you, eh? Guess the ol' Dirk can teach you a thing or two on how to throw a blade. In return you could, you know, I expect a few coins for my time, being a 'Master' an' all." He looked at his crew behind him. "An' perhaps a drink for all the lads so they don't start getting too restless."

Looking at Athinad behind the bar, I gave him a nod, then counted a few bronze coins out from my small purse.

A few moments later, Athinad came round and served drinks of brown ale from utilitarian horn mugs, plonking them down gruffly. "Just to remind you boys, no trouble, you hear?"

"We hear you, all right," Devon replied, his eyes rolling at the repeated nagging. "Now, this here is the game we'll be playing once you can hit the fat bum of a passing laur. Hit the target over there, you take a swig. Miss the target and old biddy Taper over there goes up in a huff about us damaging the walls, and ye 'ave to drink two swigs. Like so," Devon said, taking a quaff from his mug and burping loudly, to the amusement of his companions. "Now, you'll be wanting to hold yer blade like this." He held up his blade for inspection before passing me a small, simple throwing knife.

It was a very unassuming weapon, with a thin steel blade that flared a little in the middle before tapering off to a sharp point. The handle was made from wood wrapped with rawhide, and it had a small bronze guard to stop the fingers from slipping accidentally onto the blade.

Attempting to follow my new instructor's example, I placed the end of the handle into the center of the palm of my left hand, with my middle finger closing the grip and my thumb on the side. My index finger rested along the spine of the weapon at the balance point of the knife.

He grunted before taking another gulp from his mug. "Not bad, not bad at all. You pick things up quick. Now the trick is"—he stood, taking a loose stance and raising the blade behind his head—"all in the timing of the release!" he said as he threw his knife.

Without spinning, the blade flew unerringly towards the wooden target on the wall, sinking a few centimeters into the wood.

He took a quick swig from his mug and gestured for me to have a try, as if he were a director introducing a new character to the stage. I nodded to him, taking a stance that approximately resembled his.

My Dexterity was reasonably high now, considering I had started with a mere eight points, so I felt that I would have a good chance at picking this up. Lifting the knife behind my head, I tried to copy my teacher's throw, but released a moment too early and missed the target by a small margin.

Devon clapped me on the back in commiseration, encouraging me to try a few times more, then explained in his slurred voice that being drunk was the key to good knife throwing. However, totally engrossed in my practice, I did not care to drink with the others or take part in any gambling.

I did, however, continue to order a few more rounds of drinks in exchange for further friendly instruction. Devon would shift my stance on occasion and give me pointers on how to "feel" for the timing of the blade. Soon I was hitting the target more often than not, and I was granted the notification I had long been waiting for.

You have gained 1 Dexterity.
You have learned Daggers Lv. 2.
You have learned Throwing Weapons Lv. 1.
You have learned Throwing Weapons Lv. 2.

It seemed that with proper instruction, I could gain skill levels much faster than by just messing about in the dark by myself. Daggers would be a useful proficiency to have in case I ever lost my main weapons, or if I had to engage in some up-close wet work in the future. As a bonus, I had gained a point of Dexterity for my trouble and a tiny amount of experience.

"Thank you, Master Devon," I replied with a small bow, which drew laughs from Devon's crew, but I could see that Devon's face was a little flushed with more than just alcohol. With the simple word of "master" I had appealed to his pride and won him over. "Where can one get such weapons as these?" I continued. "They have a fine balance and fly true."

His posture a little straighter, Devon smiled and replied, "Go down along this road outside to yer left a little way. You'll see the sign of the Soot-Stained Pig Iron Forge. Basically, look for a black pig if you don't know your letters. Tell ol' Cillis Aideh I sent ya. She'll give you a discount if you buy ten." He slurred the last sentence, clearly inebriated, and I knew he would not be able to give much further useful instruction.

Luckily, he had forgotten about our competition, for which I was grateful.

I thanked Devon again, and the seedy-looking men behind him raised a drunken toast in my name. Though it had cost me a few coins, I was happy with my newfound popularity. But I was even happier when I saw a new notification.

You have gained 1 Charisma.

Not bad, I thought to myself as I turned to the bar and cleared my tab with Taper before heading back up the creaking stairs to my room. Entering, I saw Kidu and Elwin attending to the maintenance of our gear. The hunter had even fashioned a strap for my helm. I didn't have the heart to tell him I was thinking of trading it in for something else at the earliest opportunity.

"That's it. My turn, now," Elwin said, rising from the floor like a hound that had just been let loose, then dashed for the door.

"Try and find a place to sell the..." I tried to remind him as he passed me.

"Yes, yes, Mother. And I'll try not to sink too deep into my cups, nor will I be losing my chastity tonight!"

Upon hearing this, Kidu just grunted as he continued to diligently polish his spear, grinding out traces of rust with a coarse stone.

Sitting down by the shutter, I decided to practice my magic.

Chapter 41

A SLIGHT MISHAP

The human drive for order is evident in our daily lives, from the schedules we keep to the way we organize our physical space. We create rules and regulations to govern our behavior and ensure a stable society.

However, the predictability of order can leave us feeling unfulfilled and stagnant. We crave the unexpected, the chance occurrence that brings excitement and novelty to our existence. Our attraction to coincidence and surprise is an essential aspect of the human experience.

Therefore, while we may strive for order and structure, we must also embrace the beauty of randomness. It is in the unexpected where we find new perspectives and opportunities for growth. In the delicate balance between order and chance, we discover the richness of life.

— *The Just Realm* by Gideon de Salavia, 368 AC.

The setting sun had cast its final rays, painting the sky with gentle hues of red and orange. The streets below were bustling with people eager to conclude their business and head home. Amidst the crowd, I spotted a merchant hurrying down the road, carrying several large packs.

He collided with a tall, sturdy woman, and both fell to the ground. The bags burst open and the goods spilled out like a wave. Street urchins, ever the opportunists, swooped in to loot what they could before disappearing into the throng. As the vultures made their escape, the merchant raised his fist, hurling a stream of invective at them while the woman tried to assist him in retrieving the remainder of his possessions.

Perfect, I thought, focusing on the unlucky merchant. I started to cast a spell, carefully enunciating the first syllables of the incantation. The words tasted vile, oily, and spoke of unspeakable things of the void. My human tongue struggled to articulate the otherworldly phrases.

As I finished the spell with a dark syllable, a group of gossamer-thin threads, black as midnight, flew from me towards the merchant. I had cast the spell, Drain. The dark threads attached to the merchant, and I felt a trickle of sinister, yet essential, energy enriching my very being, satiating a hunger I had never known existed. At a primal level, I realized that I was sapping the poor man's life force like a magical vampire.

Did the spell restore Health? I had to find out, so I quickly drew a shallow cut across my forearm. My skin at first seemed to resist the edge of the blade before I was able to inflict four points of self-harm.

The man was still arguing with the woman and cursing the world in general at his poor fortune—almost frothing at the mouth, really. I continued to watch him, and I felt a single point of Health be restored. The cut on my arm began to close, and I continued to wait as the spell drained the man's life force, gradually restoring my Health to its full level.

The man looked slightly less animated now, his anger beginning to lose its rough edge as the woman kept apologizing. He shivered, perhaps from the evening chill, and looked around for the source of his discomfort, ignoring the woman's constant apologies. I quickly ducked out of view, fearful that perhaps he had noticed my arcane meddling.

Shielded from view, I took a moment to take stock and noticed that my Mana had ticked back up a single point. Simple arithmetic and deduction dictated that this new spell cost two Mana points to cast, but could also restore Mana, as well as Health. My heart was beating like a war drum, so I breathed in, slow and steady, to calm myself. A second later, I reined in the dark threads of magic and ended the spell.

Kidu, done with tending to his weapon, was now engrossed in carving a wooden figurine of a small animal. Though it was still in its nascent stage,

I could see that, once finished, it was going to be a six-legged creature of some sort. So intense was his concentration that he must have been oblivious to my breakthroughs in the magical arts. That was perhaps for the best, as I doubted he would agree to what I planned to do next.

It was imperative that I test the full potential of the Drain spell, and to do so, I needed to deplete my Stamina. Rising from my seated position, I drew my short sword from its scabbard. Pretending to practice an imaginary sword form, I cut a few times at some imaginary opponents in front of me, watching my Stamina gauge deplete with each strike.

I even used a few power strikes. The increased speed the skill gave to my strikes made my blade draw flashes of steel in the air. Keeping an eye on the lower left of my vision, I noticed that if I used the skill in quick succession, the number of Stamina points used per power strike would increase. Although I had a prodigious amount of Stamina, it was something to keep in mind.

Feeling a little self-conscious and embarrassed about my made-up and amateurish display, I took a glance at the big man. He did not seem to have noticed anything, thankfully, and was busy chewing on a bit of jerky as he continued to release the creature from the wood.

With my preparations complete, I cast Drain on one of the unsuspecting passersby below. To my satisfaction, my Stamina began to replenish at an accelerated pace. The spell indeed had the power to restore Stamina in addition to Health and Mana.

Elation surged within me as I considered the possibilities. I was still quite young, but if this spell truly drained life energy from others and added it to my own, then the vampiric nature of the dark magic and the euphoria I felt suggested it could potentially extend my life. After all, who did not want to live forever? Yet, knowing the cruel and unjust nature of this world, it could be that the spell simply restored my Health, Stamina, and Mana.

I was suddenly met with a notice that shocked me.

You have slain a Human. 20 experience gained.

What in the blazes? What madness is this? My mind was in confusion, for I was sure that no one had perished by my hand. The game's workings were strange indeed, for twenty points of experience was a pittance for killing a human. However, experience points were still experience points.

As I pondered this sudden stroke of fortune, I fancied that I heard a faint, mocking laughter from the shadows, a sinister chorus of sibilant whispers that seemed to taunt me with their enigmatic meaning.

Kidu put down his knife and the figurine and turned to me. In a serious voice, he asked, "Are you finished with your practice?"

"I perceived you observed all of that?" I stumbled, my embarrassment leading my syntax astray. "You saw all of that?"

"Hard to miss you flailing about," he answered, repacking his belongings.

"No... not that sword kata. Yes, I mean sword form. I mean, like, could you tell I was using magic?"

"Your face. It is a good tell when you are concentrating. Seen it before, too, only twice, when you are waging war on stone and when you are doing your magic... thing." He shrugged his massive shoulders.

"Kidu, speaking of magic, do you know tales of people achieving eternity with it—"

With almost impeccable timing, Elwin burst into the room, interrupting our conversation. His cheeks held the rosy hue of too much wine, and a sly grin played upon his lips as he recounted his exploits. We listened as he wove a tale of charm and subterfuge.

According to the rogue, it was his honeyed words that had won over the skeptical locals and led them to reveal the location of a fence who would buy our appropriated goods at a discounted price.

As he finished his story, Elwin removed his leather boots and made his way towards the bed. But before he could climb beneath the covers, he spun around with a flourish and slipped a small, ragged bundle into my waiting arms.

"I remember… the promise I made to tell you what I knew about the arts. The Control." He burped unceremoniously, and even at a distance I could smell the reek of cheap alcohol. "Got this on the cheap… Damaged goods… But a… Like za hat would be too much…" he finished, before falling into bed and snoring almost instantly.

Upon closer examination, the bundle revealed itself to be a damaged book, devoid of a cover and bound together haphazardly. Holding it gingerly, I could see that it was missing many pages, and the ink had bled, rendering parts of it illegible. A book, at last. True, it was flawed, but it contained precious knowledge nonetheless.

The first page revealed itself to be inscribed in the local dialect. Fortunately, it was penned in "simplified" Trade, meaning I would not need to expend much energy to comprehend its meaning.

Delicately going over the old tome, I was extra careful with my fingers when touching the brittle sections of parchment. Hungrily, I pored through the text, using Identify to reveal the meaning of the parts that eluded or frustrated me. Through magical means, deduction, and inference, I began to establish an idea of the damaged tome's essence. It was a primer of sorts, for initiates in the study of magic and Mana.

Eager for fresh knowledge, I locked the room's door and settled into my usual position. Holding the book in my hands as if it were a precious relic, I continued going over the text under the light of a dying candle. Eventually, the candle's light faded, and I was left in the darkness.

No lanterns adorned the darkened street, and the moon was obscured behind a veil of clouds. The only illumination was that which slipped out from the shutters and doors of the homes and shops that stubbornly refused to call it a day.

The city, even at this hour, was still filled with noise as people went about their business. If I listened closely, I could even hear the occasional crack of a whip in the distance, followed by a scream of pain. I shuddered, then shifted a little on my chair and looked out into the evening, trying to enjoy a moment to myself as night fell and my watch began.

Chapter 42

HONEST CITY LIFE

It is wiser to traverse the journey in solitude than to accompany a fool.

— Quassian aphorism.

While keeping myself revitalized with the Drain spell, I had borne the watch for most of the night. It was only in the very early hours of the morning that Kidu relieved me of my duties to allow me some sleep. Throughout the night, the repeated use of the Drain spell had allowed me to keep my Mana almost full. Moreover, my unwavering focus had elevated the spell's level and augmented my Intelligence by a single point. Fortunately, no one broke into our room during the night to steal our belongings, a much-needed triumph.

Most of the night was spent in contemplation of the book's contents, particularly the enigmatic diagrams that tantalized my imagination with their intricate designs. I recalled that the Identify scroll I had absorbed contained comparable patterns in certain areas. The pages were adorned with mathematical equations in a paradigm I struggled to comprehend, and much of the text was marred by damage.

Despite this, I was able to glean a rough overview of the workings of magic in this realm. It seemed that the manipulation of Mana could influence the fabric of reality, though the level of difficulty was determined by the magnitude of change required. From the incomplete manuscript, I deduced that the casting of powerful or intricate spells necessitated a greater expenditure of Mana to bridge the chasm between the caster's "intent" and the present reality.

Indeed, a fireball would have a more discernible impact on reality than a mere spark. Similarly, conjuring a blade of water in a parched desert would prove far more arduous than in a damp, marshy environment. This incongruity led me to question why my own magical abilities always had the same Mana, fluctuating solely in correspondence to the spell's level and potency.

Filled with stolen energy and lost in the contemplation of these musings, I was far too excited to find sleep. I lay there on the bed awake and staring up at an unfamiliar ceiling, simply thinking, before rousing Elwin from his slumber a few hours later.

The man slowly got up, still bleary-eyed from his rest. Despite his grumbling, I expressed my sincerest gratitude for his gift, an act he dismissively shrugged off. As it was still early, we opted to forgo the customary morning meal and instead dined on our travel provisions of tough dried laur meat. As I gnawed on the leathery jerky, memories flooded my mind of the time when the very same creature had attempted to devour me. *Survival of the strong,* I thought, washing the meat down with some water that had long since grown stale.

Our meal complete, we decided upon a plan for the rest of the day. Elwin would take care of selling the smaller, "higher-end" bits and pieces we had acquired from the charcoal-burners, while Kidu and I would sell the rest of the larger, less valuable equipment and search for work or other means of earning coin. It had also been decided that we would make a stop at a blacksmith or armorer to purchase some new gear.

Kidu had expressed the need for a decent bow, while I desired a better helmet. Although my current helmet had proven its worth time and time again, aesthetics were still important to me. After all, though a helmet was one of the most vital pieces of protection, that did not mean it had to look ugly. I now understood why the ancients had paid so much attention to the decoration of their armor.

Would my attributes and skills affect what equipment I could wear? I knew almost for a fact that they affected what skills I could acquire. These thoughts in mind, it was a good a time as any to check my character sheet.

STATUS

> **Calling:** Gilgamesh Lv. 10 Paladin of Avaria / Reaver
> **Strength:** 24
> **Dexterity:** 19
> **Constitution:** 34
> **Intelligence:** 19
> **Wisdom:** 17
> **Charisma:** 11
> **Luck:** 16

SKILLS AND PROFICIENCIES

> Pain Nullification Lv. 2
> Power Strike Lv. 2: 10
> Endure Lv. 3
> Stealth Lv. 1
> Rest Lv. 3
> Backstab Lv. 2
> Dodge Lv. 3
> Polearms Lv. 2
> Dual Wield Lv. 2
> Critical-Hit Mastery Lv. 2
> Mining Lv. 2
> Unarmed Combat Lv. 3
> Hammers Lv. 2
> Flails Lv. 1
> Maces Lv. 1

Shields Lv. 1

Medium Armor Lv. 1

Heavy Armor Lv. 1

Axes Lv. 1

Daggers Lv. 2

Throwing Weapons Lv. 2

SPELLS AND MAGIC

Heal Lv. 5: 5

Rust Lv. 3: 1–2

Identify Lv. 2: 1

Silent Casting Lv. 1

Mana Regeneration Lv. 2

Purify Lv. 2: 3

Greater Heal Lv. 1: 10

Holy Aura Lv. 1: 2

Decay Lv. 1: 1

Drain Lv. 2: 2

Entropic Aura Lv. 2: 2

GIFTS

Curse of Entropy: -20% to all starting attributes.

Mark of the Paladin: 10% resistance to Dark/Holy magic. 5% resistance to Physical.

Touch of the Void: 10% reduced resistance to Holy/Fire magic, 20% resistance to Mental Effects, 15% immunity to Mental Effects.

Experience to Lv. 11: 2447/2583

Health: 230/230

Stamina: 53/55

Mana: 12/13

I could not help but feel a sense of accomplishment as we left the room. Practicing my magical skills had boosted my mental faculties, as well as gained me some nominal experience. Learning how to throw daggers, too, had added to that total.

I climbed down the creaky stairs and went to the bar to clear our drinks tab from the previous evening with Athinad. It appeared that Elwin had been a bit too liberal with our expenses, but I deemed it necessary to view it as a business investment, for if we could find a buyer for our trinkets, the cost would prove worthwhile. Such was the price of civilization. Knowledge and information were paid for in coin or favor, and in that moment, I was not in the mood for the latter.

We emerged from the inn, then strode along the main thoroughfare for a spell. The flow of wagons and beasts was still sparse at this early hour of the morning. A curious creature, resembling a larger and gentler incarnation of the tree-laur I had chanced upon in the woods, crossed our path. Its six squat limbs hauled a diminutive wooden cart freighted with wares.

I debated casting Identify on the creature, but decided it was simply better to ask my companions first.

"Keep forgetting you don't know much about anything," remarked Elwin unhelpfully. "It's a—"

"Plains-laur," Kidu finished for him, drawing a shrug from the rogue as he continued on like a farmer plowing a field. "They make for good eating."

Elwin rolled his eyes. "Plains-laur, a bit more expensive than horses and definitely more temperamental. They got a lot more Stamina, if not quite the speed of a good horse. Can't say I care much for them—except, as my large and learned friend has mentioned, they make for good eating." He made sure to enunciate the last part carefully.

Kidu just grunted at this, then dodged a middle-aged man carrying a wicker basket over his shoulders. I grinned at the pair's trifling banter, my thoughts fixated on the potential experience points the creature would yield, rather than its epicurean value or merit as a mount.

We had reached a corner of the road dominated by a large yurt-like building when Elwin suddenly declared with a cheerful smile, "Well, gentlemen, this is where we'll be needing to part ways a while. I'll see what I can do about selling these old bits 'n' bobs with a local fence and get a little lay of the land. You two have fun selling our other junk for what you can, then let's meet back before sundown at the Twisted Boar."

"Fortune favors you, Elwin Tucker," Kidu rumbled, holding the rogue's eyes for a moment, causing Elwin to run one of his hands through what remained of his hair.

The wiry man walked off into the crowd, turning around one last time before throwing us a wave. There was no doubt that Elwin was still a bit of a mystery to me. He had proven dependable enough so far, a reliable blade to be called upon when needed. Yet, I could not help but feel a nagging sense of doubt about his motivations. The man had clearly lied about his backstory before.

Continuing down the road, which was beginning to fill up with more traffic, Kidu and I passed a stooped old man, who looked to be some sort of tinkerer, setting up his simple iron goods on a tarp along the side of the thoroughfare. Kidu and I approached him. The looming presence of my companion cast a large shadow across his humble wares.

"Oh, hello there, sir!" said the startled trader, almost jumping at the sight of the large man as he finished setting up a display. "Wh-What can I do for you today?"

I bent down before his display, touching some pots and pans—as if feigning interest in the quality of his wares—before getting down to business. "Good sir. A fine set of products, you have. And it so happens that we possess certain goods of similar quality that may be of interest to you." My tone conveyed both courtesy and purpose.

Meanwhile, Kidu, comprehending my unspoken instruction, began to unpack our array of mining tools—the trusty picks and shovels that had served us so well. It was time to see if I could pass an extortion roll.

"We have a few things you might be interested in. Of course, being an honest and healthy merchant, you will give us a fair price for these, won't you?" I had little patience to dicker over the price; the hunter's massive presence alone ensured we would be treated fairly.

The tinkerer proved to possess more backbone and mercantile savvy than I had initially assumed. His voice was unwavering as he offered his assessment. "These tools appear to be of inferior quality, lacking in any identifiable maker's mark, with considerable wear and tear. That pick in particular"—he pointed at the one I had wielded in the mines—"has seen better days. I can only offer you five bronze for the entire lot." He stared me down with steely eyes.

It could have been my lack of Charisma, or perhaps his shrewd instincts as a natural-born trader, but the man was well aware I lacked the fortitude to drive a hard bargain. In the end, it would be my loss. I really needed to work on my delivery.

"Add another five copper to the sum and we shall consider it a fair exchange," I relented.

The tinkerer's face split into an avaricious grin. "Agreed," he said calmly.

Whilst engaged in the trade with the tinkerer, I couldn't help but overhear a hushed conversation between two women as they walked by.

"Did you hear about Marda? She lost her child last night, just walking down this very street. The midwife says she may never be able to bear children again!" one of the women whispered a little too loudly, as if sharing a delicious secret with the world.

"I heard the same thing," her friend replied. "Poor Marda believes it was a curse of witchcraft, cast upon her as she passed by that accursed inn, the Curled Boar or something. Some say they, too, felt something sinister. Even old Gus was assailed by the demons of the night. It's enough to warrant the attention of an Honored One. Who knows? It could be foul magic or the handiwork of foreign spies!" Her nervous giggle faded as they gradually receded from earshot.

A pang of guilt assailed me for a microsecond, but I quickly redirected my attention to the tinkerer. He reached into a light blue knapsack that was slung over his shoulder, deftly counted out the coins, then deposited them into my waiting palm. I bade the trader farewell, inclining my body slightly in the customary local bow, while Kidu offered him nothing more than a resentful look as we continued on our way. I handed Kidu his share, which consisted of one bronze and eight copper pieces. He tried to refuse, but I insisted, reminding him of his duty to bring wealth back to his clan. Even if I had been "cheated," I would not do so with my own companions.

Chapter 43

THE SOOT-STAINED PIG

It is a fact that true malevolence weaves its way through the delicate balance of intentions both virtuous and vicious. Let us not deceive ourselves, for it is essential to acknowledge that such wrongdoing is unequivocally wrong.

> — *The Just Realm* by Gideon de Salavia, 368 AC.

Soon enough, we were able to find our way to the Soot-Stained Pig. It was a medium-sized building, two stories tall, constructed from large blocks of locally quarried white alabaster stone. A cast-iron sign hung over the entrance, depicting a large black pig and an anvil in the background. The unoiled hinges squeaked in the breeze. The sounds of the forge could be heard coming from within, rising above the general hubbub of the city.

As we entered the shop, the clanging of metal on metal filled our ears, drowning out the sound of the heavy wooden doors that closed behind us. The air was thick with the heat of the forge, and we could already feel the sweat beginning to bead on our foreheads.

Our eyes were immediately drawn to the woman at the anvil, her full figure commanding our male attention as she rhythmically hammered away at a bar of red-hot steel. Her brow was furrowed in fierce concentration, and her hair, pulled back into a simple ponytail, was slick with sweat.

Tilted coal-black eyes peered out from an oval face at the work in front of her. We stood there, unnoticed, as she deftly picked up the piece of steel with her tongs and quenched it in a liquid that glistened like oil.

As we were in the presence of a master at her craft, Kidu and I held our tongues in respectful silence, and I took the opportunity to observe our surroundings. Weapon racks lined the walls, filled with an array of vicious battlefield implements. In glass cases, delicate and ornate items, encrusted with jewels and other precious stones, were on display.

The establishment boasted a varied collection of arms and armor, from the simplest of bronze daggers to a masterfully crafted, fully articulated set of plate armor. The armor was a true marvel, a work of art that appeared as if it had been sculpted out of flowing steel.

After finishing her task, she set down the tongs and placed her gloved hands on her generous hips. Looking Kidu up and down, she greeted us with a smile on her lips. A single delicate eyebrow arched itself as she asked in an alto voice, whose timbre resonated with the heat of the forge, "Do you see something you like?"

As I lifted off my helmet, I stumbled over my own tongue, struggling to find the words. "The Dirk... I mean, Devon, vouched for this establishment and suggested we seek out an Aideh Cillis... I mean, a certain, certain Cillis Aideh for a fair price. Our aim is to barter a few items, yet primarily to purchase."

The woman's amusement was clear as she surveyed us, laughter sparkling in her eyes. "Cillis Aideh, at your service. That wily old scoundrel still breathes, I see. I fear his fondness for liquor and games of chance will lead him across the Shallow River one day, but I can't fault him for bringing me trade. So, what can I do for you?" she inquired, her tone becoming all business.

"I was wondering if I could trade this in for perhaps a new one of iron or steel?" I held out my helm.

"Open or closed?"

"I b-beg your pardon?" I stuttered, at a loss for words and not completely understanding the context.

"Helm," she said, rolling her eyes and tapping her head.

A blush crept across my cheeks. "What would you recommend for my companion and me?"

I looked to Kidu, whose gaze was still roaming over the items on display.

"Hmm." She paused, crossing her arms in thought. "Closed be a bit harder to breathe in, can't see as well either. But I'd still recommend one if you're going to be getting into lots of scraps. A visored helm would probably give you best of both worlds, but that'll cost you a pretty penny, and they can be a devil to maintain in the field."

"To be honest, madam—"

"No need for a madam. I'm not that old yet," she interjected, a slight edge to her voice.

"Well, yes, Miss Aideh, we have a budget of about four gold between us," I said simply, hoping Elwin could procure more money for us from the sale of our other loot. "We both need to be fully equipped, and we can trade these."

I spread out the laur hide, two spare zajasite stones, two pairs of echo-stalker weapon claws from the drones, and my echo-stalker scythe daggers. I also placed, albeit hesitantly, my simple length of iron chain on the counter of the shop.

Cillis surveyed our wares, her delicate lips pursed in contemplation as she caressed the scythe daggers. "A rare find, these echo-stalker claws. Exotic. There must be a demand for them somewhere, but I'm not sure where to begin. I can offer four silver for the smaller ones and six for each of these daggers if you're willing to take store credit. Three and five if you need the coin now," she mused, slipping off one of her gloves and tracing her fingers sensually over the animal hide.

"This laur hide is a beauty—a tree-laur, if I'm not mistaken. My husband, Khisam, could fashion something splendid with it. I'll throw in another silver for it. As for the zajasite stones, they're of low quality, so I can offer five copper each, and three for the chain as scrap. Just because the big chunk of muscles here is easy on the eyes." She wiped her face with the back of her hand, which left a trail of lingering black.

I could not help but notice the playful way she looked at Kidu.

Following the smith's advice, I bought a second-hand visored steel sallet with a sturdy bevor, as well as the heaviest leather and steel brigandine they had that could be easily fitted. Black canvas was riveted onto the plates of the brigandine, which also came with a cloth gambeson that had butted mail attached and sewn across the arms. For leg armor, I chose simple iron greaves with chainmail leggings. I would have to keep my leather gloves for the time being, as I simply did not have the budget for new gauntlets. Also, a further loss of dexterous motion might prove fatal in a future conflict.

I tried to persuade the smith to craft a flail out of the chains I had placed on the table, but she found the whole notion absurd. Instead, still perplexed by my choice of weapon, she proffered me a reasonably priced spiked iron flail that exuded a menacing aura, and she paired it with a basic kite shield that I could easily sling over my shoulder.

The pommel of the weapon bore a sharp spike, while at the juncture where the chain met the handle, mean flanges of iron construction were affixed, enabling the weapon to also function as a simple mace. The ball of the flail was forged of heavy metal, had five small spikes on its rough surface, and was attached to the handle of the weapon by a short, heavy chain. The weapon was called a *tsengelt-tum*, and the smith promised to teach me the basics of its use later for another two bronze.

I also decided to buy an old leather sword belt that sported a bronze buckle, as well as hooks for suspending weapons and gear. In addition, I procured a set of three well-balanced throwing knives. As a final thought, I exchanged my looted short sword for a parrying dagger. The dagger was marked down due to it being one of her apprentice's initial works, and its quality was uncertain. However, it was an eye-catching piece.

The weapon bore a striking resemblance to a fifteenth-century blade, with recurved bronze quillons that angled slightly upwards towards the blade. A groove at the base of one side of the blade permitted the thumb to obtain a firmer grip, while a shallow fuller ran across half its short length. The blade itself seemed to emulate a lethal serpent in motion. Upon observing my inquisitive expression, Cillis divulged that the ripples in the blade were designed to weaken the impact of a strike against the weapon and slow down an adversary's blade.

Now that we were properly equipped, Cillis faced the stairs and bellowed, "Khisam! I need your help with some fittings!"

A slender man descended the stairs, stumbling over his own feet as he struggled to carry various items.

Khisam was a shrew of a man, and I found myself perplexed by his match with Cillis. Despite his relative youth, he had begun to bald well before his time. His furtive nature, slightly hunched back, and large bespectacled eyes only added to his shrew-like countenance. He followed his wife's orders almost without question and with mechanical efficiency, his hands a whirlwind of activity as he fit my gear to me, occasionally informing his wife of my measurements.

The raven-haired woman took her time teaching me how to properly equip my arms and armor, as well as how to maintain them. Her hands lingered a little too long in places, doing so in front of her husband, as if she enjoyed the thrill. She also—with much amusement at my expense—showed me how I could relieve myself while fully armored. I was relieved to discover that my gear, though weighty, was not as unwieldy as depictions in contemporary media had led me to believe. Adorned in thick layers of leather and sturdy metal, I felt considerably more secure.

Kidu, after much consideration, settled on a scale mail cuirass and chainmail protection for his arms and legs. He was adamant about not wearing a closed helm, citing the importance of his senses in combat. However, after some persuasion, he agreed to don a chainmail coif.

Instead of a shield, he opted for a thick steel gauntlet, complete with articulated fingers and metal plates covering his arms. Cillis referred to it as a "shield-gauntlet," and it brought to mind the fierce Murmillos of Ancient Rome. For his weapon, with great reluctance, he exchanged his old one for a steel boar spear, with small iron lugs that sprouted underneath a long leaf-shaped blade that ended in a sharp tip.

It would take some time for Khisam to make the necessary adjustments for Kidu's large size, so Cillis invited me to the back of her smithy, where I found a small open area surrounded by a fence.

Approaching a straw training dummy, she turned around to give me a dazzling smile. "Now, I would be a poor smith indeed if I didn't understand how to use the tools that I make. Make no mistake, boy, these are tools and nothing more. The flail is a difficult weapon to master, and lacks a little power because you can't put your full weight behind it. But it's a tricky thing, the flail, capable of wrapping around someone's guard or letting you attack from a different angle. Now, remember that when you hit a solid target, you'll need to follow through..."

I didn't know whether it was my single point of proficiency in flails, my higher Dexterity, or the combined experience from all of my fights until now, but Cillis's instruction came easily to me. She pointed out flaws in my stance with a whisper close to my ear, warning me to always keep my shield up and not rely on my weapon for defense as one would with a sword.

After what felt like hours of training, the world finally informed me that I had gained in skill.

You have learned Flails Lv. 2.

I was a little disappointed I hadn't had an increase in attribute points, but was still pleased that I had made some martial progress. Though nowhere near a hardened warrior of legend, I felt I had at least begun to take the first tentative steps on that path.

Emboldened by my recent achievement, I turned to the attractive raven-haired smith with a playful grin.

"You know, you are very pretty," I started lamely. "So, you and Khisam, how come you two…"

She silenced me with a finger to my lips. "I'd prefer the big man, but you'll do. This will be just a little secret between us. Come."

Like a sacrifice, she led me by the hand to a tool shed in the corner of the yard. *Is this a trap, some ploy, or scheme?* I wondered, before the raw power of the moment pulled me from my thoughts.

Her fingers traced the line of my face, gentle and delicate like a butterfly's touch, as her lips drew closer to mine. I could feel my heart racing in my chest.

"You are very young, aren't you," she said, a devilish smile playing on her full red lips. Her eyes bore into mine, lined with mischief and seduction.

She kissed me aggressively, her tongue forcing its way into my mouth as I reeled in shock. Her grip was surprisingly fierce, pulling me closer. The smith's eyes bored into mine as she pulled slightly away.

"If you promise me one thing… I might be willing to teach you something else…" Her voice was low and enticing as she pushed me back against the rough wooden wall of the shed.

My mind went blank as I hung on her every word, completely under her spell. But even in the heat of my lust, a dark part of me wanted to wrap my hands around her delicate neck and extinguish her life. How easy it would be to gain some quick experience. How sweet and satisfying it would be…

But suddenly, a call shattered the moment, coming from outside the shed. "Cillis!" cried Khisam in his shrill, whiny voice.

"Yes, dear!" Cillis answered hastily, leaving me behind and abandoning me to my unsatisfied desire.

For long moments, frustration welled up inside of me. Drinking deeply of the stale and musty air of the shed, it took all I had to force cold clarity to return. As much as I wanted her, I could not deny that it was probably for the best. Yet still, I damned Khisam for interrupting us.

Humiliated—no, emasculated—was what I felt as I joined the others back in the shop.

Kidu's gear, now adjusted to his size, stood out in stark contrast to his rugged form. Studiously avoiding Cillis's gaze, I paid her for her time, training, and goods in a weak voice tinged with guilt. I could barely meet her eyes as I promised to return if we needed any more purchases in the future.

As if offering a parting gift, Cillis even recommended a stall in the market to acquire archery gear for the hunter—all the while acting as if nothing had happened between us.

With our business concluded, we left the shop quickly, driven by my yearning to be anywhere but in the Soot-Stained Pig. After all, we still had chores to finish before the day was done.

But even as I wallowed in my embarrassment, I couldn't help feeling that in this world, I could experience the full range of human sensations. Hopefully, pleasure would be included among them.

Chapter 44

A MEASURE OF VENGEANCE

Elven mages felt the horror of the void for the first time as it touched their minds. Many of their number went mad and unleashed the sum total of their magical energies. Those who kept their sanity failed to shield the rest of their brothers and sisters, their own defenses overwhelmed with the outpouring of wild entropic magic that ate away everything it touched.

— On the Cataclysm by an unknown Quassian Scholar, circa 103 AC.

My heart continued to thump wildly in my chest, and my body felt uncomfortably warm. Gasping for air, I lifted my helm from my head and secured it to my belt, hastening my stride to match Kidu's. Though my thoughts repeatedly strayed to the shapely contours of Cillis's form, I forcefully banished her from my mind and calculated our remaining funds.

Our acquisitions and trade dealings had left us with five and a half silver coins of various denominations. This was a sum that was, according to the couple, more than sufficient to acquire a decently crafted bow and a modest number of arrows from a recommended bowyer in the market. To help save some money, Kidu even told me he could make his own arrows, provided he had the tools and materials.

It was around lunchtime by the time we made it to one of the markets near the central Ark, which loomed even more as we moved closer. The scale of the beached ship simply blew away the mind; its sleek lines and sheer size defied engineering for a culture at this level of technology. Such a creation could only have been achieved through magical means.

The market square was much as I remembered it, busy with the sound of trade conducted by scores of merchants from all across the Grieving Lands. All sorts of goods were being sold here, from mundane kitchenware to purported magical artifacts and relics of mysterious power.

At the other end of the market, there stood a structure that I surmised to be a temple, chiseled from the indigenous white alabaster rock. A golden dome, towering towards the heavens, competed with the Ark for supremacy in the city's skyline. Minarets, like sculpted stone sentinels, were situated at each of its corners.

Positioned at its entrance were two guards adorned in shining suits of heavy plate armor and wielding towering bladed polearms. Devotees of the faith walked between them into the inner sanctum, bowing in veneration as they crossed the threshold. The deity or deities worshiped inside would, however, remain a mystery to us, as we had more pressing concerns to attend to.

Our stomachs rumbled, and Kidu and I were then focused on one thing alone. The alluring scents of barbecued meat and exotic spices drifted through the air, tempting us with their delectable aroma. Scanning our surroundings, we eventually pinpointed the origin of these smells.

On a hot, sizzling griddle, a hunched-over man of indeterminate age was cooking thick pieces of meat on a stick, basting them on occasion with a honey-colored glaze. Kidu and I ordered one each in exchange for a few coppers, and we bit down on our meals in excitement. The hot and spicy taste was rounded out with a unique grassy finish. Kidu, unaccustomed to such flavors, found himself in the midst of a gastronomic epiphany, his eyes almost glazed over in bliss, much to the amusement of the seller. We quickly placed another order.

As we indulged in our meals, two merchants across from us were caught up in a lively discussion regarding an upcoming event, "The Festival of the

Undrawn," which was to be held in a far-off city whose name escaped me. I listened as their words ebbed and flowed, the topic piquing my curiosity. Yet, for now, I remained content to bask in the flavors of the moment.

Once our considerable appetites were sated, we rinsed our hands in the lemon-scented bowls of water kindly provided by the cook. I adjusted the shield strapped to my back, feeling that I was finally being rewarded for all my suffering. This was the fantasy I had always yearned for! The sight and sounds from this exotic and alien world captured my senses, and I was glad to be present in the moment without the distraction of a connected device. In my previous life, I would have feverishly recorded the meal on whatever gadget was currently in vogue, instead of living and savoring the memories and experiences. Such thoughts, however, were nothing but an elegiac lament for a way of life now lost.

No, that was merely a polite deception. I did not harbor much sorrow for the world I had left behind, for I had traded trivial pleasures for the opportunity to pursue power. This trial had given me a precious gift: a chance to forge a new identity and become someone of worth. Here, I could find purpose.

My mind returned to the present, recalling our primary purpose for visiting the market. Following Cillis's instructions, we soon found the bowyer displaying his wares on a wooden stall. The bows on exhibit ranged in length and type, from one-piece longbows to composite recurve short bows made of exotic-looking horn material, wood, and metal. Each was securely fastened to the stall with a length of small steel chain.

In one corner, an ornate crossbow drew my eye. Its sleek lines and steel wings emanated raw threat and deadly purpose. I knew from my studies that training an effective archer could take many years, but a crossbowman could be trained in just a few weeks. My mouth was almost salivating at the thought, and I knew I simply must have one like it someday.

Behind the wooden stall, sheaves of arrows and bolts lay in wooden barrels arranged in a neat row, with their prices written in the local script.

Noticing my interest, the man behind the stall rubbed his hands together and came closer.

I greeted the bowyer, who looked no more than thirty, except for the lines around his eyes and the hollowness of his cheeks. He was a dark-haired man of above-average height, but he looked positively small standing next to the blue-eyed giant that was Kidu. His hooded, calculating brown eyes met mine as he returned my greeting.

"Hello there, the name's Ashan. I am a humble bowyer of Ansan City, selling the finest bows in all of the Grieving Lands," he said, his lines coming off as rote despite his friendly tone.

"Looking for a bow," Kidu rumbled in his deep voice, looking down at the man.

"Yes," I added. "Cillis, the smith of the Soot-Stained Pig, recommended you to us, Ashan. What can we get for three silver for my friend here? And, out of curiosity, how much is that crossbow going for?"

"Ah, you have a fine eye, good sirs! And a friend of Cillis is a friend of mine. That is a weapon from the faraway island of Quas, all the rage these days with the nobility, they say. A fine specimen like this one? For you, a special price, just a single gold piece!" The merchant smiled and rubbed his hands together. "As for a more modest choice for this large gentleman, I would recommend this excellent weapon here," he answered, gesturing with exaggerated motions to a single-piece unstrung longbow almost two meters in length.

"This is what I require," said the giant simply to the merchant, looking him steadily in the eye.

"We'll take it if you can throw in the string for the bow and a discount on some arrows," I said quickly, not really wanting to bargain and eager to conclude our business.

"Very good, sir," Ashan said obsequiously, pathologically rubbing his hands. "That will be three silver for the bow, and half a silver for some hunting arrows and a spider-silk string from the Sainba. Consider the quiver a gift for a first-time customer."

I paid the merchant his money. Kidu held his new bow, unstrung, like a staff as we walked. It was clear that our funds were dwindling, and as we strolled along the outskirts of the busy marketplace, the thought gnawed at me like a hungry animal. Putting all our trust in Elwin's assurance of finding a fence would be unwise. I couldn't help but wonder if there was a quick way to earn some much-needed coin.

I stopped in my tracks for a moment as the scene before me became suddenly familiar. I had witnessed this very street from a wholly different vantage point while I was imprisoned in the cold confines of a cell. A wave of anger threatened to overwhelm me, for we were near the jail where I had been incarcerated when I first came to the city of Ansan.

The guards at the entrance were lazily leaning on their spears, indifferent to the bustling traffic passing by. Their faces were vaguely familiar, but distinguishing one local from another proved challenging. We walked past them, and I pulled my hood further down, hoping to avoid recognition.

However, a small part of me longed for them to recognize us, yearned for a quick and violent confrontation. As compensation for their failure to recognize me, I made a point to etch their faces into my memory and vowed to return one day. The temptation to incinerate them in their metal armor almost overwhelmed me. I forced the impulse down until my anger grew cold and calculating.

The gods or fate, however, would soon deliver unto me a welcome present. A lightly armored man was retching into the mud in an alley between two wooden buildings, just opposite the jail. I smiled at Kidu, a knowing grin tinged with a hint of madness. The wild man looked at me quizzically, but followed me nonetheless as I stalked towards my prey.

Softly whistling a forgotten tune, I cast Identify at the poor man struggling with the contents of his stomach. My confidence grew with each stride as I closed the distance.

Bataar Jargal - City Guard Recruit (Human Lv. 7)
Health: 62/71
Stamina: 18/25
Mana: 7/7

My eyes quickly assessed the man's weakness and vulnerability as I placed a comforting hand on his shoulder, feigning friendliness. Murmuring his name in a concerned tone, I drew my newly acquired dagger with a swift and fluid motion, slicing his throat. Blood and vomit mixed as he gurgled his last breath, and I propped him up against a building, his mouth frozen in a silent scream with crimson liquid flowing down his front. My deception was seamless, and to any casual observer at a distance, I was simply a concerned friend.

A few moments passed as I watched the light slowly fade from his eyes. I saw fear there—fear of the end—and a part of me resonated with that emptiness. A breath later, I received a notification of the man's death, accompanied by a paltry twenty experience points. I tsk-tsked to myself as I rifled through his purse, which contained only a handful of copper coins. Truly pathetic, in every sense of the word. For a fleeting moment, I pondered whether the reward for experience points was proportional to the difficulty of the kill.

Whatever it took, I was determined to avoid meeting a similar end. Death, with its dark oblivion, terrified me. The voices within concurred, pleased with my conclusion.

My heart pounded in my chest for what felt like an eternity as we made our way down a few streets. Suddenly, Kidu's eyes hardened, and his mouth formed a grim line. He spoke rare words to me, his hunger evident in his gaze. "That was a well-struck blow in the name of vengeance."

A guffaw escaped me, grateful as I was to be spared a sermon on the inviolability of mortal existence. "I vow that the next one shall be yours," I offered, to which Kidu responded with a resonant earthy chortle. It seemed as though a shadow had been lifted from him, a darkness I had not perceived until that moment when his smile broke through, sincere and unfeigned. At long last, he was unshackled from the chains of impotence that had bound him.

Chapter 45

THE SANDS ONCE MORE

Every strike must be filled with the deadly intent of damaging your opponent. Your attacks your defense, your defense your attacks. You must be the discord in your opponent's sword song.
— *The Living Sword* by Fen Vaigorus, circa 520 AC.

We flowed with the tide of the cloth city, distancing ourselves from the scene of the crime, my mind understanding what I had just done and my steps growing lighter. My senses soon picked up on another rumbling as my eyes landed upon a large gathering of people, the sounds and howls of combat familiar to my ear. Kidu and I made our way towards the origin of the sound.

A crowd surrounded a large primitive fighting pit dug into the ground with crude wooden walls around its perimeter. Its floor was lined with coarse sand the color of bleached bone, with rough benches and boxes to hold the spectators. The fervor of the crowd swelled like a living, breathing beast, its very pulse stirring the air with a palpable ferocity. The place was bereft of the scale and thin veneer of civilization, as well as the pomp of the place where I had made my first kill. This sordid arena was just a place to satiate man's bestial base desires.

Two men, clad in archaic-looking armor and weapons resembling the Greek hoplites of antiquity, were fighting to the raucous cheers of the crowd. Money was constantly changing hands as people looked to make their fortune on the next clash of steel.

I asked Kidu to clear us a way to the edge of the pit so that we might observe the fight more closely. His bulk parted the crowd like a leviathan of the deep cutting through a school of lesser fish, and I followed closely in his wake until we reached a good vantage point.

A man with a spear and shield was facing off against a man equipped with two straight swords of differing lengths. They seemed evenly matched in terms of speed and skill, but the sword wielder appeared to be tiring. The spearman was willing to accept the brunt of his attacks, keeping his distance and baiting the swordsman with his spear's longer reach.

The two fighters disengaged from each other, and I took that moment to quickly cast Identify on both. The magic came to me easily, but for the first time more slowly, as if the energy were flowing through a resistor. I surmised that my slower casting may have something to do with my thick new armor.

Arvan Azzarik - Gladiator (Human Lv. 13)
Health: 191/191
Stamina: 24/39
Mana: 9/9

Gaven Tolaris - Gladiator (Human Lv. 15)
Health: 187/187
Stamina: 12/38
Mana: 7/7

The two fighters were, unsurprisingly, gladiators. The casting confirmed what I had previously observed without the aid of my spell: they were closely matched in ability. However, the spearman, Arvan, having more Mana than the swordsman, Gaven, seemed to be the "smarter" fighter. His wily tactic of baiting his opponent into making ineffectual attacks was slowly draining away the Stamina of his enemy.

Suddenly, the swordsman engaged in one last desperate gamble. He seemed to split into two identical images as he began his new assault against the spearman. Gaven's blade became a whirlwind of steel, crashing against Arvan's guard in a lightning tempest of blows. In turn, Arvan's shield became a blur of motion, intercepting all the savage blows. The display appeared to be as if born from magic, well beyond the scope of normal martial prowess.

Why isn't he shouting the Skill?" I whispered to my companion, remembering my own fight with Jongshoi.

Looming over me, Kidu had to hunch, his armor forcing him to bend at the knees as he half-shouted in my ear over the roar of the gathered crowd. "Only those who have just started down the Path Martial do so as a way of learning the weapon forms. Once one becomes adept, it is as instinctive as breathing."

I realized now the distinct advantage I had gained by having progressed along both the magical and martial paths. The gamer inside me concluded that I had created a synergy of sorts; I could use power strike with Silent Cast to mimic the effect of a higher skill proficiency. This also meant the two fighters in front of me, as well as my companions, were, at the very least, adept fighters in skill.

The fight would be decided soon. The swordsman was exhausted after his last roll of the dice, drawing great gasping breaths, his twin swords now lowered from exhaustion. The spearman led with his shield first, bashing through his opponent's guard and finishing with a serpent's spear at Gaven's neck, forcing him to drop his weapons and yield. Half the crowd went wild, and the others threw now worthless pieces of paper on the ground in disappointment.

The two fighters exchanged comradely handshakes before leaving through iron portcullises at opposite ends of the fighting pit. Soon after, a woman just before her middle years, with auburn hair that seemed to glow in the afternoon sun, sashayed seductively across to the center of the pit.

She was clad in a clinging green dress that left little to the imagination, accentuating the graceful lines of her magnificent figure and exuding a subtle feminine power with each step. A silk sash of deep crimson encircled a delicate waist that widened into full hips, and gold bracelets, inlaid with precious stones, jangled at her wrists.

Between her generous bosom was a large, even more heavily jewel-encrusted medallion, stylized in the design of the twin horns of an auroch. Skin, an ochre like the mellow brown light that had bathed the forest, colored a still-comely feminine face that spoke of a once unrivaled beauty in her youth. This beauty was juxtaposed by a jagged scar that ran across a now blinded white orb of an eye. The woman's good eye was a deep jade green, and an elegant patrician's nose lay above a set of sensuous red lips that were arched in a knowing smile.

Raising both hands, she began to address the crowd with a ringing voice that echoed around the fighting pit. "People of Ansan, the next event is the match that you have all been waiting for! Today's fight to the death! Wily human versus savage orc! Who will be victorious?" She paused as the crowd's roars drowned out all sound. She allowed time for the crowd to quiet down, silence eventually pervading the prolonged gaps before she continued. "I give you the Bonegrinder, of the Longfang tribe! He comes to Ansan, the jewel of the Grieving Lands, to win wealth and renown for his people. Many have fallen before his mighty blade, and he wishes to test his might against only the strong!"

Again the crowd went wild, the much-anticipated spectacle of blood drowning out any semblance of human reason or reserve. A portcullis was raised and a huge olive-green orc, clad in thick, heavy hides, burst into the arena with a bestial roar that challenged the crowd. The orc had large ivory tusks that jutted out from an extended underbite, and his porcine eyes searched the crowd for any who would challenge his dominance as he continued to beat his chest with one hand. His other hand held a massive, fearsome war cleaver, almost a meter and a half in length from handle to tip, the edge of its dark iron blade pitted and worn from a hundred battles. I made sure to cast Identify on the orc, eager to know his strength, and once again it took longer to complete the spell than usual.

Gnarlug Bonegrinder - Warrior (Orc Lv. 14)
Health: 280/280
Stamina: 47/47
Mana: 4/4

Such was her control that the woman simply raised a single dainty hand, crusted with fine rings, to cast a silence over the crowd. Another portcullis was hoisted with a grinding of gears.

"I also give you Vidone Amantea, of the island of Quas! A philosopher-soldier of the great university! Today, will intellectual might best ferocious savagery? Will this down-on-his-luck student be able to pay the fees of that most hallowed of institutions?" she announced in a loud, clear voice to the laughter of the boisterous crowd.

The woman was playing the crowd well, teasing out their steadily rising excitement like an experienced conductor. A willowy young brown-haired man nearly danced into the arena with a winning smile that dazzled, then bowed deeply at the hip to the astonished crowd.

How could this thin wisp of a man ever hope to defeat the dreadful-looking orc?

My question was soon answered. As he executed a flamboyant sword flourish to the "oohs" and "aahs" of the spectators, I cast Identify on him.

Vidone Amantea - Duelist (Human Lv. 22)
Health: 341/341
Stamina: 47/47
Mana: 12/12

As I finished the spell, the wiry man looked worried for a moment, his smile faltering slightly as he searched the crowd for a hidden threat. Had he felt the touch of my magic? My brow furrowed. *This is most disconcerting...*

Vidone was elegantly clad in a finely cut blue cloth jacket and trousers, with brass buttons to complement his high leather boots. His hair was tied back in a simple ponytail, and white ruffles adorned his jacket and shirt at the neck and cuffs. Warm amber-brown eyes were set in a gaunt and hawkish olive-brown face with a strong aquiline nose.

Adding to this, his jawline, ending in a sharp chin, and predatory, casual grace gave the overall impression of a bird of prey. In his left hand, he carried a long needle-like rapier with a basket hilt and a bejeweled ruby pommel, its flashing blade tracing a line of steel as he executed another sword form.

Vidone was an obvious plant. The human's physical attributes were distinctly superior to the orc's, despite appearances seeming otherwise. He was also eight levels higher, which cemented his chances of winning.

Thanks to my magic, this was clear to me; although apparently not to others in the crowd, who clamored to place their bets with a bookkeeper behind a long wooden counter under the watchful eye of two burly guards.

On the other end, at a different station, a bored-looking man was shuffling papers and taking a few bets from the braver members of the crowd, who placed their fortunes on Vidone's delicate blade. Kidu and I moved over, and the bored man behind the counter looked over at us before greeting us in a voice bereft of interest.

"How much... and your name, please? Odds are twelve to one on the Quassian," he said, barely looking up to meet my eyes.

"Two silver. The name is..." I paused for a fraction, suddenly realizing it wouldn't be the best of ideas to give my real name. "Elwin Tucker," I finished confidently, causing Kidu to tense up for a moment before relaxing again.

Placing the lion's share of our remaining funds on the counter, I gave the bored man an assured smile. He quickly wrote the amount—alongside the false name I had given—on a small piece of parchment before marking it with a stamp that glowed a dull blue as it made contact with the paper. This was the third magical artifact I had encountered since coming to this world, and for a few moments, I gaped like a fish out of water.

The betting clerk, noticing my reaction, explained matter-of-factly, "A truth-seal, which guarantees that bets are honored at Ansarai's Fighting Pit." He passed the slip of paper to me before turning to take the bet of another man.

I had to fight to suppress my excitement. I had never gambled in the old world, preferring to always play things safely. For the first time in my life, I felt the seductive thrill of truly risking something, similar to how I had felt when I had been engaged in battle. It was even better, for I was almost one hundred percent certain I would win, and at that moment, I understood why some fell to the addiction.

An unspoken communication was made between the bookkeepers and the woman who was strutting on the sands, her mix of latent violence and sexuality still intoxicating to behold. The woman exited the fighting pit, and the crowd returned to the edges of the ring as the two fighters began to warily circle one another.

The orc beat his chest in savage fury, challenging the diminutive man. In response, Vidone simply raised his rapier to his face, kissing the hilt before adopting an *en garde* position. The bestial brute then charged directly at Vidone, waving his giant cleaver in front of him in wild arcs, seeking to overpower the Duelist with his raw strength and brutality. But wherever the orc swung, the small human simply wasn't there, the green monster's dark iron blade missing him by inches as he swayed left and right, ducking and weaving through every blow.

The crowd went wild, lusting for blood.

Dodging a particularly clumsy thrust, Vidone took a moment to bow to the crowd. Like a lone matador baiting a bull in the *tercio faena*, he knew how to put on a show. He danced around his opponent with eminent skill. The orc was beginning to weaken as exhaustion took its toll.

The Duelist met Gnarlug blade to blade, needle-thin rapier against brutish war cleaver, parrying each and every one of his attacks with a delicate flick of the wrist. This time, Vidone was beginning to draw blood with blindingly fast two-tempo counters. His elegant sword wrote the script of death in sweeping strokes and flourishes, leaving shallow red lines across the barbaric warrior's green skin.

Seeing the vast difference between physical skill and ability, I knew then that the orc's loss was all but certain. Still, with the likelihood of him losing, I did not want his potential death to go to waste, so I readied a spell. His death would add to my power.

Gathering my magic to me, I cast Drain silently, sending the thin threads of the darkest gossamer midnight to attach to the now rabid orc as he swept a mighty horizontal slash at the small man. Unlike my use of Identify, my Drain spell seemed to be unimpeded by my new equipment. I surmised that perhaps this was because they were different types of spells.

I would have to leave such musing for later, as I observed the results of my magic come to fruition. Sensing something afoot, the skilled swordsman paused for a fraction of a moment, which threw his next parry off. Unable to divert the kinetic energy of an upwards slash, the lighter blade failed to stop the cleaver from smashing into the Duelist's guard. Although the two combatants were probably similar in raw strength, the same could not be said for mass, as the force of the blow lifted the willowy man several meters into the air, only for him to crash down a second later.

I kept my spell going, still reeling from surprise as I held my breath, praying for the slight man to get up as the orc's life energies kept flowing into me.

Vidone struggled to his feet, a trickle of blood dribbling from the corner of his lips. To the casual observer, the Duelist was done for.

The crowd was silent until Gnarlug followed up with a smashing blow, seeking to end the life of the Duelist. By some miracle, Vidone evaded it by a hair's breadth, desperately rolling to his left with none of his practiced elegance, causing the crowd to go wild once more.

The playfulness had left the smaller fighter's eyes. Gnarlug's lucky blow had served as a call for greater caution on the pearl sands, the Duelist's confidence clearly shaken. Through a gash in his elegant blue jacket, I saw the silvery flash of delicate chainmail that had stopped the edge of the blade, if not the full force. The blow that connected must have been so powerful that, even partially deflected, it had grazed his chest.

Vidone's moves were now less flamboyant and a lot more practical as he lightly avoided his opponent's attacks, his facial expression growing more serious as the exchange drew on. Then, almost without warning, it was suddenly over. The small man bent slightly at the knee and then moved so quickly that he simply seemed to appear behind Gnarlug before plunging his thin, silvery blade through the back of the orc's heavy skull.

You have slain Gnarlug Bonegrinder. 75 experience gained.
You have gained 1 Intelligence.

A great silence descended on the crowd. As the notification of the orc's death filled my vision, the giant monster slumped to the white sand with a heavy thud. My eyes darted over the scene before me; those movements were too fast for someone of the mortal realm to accomplish unaided. I shifted uneasily, the realization dawning that, beyond doubt, some form of the arcane arts had been employed to assure Vidone's victory.

Chapter 46

FORTUNE'S FAVOR

The short-lived races too were ravaged by the horrors of the great beyond, their delicate psyches overwhelmed by the total fear of the end of all things. Those who had the gift of magic were consumed in a conflagration of magical energies, which started a chain reaction throughout the rest of the world. Only those who had fully given themselves to the path of necromancy had any defense against the great psychic cry that consumed any of those who had a spark of magical aptitude.

— On the Cataclysm by an unknown Quassian Scholar, circa 103 AC.

I gasped in sweet, blessed relief as my lungs remembered to breathe with the notification of the brute's death. Placing my hands on my knees, my armor suddenly felt heavy as I grew a little weak. After the relief came euphoric joy. I punched a fist into the air, delighted my gamble had paid off.

Kidu, unsure at first, finally joined me in my celebration, whooping and hollering like a drugged loon. After a while, once our jubilation returned to a manageable level, my sense of practicality took to the fore once more, propelling me to collect my winnings. Kidu and I hurried over to the betting counter.

Despite the joy flooding me and despite realizing my good fortune, I could not shake a lingering sense of fear. Beneath my excitement, a foreboding feeling was already gnawing at the back of my mind. It reinforced my desire to make sure my Health was never reduced to zero, whether by an enemy's hand or the specter of death on the distant horizon.

Death, I realized, was the poison we drank the moment we were born: sometimes it was swift, sometimes slow, but always certain. And, like many things in this world were, even death was reduced to a simple number heavy with meaning.

My mind wandering, I almost bumped into the counter. The bookkeeper looked at us over horn-rimmed spectacles as I handed him my betting slip.

"Got lucky, didn't we? Who would have thought that he could have won against the orc, eh?" His tone was a lot more animated now, and he seemed a little nervous. "Still, we always honor bets placed at Ansarai's," he finished quickly, sneaking a look at the hulking guards behind him wielding long halberds that gleamed to a polished shine. The guards were clad in heavy and well-worn coats of plate, their hard eyes looking at us as if drinking in all the information they could for later recollection.

"Aha, that comes to two gold and two silver pieces," he said, almost sweating. "That was the biggest wager placed today on the Quassian. Congratulations... ahh... err... Mr. Elwin Tucker."

A few moments later, he reached into a sturdy-looking metal money box and handed me my winnings.

I noticed the money was a little short.

"I think—"

Used to this common question and reading my expression, he answered succinctly. "Gambling tax, a city ordinance here in the pits for winnings over two gold pieces."

Looking at the guards, I tried to read their expressions, but they all looked like marble statues staring into the distance. I would get no quick answers there, and I did not want to cause a scene.

Pocketing my money, I was delighted by an unexpected notification.

You have gained 1 Luck.

Smiling to myself, I realized there was still much I did not know about this gamified world. How on earth was it possible to train Luck? It seemed that, in this world, gambling was the answer. But in what way did Luck even affect me here?

Such musings would have to wait for another day. The shadows had started to grow long, and it was high time we made it back to the inn to regroup with Elwin. I had to get used to living in a world where civilization had not completely conquered the night.

I made sure to split my winnings evenly with Kidu before we started to make our way back. Never having had a lot of material wealth, a loose attitude towards money was one of the things I could never stand in the old world and was the cause of some friction in my previous relationships. Still, having a gold piece in my pocket put me in a more financially secure frame of mind.

On our way back we had another celebratory meal of some spicy meats-on-a-stick at a small food stall, savoring the sweet flavor of victory. We learned that the stall owner's name was Elbeg, and we promised to come again. On a whim, I also bought a rough gray linen robe from a clothing seller who had tried to convince me to buy some fancy-looking garments that were beyond my means. Inspired by Vidone's performance, the usefulness of hidden armor was what probably powered most of that decision. Also, my initial starting robe had been stolen from me when I was inducted into the life of slavery. A sentimental part of me wanted a symbol, if nothing else, of freedom.

We didn't pass any more of the plains-laur, which disappointed me a little, as I wanted to take the time to cast Identify on them. Instead, I spent my excess Mana casting Identify on the script I could see written on shop signs, understanding now that, thankfully, the Trade language was phonetically written. I shuddered to think of the amount of Mana I would require were it to have used ideograms.

From a young age, I had always enjoyed reading, even taking the time to read the cereal boxes at breakfast. At the very least, now I could understand the shop signs and simple notices, but what I really wanted to sink my teeth into were books. Elwin's "present," though extremely insightful, was growing limited in the knowledge I could glean from it. I wanted to know more, and not just about magical equations and arcane knowledge. I wanted to know more about this world outside my limited scope! I was almost chomping at the bit to get my hands on a book, even a mundane one, so I could read the stories and histories in written form.

While these idle thoughts and wishes were running through my head, we made good progress along the eastern main road that would eventually lead us back to the inn. Of note was a purple-colored yurt that was belching ochre-colored smoke from a stone chimney set in its center, much to the disgruntlement of its neighbors.

Two wizened old wives, hunched and stooped, were deep in conversation next to the yurt. They wore what seemed to be the traditional clothes of the Children, colorful deels with wide open sleeves tied with silk sashes, and they gossiped and complained about the noise and smell of their neighbor. I read the sign that was staked in front of the strange yurt, which read, "Hamsa's Wondrous Apothecary."

Interesting, I thought as we walked past. This was probably where I could acquire potions like the one that Degei had force-fed me after my torturing. The memory alone brought to the fore of my mind emotions and feelings that induced, in equal part, both rage and a powerful urge to vomit.

Turning the corner back to the main thoroughfare, I accidentally bumped into what I thought was a wall of hulking metal. I caught myself before truly losing my balance and looked up to see a man clad in heavy steel scale armor. The edges of each overlapping section were trimmed with bronze or copper and polished to a mirror shine, giving the impression that he was clad in the hide of a mythic sea creature.

His helm was in the form of a snarling reptilian beast. The face that looked out from within was a patchwork of fights won and lost, grizzled features scarred by battle, with cruel Asiatic eyes that looked down at me with casual disdain. He held a long halberd in his left hand, its fearsome curved blade erupting from the mouth of the dragon at the end of the shaft.

"My pardon," I began to mouth automatically, modern-day politeness still ingrained in me even as my companion, who was flanking me, began to grow tense.

It seemed that the man I had inadvertently bumped into was but one of many, an escort for a well-to-do couple. The escort numbered four men, all clad identically to the man before me. At the center of their formation was their master, a rich-looking man with a long thin mustache. He wore a rich sunset-orange deel that was of an expensive cut. At his waist, a scarlet silk sash circled a portly frame grown to excessive fat. The master accepted my apology with a nod—no doubt to him a form of magnanimous noble largesse—and waved away his formidable guard.

The woman at his side looked at me in shock, however. Gasping, she covered her mouth as if she had seen a ghost. The woman was perhaps just on the cusp of middle age, and beautiful golden rings decorated her crow-black hair. *She must be shocked at my impertinence at delaying her progress through the city,* I thought.

Seeking to avoid further insult, I ground my teeth and hurriedly added, "Apologies to you and your guard. We had best be on our way." I bowed low and as ingratiatingly as possible, drawing a haughty snort from one of the guards.

I indicated with a few hand gestures to Kidu that we should make our exit quickly.

Kidu shot the armored entourage a brief, defiant glare, ensuring he didn't appear intimidated, yet avoiding provocation, before trailing behind me.

We finally arrived back at the inn sometime in the late afternoon to find Elwin drinking a stein of ale at the bar. He gave us an insouciant smile before finishing one of his tall tales with Devon. They were both laughing with each other, trying to outdo the other with their tall tales of derring-do. Once he was done, he turned from his drinking companion and greeted us.

"Finally! You lot are back? I see you are going for a new look. Hmm, yes, very menacing. We were just talking about you. Why don't you pull up a seat and let's exchange stories? I had a right-old fine time today, I tell you!"

"Thank you, Elwin, but no," I answered. "I think we should *all retire to our room* for a moment to catch a breath. We would, of course, be *delighted* to hear your good news there."

The earlier encounter with the local nobleman and his guards still lingered in the background of my mind. My thoughts kept replaying the scene, my mind grasping for something that kept floating out of reach. There was something missing, but I was distracted from my ruminations as Elwin finally answered me.

"Ah, I see, of course, pardon me," he replied, draining his drink and patting Devon on the shoulder. "Was lovely talking to you, old pal." Surprisingly steadily, he got to his feet and followed us up the stairs to the room.

Upon entering our humble lodging, I resisted the urge to flop down on the bed in full armor, instead settling for the chair by the shutters, which I opened. Kidu chose a comfortable corner, his bulk completely filling it up, while Elwin sat on the bed with his hands steepled together as if deep in thought.

"All right, let me start." Elwin coughed. "I was able to meet up with several fences, or merchants that didn't ask too many questions. None of our pieces of loot were particularly special, but you never know, eh? Anyway, I was able to get together just a little over two gold pieces. How you lads do?"

Two gold pieces were a lot more than I had been expecting. I thought he would have gotten a few silver at most, so I couldn't help praising the rogue for a job very well done. Perhaps he was worthy of trust after all.

I told him about my adventures of the day—minus my moment of raw intimacy with Cillis—which impressed him to no end. We split the proceeds of the sale among us and he offered to place a few silver on my bets in the future.

However, gambling could not be our main source of income. It would simply draw too many eyes, and if word got around that I was using magic to ease the odds in my favor, things would not end well for me. I decided to make my position on the matter clear.

"There is no harm in gambling for the occasional bit of coin, but I would prefer it if we didn't draw too much untoward attention. We'll need a way to make some honest money. Now, I'm not much into the gig economy"—they both looked at me, a little puzzled, before I continued—"One-off odd jobs, I mean. We'll need something a little more stable. Remember Taper downstairs? Didn't he mention something about an 'Adventurers" Guild?'"

Kidu just shrugged, willing as always just to follow my lead, but Elwin, equally as always, had something to say. "Probably means we'll have to head back there." He pointed in the general direction of the forest. "The Grieving Lands are a dangerous place for adventurers. Hunting beasts to fill a rush order from a tanner or to get ingredients for an eccentric alchemist is one thing, but monsters are, well... It's in the name, isn't it? They're dangerous, I tell you!"

"What is the difference between an animal and a monster anyway?" I responded, a little confused. The pair looked at me, dumbstruck, before Elwin slapped himself on the head after he remembered my background.

"Of course; we have a budding scholar on our hands, after all. An animal is a creature that is a natural product of nature, and more importantly, they all fear, or at least interact with, the races of man as nature intended. A monster is something that will purposefully go about to harm man, beyond the simple reasons of food and territory." He said this with great patience, as if talking to a child.

"You mean, just like mankind?" I flippantly commented, enjoying the reaction on his face.

"A philosopher too. We're actually the real monsters?" He snorted, waving both hands in the air in a mocking fashion. "You truly know nothing. There are things out there that will give you nightmares for the rest of your life. But if you must know, they say that somewhere in Quas there is a book with all the known species in it, recorded before the first Cataclysm. They say anything after that, anything that Iasis created in her twisted mind, is categorized as a monster." He finished on a tired note, which put an end to my impromptu lesson, reminding me of just how little I knew of what was considered common sense in this world.

"Well, if it's good money, I say that we at least have a look, maybe even register. At the very least, I would assume that being a member should provide some protection against possibly being *enslaved* after being lulled into a false sense of security by being plied with drinks in the late afternoon." I said the last pointedly, but I was all too aware of my own little hypocrisy. Besides, something in my gut told me it was an avenue worth pursuing.

I made sure, however, to add something I knew would be dear to the rogue's heart. "There is bound to be treasure somewhere along the way!"

Elwin grinned at me, and even the taciturn Kidu seemed to spruce up at the mention of treasure.

"Well, I guess a few nights in the rough can't be too bad," the rogue said, testing the waters.

"Where you go, I will follow. I am sure there will be worthy opponents to wet my spear," intoned the giant man in a voice that rumbled like a big cat, loyal as always.

And so, it was decided—we would become adventurers.

Chapter 47

SYMPHONY

The high elves, in their hubris, think themselves at the pinnacle of all things cultural, yet when was the last time their bards composed a new song? Their poets a new verse? Their tailors a new cut of fashion? Theirs is a legacy of stagnation that permeates all aspects of a society that has not seen change in millennia. What I have done in ten years their best could not do in a hundred. They call us the "children of the day," but I view them as nothing more than a collection of youthful-looking old men set in their ways and bitter crones lamenting a world that once was. It is not the length of one's life that is the measure of one's legacy, but one's accomplishments.

— *The Fanciful Travels* by Beron de Laney, 376 AC.

Still excited by the day's events, we mutually decided our trip to the Adventurers' Guild could wait until morning—there were, after all, only so many hours of daylight. Kidu wanted to familiarize himself with his new equipment, and he held his new spear almost as if it were a lover. Elwin, on the other hand, wanted to go shopping and see more of the city.

I wanted to voice my disagreement but realized he was a man, fully grown, and could take care of himself. What else helped sway my opinion was that he was able to purchase some new casual linen clothes, including simple tunics and loose trousers for Kidu and myself. Before the evening meal, I chose to practice some of my skills, then ventured downstairs to request a few favors from the inn's proprietor.

Clanking down the creaking stairs, I saw that the common room was half-full, the locals already beginning to fill the place as they finished their shifts. I spied Taper, the innkeeper, mopping up a recent spill on the floor with an irritated look on his face. Waiting for him to finish his chore, I sat down next to the bar.

Eventually, he finished, then served another customer a large measure of ale in a horn stein before finally turning to me.

"What can I get for you? Evening meal's not for about another two hours or so. I'll take your order now, then, if it pleases quick, gots to check on the stew in a bit, see if it's nice and tender. Oh, I can see you've got some new gear, hardly recognized you," he said perfunctorily, barely looking me in the eye.

"Actually, I was wondering if you had something that I could measure time with. I'd be willing to make it worth your while if you had perhaps a sand clock or something?" I said as casually as I could, relaxing on my stool.

He looked at me a little curiously. "Most folks here just look up to the sun, lad. But, if you're wanting to be a little more precise, I can sell you an old cooking timer. Measures about one hour. Let's say for about three bronze pieces. Don't have much need for it these days."

"That would be much appreciated, Taper," I expressed, genuinely pleased, and slid three bronze coins across the bar.

"Two more ales, good innkeeper," one of the locals shouted from somewhere near the back.

"Be with you in a moment, Jefra, just getting something," the innkeeper replied tersely, pocketing my coins before heading to the back room.

I waited for perhaps a minute or two before Athinad returned with a small bronze hourglass filled with fine black sand, perhaps fifteen centimeters in height at a rough guess. It was not particularly beautiful, but it certainly looked practical, with small indents on the glass that demarcated ten-minute intervals up to an hour.

Placing it on the counter, he looked at me and inquired, "Have no idea what you're wanting with this, and for three bronze I really don't care either way. But can I do you for anything else?"

"No, thank you kindly. This will do just nicely," I said as I got up off the stool, feeling a little stiff around the waist due to my armor. I stretched for a moment before cradling the hourglass in my hand. I nodded once more to the innkeeper, who was already taking another drink order, and made my way back to our room.

Athinad's shrill voice followed me up the stairs. "Don't forget! The evening meal's in two turns of that glass!"

I couldn't help but smile to myself at finally having a way to measure time. This meant I could more precisely measure the scope of my abilities, instead of relying on blind guesswork. The game world seemed to agree, as I was gifted with another notification as I clanked my way back up the stairs.

You have gained 1 Wisdom.

Opening the door, I was met with the sight of Kidu inspecting his new weapon. I greeted the wildman and was given a small grunt in return, as he was engrossed in his work. Checking my Status, I made note that my Mana was at two points after having cast Identify at multiple shop signs throughout the day. I settled into the chair, took off my gloves, and cast Identify on a random passerby to bring my Mana to exactly one point before turning over my new hourglass.

Hallise Randefor - Baker (Human Lv. 8)
Health: 88/88
Stamina: 29/29
Mana: 9/9

I quickly dismissed the unimportant information and, with a little time on my hands, decided to join Kidu in the maintenance of our gear. I stood up from the chair and took off my robes and armor, feeling a small sense of relief as I removed my heavy brigandine. Next to come off were the gambeson, bevor, and my visored helm, followed slowly by my iron greaves and chainmail leggings. Looking at my equipment, I couldn't help but feel a little impressed with my layers of protection.

Remembering Cillis's instructions concerning the maintenance of my armor, I checked over my new equipment. I did this more out of a need to form a habit than actual necessity. This did not last long, as often my thoughts would wander back to my time with the smith in the tool shed. Shrugging off those distracting thoughts from my mind, I focused back on the task at hand and finished my inspection.

As my hands roved across the hard surfaces, I could see now why the warriors of antiquity had a very personal relationship with their armor. Each piece was designed to soften a blow or turn a blade to protect the wearer's life and was deserving of respect and care.

Once I had finished the ceremony of the maintenance of my arms and armor, I gazed fixedly at the hourglass. The sands continued to trickle down until, finally, the top half emptied, marking the end of an hour. Soon afterwards, my Mana ticked up by a single point, signaling the success of my experiment and establishing a baseline for my Mana regeneration. I did not require "rest" in the traditional sense of most games to restore my magical energies.

With another hour to go before the expected evening meal, I flipped the hourglass over and informed Kidu that I would be going downstairs to take a bath. He just grunted and nodded knowingly as he continued sorting out and familiarizing himself with his own gear.

After going down the stairs again, I tried to pay Athinad for the use of the baths. However, the innkeeper waved away my payment with a quick smile, saying that it was included with the clock I'd bought. Soon after, he called the boy to see to my laundry. Again, just the mere mention of that boy drew feelings of irrational suspicion to the fore of my mind.

Entering the baths, I was able to ease some of the tensions of the day as the hot water began working its magic on my knotted muscles. I would have to ask the innkeeper later how he heated the water. The Children of the Tides, for all their barbarity, definitely had a good understanding of water and plumbing. It would be interesting to see how magic had affected this society's technological development, or lack thereof.

After a good soak and a stay in the dry room, I returned to our rooms and left my borrowed bathrobe at the door for the boy to collect. I felt another stab of irrational fear; was the boy spying on us again? I quickly dismissed that thought and conversed with Kidu, asking him about his life in the north of the continent whilst he helped me don my armor once more.

Kidu spoke of his people, who inhabited a massive area of frozen tundra known, in his language, as the Kar-Kaphon, which directly translated to the "Trial of Man." The group of people who lived their lives there were called "The People of Trial," or "They Who are Tested." The people of the North were then broken down into many independent tribes, each named after their totem animal. Kidu's own tribe was named after the great bears, which they venerated.

Like the Eskimo of Earth, with their vocabulary for snow, the Northern tribes had many different words for the myriad tests their savage land brought. The elements tested their fortitude; the beasts and ever-hungry, semi-sentient ice drakes tested their cunning; and the harshest of winters, requiring great sacrifice from the older members of the tribes, tested their resolve as a people. There was even a word for leaving the arms of a passionate lover to enter a cold blizzard for the good of the tribe.

Life in the farthest reaches of the North was difficult and short, with every day a raw struggle to survive in the icy wastes. So harsh were the conditions there that the mothers of the tribe would hold a funeral ceremony for each babe on the day of their birth, and would give them a name only once they had reached their tenth birthday. They only celebrated each decade of life, and a man or woman who had seen five such celebrations was seen as a venerable elder of the tribe, earning the title of "Icewalker." These highly esteemed people were well respected, and their voices were heard and given due weight at tribal gatherings.

Their women, more resistant to the rigors of the cold, were highly regarded, and often held positions of great esteem within the tribe. When the survival of the tribe depended on level-headed rationing and easing tensions in crowded tents in the bitterest of winters, it was the women to whom the tribes looked.

Some were even trained as "windspeakers" to guide their tribes through the frozen storms and to preserve their laws, oral histories, and ancient traditions. So in tune were they to the frozen wastes that a rare few were even able to call upon the raw elemental power of the ice and storms to protect the interests of their tribe. Thus the culture of the North was, for the most part, a matriarchal society.

Their whole culture was based around two eternal constants: the freezing cold and the massive cronir. These heavy, six-horned, and muscular deer-like animals were, according to Kidu, almost forty hands high, and moved across the frozen north like the caribou of Earth would. The cronir provided them with their meat, clothing, and primitive weapons, and even their fermented blood provided the tribes with a form of strong alcohol they called "kazass."

Permanent settlements were few and far between, all of them centered around rare hot springs that gushed from the ground and provided warmth for the tribes. These settlements were exclusively neutral grounds that were used as trading centers for the people of the North, and were not owned by any single tribe.

These hardy folk were cousins to another group called the Nords. While Kidu and his tribes followed the migratory herds of cronir across the tundra and forests of the North, the Nords followed the currents of the seas, and were eminent sailors. The would-be bully, Harun—Gunne's protector—was one fine example of a bellicose Nord. I still occasionally savored the taste of his death and the cathartic power it had brought me.

Both peoples were also skilled raiders who would send parties to what they called the "Hot Lands," or "Warm Lands," to bring wealth and honor to their tribes. On occasion, they would venture down as mercenaries or swords for hire, their skills forged in the frozen north and then forged anew in the heat of battle of the internecine wars of the South. Not all would make it back, either fallen in battle or seduced by the easy life of the southern lands.

With the hourglass finally emptying and the evening now upon us, I judged it to be a good time to head downstairs for the evening meal. I thanked Kidu for telling me about his people and apologized for not being able to say much about my own. I promised him and myself that one day I would tell him everything, but for the sake of simplicity, that day was not today.

Hauntingly beautiful music echoed up to my ears as I opened the thick door to our room. I followed the trail of musical notes down the stairs to the common room and was greeted by a strange and mysterious sight. An armored man of average height and build, clad in chainmail and boiled leather scale armor, sat cross-legged in the corner. His raven hair splayed across his shoulders like a dark waterfall, and his brown eyes glowed warmly, reflecting the fire's light.

He sang in a resonant tenor, filling the room with the enchanting beauty of his melody as his fingers danced across the strings of his delicate, lute-like instrument. I did not understand a single word of his song, but understood fully the beauty of his message. The song was about life, death, loss, and the siren's call of finality. The room fell into a respectful silence as the final notes of his song died in the air. Moments later, the solemn atmosphere was burst apart by thunderous applause.

"First time I have seen a true bard," a familiar voice whispered in my ear, causing me to jump, almost embarrassingly, in my heavy armor.

"Elwin!" I said, thoroughly surprised at what I saw before me.

Elwin had bought what looked like a set of dark-colored armor made from boiled leather scales. The whole ensemble came with a cloth-padded hooded jacket. Around his waist was a new belt with an array of deadly-looking knives in small sheaths. Now, after his shopping spree, the man really did look like a rogue.

"Thought I'd get back to join you all for the evening meal," he replied, as if it were the most normal thing in the world. "Was pleasantly surprised to listen to music from a bard. Seems that there is light at the end of the tunnel."

"Yes, the music was rather lovely. I can see that you decided to enrich some of the local merchants."

"Ha!" he said, tapping the side of his nose knowingly.

Curiosity possessed me, so I walked up to the bard as he was drinking ale from a large mug in great lugs. My sallet held under the crook of my arm, I greeted him.

"Hello there and good evening, good sir. My name is Gilgamesh of Uruk," I said formally, feeling that a little ceremony was required. "I have a favor and request to ask of you."

He arched a single eyebrow before looking at me directly as he put down his wooden mug. "The name is Darren Kragain of Haylesland, a pleasure to meet you. Your manners serve you well, so please do go on," he replied in a cultured tenor voice that was as smooth as spun silk.

"Your song was most beautiful, the best I have ever heard in these lands, and has given me a yearning for the sounds of my own home. I would like you to play a song from my homeland, if it is not too much trouble?" I asked, a little awe in my voice as I placed half a silver beside his instrument. Being this close to it, I could see that it was almost a magical thing. Intricate whorls and patterns flowed across its body, and entwined plant and animal designs gathered around the rose and ran up to the neck.

"Tell me the name of the song," he said, looking a little bored.

I was sure that the bard often got requests like this.

"You will have never heard of this song," I continued, and the bard perked up a little, his interest now piqued. "It is a song from a faraway land, and it goes a little like this…"

Humming as best I could the parts of the song from the intro to the outro, I was lost for a moment in the memories of better times. Having no ear for music myself, I wondered if I was properly able to convey the song. But even with my lack of musical talent, the bard looked absolutely enraptured by the catchy melody.

"Yes, yes… I believe it would be easy to do. This is a whole new style of music!" His eyes were alight as he re-tuned his instrument before sitting down cross-legged once more.

His fingers played across the strings as a melody, both different yet hauntingly familiar, echoed around the common room, and people grew silent once more to listen. The bard had added his own flourishes to the tune. For one, the lyrics of the song were now markedly better in comparison to the trite, childish nonsense of the original, and the notes flowed together like an ocean wave. However, the soul of the music was there, and it brought back memories of a world now lost to me. A wave of homesickness crashed over me, and I felt that it was almost worth the half a silver I had paid to inflict this world with pop music.

Once the music had ended to another thunderous applause, I thanked the bard once more for his gift and ordered him another drink. I was surprised when he, in turn, thanked me, placing my coins back in my hand while saying it was I who had given him a great gift. According to his tale, he was on a journey to find new inspiration so that he might complete his quest to become a master bard, and thanks to me, he had found it.

My good use of manners rewarded me with a notification.

You have gained 1 Charisma.

Extricating myself from the bard's pleasant company, I rejoined my companions for the evening meal and placed my heavy helm on the table. Taper served us a delicious-looking stew in wooden bowls. The stew was spicy and was filled with a wide array of tender meat and freshly boiled vegetables with a peppery aftertaste. It was very filling, but we all still ordered seconds as it was a true gastronomic delight.

Feeling rather pleased with myself, I decided to act on a whim and do something spontaneous. Cillis's words echoed in my mind, her voice haunting my thoughts. The time I had spent with her had been a rare comfort in my life of relentless struggles. Driven by a burst of youthful recklessness, I resolved to do something wild, consequences be damned.

I turned to Elwin and mentioned that I needed some fresh air. He looked at me with surprise, but his cheerful mood prevented him from probing further. It also helped that he was drinking like a fish.

Filled with the heady optimism of youth, I made my way to the Soot-Stained Pig. Despite the late hour, the rhythmic sounds of labor at the forge reached my ears. I entered and, seeing that the smith was busy, waited patiently near the entrance like a petitioner.

Once she was done with her work, she finally noticed me.

"What brings you here at such a late hour?" she asked with a quizzical smile.

"I... I... was wondering if we could see more of each other," was my weak and banal response. I cringed inwardly.

She crossed her arms, sighing as she did so. "You speak as if you want to court me. Me, a happily married woman?" She laughed, inadvertently smudging her face with soot as she covered her mouth. To my ears, her laughter seemed joyous, yet tinged with condescension.

"But I thought... You and I. I thought we had something, or could have something together," I continued lamely, cursing myself even as I did so.

"You're serious, aren't you?" she said, her eyes widening. "Now there, young Gilgamesh, all we did was have a little fun. I'm sure you... we... both enjoyed whatever it is that you think happened. But that was all it was—just a little thing. And that is all it will be. Now… I have things to do. If you could please leave, I would be most grateful," she said sweetly, hanging up her leather apron on a peg.

"Who's there?" came the distant voice of her shrewish husband.

"No one important. Just sorting out a bit of business," she answered. "Gilgamesh, you're a young man, and it's flattering that you think so highly of me, but there can be nothing between us."

Like a scolded child, I excused myself and quietly closed the door behind me. I made my way back to the Twisted Boar, the walk back feeling like a hundred leagues, then ascended the stairs to our room, my spirit as heavy as my footsteps.

There I found my companions beginning to settle in for the night. Voice hollow with defeat, I volunteered to take watch, taking my customary position by the shutters to stare out into the night streets. I cast Drain a few times during the long hours of my watch, when my Mana allowed for it, at some passersby who were making their way back home. A perverted joy came to me as I released some of my frustration on random strangers. I realized that rejection was a bitter thing, made ever more so by a small dose of hope.

I hardly noticed the dark voices of my magic anymore, their promises and threats falling on deaf ears; but I did notice that, with my spell having increased in power, there were now more threads of darkness made with each cast. *Progress in the dark arts,* I thought, grinning ruefully. Who would have thought? My body was thrumming and jittery with stolen life energies by the time I was snapped from the training by a heavy hand on my shoulder.

Kidu relieved me from my watch, and I, too lazy to care, simply fell onto the large bed. Despite feeling mysteriously tired, I also felt strangely stimulated. With my rest skill, however, I was able to quickly fall asleep to the embrace of familiar nightmares that stalked me in the night.

Chapter 48

THE NAME BEHIND THE MAN

Seas rose and continents cracked under the energies that ravaged the world. The sky itself burned in places that scoured the very ground beneath all life. Great volcanoes spewed mountains of dark ash into the air, covering the world in primordial darkness. In the deep places of the ocean, there was to be no refuge. The water boiled, killing all but the hardiest of creatures, and the people of the Mer suffered greatly.

Thus was how the first Cataclysm started, and the game board set anew for the unending game of the thirsting gods.

— On the Cataclysm by an unknown Quassian Scholar, circa 103 AC.

Dawn had yet to cast her rosy fingers across the sky before I was woken without ceremony. The rogue, his breath still scented with strong drink, shook me awake from my dreams, in which something unwholesome stalked me through the corridors of my mind. Shaking off the last vestiges of sleep, I did my business in what passed for a toilet in this place, squatting like a savage. Being civilized and hygienic, I made sure to wash my hands.

"Good morning to you, muse of music!" chirped Elwin. "Since I didn't want to be eating jerky all the time on the road, I bought us a few other trail snacks. Think of it as a thank-you present!" He ran a hand through what remained of his hair and handed over a simple leather satchel filled with traveling provisions.

"And to you too," I unenthusiastically replied. After the events of the previous night, I was still feeling a little raw. "We'll make our way to the Adventurers' Guild and see what it's about, I suppose. We will have to find some sort of work to pay for a caravan or transport out of this town to head for more civilized climes," I said, still struggling to find some motivation.

As my companions gathered the rest of our provisions and supplies, I mentally looked over my character sheet. Sleeping in my armor during the night had given me a level in the heavy armor skill. The effect of the improved skill was already apparent, as my equipment felt a little less cumbersome while we went down the stairs.

The innkeeper of the establishment was waging war with the remnants of last night's revels. He was mopping spilled ale and vomit and hitting his still-sleeping customers to wakefulness with the business end of his mop. The bard from last night was nowhere in sight, as was to be expected from a man of his caliber. The regular customers were just making their way out when we noticed there seemed to be a smell of something cooking wafting up through the air.

"Good morning, Taper," I said, trying to muster up some goodwill and energy. "I see that business was good last night."

"Business is always good when there's a bard about. This sorry lot is always looking for an excuse to celebrate and drink," he replied as he put his mop away. "I'll be serving breakfast soon. The usual three coppers, if it pleases you."

I sat down with my companions at the counter, placing nine dull copper coins on its impeccably clean surface. I asked the innkeeper for directions to the Adventurers' Guild, even though I was pretty sure the building I had passed on my way to my fight with Jongshoi was the same one.

The innkeeper gave me some rough directions from the inn, which confirmed my suspicions. In the old world, I was never much gifted in the art of map reading, let alone directions, but thanks to my increased

Intelligence, I had a much clearer picture in my mind of where the guild should be.

Soon enough, Taper served us some form of gruel with a dollop of honey in the center. It was a simple and filling fare, and Kidu even asked for seconds, counting out three coppers from his purse. We waited for Kidu—who finished his meal with a resounding burp that amused Elwin to no end—and then we exited the inn.

The morning light had fully taken the sky now, and with the risen sun came the sounds of a city waking up. There had been a light rain during the night, and the streets were muddy as we started off in the direction of the Adventurers' Guild. The mud did little to hamper the number of people who were making their way about their daily business.

We plowed on through to the market square as I retraced my steps from the jail to the Adventurers' Guild. Turning a few corners and passing many yurt-like buildings, we finally arrived at our planned destination. I accidentally stepped into a puddle and sank down to my ankles, much to the amusement of my companions.

The building was as I remembered it and where Taper had described. The guild hall was carved from large blocks of simple white stone. Over its heavy wooden iron-banded entrance hung a sign bearing the symbol of a crossed sword over a wooden burning torch. We entered the building to find the common room surprisingly well lit, with a large fireplace bathing the room in its warmth. The floor was made of worn wood, and there were several brushes by the door, which I saw people using to wipe the road from their boots.

The people inside seemed to come from all sorts of backgrounds and walks of life. Some were armored to various degrees, from full plate to ratty-looking worn leathers, and all of them were armed with an eclectic mix of ranged and melee weapons of varying quality and origin. What drew my eye were the few who were dressed in mystical garments of many hues and wielded magical-looking staves and wands.

A man in a red robe and wide-brimmed "wizard's hat" patterned with yellow stars gripped a staff tipped with a scarlet crystalline point. He was smoking from a delicate wooden pipe, the smoke from which was so dense that it looked like an extension of his bushy gray beard that reached to his chest.

Serving girls wended their way through large wooden tables, delivering stacked trays full of delicious-looking food and ale. It seemed that the Adventurers' Guild also doubled as a tavern in this city. *A smart move,* I thought.

Several groups of people were sitting at tables, discussing amongst themselves and exchanging information. Not everyone was in a group, and not everyone was human. Alone at a table, a dark-skinned humanoid with the characteristically pointed ears of the elves and platinum-silver hair sat nursing a drink. My hackles rose at seeing the elf, and I had to pointedly refrain from reaching for the flail at my side. I had not had a good first impression of their kind.

At the other side of the hall was a wooden counter, where several people were queuing up. Behind the counter, smartly dressed employees in elegantly cut clothes were busy with clerical work as they tallied, counted, and calculated. Next to the counter was a large board with various pieces of paper pinned onto its surface.

"Nice setup they got here," Elwin chimed in as he whistled in awe.

"It certainly looks like an Adventurers' Guild—not that I have seen one before, mind you," I commented, making sure to correct myself.

Kidu, taciturn as always, just grunted knowingly.

Still unsure of the social niceties required and not wanting to cause a stir with a potential *faux pas*, I sent Elwin to find some information. Meanwhile, Kidu and I finished cleaning our shoes and now waited at an empty table. In due course, one of the serving girls came to us.

The girl was perhaps in her twenties, young and fair-skinned with a sprinkling of light freckles around her nose. She had flame-red hair tied in a bun, but had the Asiatic eyes and small nose so common to the locals here. Our server was pretty in a homely sort of way, offering us a pleasant smile while she asked for our order.

"Hello there! Nice to see some new faces," she began cheerfully in a high singsong voice as she eyed the massive Kidu up and down, stifling a giggle. "What can I get for you?"

"Do you have anything that is non-alcoholic? Juice, or milk, perhaps? And a light snack, as we have just eaten?" I asked, not wanting to start drinking so early in the day.

Her bright smile grew in amusement. "We got a little lanelo juice and some rockcrab legs," she said, as if rummaging through the back of her mind.

"That would be lovely," I said gratefully. Wistfully, I couldn't help but recall my struggles with complicated menus in the past.

"That will be twelve coppers, then, for three of you. I'm assuming you'll be wanting to order for the man that came with you, too?"

I realized she was the type that grew prettier when they smiled. Now that Elwin was elsewhere, scouring for information, I was able to summon up a little courage. "What's your name, if I may be so bold?" I blurted out a little too formally, placing twelve copper coins on the table.

Red stained my cheeks as I removed my helm and set it beside the coins, and I grew conscious of my appearance.

"Aren't you a dear! My name's Halena Aster. Nice to meet you, adventurers." She smiled, eyes lighting as she played with a loose strand of hair.

"Kidu Kreshin," the big man rumbled.

For the first time, Kidu had introduced himself with a second name. I had known about this additional part of his name for a long time now, having cast Identify on the wildman during our days of enslavement. Perhaps it held some significance? I would have to ask him about it later.

"Well, aren't you both the strapping sort! I'll be right back with your order." She gave us a wink, dexterously scooping up the coins in one smooth motion before turning around and walking towards the kitchens.

I noticed she had never asked for my name, and that Kidu was looking at her retreating form for a few long moments before I coughed.

"Kreshin?" I asked, curiosity apparent in my tone.

"On the ice, we receive the name of the first kill as our second name so that we may never forget the struggle and the test. The Kreshin brought me great honor among my tribe," he said solemnly, successfully tearing his eyes away from our server.

"So, no family name?"

"All in the tribe are one. My family is the Three Bears," he said stiffly. He probably thought this must be common knowledge—and he was currently distracted by our waitress.

I was soon saved by Elwin after he had navigated through the groups of people back towards our table, a roguish grin plastered to his face. He plopped himself down and looked us both in the eye before he began.

"So right, the thing is, first of all, before we start doing jobs for the Adventurers' Guild is that we got to register and pay the membership fee," he said, pointing a thumb at the wooden counter where the people were lined up. "That's three silver each, but from what I heard, only one of us needs to be a member to take on jobs, so that saves us six silver. Though if we'll be doing work a little bit on the regular side, they advised that we all register." He shrugged noncommittally. "'Course, the pay's all the same split three ways, but some jobs require a minimum number of members. Once we register, we'll have to meet the guildmaster and be given a badge designating our rank. It's the same system like the guilds where I come from. We can take any jobs from the board as long as they are within one rank of our badges, and the guild gives out a death payment only on jobs of the same rank. I don't plan on dying anytime soon, so this doesn't really matter, I guess..." He finished just as Halena returned with our food and drinks.

"What rose blooms in this here sad garden?" Elwin asked lasciviously, looking the girl up and down as he made to touch her shapely rear.

Halena, with a stony, fixed smile on her face and a veteran of a hundred such advances, adroitly dodged his questing hands while placing our items on the table.

"Anything else?" she asked, a little annoyance clouding her voice.

"No, thank you," I quickly added.

She had already begun to turn away to take another adventurer's order before I had even finished.

"I can tell that one likes me!" Elwin guffawed, which drew a simple grunt from Kidu.

We drank our purple lanelo juice, which was sweet and tart, and ate our deliciously spiced salty rockcrabs, which made us order even more juice. Elwin, uncharacteristically, didn't even complain that the drinks weren't alcoholic.

Once we had finished our light meal and drinks, we made our way to join the queue at the counter. In front of us was a line of about ten people. As we waited, the dark-skinned elf, who was at the front of the queue, briskly handed over a bundle of herbs and plants to a busy-looking clerk, who then stamped a few official-looking papers.

Moments later, and with great clerical efficiency, a few silver and bronze coins were presented on a tray, which the elf quickly picked up with dexterous fingers, placing them into a small purse. Even hooded and cloaked, I could see clearly that the lines of the elf's body under the tough-scaled leather armor were of a more feminine persuasion.

She walked with an unconscious, yet confident, sway in her hips that challenged every man in the room, exuding competence and deadliness in equal measure. The elf shot one last glance around the guild; our eyes met for the merest fraction of a second as she exited the building through the thick iron-banded doors.

With time to burn and curiosity to be sated, I asked the man in front of me about the sight I had just seen. He was a distinctly average specimen of Asiatic persuasion, of medium height and girth, with a round, homely face. Brown hair fell from a wide-brimmed kettle helm, and he was clad in a mixture of old scaled leather, coarse homespun linen, and patchwork chainmail. At his waist, though, was a deadly-looking unadorned bearded axe of dark wood and darker black iron of exceptional quality.

"Oh, her. She caught your eye too? She's a famous one, Lanarisa. We all just call her Lana, which she hates." The boyish man grinned. "Name's Gan Garamgai. You can call me Gan if you like—that's what everyone else does, anyway. Say, haven't seen you around before. What's your name, if you don't mind me asking?" He stuck out his gauntleted hand in greeting.

I regretted my decision to ask the overly familiar man almost immediately, and I looked at his gauntleted hand for a moment as if it were a snake. Something about him simply grated on me. But my goals depended upon me not standing out or causing a scene, so I swallowed my regret and remembered my manners. I held a special place in my heart for all the Children of the Tides, and Gan Garamgai, with his stupid name, was no exception.

Gilgamesh of Uruk would have to play the friendly individual for a while; then perhaps sometime in the future, I could convert Gan into experience points. Somewhere in a hidden corner of my mind, a dark thing silently voiced its agreement as I reached to shake Gan's armored hand and introduce myself. Something must have reminded the dolt of his own lack of manners, and he stopped himself before finally removing his own gauntlets.

"Name's Gil. Pleasure to meet you, Gan," I said with a smile that probably didn't quite reach my eyes. "Are you a regular member of this guild?" I asked casually as I clasped the now unarmored hand.

"Oh, that I am. Just a bronze, though," he said, pointing to a small bronze badge on his chest depicting a crossed sword over a burning wooden torch. "Still, started way back when I was a copper. Dad couldn't work the farm, so I had to step up." His chest puffed up a little.

I had to bite back a scathing reply suggesting he could have worked the farm, instead choosing to be tactful. "And how, exactly, does one gain in rank?"

"Well, continue to do jobs and help out the guild and the guildmaster will promote you when he, like, sees you do real well. Remember Lana? She's the only silver adventurer here. Always takes on jobs by herself too, and almost always completes them. Doesn't do much on speaking, though," he continued inanely.

The conversation continued to meander this way and that. Gan told us in annoyingly exquisite detail about the members of his extended family, going to great lengths to extol the virtues of one of his younger sisters. According to his description, she was basically the goddess given flesh once more.

I was able to glean another useful nugget of information out of the country bumpkin: it seemed that the guildmaster, a man called Darcen Tsend, had a means of telling if someone spoke the truth. It was probably one of the reasons he had ascended to his lofty position.

Elwin tried to insert himself into the conversation, asking if Gan's sister was, in his words, "a looker," which thankfully caused Gan to clam up until it was finally his turn at the counter.

Gan, finishing his business, offered to group up to do a few board jobs with us someday, then waved goodbye.

Perhaps I would take him up on his offer.

Chapter 49

BUREAUCRACY

Bibsi, also known as rain-bringers or callers, are only found in one sacred pond that grows into a great lake with the coming of the rains in the Grieving Lands. To gaze upon them is said to be akin to receiving a blessing from the goddess herself.
— *The Fanciful Travels* by Beron de Laney, 376 AC.

At long last, it was now our turn. Behind the counter stood a thin, dark-haired bookish man clothed in an elegantly cut shirt with a silver bolo tie with a dark emerald at its center. Calculating gray eyes behind small horn-rimmed spectacles looked up from his papers and gazed over us.

The clerk coughed, a dainty, white-gloved hand rising to his mouth. "How can the Adventurers' Guild be of service to you, gentlemen?" he asked in a smooth baritone.

"We wish to register as new members of the Adventurers' Guild," I replied simply, mentally slapping myself for forgetting the earlier idea to just register as one member.

"Names, please?" he asked in a no-nonsense voice, all professional now as he filed through a different set of papers for registration.

"Gilgamesh of Uruk, Elwin Tucker, and Kidu Kreshin," I said slowly, careful to enunciate the names correctly as my companions simply nodded behind me.

"I see. Gilgamesh and company, that will be nine silver in total. You are lucky. The guildmaster has nothing scheduled today and will be able to see you soon for the induction process. My name is Taciano, and, since you will be becoming adventurers, I believe we will be seeing each other more often." He cracked a smile incongruous with his earlier attitude. "Please pay the requisite fee and wait a while to the side while I inform the guildmaster." He gestured to the side of the counter.

My party and I paid the requisite silver. We followed Taciano's instructions to the letter, waiting quietly to the side. With nervous energy that belied his usual confidence, Elwin spent the time throwing and catching a sharp knife that rose and fell, glinting with a deadly metallic light.

It was after a few long minutes when Taciano called us over in a quiet, formal voice. "Guildmaster Darcen Tsend will see you. Please follow me."

I nodded in assent, and he guided us up a sturdy flight of stairs before knocking respectfully on a wooden door. After waiting for a few moments, he opened the door and ushered us in.

We were greeted by a formidable sight. A lean, silver-haired, rugged man clad in the local style—a deel fashioned in hues of gold and red—positively filled the room with his presence. On anyone else, it would have looked like a colorful peacock's display, but it hugged his formidable frame and seemed like another form of armor. He stood behind a finely carved wooden desk with his hands behind his back.

Atop his desk was a purplish crystal ball, a mysterious mist moving eerily in its depths. The desk itself was delicately patterned with mystical creatures, and various trophies from past adventures decorated the walls. A massive one-eyed monster's head directly behind Darcen drew the eye, its large fang-filled mouth frozen in a roar. Tentacles circled around its single eye like a medusan mane.

The lines of his face were hard, and scars ran down one sun-browned cheek, crossing lines carved by age and old victories. The guildmaster exuded a restrained sense of danger and authority, like the head of the pack that had seen many hard winters but was content for now. He was also wolfishly handsome, and he greeted us all with a wide canine smile.

"Good afternoon, prospective adventurers. I welcome you all formally to the Adventurers' Guild. My name is Darcen Tsend, and I am the guildmaster of the Ansan Branch." He paused for a moment; I could feel a sort of energy work its way through me, as if searching for something.

"Ah, you noticed the watcher," he said somberly. "One of my earlier victories. Terrible things. They say they are creatures of the void. My party and I were contracted to clear out a nest of them. I lost many friends to those creatures." Switching gears, almost jarringly, he continued, "You all look like capable sorts, so I will induct you immediately. Speak to the fellow Taciano for an explanation of the rules. But the biggest rule of all—this isn't really part of the rules of the guild, but still—do not think to deceive me, for I can smell a lie." His wolfish appearance gave credence to his claim, and it seemed for a moment the small room was filled with his presence.

Elwin smiled nervously and almost visibly gulped as he said, with a courage I did not yet possess, "The sky was purple this morning."

Darcen just guffawed at the rogue's temerity. "I like your style," he exclaimed as he slapped him on the shoulder, which almost brought Elwin down to his knees. The bigger man chuckled throatily all the while.

"Now, place your hands on the bonding crystal, and I'll hand over your first badges," he said as he gestured to the purple crystal ball on his beautifully crafted desk.

"What does that... thing do?" I asked, apprehensive at the thought of touching something clearly magical.

"It merely registers you as a member of the guild. Trust me, it is for your own protection. Wouldn't want you being carted off to somewhere like the flesh pits or the mines, right? The crystal is also imbued with minor magics to inform the guild of an adventurer's death, and in such a case we will pay the death price to their next of kin." The guildmaster's tone was serious. I couldn't help but feel that he had given this speech many times before.

Against my better judgment, I felt a need to win this man's approval, so I moved to be the first to touch the stone. Taking off my gloves, I touched the purplish ball with the bare skin of my fingers and felt a jolt, almost like static electricity. I looked to the guildmaster to see if this was normal, but he simply nodded.

A few seconds later, the wolfish man tapped a copper badge, similar to the one Gan possessed, to the crystal's now opaque milky surface. Darcen gestured that it was all right to let go, so I removed my hand, and golden script etched itself onto the copper badge as if an invisible pen were writing on it. Soon enough, I could read my name clearly in the Trade language and was taken aback by the casual display of magic as the ball grew clear once more.

"First encounter with magic?" asked Darcen, moving to hand over my newly minted Adventurers' Guild badge.

I smiled, feigning awe and avoiding directly answering his question. Being wary of his ability to sense the truth from a lie, I was unwilling to show my hand just yet.

"Now, there is a quick thing called the Adventurers' Guild oath. It is very simple. You just need to swear that you will do your very best to always uphold the reputation of the Adventurers' Guild. Do you so swear, Gilgamesh of Uruk?" Darcen looked me squarely in the eyes, just a few moments shy of handing the badge over to me.

"I swear to uphold the reputation of the Adventurers' Guild to the best of my current abilities," I said as firmly as possible, trying not to let reluctance enter my voice.

I must have really meant it, or the guildmaster's truth-sensing ability was imperfect, because he simply looked me up and down and handed the badge to me with a comradely smile. Still, he decided to slap my shoulder, as he had done with Elwin, in an unconscious show of dominance. I was ready and expecting it, however, and with a thin and annoyed smile, I absorbed the shock of the blow through my knees and a shifting of my own weight. As a student in my old world, I had dealt with his type many times before.

Kidu, following my example, was next to step up to the desk. Taking off his gauntlet, he grasped the crystal with his giant hand almost as if to crush it, which drew a chuckle from the guildmaster. As he had done with me, he tapped a copper badge to the crystal before asking Kidu to repeat the oath about not tarnishing the reputation of the guild. Kidu's name magically appeared on his badge in the same manner it had on mine. Darcen looked at the badge and read out Kidu's name.

"Kidu Kreshin. Kreshin, now that is an impressively fierce creature for one's first kill. Gilgamesh here must be something special to be in the company of a hunter so gifted," the guildmaster said thoughtfully, a new respect in his eyes.

I barely registered the guildmaster's comment, my own mind already analyzing the oath I had taken. Was it a simple honor system, or was it magically enforced? At first, the oath seemed pretty vague, but after analyzing it a bit further, I realized it actually encompassed a rather wide range of things, from my interactions with other NPCs—people, I had to remind myself—to the manner in which I completed requests. On the other hand, as long as I was never found out, I could do, for the most part, whatever I wanted. This was probably why the guildmaster had some sort of truth-sensing ability. My enhanced Intelligence helped me realize it could be a loophole that I could potentially exploit in the future.

It was Elwin Tucker's turn next. If anyone had secrets to hide, next to me, it would be the rogue. With great hesitancy, he reached for the crystal, stopping just a hair's breadth before touching it.

"This doesn't hurt, right? Had enough pain to last three lifetimes. Not enough drink in all the Grieving Lands to numb what I've been through," he mumbled.

The guildmaster simply smiled, then grabbed his hand and forced it to the crystal with such speed I was barely able to track it. Elwin's mouth opened in stunned silence, forming a big "O" in surprise. Again, Darcen made Elwin repeat the guild's oath before finally handing over his copper badge.

"I welcome you all to the brotherhood that is the Adventurers' Guild. May you always find that which you seek," Darcen intoned in a voice that weighed heavy with the guild's authority.

Not knowing how to respond, we all just quickly looked at each other and nodded.

"All right, then, that's out of the way! You best make your way back down to Taciano. He's a good lad but a little weedy. Also, could do with a bit of toughening up. Spends far too much time indoors. Nonetheless, he's a reliable sort, and you could have done a lot worse. One of the lads from the last batch we hired was a right sod. Now be off with you!" The smile on his face made a lie of his stern tone.

Hurriedly, like schoolboys being dismissed, we exited Darcen's office. The whole encounter gnawed a little at me, but I was grateful for the protection the guild offered. My companions and I all took a deep breath before going down the stairs to find Taciano, who had, as of now, been assigned to us.

The clerk had been dutifully waiting for us, holding a thin sheet of rectangular wood to serve as a board for him to write on. On the bottom of the board was a small pot of ink, in which he dipped his fine feathered quill.

"Interesting," I said, pointing at his board. "But what would truly add to its usefulness would be, perhaps, a clip at the top to stop the parchment from moving."

His brow furrowed in thought as he considered my suggestion, before his eyes lit up. "Yes! What a brilliant idea! How could I have not thought about it before? Why, thank you, Gilgamesh... Now, to ask the smith if he could fashion a spring of some sort..." He shook my hand vigorously, his actual duties temporarily forgotten as he pondered my idea.

It seemed that my words must have been of some significance, as I received a notification.

You have gained 1 Intelligence.

Checking over my character sheet while the clerk was still distracted—and trying to keep at least half a mind in the present—I noticed that my maximum Mana had risen to a respectable fifteen points. I didn't have enough time to look over the full extent of my current Status, but I was pleased to learn that, thanks to my general activities, I had gained many experience points and was very close to level eleven. I hadn't quite locked down how the system worked, but outside of gaining levels, gaining attribute points was definitely linked to activities, skill use, and meaningful practice.

STATUS

Calling: Gilgamesh Lv. 10 Paladin of Avaria / Reaver

Strength: 24

Dexterity: 19

Constitution: 34

Intelligence: 21

Wisdom: 18

Charisma: 12

Luck: 17

SKILLS AND PROFICIENCIES

Pain Nullification Lv. 2

Power Strike Lv. 2: 10

Endure Lv. 3

Stealth Lv. 1

Rest Lv. 3

Backstab Lv. 2

Dodge Lv. 3

Polearms Lv. 2

Dual Wield Lv. 2

Critical-Hit Mastery Lv. 2

Mining Lv. 2

Unarmed Combat Lv. 3

Hammers Lv. 2

Flails Lv. 2

Maces Lv. 1

Shields Lv. 1

Medium Armor Lv. 1

Heavy Armor Lv. 2

Axes Lv. 1

Daggers Lv. 2

Throwing Weapons Lv. 2

SPELLS AND MAGIC

Heal Lv. 5: 5

Rust Lv. 3: 1–2

Identify Lv. 2: 1

Silent Casting Lv. 1

Mana Regeneration Lv. 2

Purify Lv. 2: 3

Greater Heal Lv. 1: 10

Holy Aura Lv. 1: 2

Decay Lv. 1: 1

Drain Lv. 2: 2

Entropic Aura Lv. 2: 2

GIFTS

Curse of Entropy: -20% to all starting attributes.

Mark of the Paladin: 10% resistance to Dark/Holy magic. 5% resistance to Physical.

Touch of the Void: 10% reduced resistance to Holy/Fire magic, 20% resistance to Mental Effects, 15% immunity to Mental Effects.

Experience to Lv. 11: 2572/2583

My mind was quickly drawn back to the present as Taciano finally remembered his primary duties.

"Can find jobs on the board over there," he said, pointing to the large board pinned with many requests. "You can take jobs at your rank, one rank above, and all ranks below. However, should you perish whilst attempting to do something one rank higher than your own, the death payment will not be given to your next of kin or chosen recipient."

I selected my mother and father as my next of kin, sure in the knowledge that the potential windfall of my death would never reach them anyway, and I would, of course, do my utmost to keep myself alive. Elwin wrote another Tucker's name down and gave the city name of Brownwood. Kidu surprisingly wrote the Three Bears Clan and "the North" for the address. I was genuinely surprised, as I had thought the large man to be illiterate. It seemed that I had kept a few of the prejudices of my old world with me.

With this part out of the way, Taciano went on with his explanation. "If certain proof needs to be provided for the completion of a job, you will need to hand them in at the counter to me, or to another adventurers' clerk that is on duty. Please wait for us to sign, stamp, and verify that you have completed the request, and you will be paid, minus any city taxes and ordinances.

"One of the advantages of membership is that we enjoy friendly relations with many of the traders and merchants of the city, who will be more than willing to offer you a discount. This will, however, be in relation to your current rank and, of course, your current standing with the guild. As your group does not have a healer, I would suggest that you also make it a point to buy healing supplies from a skilled alchemist. Here, let me write down directions for a few reliable sorts."

The clerk wrote down the directions, which he handed over to us on a scrap piece of parchment.

"I am also here to advise you on future ventures and so forth, so if you have any further questions, please do not hesitate to ask. On that note, I would advise that you first take a copper-class job that you feel a three-man group like yourself can easily accomplish. Any questions?"

We all uniformly shook our heads, and Taciano gave us one final, formal smile before he turned back to the counter to continue his normal duties. My own group, as advised, walked up to the jobs board, and one particular small notice in the center drew my attention. I could not read it clearly, but the part that I could was definitely of interest. My knowledge of the Trade script was still patchy, so I cast Identify on the words.

"(Bronze) Information on what is targeting the charcoal-burners of Ansan. Reward: one gold coin."

Without warning, the golden script of a new quest flashed before my eyes.

New Quest: Warn the Adventurers' Guild of the Echo-Stalkers' nest?
Yes/No

Finally, I thought, *a quest that aligns with my own goals.* I quickly accepted it. This was, basically, the world being slightly helpful for a change. I took the notice from the board and went back to the counter.

A few moments later, a slightly annoyed Taciano came back and asked tersely, "Yes, did you forget anything?"

"Not exactly, but I believe we have completed our first job for the guild," I said as seriously as possible, handing over the slip of paper with the request.

He looked at me as if I had suddenly grown new arms, before actually reading the slip that I passed over, his eyes narrowing. "So, you have information in regard to the recent attacks?"

Gambling with the die of fate, I told Taciano about the echo-stalkers we had seen in the Sainba, leaving out the obvious parts that would incriminate us. Our reason for being there was a little weak, something about Kidu wishing to test himself, but the clerk brushed this off as he was more interested in the possible location of the echo-stalkers' nest.

He asked if we had any physical proof, so we referred him to the Soot-Stained Pig and the echo-stalker parts we had sold to Cillis and her husband. Kidu also gave him a rough account of where to find the nest, a task impossible even for my enhanced intellect, which Taciano dutifully wrote down.

Taciano also informed us that we would have to leave a deposit of a silver piece while members of the guild checked the veracity of our story, due to both our junior rank and the fact we were brand-new members. I simply shrugged, then handed him over a silver coin from my own purse. Such were the responsibilities of a leader.

"Are we allowed to take another job while we wait?" Elwin asked greedily, posing the question we were all thinking.

"It is usually frowned upon to do two jobs at once. But I am sure you don't want to wait, and in the light of the circumstances, I don't see why not. Please go ahead and choose a different job. Remember to keep it to the copper requests, though; I'd rather not attend another funeral this week," said the clerk in a flat voice.

We nodded our assent as we went to check up on the board again for different jobs. The whole thing reminded me of the minutiae of dealing with forms and papers in my old world. Pretending to be completely literate to save face, I tried to make out the words, but I could only recognize one letter in four. Elwin would, however, save the day once more.

"How about this one? Says collect some moon moss from the Sainba Forest. No monster slaying for a start, and I can find us some moon moss no problem, I'm sure. A two-day job at the most and it pays three silver!"

With no other options, I had no choice but to pretend to think it over before agreeing with the rogue. "It definitely fits our initial objectives. We should set out immediately," I said, wanting to retake the initiative as the leader. Something, however, was niggling at the back of my thoughts, though I could not yet place it.

"There are three of us. Why not three jobs?" rumbled Kidu, surprisingly insightful, and my mind snapped back to the task at hand.

"That's an excellent point," I commented, nervousness stealing into my voice as I desperately searched the board for another notice I could understand.

My eyes were drawn to an illustration of a plant, its leafy fronds sprouting from a thick, bulbous base. I assumed it was a notice for a gathering job. Curiosity aflame, I hastily cast Identify on the notice, channeling magic towards the plant's depiction. The energies stretched out, their tendrils probing the object longer than usual before completing their task.

The notice read, "(Copper) Gather three heads of river root. Reward: two silver." I looked at my companions and noticed that they had grown slightly reticent.

"Why all the long faces?" I asked, confused by their reaction.

"Well, it's not so much the river root that's the problem," said Elwin, his usual smile growing strained. "Just that lurkers can sometimes be found near river root. Right fearsome beasts they are. Not always, mind you, just sometimes. But it's always the sometimes that gets you."

The wildman, on the other hand, seemed to take this as some sort of challenge. With one of his giant hands, he took down another notice with a picture of a large, fearsome lizard on it. I gave the picture on the notice a look over and almost gulped. It was certainly a terrifying sight to behold, even on paper.

The great lizard resembled a crocodile or alligator with six muscular, stubby legs that each ended in four sharp-looking claws. From the neck down to its tail were spiked ridges and bony, armored plates. The artist had captured the beast's mouth open mid-roar, and serrated, dagger-like teeth lined its gaping maw.

I took a moment to look at the notice and pretended to read it in detail. While I did this, I silently cast Identify on it, growing frustrated at my slower casting speed. The notice simply read, "(Bronze) Three river-lurker hides. Reward: six silver." We would be well rewarded for the task. Hopefully, we could complete all three jobs at the same time.

"Two birds with one stone," I said with a slight grimace, waiting for the quest messages to come.

When they did not, I let out a relieved sigh.

"I've never heard that before, but it certainly sounds apt. I guess if you got a sling and swung really hard..." quipped Elwin, regaining a little of his usual verve.

"They will make for worthy prey," said the hunter stoically, nodding as he gripped his unstrung bow in his ham-sized hands.

Chapter 50

A NEW COMPANION

"She blesses the poor by letting them lose their favored beast, only to aid them in finding it again."

— Attributed to Cardinal Mauros.

All in agreement, we exited the building. Following Taciano's directions, we headed towards a local alchemist who could provide us with some healing potions. I remembered the taste of the potion that I was force-fed by Degei, the slave overseer, a memory that almost caused me to dry-heave at the mere thought of drinking another.

In good time, we made our way to the purple-colored yurt that I had seen before. Strangely colored smoke was flowing up from a stone chimney at its crown. Girding my courage, I pushed back a heavy cloth to enter the colorful yurt, and my nostrils were hit by a foul smell that assaulted my senses.

Almost gagging, I had a look around the dimly lit yurt. Patches of morning sun streamed in weakly through openings in the side. Across the beams of giant horn, several wooden poles lay stretched across the room. Dangling from them, like shriveled mystical grapes, were a plethora of drying ingredients, ranging from herbs to unknown animal parts. At the far end of the yurt, a bald man, old and hunched, was mixing glowing liquids with the aid of various alchemic apparatuses at a sturdy-looking white stone table.

The man muttered to himself, the deep lines of his face creasing in frustration as he drained an alembic filled with a pus-yellow liquid into a glass vial filled with a viscous red substance. There was a flash of light and puff of smoke, followed by the alchemist's cry of success.

"Fantastic! A mid-grade healing potion made from only common ingredients. I daresay I have simply outdone myself!" he said in a cultured voice, raspy from the various fumes.

"Excuse me," I began.

The alchemist jumped, the newly made concoction almost slipping from his gloved hands. Peering at us from across the smoky room with squinted, bespectacled eyes, he finally realized that he had customers. He stopped for a long moment, looking me up and down, and I felt a small chill and sensed an echo of a feather's touch upon my soul.

"Welcome, honored customer, to Hamsa's Wondrous Apothecary," he managed to finish before he was wracked with a round of coughing, completely destroying the air of esoteric mystery that had previously surrounded him. "The finest potions in Ansan at an affordable price," he wheezed, waving a hand to disperse the foul-smelling smoke. Somewhere towards the back of the dark tent I could have sworn I saw something small scurrying away, but I dismissed it from my mind and focused on the alchemist.

The alchemist's skin looked sickly pale in the poor light, and his pate was completely bald, like a freshly peeled egg. He didn't have a single strand of hair upon him, not even eyebrows or a hint of facial hair. Hamsa's smoke-gray eyes looked at us through the cracked lenses of gold-rimmed spectacles, which he wiped absentmindedly with a dirty cloth from his pocket. The hunched man was wearing a tough-looking leather butcher's apron, worn with age and bearing chemical stains from a thousand experiments. He wore thick cloth vestments of coarse linen to protect his exposed skin, and thick leather gloves protected his skilled hands.

I nodded to a queasy-looking Elwin, urging him to take the initiative and begin negotiations. The rogue understood my intent and approached the alchemist in a relaxed fashion, hands behind his back.

"Good day to you, master alchemist," he said with a smile plastered to his face. "My name is Elwin Tucker, and my companions and I are planning a little trip into the Sainba Forest to gather a few herbs and materials. We were wondering if we might peruse your stock of Health potions before we begin our new venture."

The shop owner visibly preened at this and stood a little straighter. "I, Hamsa, do so swear that you have come to the right place. Only the finest potions here. I even have a small sample of troll blood that could perk up the dead." He glanced at our new copper badges, and his earlier enthusiasm wilted a little. "But for hasty people still new to the trade, I guess something a little more affordable would be in order—at a small discount for the guild, of course," Hamsa said with a sigh.

My mind tried to understand the chemical properties of the potion that I had been force-fed by Degei. Through the lens of modern science and understanding, I simply could not understand the mechanics of such a phenomenon. To be able to heal internal and external injuries in such a fashion was nothing short of miraculous. However, I did not have to understand the workings behind the potions to understand their efficacy.

"Forgive me, Hamsa, but are there any side effects to taking such potions?" I blurted.

Out of the corner of my eye, I could have sworn I saw a shadow move behind some shelves at the rear of the shop. However, it must have been my eyes playing tricks on me, for my companions registered nothing.

"Not for one such as you, though perhaps in the future if you decide to grow a cleft instead of a dangle it might affect your pregnancy," chuckled the alchemist before he patiently continued, blocking my view of the rear shelves. "But I would still stick to only one potion a day, at least until your body grows a tolerance for their effects.

"Oh yes, most importantly, the body can only tolerate taking a certain number of concoctions, depending on one's vitality. That brute of a companion you have"—he nodded towards Kidu, who simply adjusted his quiver, the little action effecting an air of menace—"could perhaps take three potions without ill effects, but Master Tucker here, perhaps one, or two at the most. You will, of course, forgive my impertinence, Master Tucker." Hamsa bowed in a half-apology. "Now, if it is of no offense, may I know the name of the one I am addressing?"

Now I felt a spike of worry at the prospect of imbibing a single concoction, let alone multiple. What did they do exactly to the body? What was the price that one paid for their miraculous effects? What happened when you went over your limit? The alchemist had sidestepped the potential issue of side effects, but for the moment I didn't feel like pressing him for a proper answer.

"The name is Gilgamesh of Uruk," I offered candidly.

Exchanging a quick look with Elwin, I simply nodded to him, and he began the next round of negotiations.

"How much for three lesser healing potions, and a single Mana potion?" the rogue asked, finally getting into the swing of bargaining.

"I see the need for three potions of healing... but, forgive my haste, I do not see an Honored One among you for the Mana," commented Hamsa uncertainly.

"It is for another member of the guild. Something of a favor to a friend of a friend and a minor errand," Elwin said offhandedly, brushing off some nonexistent dirt from his tunic.

"Of course, forgive me for prying. Just idle chatter from an old man. Three minor potions of healing should come to six silver, and a Mana potion for another three silver."

The rogue, now fully in his stride, continued to bargain. "But this is the first time we have visited your magnificent shop. Perhaps if we promise to do business only here and put in a good word with our fellow adventurers, you could help us in the matter of getting a good price?"

"Bah! You would buy colored water from those peddlers at the market square? Nonsense! Charlatans and thieves, the lot of 'em," replied Hamsa, real vehemence in his voice. "I would have you know that I graduated from the University of Quas in my youth. Ha, but I see what you are trying to do. If you could get me a few broomshead mushrooms from the forest, I could bring it down to five silver. What say you?"

"Are you sure we won't get in trouble with the guild?" I interjected.

"A straight arrow, eh? I will have a word with them myself. The guild will always get their cut somehow," he said, brushing me off.

I simply nodded to this, and we divided up the price of potions, my enhanced Intelligence allowing me to swiftly do the arithmetic as I took one silver, one bronze, and one copper coin from each of my companions. I paid the rest of the sum myself, sure in my calculations and not wanting to quibble any further. But I couldn't help but feel that I was missing something—like my mind was searching for a connection.

My eyes were drawn to a knotted herb that was hanging in the corner. The roots looked like a clump of ghost-white snakes, and the leaves were broad blades of a deep, poisonous purple. The eccentric alchemist noticed my interest and said, "Three gold for the dragonsbane, and another five silver if you want me to process it into a concoction for you."

He must have noticed the look of stupefaction that had crossed my face, as he decided to explain, a little annoyance entering his voice at my obvious ignorance. "Dragonroot, one of the strongest poisons in the world. They say it was one of the only things that the flying lizards feared, as it—according to the stories, at least—robbed the beasts of their flight. The Hero himself is said to have discovered its many varied uses. It disrupted the flow of Mana in their wings, messed with their Mana pathways or some such nonsense, according to the sages of old. Diluted, it can cause paralysis in all but the strongest of constitutions, and a single drop of this in its purest form can kill a man in a few heartbeats. In lower circles, it is called the Final Gift."

I simply shook my head and made a weak promise to hopefully buy some of the herb if I was ever able to scrounge up the money at a later date. Then, carefully, I counted out the money on the counter in front of Hamsa.

The alchemist pocketed the money with a snort, then handed over to us three thick red vials and one blue vial. We thanked Hamsa, and, after confirming where we could find the broomshead mushrooms, we left the foul-smelling yurt.

I shielded my eyes from the strong late-morning sun as we exited Hamsa's establishment, adjusting my tear-shaped shield across my armored shoulder. Then I divided the potions with my group, keeping the single blue Mana potion for myself.

"How big are lurkers supposed to be, anyway? Anything I should know about them?" I asked Elwin as I took care of a recent crick in my neck.

"Not too big. They can grow about six paces from snout to tail. Their mouths are mostly filled with daggers for teeth and can shred just about anything. The trick is to get them out of the water where they are ever so slightly slower," answered the rogue, his eyes scanning the streets.

"Then I guess it's going to be a bit beyond us to carry their hides by ourselves," I said with a smile. "We will need to invest in a beast of burden." Perhaps we could even get an exotic creature, like a domesticated laur.

"Yeah, I'm with you on that," replied the rogue, eager to make his life easier by any means necessary. "Let's head off to the market and see what we can find."

We continued in relatively good spirits and made good progress through the streets to the market. Once there, we entered the section where a large selection of creatures were being sold. Some were predators that hissed at us from behind the thick metal bars of their cages, displaying fangs, talons, and claws that could easily rip flesh and tear bone. Others were more placid and docile, like the sleepy rodent-like creatures called catyids, according to Elwin, at least. These beasts looked like an even larger version of a Terran capybara but with a long and sinuous scaled tail.

What drew my eye, however, was a wretched creature that was being led to a butcher's block. It was a donkey, and one of its legs was lame or broken.

The owner, a turbaned man with an impressive handlebar mustache, probably wanted to cut his losses on future feed and grain.

Sensing a potential bargain, I called out to the man, "Hey! How much for that donkey?"

The man turned around, surprised that someone had interrupted him, and looked at me, perplexed, before finally answering. "This beast's no good. Lame leg, only good for glue or stew now." He sighed as the donkey brayed in a panic, almost as if it understood its fate.

"How much for the donkey? And some feed and grain?" I continued, undeterred, the seed of a cunning plan forming in my mind.

"Stubborn one, ain't ya? Well, guess I could get half a silver from the knackers, so I'll do you for that? Throw in some feed for another two bronze? Throw in a carrot or two if you like," answered the man, almost licking his lips with glee.

My companions looked at me as if I had gone soft in the head as I handed the man seven bronze coins, not even bothering to dicker about the price. I smiled at the man as we completed our transaction, and he kept looking at me as if at any moment I would seek to renege upon our bargain. I quickly had a look at my purse and counted out my remaining coins. After all the various fees and expenditures, I calculated that I had a bit over one gold in various shrapnel—my father's word for coins. It was strange that I could remember his words while his name and face eluded me.

I was no expert on equines, but even I could see that our newest party member was rather on the large side for a donkey. A frail-looking thing, mostly skin and bones, she stood sixteen hands high and was bigger than some of the horses I had seen. She was a dull black, except for white fetlocks that looked like socks, and went white again around her mouth and forelock. Her entire coat looked unhealthy, and there were several bald patches, probably due to malnutrition or stress. The donkey stared at me as I fed her a slightly wilted carrot, which she half-heartedly chomped down on.

"I think I'll call you Patches. A bit of a boring name, but it suits you," I told my new donkey, her eyes full of soul.

* * *

It was slow going on the way back to the inn, as our donkey was lame and we had to stop off to buy a harness and tack for half a silver, which Kidu was forced to carry, much to Elwin's amusement. The pair of them looked at me as if I had gone crazy. After all, what was the point of buying a beast of burden that couldn't carry anything? Still, I assured them that there was a method to my madness, and even Elwin stopped with his frequent protestations and suggestions about making donkey stew.

We entered the empty stables, and I told Elwin to watch the street to make sure no one else followed. Kidu saw to the donkey while I filled a trough with grain and another with water from a dark wooden barrel. The donkey started to eat with gusto and was looking decidedly better.

Once Patches was happily fed and watered, I decided to put the plan I had been brewing since the marketplace into motion. First I drew my power inwards, focusing on the warm luster and, pushing from my center, the golden energies that constituted my strongest healing spell. Silently I cast Greater Heal, going through the ceremony of its long cast entirely in my mind.

With the spell complete, I released the invigorating light slowly into Patches's broken body. First, her lame leg straightened with an audible "pop" as the limb was forced to take on a healthy shape. The golden light continued to flow around the donkey, repairing the damage of the long, cruel years under an uncaring master. Both within and without, the magic restored the animal to its best possible form; her dark coat regained its luster, and there was a new sparkle to her intelligent eyes as she brayed with joy.

The spell had taken a full two-thirds of my Mana, but I was overjoyed that my little experiment had worked. Patches nuzzled my hand, recognizing that I was her source of good fortune. Kidu just nodded in understanding, his faith in me reinforced.

"That was well done," the large man praised. He ran a hand across the donkey's back before beginning to load Patches's tack.

A warm feeling began to suffuse me, and I nodded to Kidu in appreciation. I simply couldn't help myself as I cast Identify on my new pet.

Patches - (Donkey Lv. 12)
Health: 264/264
Stamina: 51/51
Mana: 4/4

Well, that was just great. Even the donkey was stronger than me, or at least was at a higher level. In a way, it sort of made sense, as animals were generally physically superior to humans. I still snorted a little in frustration, and the donkey brayed in affection, displaying large, perfectly white pearly teeth.

Once Kidu had finished mounting the tack on my donkey, we left the stables. Elwin almost shouted in surprise at Patches's new and improved form before Kidu hissed him to silence.

"What happened?" Elwin asked curiously, bemusement all over his face.

"The blessing of the gods," said Kidu almost reverently, which caused Elwin to bluster a little before he finally caught on.

Now that Patches was no longer lame, we were able to unload our camping supplies onto the donkey's packs. In good spirits, we made our way at a rapid clip along the eastern road, past the gate guards. With a wave and a smile, I greeted the corrupt Dagesh, the same guard who had introduced us to the Twisted Boar.

I turned back to look at the city, still stained with the light of morning, a mix of emotions filling the pit of my stomach. Here, I had a feeling that if I could rise above the rabble, I could achieve anything. I felt the first buds of something unfold—a lofty and somewhat vague goal, but a goal, nonetheless. Blown about as I had been, it gave me a point to fix upon, a path to pursue.

The gods had sent me here for their own purposes, twisting my fate as they saw fit. I needed power to resist their meddling. I had to make sure not to seek power for power's sake. Down that road lay only evil and corruption. No, I would seek just enough power to be free—and perhaps, if possible, a sliver of the Divine's eternity. That would be my vengeance.

A sliver of eternity, something to allow me to live forever—it certainly had a nice ring to it. Even if all of this was simply a manifestation of my madness, a coma dream, time, I was coming to realize, was a precious commodity. Time's true length did not matter; only how long it was perceived to be did. The longer I had with my turn, the better. My brushes with oblivion had taught me of the alternative.

Whether this world was real or not, a man needed a goal, a higher purpose. Immortality would be the ultimate form of survival.

Soon we would be entering the domain of the great Sainba Forest, where my companions and I would be put to the test once more. I gazed upon the verdant forest in the distance and remembered the woman, her shocked expression at the arena, as my mind finally made a connection. I remembered a mother's grief, which had shattered the Tides's ancient rite of passage with its great lament.

Epilogue

"Exquisite" could not begin to describe what Mauros saw before him. The strokes and subtle application of line and shadow, each accent and touch a study in technique, were both effortless in their execution yet perfect in style. The colors drew the eye here and there, a new shape for the imagination to take in before drawing them back to the overall piece and its true magnificence. Each time he looked upon his work he saw new aspects that he had never seen before. It was perfection, and thus would go unappreciated by those who saw it only with their eyes, and not through the lens of their soul. The true aspect of the divine transcended brush, paint, and canvas.

The artist began to add imperfections to his work, his heart breaking with every distortion he was made to render. When he could finally take no more, he forced himself, exhausted, to a lemon-scented bowl of water placed near his desk by one of his aides, where he splashed himself.

Then the horror came back. The horror that had haunted him through childhood, that propelled his art to levels that debased, created, and molded him. He saw his own face distorted across the water's surface, the colored oils twisting his visage into a monster as he saw the stigmata of the goddess. It would seem that no matter what heights he reached, to whatever new levels of artistic or spiritual nirvana, the mark would always hold him back, even as it propelled him up the ranks of the ecclesiarchy.

Jealousy—once hot but grown cold with the passing of the years—flared, before he was interrupted from his thoughts by a knock at his door.

"A hundred pardons, Your Eminence, but you asked to be informed if there was any news of the location of Her Champion," said a tonsured bookish man, bowing low as he entered the room.

"Then spit it out, Fedius. You have yet again interrupted my meditations on the nature of the goddess," said the artist, stealing a glance at his latest work before donning the robes of his office.

"Yes, Cardinal Mauros. One of our assets in the Grieving Lands, in the heathen city of Ansan, has detected the God-spark of Her Champion," said the nervous aide, looking with awe at the cardinal's latest piece of art.

The oil painting showed the veiled Goddess of Justice with an expression of righteous anger. However, the lines of her body displayed the welcoming warmth of compassion, like a mother's invitation. In her right hand, she held the long, heavy Sword of Judgment, and in her left she gripped the short Knife of Mercy. The whole painting was truly sublime, showing movement and motion shackled in a single moment, frozen forever in the stillness of eternity.

Mauros, one of the highest-ranking members of Her Church, stopped for a moment. New emotions added to his seething mixture of annoyance and threatened to spill over into violent rage. With a supreme effort of will, he stopped himself from throwing something at the bearer of the news.

"You have, of course, verified this?" said Mauros, his anger turning into the cold, professional calculation that had allowed him to reach his high rank.

"Yes, Your Eminence. They are one of our most trustworthy agents. However, there was an irregularity..." He bowed even lower, fearing the ire of his master.

"You do say..." the cardinal replied, raising a cultured eyebrow.

"The God-spark was detected, yet disappeared after a few hours, according to our source. It is posited that perhaps the Champion has found a way to shield his or her divine grace," continued Fedius, his head now touching the floor.

"No matter. We must pursue all leads in regard to the God-spark. We will send a team of our best inquisitors and knights to the region, but do be sure that they go under no banner and that the rites of secrecy are observed.

By our very best, you will also see to it that the Light of the Faith leads them. Also, be sure to send that overly zealous hothead, the one the lay-priests call the 'little goddess' as well. I believe that she is used to dealing with the locals there. You will collar the bearer of the God-spark with blessed metals and bring him into the loving arms of the church; the goddess will have it no other way," proclaimed Cardinal Mauros, the authority of his office echoing with each word like the judgment of the hammer.

"It shall be as you command, Your Eminence. As the goddess wills," intoned the aide reverently, with no little relief.

"Yes, as the goddess wills, my child," the cardinal replied, sure in his conviction and interpretation of the divine will. Inwardly, he still seethed; for all his efforts, and despite a righteous life lived, he could never be her chosen.

How dare they go against Her great will, he thought. He would chain Her rebellious Champion to Her divine intent. Even if they chose to cross to the other side through the veil of death, he swore that he would bring them back, a thousand times if necessary.

Glossary and Dramatis Personae

Aditi: The old female cook in the slave pits of Ansan. It is thanks to her that Gilgamesh is able to survive.

Adventurers' Guild, the: An organization specializing in slaying monsters, gathering rare and precious materials, conquering dungeons, and protecting the weak. They are rivals of the Mercenaries' Guild.

Aeyory: Sacred trees of Avaria. Except for the trees blessed by the goddess herself, which are in bloom throughout the year, the aeyory trees usually blossom when the snows of winter thaw. Since military campaigns usually start in spring, the blossoms of the tree have come to symbolize war.

Ancestor Spear: An object of reverence for the Children of the Tides. It was Gilgamesh's first weapon.

Ansan: Seat of power for the Children of the Tides. The City of Tents is built around an ancient Ark made of mystical living witchwood. It is a nexus of trade.

Ansarai's Fighting Pit: A seedy fighting pit in Ansan. Gilgamesh wins a lot of money here by placing a bet on Vidone Amantea, a plant from the organizers.

Aranthia: A kingdom far to the west of Ansan.

Arbitrator: A man responsible for dispensing justice in the borderlands of Aranthia.

Arimea Lostariot: An elven spellsinger. Gilgamesh and his companions barely survive a hostile encounter with her and her entourage just outside of Ansan.

Arvan Azzarik: A gladiator in Ansarai's Fighting Pit.

Avaria: Goddess of Justice. Known in the North as "Vari, Chooser of the Slain." She is often symbolized wielding the Sword of Judgment and the Knife of Mercy.

Beacon Mountains, the: An active volcano range and the home of Durhit Coal, a companion of Gilgamesh.

Beron de Laney: Author of *The Fanciful Travels*, an account of his travels and adventures across the world of Gesthe.

Bibsis: An amphibious monster sacred to the Children of the Tides due to their control over the element of water. Also known as rain-bringers or callers. It is believed that they have a link with the torrential annual rains that sweep the Grass Sea.

Blooding, the: Part of the Winnowing.

Bogurchu Batbayar: A waverider of the Children of the Tides. He is one of the first people that Gilgamesh encounters.

Bone-Dragon: A necromantic creation made from the flesh of a newly deceased dragon.

Breaking, the: Another term for the Cataclysm.

Bronzegate Hold: The place Durhit mentions as he dies.

Broomshead: A type of mushroom that the alchemist Hamsa requests Gilgamesh find for him.

Calling: The calling to which one's soul is naturally inclined. It is a path of fate.

Caru nut: The seed from the caru tree. When falling from a great height, these large nuts can kill. The remains of those killed then act as fertilizer for the new tree.

Cataclysm, the: An apocalyptic event. The last Cataclysm was caused by the Seed of Oblivion being brought into the world of Gesthe.

Catyid: A large, docile rodent that resembles a capybara but with a scaly, sinuous tail.

Charisma: The attribute that governs how effectively one can interact with others. It includes confidence and eloquence, and it can represent a charming or commanding personality.

Cillis Aideh: Smith of the Soot-Stained Pig. Supplies Gilgamesh and his companions with a new set of armor and equipment. Trains Gilgamesh in the use of flails.

Concord, the: An agreement between all of the higher beings.

Constitution: This attribute encompasses a character's physique, toughness, general health, and resistance to disease and poisons. It also determines the number of potions one can consume without ill effect. The Constitution attribute greatly affects both Stamina and Health.

Cronir: A large animal found in the North. They are hunted by the people of the Kar-Kaphon and the ice drakes.

Dagesh: A corrupt guard in Ansan. He recommends that Gilgamesh stay at his cousin's inn, the Twisted Boar.

Darcen Tsend: Guildmaster of the Adventurers' Guild branch in Ansan. Reputedly, he has the ability to detect lies.

Darren Kragain: A bard whom Gilgamesh encounters in the Twisted Boar. Gilgamesh inspires Darren to create a new type of music by introducing him to melodies from his own world.

Deeptakers: An elite group of dwarven warrior miners who explore the Everdark in search of treasure and long-lost artifacts.

Degei Ganbataar: Slave overseer of the slave pits of Ansan. Disciplines and tortures Gilgamesh after he kills Harun.

Devon the Dirk: A drunken regular of the Twisted Boar. He taught Gilgamesh how to throw knives.

Dexterity: This attribute is a reflection of a number of physical abilities including hand-eye coordination, agility, reflexes, fine motor skills, balance, and speed of movement. Dexterity also moderately affects maximum Stamina.

Durhit Coal: A dwarf from the Beacon Mountains. He became a slave in Ansan as his sister Evenes was unable to pay for his war ransom. He is slain by a chameleonic variant of the echo-stalker.

Dragon: Capricious, sentient winged lizards that possess great physical and magical might. They are some of the most powerful beings on Gesthe and their might is said to rival the gods themselves.

Dragonroot: A highly valuable alchemical ingredient. It can be used to craft a poison that is said to be able to kill a dragon. Dragonroot has wide-bladed purple leaves and white roots. The plants are guarded by the monstrous jaderock bees. The poison concocted from this ingredient is also known as "widow's mercy" or the "final gift."

Earth-Mother: A dwarven term applied to the element of Earth, the soil, the rocks, and the mountains. Dwarves believe that all creatures are of the Earth since they all must return to it one day.

Echo-Stalker: A monstrous, multi-limbed insectile creature found in the deep parts of the world.

Elves: A long-lived humanoid species whose origin is shrouded in mystery. The elves refer to themselves as the "First Children." They are allies of the fae. There are several varieties of elves.

Elwin Tucker: Gilgamesh meets Elwin in the slave pits of Ansan. He professed to be a forester, but is, in fact, a rogue.

Entropy: One of the first primordials. Entropy, as a higher truth, is present in almost all things in the universe.

Evenes: Durhit's sister. She could not pay Durhit's ransom when he was taken as a prisoner of war. This led to the dwarf becoming a slave in Ansan.

Everdark, the: A vast subterranean realm beneath the surface of the world.

Fae: The inhabitants of the In-Between.

Fen Vaigorus: Author of *The Living Sword*.

Festival of the Undrawn, the: A martial tournament in an unknown city.

Gaven Tolaris: A gladiator in Ansarai's Fighting Pit.

Gesthe: The name of the world our protagonist finds himself in. The word means "Garden" in the language of the elves.

Gideon de Salavia: An academic and scholar who authored numerous books exploring topics such as justice, morality, and humanity's place in the world.

Gilgamesh of Uruk: The first hero and protagonist of our story. In certain translations, Gilgamesh is also known as the "Watcher of the Deep Places."

Girabis: A large, gentle creature used as a pack animal.

Glass Fire Sea, the: An area of ocean protected by sentinel crystals that burn incoming ships to a crisp.

Gnarlug Bonegrinder: An orc in Ansarai's Fighting Pit. He is slain by Vidone.

Goblin: A small and green feral humanoid. Thought to be cousins to the orcs.

God-touched: The name of those who suffer from epileptic fits.

Grass Sea, the: The domain of the Children of the Tides. Travel across this vast expanse is difficult, as a water mage is required to conjure drinking water.

Great Crawler: A large underground creature. It is believed that they are the cause of some earthquakes. Also known as earth dragons.

Grieving Lands, the: The name of the region where Gilgamesh is initially transported to.

Gunne: A boy who had sworn vengeance against Gilgamesh for killing Harun the Iron. On Durhit's request, Gilgamesh kills Gunne out of mercy.

Hamsa: An eccentric alchemist in Ansan.

Harun the Iron: The first human our protagonist kills. Gilgamesh kills the large man after he cuts in front of him to wash.

Hassan: Gilgamesh encounters this man when he becomes a slave. Hassan is charismatic and sanguine, but tremendously obese.

Healing Potion: An item that, when imbibed, restores Health.

Health: The measure of one's current physical status.

Ice Drake: Lesser cousins of the dragons. They prey upon the cronir. They grow more vicious and powerful as they age.

Icewalker: The title for those who have lived for fifty years or more in the North.

Intelligence: The attribute that measures mental acuity, the accuracy of recall, and the ability to reason. It significantly affects maximum Mana capacity.

Inverse Mountain, the: A legendary place in the Everdark.

Iron Slave Collar of Obedience: A magical collar that can cause great pain to the wearer.

Jongshoi Aigiam: A boy that Gilgamesh is forced to kill in the Winnowing.

Kar-Kaphon: How the people of the North refer to their home of endless tundra and ice.

K.D. Fidditch: Author of the book *Monsters of the Mortal Realm*. Staple reading for adventurers.

Kazass: Strong drink made from the fermented blood of cronir.

Khisam: Husband of Cillis Aideh.

Kidu Kreshin: A peerless warrior and hunter of the Three Bears clan from the far North, or Kar-Kaphon. He is a loyal companion of our protagonist. Gilgamesh encounters Kidu in the slave pits of Ansan.

Lanarisa: An elven adventurer in Ansan. She is currently one of the highest-ranking members of the Adventurers' Guild.

Lanelo: A purple fruit that is commonly used to make refreshing fruit juice.

Language of the Knots, the: In ancient times, the Children of the Tides traveled the seas. Since paper could get wet and rot easily at sea, they used knots to record things and communicate. In the modern era, many people across the Grieving Lands still use knotted pieces of string, with the knots representing words and ideas.

Laur: A genus of six-limbed, warm-blooded creatures. They look like a cross between a wolverine and a warthog. Some laur species have been domesticated.

Luck: How this attribute works remains a mystery to Gilgamesh.

Mana: The source of magic for the world of Gesthe. It is called the god-gift by the many races of Gesthe and is associated with life itself.

Mana Potion: An item that, when imbibed, restores Mana.

March Reaches, the: A borderland region of the Kingdom of Aranthia.

Mercenaries' Guild, the: The rival of the Adventurers' Guild.

Monsters of the Mortal Realm: An encyclopedic book detailing the monsters of the world of Gesthe.

Navigator: In ancient times, the Children of the Tides relied on the skills of the navigators to cross the great seas of Gesthe. However, in the modern age, navigators are relied upon to chart the best course of action for their people.

Necromancy: The art of raising the dead and bringing them back into a state of unlife. This school of magic was discovered by the ancient Republic of Arastia before the last Cataclysm.

Nord: Cousins to the people of Kar-Kaphon. Nords are the seagoing people of the North.

North, the: A vast expanse of ice and tundra. Also known as the Kar-Kaphon.

Olai: A navigator for the Children of the Tides. Condemns Gilgamesh to fight in the Winnowing.

Orc: A powerful, green-skinned race of humanoids. They grow stronger and more powerful if they are injured or go into a bestial heat.

Patches: The large donkey that Gilgamesh saves from the butcher's block.

Quas: Name of both an island and the city on it. It is famous for being a center of learning.

Quassian: The name of the people and the language of Quas.

Rawesan: The blessed land of scripture.

Republic of Arastia, the: The nation that fought against the Alliance in ages past.

River God, the: The god of time and prophecy. Also known as the "God of the Wend and Way."

River-Lurker: A six-legged crocodilian. They can often be found near where river root grows.

River Root: An alchemical ingredient. It is part of a request that Gilgamesh and his companions accept as one of their jobs as adventurers.

Rockcrab: An edible land crustacean. They are commonly found scavenging through the waste and detritus of cities and urban areas.

Sahel: The name of the sun that the world of Gesthe orbits.

Sainba Forest: A large, ancient forest filled with gigantic trees.

Seaguard: A coastal town with high walls, ruled by Lord Farilse.

Seed of Oblivion, the: An artifact that was brought into the world of Gesthe from another plane of existence.

Shallow River, the: The river that represents death.

Soot-Stained Pig, the: A smithy and armory in Ansan City.

Stamina: The capacity to engage in physically demanding activities. When certain conditions are met, Health can be used in the place of Stamina.

Stone-Eater: A derogatory term for a dwarf.

Strength: The Strength attribute is a measure of muscle strength and endurance. Strength moderately affects Stamina and, to a much lesser degree, maximum Health.

Taciano: Clerk at the Adventurers' Guild branch in Ansan. He is assigned to Gilgamesh's party.

Taper Athinad: Proprietor of the Twisted Boar, an inn and tavern in the city of Ansan.

The Living Sword: A treatise on how a warrior should train in the use of a sword and a commentary on martial arts in general. Written by Fen Vaigorus.

Three Bears, the: A Tribe of the North.

Time of Trials, the: A period when the North is especially cold and unforgiving.

Trade: The common language and *lingua franca* for the Grieving Lands.

Truth-seal: A piece of paper that is used to confirm bets in Ansan.

Tsengelt-tum: A hybrid weapon that can act as both a simple mace and a deadly flail. The chain is short enough that it will not hit the wielder's hand.

Under-Kingdoms, the: The ancient realms of the dwarves before the Cataclysm.

Vidone Amantea: A Duelist from Quas. He slays the orc Bonegrinder in Ansarai's Fighting Pit.

Vizzeks: The first bone-dragon.

Waverider: An officer in the standing army of the Children of the Tides.

Wildlands: The untamed area beyond the Sainba Forest.

Windspeaker: Keepers of the oral traditions and lore of the Kar-Kaphon. A few of them can harness the elemental power of Mana.

Winnowing, the: The sacred act where the young men of the Tides must prove themselves capable of taking the life of another man.

Wisdom: The attribute that governs willpower, common sense, perception, and intuition. It moderately affects maximum Mana and Mana regeneration.

Witchbound: A term describing a magical tool or item.

Witchwood: A near-legendary substance grown from the groves of giant sentient trees that have their roots in both the world of Gesthe and the In-Between. Sacred to the elves and the fae.

Zajasite: Glowing crystals that are mined from the earth.

You may also enjoy...

Waking up in a strange world with a spear in his chest was not on Glenn's bingo card.

Then again, neither was being possessed by a sarcastic demon who insists they're partners.

But that parasitic nuisance becomes the least of his worries when he discovers the place he's been tossed into is filled with bizarre monsters, overzealous cults, and other entities hell-bent on making his life... Hell.

Now, Glenn must uncover the reason he's here and satiate his new partner if he wants to survive long enough to do something about it.

Grab your copy of Symbiotic Ascension, a Progression Fantasy Adventure where one man's only hope lies in trusting the demon bound to him. Perfect for readers who enjoy gritty fantasy, sharp humor, and magic with a price.

Available on Kindle Unlimited and Audible!

Thank you for reading a MoonQuill original novel. More exciting stories can be found on our website, www.moonquill.com.

We would greatly appreciate it if you would take a moment to leave a review. Each one helps the author and supports their ability to continue writing fantastic books for everyone to enjoy!

If you're looking for more great books to read, join our mailing list by scanning the QR code or clicking the link below. You'll get 4 books for free!